PATRIARCH

COIREE GUARDIANS

BOOK THREE

MARI MINIATT

ANIMATED LIAR MEDIA

This is a work of fiction. Names, characters, businesses, places, events and incidents are either the products of the author's imagination or used in a fictitious manner. Any resemblance to actual persons, living or dead, or actual events is purely coincidental

Printed in the United States of America

First Printing, 2012

ISBN 978-0-9826660-4-3

Animated Lair Media

Syracuse, NY

Book design and production by Animated Liar Media

Editing by Animated Liar Media and Josh Shear.

Dedication

There are many people I want to thank:

My husband and boys, for putting up with me writing while you want to play video games.

The staff at the Enchanted Bazaar, for pushing me to finish this.

My small handful of fans that kept asking me about this book and being patient.

Thanks to all of you.

CHAPTER 1

A white van turned the corner at high speed, making Steopa jump back onto the curb. The filthy, melting snow splashed onto him. The car that the van had cut off swerved and sounded the horn. Steopa reached back and laid his hand on Rebecka's shoulder.

"Are you all right?" he asked.

Rebecka patted his large hand. "You were nearly run over, not me."

He watched the white van as it sped away from them. He took Rebecka's hand with one hand and with the other wiped the slush off his green overcoat. They walked down the street, following the van. People moved out of his way as he picked up his speed. His stature, seven feet tall and broad shouldered, would make anyone want to avoid being run down by him. But the people on the street did not see him.

Steopa and Rebecka blurred as they hurried. Shadows covered both of them as they stayed on the white van's path. Both of them kept pace with the vehicle, speeding past the pedestrians on the street as if the world had froze. Its path, turning down one street, then another, along with the darkened windows, had piqued his attention. A shroud, the dark cloud that vampires could see, covered the van. Someone in that van wanted to die.

The van rode low to the ground, so low that if it hit a large bump, it would be damaged. The blackened windows did not allow anyone to see how many people were inside the vehicle. From the interior you could feel, before you heard, the heavy bass lines echoing from a hip hop song.

Steopa strained to hear, over the bass and engine, the heartbeats of the occupants. He heard three. The strongest, a steady beat, with a slight irregularity, almost drowned out the other two. Those beats were fast. Steopa raised his eyebrow. Two of the occupants were frightened.

The van slowed. Steopa paused on the street. He pulled out a hair tie from his overcoat pocket and tied his long black hair back. He started to move; Rebecka did not. She motioned with her head.

Across the street, a group of men, all wearing the same shade of red, watched the van roll past. The van turned down another street and the group of men followed it. Steopa growled. Rebecka grinned; the points of her fangs peeked out of her mouth.

Steopa faded into the shadows, as did Rebecka. They jumped across the street, then followed the men. Most of the street lights on this side had been broken, leaving the area in darkness. Steopa caught up with the last man of the group. He walked an arm's length away, but did not reach out to take him. There were no witnesses in the area he could not dispatch. They are up to something, Steopa thought. This will be interesting.

The van turned into the parking lot of an abandoned factory. The wheels spun as it broke through the last of the snow that had been piled in the lot. It drove through a set of open double doors and shut off its engine. The music echoed through the empty building. Most of the men followed the van. Two of them stayed outside. They shut the double doors and turned to watch the street.

Steopa and Rebecka paused at the corner. He studied the building. The factory had four floors. The third floor sat back from the edge of the lower floors. Most of the windows in the building wrapped around that floor. At one time it may have been the only light source in the building. Now, most of the windows were broken, and panes were left to rot in the elements.

He jumped and landed on the small ledge. Rebecka joined him. He leaned over the empty window frame and watched the scene. The van had pulled into the middle of the factory floor. The group of men surrounded it. One of them walked up to the driver's side door.

Rebecka put her arm through the empty window pane, then pulled it back. Steopa gave her a single nod.

"It is abandoned," he whispered.

"You never know," she said.

The driver got out of the van. Unlike the other men in the factory, the driver wore a suit coat over blue jeans. The one that had walked up to the van and the driver walked over to the side door. They were engaged in an animated conversation.

Steopa could hear parts of the conversation. They discussed a payment. Money exchanged hands. The driver opened the side door. Steopa grabbed Rebecka as she lunged forward.

Two children were bound and gagged on the floor of the van. Steopa growled. Each of the men grabbed one of them and pulled the children out of the van. Two of the red-hooded men came forward and took the children.

Rebecka pried Steopa's fingers off her arm. Steopa grabbed her wrist. She glared at him. Steopa whispered, “Wait.”

“Why?”

“When I come back, get the children.” Steopa jumped down to the ground.

He hurried around the building, checking for any exits that could be used. Most of the lowest level had been boarded up with warped pieces of plywood. He found one door partially open. He shut it. A piece of reinforcing bar jutted out of the concrete. Steopa ripped it out of the pillar. He wrapped it around the door handle and shoved the ends into the door frame.

He found one widow that had been broken. The warped boards laid on the ground. He glanced into the factory. Steopa could see the men as they jostled the children. He left that window alone.

The two men stood guard outside the double doors. Steopa forced his fingernails to grow. Then he leaped. He slashed one man's throat. As the other turned to see his companion fall, Steopa twisted his neck. The sound of two bodies hitting the frozen gravel broke the silence of the late winter night.

Steopa shoved a large empty industrial garbage bin in front of the doors. He returned to the open window. It looked as if the men had not moved. Steopa grinned. It had taken him moments to secure the building.

He jumped into the open window, making no sound as he landed on the floor. Steopa crouched down behind some of the discarded machinery.

“Boy and girl, just what we ordered,” said the red clad leader. “She will be happy.”

“I just deliver,” said the driver.

“That's right.” The leader pulled out a gun and shot the driver between the eyes. When the body hit the ground he turned to his men.

“You and you, take the kids. The rest of you strip the van, all evidence destroyed."

Two of the red-clad men pulled the struggling children to the other side of the factory. Steopa could not see anything there, only the empty floor. He glanced up at Rebecka. He pointed to the two men with the children. He saw Rebecka tense.

Steopa stormed up to the leader. He gripped the leader's head and twisted it until the spine snapped. The leader's body hit the ground. Steopa growled. The group of men that had surrounded the van stopped. A couple of them reached into their jackets.

He heard two thuds behind him. Two of the men in front of him opened fire on Steopa. Bullets hurt him like multiple bee stings. He walked straight for one of the men. He crushed the man's hand, twisting it so the gun barrel became pressed against his throat. The rest of the clip emptied into the man's skull, spraying bones and blood over the floor.

The three men that were left glanced at one another. The one with the gun fired it at Steopa as he ran toward the double doors. Steopa had the semi-headless body in his grip. He flung the body toward the two who had not moved.

The body slammed into the two men and knocked them against the van. Steopa picked one of them up and threw him across the old factory floor. He picked up the other man.

"Rebecka!" he shouted, motioning with his head to the last one. She blurred as she attacked him.

Steopa hissed at the one in his grip. "Are those your children?"

The man opened his mouth and made strange noises. Steopa shook him. "The children!"

The man tried to pry Steopa's fingers off his neck. Steopa pulled him closer and growled in his ear. The man pissed his pants.

"What?" he choked.

Steopa lifted him up by his neck. He forced him up the van and then up to the ceiling. At the roof, he tightened his grip. "How much?" he asked.

"Five hundred," the man choked.

Steopa let go of the man. His body dropped and bounced when it hit the concrete floor. Steopa lowered his body. Rebecka stood, the body of the one who ran laid in pieces at her feet.

"Where are the children?" Steopa asked.

Rebecka pointed to the old machinery. Steopa stepped over the bodies, making his way to the children.

"They've destroyed those kids' lives," Rebecka said. "They will always remember."

The children held each other in a corner of the factory. Their bounds and gags had been removed. Both of them cried, but the boy looked up, his eyes traveling up Steopa's frame. Steopa stood a distance away from them. The girl turned her head. They stared at him with tear-stained eyes.

"What are we going to do now?" Rebecka asked.

"Call the police," Steopa said. "We cannot take them."

The boy, who looked older, wiped his face. "Where are we?"

Steopa glanced at Rebecka. "Deerbow City," he said.

"Can we leave?"

Rebecka came closer to the children. They backed away from her. She stopped. "We are calling the police. But stay here. You shouldn't see..."

She lowered her head. Her brown curls slid down around her face. "Please stay here until the police come."

The boy glanced around her. He saw something that made him grimace. He pulled the girl closer to him while she cried. Rebecka pulled out her cell phone and made the call. Steopa turned and looked over the carnage that Rebecka and he had made.

"Can I see my mommy?" the girl cried.

Steopa walked over to them. The boy pulled the girl back. Steopa got on one knee. "We will stay until the police come," he said.

"You killed all of them," the boy whispered.

Steopa stood. "We did what we had to do."

Rebecka turned her face toward the double doors. "I already hear sirens. That was fast."

Steopa jumped to the third floor. Rebecka followed a few moments later. Three police cars pulled into the parking lot. Steopa and Rebecka waited until the police found the children, then they left.

They walked away from the crime as an ambulance roared past them. Rebecka took Steopa's hand.

"I wish we could have taken them out of there," she said.

Steopa nodded.

"There are some really sick people in this world."

"There are fewer of them now," Steopa said.

"Don't joke," Rebecka said.

"I am not."

He turned down the street that would take them back to Konakove. Rebecka wrapped her arm around him and laid her head on his chest. Steopa paused and kissed her forehead. "Do you want to retire?"

Rebecka shook her head. "Those were strange gang members."

"What do you mean?"

"They were dressed like gang members. But that one did not speak like any gangsters we have run into."

Steopa ran the conversation that the driver and the leader had through his mind. "You are right," he said.

"I wish we could have done more," Rebecka said.

"It was best that we left them there. Where would we have taken the children?"

"Teodor's?"

"I am sure that they would have taken the children in, but too many questions."

"I suppose."

He stopped on a pedestrian bridge. "Rebecka, as much as it would have been the right thing to do, to take the children away, we could not."

"It would have only been for a short time," Rebecka said.

Steopa shook his head. "I only had my daughter for a few hours and that was difficult."

"You never told me that."

"It is the past."

"But-"

"The families that lost them will be eager to find them again. We would only be interfering with their reunion."

Rebecka bit her lip, then said, "You're right."

Steopa pulled Rebecka closer to him. "They will be safe, safer than what we could have offered."

She laid her head on his chest. Steopa placed his large hand on her brown curls. A passing couple glanced in their direction and smiled at Steopa. He lifted Rebecka's chin and kissed her lips.

Rebecka ran her hands up his chest. Steopa placed his hands on hers. He stepped back. "We should go home."

Rebecka nodded. They continued over the bridge back to their home.

CHAPTER 2

Months later, Steopa rolled over and laid his arm across Rebecka's side. She pulled his hand up to her chest. He rested his chin next to her ear.

"I would like some pirogies," he said.

Rebecka giggled. "Didn't you eat enough last night?"

Steopa raised his hand and snapped his fingers. The candles in their room lit. Rebecka rolled on her back. She reached behind her and ran her finger down the wood post. "Where do you want to go?"

"The usual."

"All right."

Steopa got out of the four-poster bed and went over to his standing wardrobe. He heard Rebecka get out of the bed. She opened her dresser.

"I was thinking we should stop in and see John," she said.

"Perhaps, it has been a while." As he pulled on his pants he felt a strange sensation in the back of his head. He paused and tilted his head. It felt familiar. But why would she try to contact me? he thought.

"What is it?" Rebecka asked.

"I am not sure." He tucked his shirt into his pants. "Would this be appropriate for the nightclub?"

"For us I don't think it matters." Rebecka finished dressing. She looked at him. "Are you sure it was nothing?"

"I thought it was my daughter."

"Her name is Nastenka, right?"

He nodded. He sat down on the bed and pulled on his boots. He noticed a rip along the seam on the right one. "I will have to replace these soon."

"How long have you had those?"

Steopa thought. "Twenty years. I had to get them specially made."

"That might be a problem now, but we could check online."

"We could?"

Rebecka nodded. She waited beside the metal door. Steopa walked over and turned the large wheel. It opened to the room they used as a living room. He snapped his fingers and the candles in their bedroom extinguished. For a moment, Steopa could not see anything, then his eyes adjusted to the pitch blackness. He could see everything in the room with a monochrome view. Rebecka walked around him to her small table.

She unplugged her cell phone. As she pulled the plug out of the phone, there was a quick flash where the electricity had been disconnected. The cell phone had a slight red glow due to the heat it generated.

Rebecka pocketed her phone. She turned around and smiled. "Pirogies or my brother?"

"Pirogies."

"How can you still eat them?"

Steopa chuckled. "It is a little vice, that is all."

"And the vodka?"

"Rebecka, you surprise me. I lived in St. Petersburg for over a century, I learned how to drink vodka like water."

"It just..., I can't even pretend to eat one. I taste that oil and I want to retch."

Steopa chuckled. "It will take a few years."

He put his arm around her and opened the exit. After he secured it by placing a large column of concrete in front of it, he took Rebecka's hand. She had pulled her hair back. Her curls piled on the top of her head like a crown.

Steopa leaned over and kissed her forehead. "I like your hair up."

"Now that it doesn't look like a tangled mess..."

They walked down the long corridor, then up into the parking garage. The fluorescent lights flickered and buzzed, casting intermediate shadows over the pavement. One homeless man shuffled past them as they exited the building. He glanced over, then hurried away from them, leaving the scent of urine and beer hanging in the air.

Rebecka giggled. "I remember when I first came to you. I almost thought you lived in the old base."

Steopa stopped. "What base?"

"Those urban legends, about the base under Deerbow."

Steopa glanced back at the parking garage. He squeezed her hand. "I would like the pirogies."

As they crossed the street, another feeling hit him, strong, like smelling a heavy perfume. He felt a slight pain in his temple. He raised his hand to rub his forehead. As the feeling intensified, he recognized it. This was not Nastenka. At the corner he stopped. Rebecka waited. He glanced at her. How do I tell her? he thought.

"Rebecka," he said. "We must go. I have to explain on the way."

Rebecka let him take the lead. How could she understand? Steopa thought. Start at the beginning. The feeling felt stronger as long as he faced the East. Steopa used it like a homing beacon.

"I spent some time with Nastenka after she married. Her husband was an intellectual. To him, I was a puzzle of nature." Steopa cut through an open lot that led to one of the high schools. He hurried across the football field. Their path cut through the fog like the wake of water along the prow of a ship.

"She had three children. Then one day, she was thrown from a horse. A day later she was hunting with me."

Rebecka stopped. "That's right, you told me. She pulled off the shroud and laughed."

Steopa nodded. "Two of her sons also became vampires, when they passed. Her daughter moved to the United States." Steopa pulled Rebecka along again. "From that family line, more vampires came."

"So every time one of your descendants dies, they become a vampire?"

Steopa shook his head. "Only the ones that die in accidents or have untimely deaths."

An overpass came into view. It showed the unofficial dividing between the city and a large protected forest called Greenwoods. Steopa paused under the overpass. He stood for a moment and closed his eyes. "I have lost count of how many of my descendants are vampires now."

He could sense who they were, but not clearly. This descendant felt young. Steopa got the sensation of water. He or she wasn't drowning, but there was water around them. Soon they would change, Steopa could feel that death waited for them.

He grabbed Rebecka's hand and ran across the road. He

followed a deer trail into the woods.

"What does this have to do with us running?" she asked.

"When one of my family dies and becomes a vampire, we can feel it. Somewhere near here, I can feel one."

"That's where we are going?"

Steopa nodded. "The closest family member tries to come when the change happens."

He led the way, using the feeling in his head to guide him. He could feel water surrounding whoever it was. He paused.

"Is there a lake in here?" Steopa asked.

"No, just the swamp."

"Where is that?"

Rebecka pointed down the path. "We are heading the right way."

Steopa started to hurry down the path when a large deer came out of the brush and stood in his way. The buck snorted and shook his head. The green antlers glowed in the moonlight. Steopa cursed.

"Not now, Perun," he said.

"What?" Rebecka asked.

The deer lowered its head, then changed into an average-sized man with wild brown hair that had sprouts of moss and plants growing along the twisted masses. His green eyes shined, reflecting the moonlight. He smiled. The width of his grin seemed to split his face in half.

"It has been ten years since you came for a visit and you don't have time to say hello?" Perun laughed. His eyes fell on Rebecka. "Ah, you have a woman."

"I am sorry, but I have pressing matters."

"You are here for that car crash?"

"What car crash?" Steopa asked.

Perun motioned with his head. "I heard the crash. I was going to see myself."

"Show me."

Perun ran a little further ahead. Rebecka caught up with Steopa. "Um, What's up with his feet?" she asked.

Steopa glanced down as Perun bounced over the ground. He had forgotten his feet. Perun wore no shoes. His feet were stretched and elongated like a dog's. He left tracks in the dirt, like a deer would.

"He is a leshy," Steopa said.

"A what?"

Perun glanced over his shoulder. "A leshy. I watch over these woods."

"I've never heard of that. I mean him," Rebecka said.

"You never told her about me?" Perun asked. "Were you scared she would want me?"

"Perun," Steopa said, growling.

"Good taste. She's got great tits."

Rebecka stopped, her mouth fell open. Steopa smirked, then grabbed her hand.

"Perun, the car crash."

Perun chuckled. He bounced ahead of them. The path went up a small rise. A strange light glowed, illuminating the open ground beyond the rise. Steopa smelled gas, oil, and melting plastic. They came to the crest of a drop-off. The banks of the bog rose up at a steep angle, making it difficult to enter.

In the middle of the swamp, an overturned car's lights glowed through the gloom. The path the car had taken could clearly be seen. Branches had been ripped off the trees. Two large trees showed signs of the car ramming into them.

Rebecka pointed to the other side of the bog. "There is a road over there. My God, how fast were they going?"

Perun shook his head. "That gunk from the car is poisoning the water."

"I have to get down there," Steopa said.

"What's the rush?" Perun asked.

Steopa didn't answer. He made his way down a bank. Rebecka followed him. Perun changed into an owl and flew over to the car. Steopa stepped on to the moss. He did not sink. He lifted his weight above the water. He made his way across the bog using the vegetation. The standing water did not get disturbed as he stepped over the small pools.

The impact of the crash had buried the roof of the car into the wet ground. It sank as Steopa approached. Bubbles rose up, while the sound of the car sinking became the only sound in the swamp. Perun flew off and then changed back into his human shape. He stood on a tuft of moss, pulling his leather legging up, so the edges would stay out of the muck.

Steopa got down on one knee and looked inside the car. There were three people. The steering wheel and the air bag had pinned the driver to his seat. The impact had forced his head down to his chest. The steering column smashed his face. The roof of the car had been crushed in, pinning his head in place.

On the passenger side, a woman hung from her seat belt. Steopa could hear her breathing. When she took in a breath, he heard a gurgling noise. The passenger side window had broken and made a deep gash in her upper arm and upper chest. Her once-blue blouse had turned a deep purple with her blood.

Neither of them was about to turn into a vampire. Steopa moved so he could see the back seat. The young man in the back had been tossed to the side. His seat belt had stopped his body from sinking into the water that seeped into the roof of the car. The water had rose to the young man's nose.

Steopa pulled the back door off and threw it into the bog. He heard Perun protest, but he ignored him. He grabbed the leg of the young man. Except for the rib poking out of his chest, the young man looked as if he was asleep. Steopa pulled him out of the car.

He stood up, cradling the young man in his arms. He could see that the young man had the familiar features that seemed to bless all his descendants who turned at death. The black straight hair, the square jaw, and large hands.

"We should get out of the mud," Perun said.

A voice came from the car. "Hello, we have registered an air bag deploy, is everyone alright?"

Steopa stared at the car. Perun ducked his head into the passenger side. The voice had sounded like it had came from the radio.

Rebecka smirked. "It's a service some people pay for," she said. "It monitors your car. It will be reporting this accident soon."

Steopa jumped with the boy in his arms. He landed at the top of the ravine. He laid the young man on a cleared piece of land. The young man's breath rattled. A few more moments at the most.

"Do you have any idea who he is?" Rebecka asked. She had gotten down on her knees next to the young man.

Steopa shook his head.

Perun twirled his hair in his fingers. "He's changing."

Steopa could feel it. The heartbeat slowed, then stopped. The young man's breath rattled. He gave out one last rasping breath. His head lolled to the side. Silence filled the woods, except for the sound of the car sinking into the bog.

"Have you two mated yet?" Perun asked.

Steopa glared at Perun. "You know that is impossible."

"No it isn't." Perun grinned at Rebecka. "You look more than capable."

"This is not the time." Steopa growled. "I can feel this boy is changing."

"How long?" Rebecka asked.

"A few minutes," Steopa said.

"It took me days."

"It's happening now," Perun said, his voice serious. The smile had faded from his face.

A soft sound, like a straw being slid through a milkshake, made Steopa look at the young man's chest. The rib moved back into the young man's body. The blood that had coated his face and skin disappeared. His hands shot up in front of his face and he cried out.

Steopa took the young man's hands in his and lowered them to the boy's chest. He opened his eyes. They were the same shade of green as Steopa's. He looked at each of them, then shook his head.

"Oh God, what happened?"

"You were in a car wreck," Rebecka said in a soft calm voice.

The young man stared at her for a moment. Then at Steopa. "Where are my parents?"

Steopa pointed to the bottom of the ravine. "They are dead."

The young man stared at the sinking car. "Can't we save them?"

"No," Perun said.

The young man turned his head and started when he saw Perun. Perun grinned. The young man's eyes became wide. He studied Perun's features then turned to Steopa.

"What's going on?" the young man asked.

"What is your name?" Rebecka asked.

"Jimmy Martin," he said.

Martin? Steopa thought. Which family line did this young man belong too? I do not remember a Martin. "We should go," he said.

"Wait," Jimmy said. "Who are you guys?"

"Did your parents share any family history with you?" Steopa asked.

"No, I was adopted," Jimmy said. "What the hell does this have to do with anything? My parents are trapped down there."

"They are dead," Steopa said.

Jimmy shoved Steopa away. Perun leaped and block Jimmy from running down into the ravine. "You need to listen now."

Steopa stood. Jimmy craned his head to look Steopa in the eye.

"You are dead, too," Steopa said.

Jimmy scoffed. He glanced at Perun, then his eyes traveled down and stared at Perun's feet.

Rebecka brushed the dirt off her pants. "Jimmy, check your teeth."

He ran his tongue over his teeth. He winced when his tongue got cut on the fangs. He pressed his fingertip against one of them.

"They are real," Steopa said.

"This is a sick joke, right?" Jimmy asked. "I'm on a reality show, right?"

Rebecka shook her head. "You might want to check your pulse, too."

Jimmy felt his neck, then he grabbed his wrist. He dropped his hands to his sides. "What the hell is going on?"

"I will explain. But we must leave here," Steopa said.

"My parents..." Jimmy said. He looked down at the middle of the bog. The car listed to the side that had the open door, then it flipped and sank deeper into the bog.

"There's nothing we can do," Rebecka said.

Perun looked away, scratching his beard.

Steopa patted Jimmy's shoulder. "We have to leave. If we stay, there will be too many questions."

"Are you two..?" Jimmy asked.

"Vampires," Steopa said.

Jimmy felt his neck.

Rebecka laughed. "No, we didn't bite you."

"Then how?"

Steopa paused. He tried to think of the best way to explain it.

Rebecka said, "Since you were adopted, you might not know your real parent's health history. Let's just say, instead of diabetes, you got vampirism."

Jimmy's face lit up with a wide smile. "Like a dhamphir?"

"Not entirely correct, but not wrong, either," Steopa said.

“Don't worry about anyone looking for your body,” Perun said. “That bog can hide many things.”

“You're not a vampire,” Jimmy said.

“He's a smart one.” Perun chuckled. “Follow me. I have a place you can talk.”

“Then what are you?” Jimmy asked.

Perun walked ahead of them on the deer path. He threw his arms up. “Soon those rescue vehicles will be here, messing up the forest.”

“This has happened before?” Steopa asked.

Both Perun and Rebecka nodded.

“Cars crash on that corner a lot,” Rebecka said.

Jimmy walked in front of Steopa with his mouth open. He would stop and stare at something for a short time, then smile and hurry to catch up with the rest. They came into a small clearing. Jimmy looked up and smiled. “That's trippy.”

The full moon hung above the trees. At first, Steopa did not realize what Jimmy meant, then he remember how strange the moon looked when he first changed. It had become brighter and had a blue halo around it. The halo had become so normal to Steopa that he forgot humans could not see it.

Perun pointed across the clearing. “Over there, the old village.”

“Where?” Rebecka asked, scanning the ground in front of them.

Perun raised his hands. He sang in a guttural voice. Steopa could not make out any words. The language did not sound familiar. Across the clearing the brush trembled. The branches slithered and twisted away. A path cleared in front of them. Framed in the open brush, a corner of a large house could be seen in the moonlight.

“My home. I share it with Jeremiah and Mak,” Perun said.

“Jeremiah is still here?” Steopa asked.

Perun nodded and chuckled.

“Was that the heavy-set vampire you introduced me to?” Rebecka asked. “When Vincent had that fight in Forest Grove?”

Steopa nodded.

“He won't be here tonight,” Perun said. “He had to hunt.”

“Hunt?” Jimmy asked. “As in finding some blood to drink?”

“Yes,” Steopa said.

“So I have to drink blood, right?”

Steopa nodded.

Jimmy lowered his head and scratched his cheek. "Blood? Hmm," he said in a lowered voice.

"Have you seen Teodor?" Perun asked, leading them down the path.

"Yes," Steopa said. "One of his sons is marrying a friend of Rebecka."

Perun smiled. "You know what that means. More werewolves. They are going to outnumber your kind soon."

"That will not be a problem."

The path opened into a flat piece of ground. Old homes in various states of decay lined the sides. A large, empty fountain sat in the middle of what might have been the center of the village. On one of the porches, a dark-haired vampire watched them. He raised his hand. Perun waved him away.

The vampire stood up, wrapping a deer hide around him. Steopa could tell by his features he was a Native American. He recognized him. He had also come to the fight at Forest Grove, but had not said much. The vampire went inside one of the old homes.

Perun motioned to a large porch covered in grape vines. "Wait here. I have something for us, Steopa." He hurried into the house.

"You have questions," Steopa said to Jimmy.

Jimmy held his hand out in front of him, studying his thick fingernails. "Yeah."

"You do understand what happened?" Steopa asked.

Jimmy nodded. "I died because my adopted dad decided to drink and drive. But then a real relative of mine shows up, and I come back from the dead a vampire. I have to say, this is one of the coolest things that ever happened to me."

"I suppose it is cool," Rebecka said.

"Are there any vampire clans? Do I have to introduce myself to an elder?"

Rebecka laughed. Steopa shook his head. Rebecka put her arm around Steopa. "It's not like in the role playing games, or the books. Well, most of them."

"I suppose you're my elder, anyway," Jimmy said with a twinkle in his eye. "Are you my real parents?"

Steopa shook his head. "I am your many-great grandfather. Rebecka is my love."

"So I am your step-many-great grandmother." Rebecka said with a slight laugh.

"Would that make me his uncle?" Perun asked as he came out of the house. He sat down beside Steopa, two clear bottles clinking in his hand. He handed one bottle to Steopa. "Vodka."

"Where did you get this?" Steopa asked.

"Those college kids like to party in the woods. Sometimes I join them. Sometimes I just take their drinks." Perun opened a second bottle. "It not like in the past. People would give me this."

"Why?" Jimmy asked.

"Because if they didn't, I would make their time in the woods... difficult."

Steopa took a deep drink of his bottle.

"Can I have some?" Jimmy asked.

"No," Steopa said.

"Because I am underage?"

Rebecka shook her head. "You don't need it. Besides, it would taste like rocket fuel."

"This is the good stuff," Perun said.

Jimmy ran his finger along his fangs. "These feel weird. Whoa, what is this on the end of my tongue?"

"Your body has changed," Steopa said.

"It's like a straw," Rebecka said.

"Cool."

"How did this happen?" Perun asked. He pointed to Jimmy.

Steopa leaned back on the steps. He took a swig. "I had been attacked in the woods next to my home. I killed that vampire, but I had been bitten. I did make it home. I saw my wife."

Perun chuckled.

"Yes, we had not seen each other in a long time."

Perun laughed. "Was it good?"

"I died."

"That's how I would want to go."

Steopa glared at Perun. "My wife became pregnant."

"Your daughter?" Rebecka asked.

"Nastenka."

Perun raised his bottle. "Congratulations."

"I see," Jimmy said. "Does it happen all the time?"

"No."

"You must be hungry," Rebecka said.

"Thirsty," Jimmy said.

"That's how it starts."

Steopa handed the half empty bottle back to Perun. "We have to leave."

"Don't be a stranger. Rebecka, make sure he comes by or I might have to get nasty," Perun said.

"I can try," she said

Steopa shook Perun's hand. They left the old village. When they walked into the clearing, Steopa turned around and saw the brush and trees move so the only path to the village became invisible.

"Where did you meet him?" Rebecka asked.

"I will tell you later," Steopa said.

"Where are we going?" Jimmy asked.

"To the city."

"Great, I was never allowed to go."

Steopa pointed to the lights of the skyline of Deerbow. "That is where we hunt."

Jimmy smiled. His fangs glistened in the moonlight. "I can't wait."

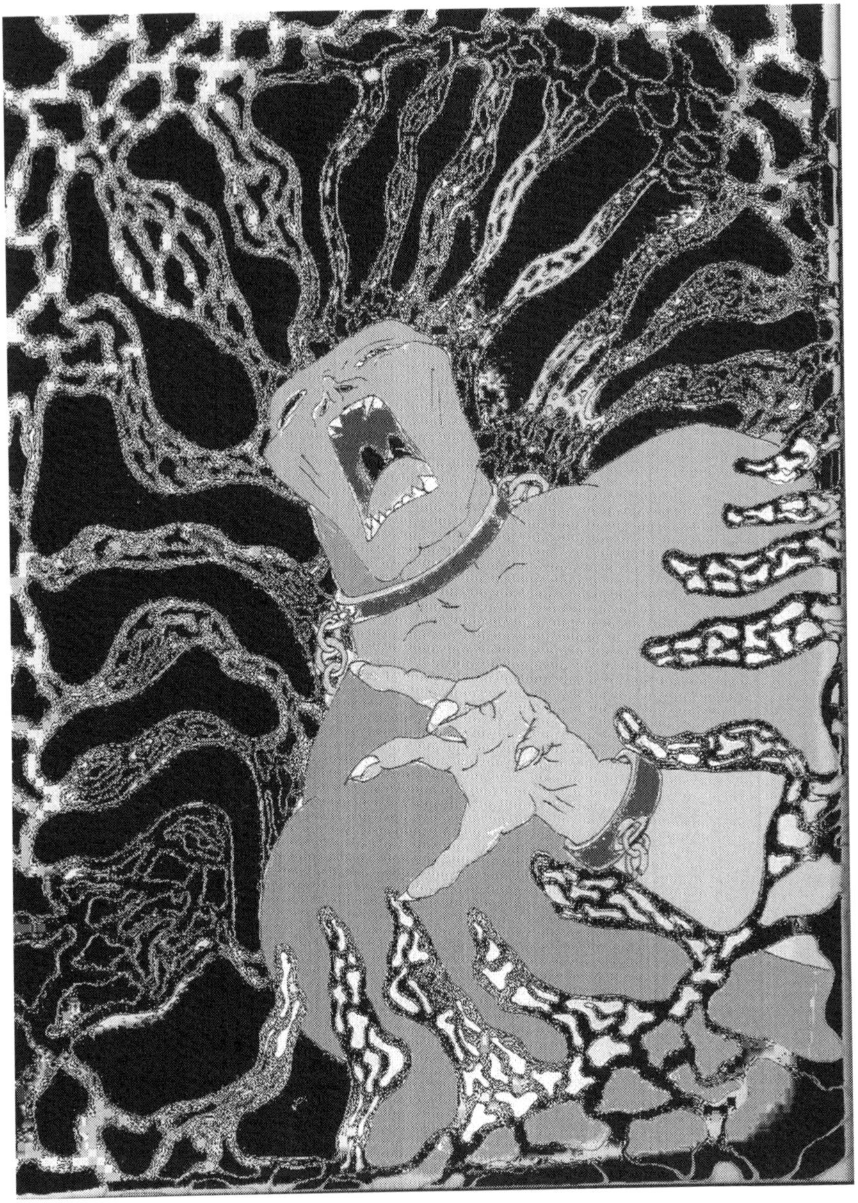

CHAPTER 3

The sound of the music from the jazz club drifted across the street. Steopa stood facing Rebecka as Jimmy scared a feral cat. Steopa crossed his arms. "I do not think it would be a good idea."

"Why not?" Rebecka asked. "Vincent won't mind."

Steopa shook his head. "But we are asking him to accept Jimmy." He glanced at Jimmy. Jimmy left the cat alone and stared at the street lights. The jazz club door opened, amplifying the alto sax solo.

"Come on, I know Vincent."

Steopa shook his head. "Not tonight."

Rebecka ran her finger down Steopa's lapel. "Are you sure?"

He raised his eyebrow.

She grinned. "Tell you what, why don't you take Jimmy out and show him the ropes. I'll go visit my brother and Vincent. I will see you at home later."

"That is acceptable."

Rebecka stood on her tip toes to kiss Steopa. She opened her mouth and ran her tongue along his fangs. She pulled away, then turned to Jimmy.

"Make sure you listen to him," she said. "He taught me everything."

"Where are you going?" Jimmy asked.

"Somewhere else, but I will see you later."

Jimmy grinned. "See ya, Grandma."

Rebecka stopped and her mouth dropped open. "Please don't call me that."

Steopa hugged her with one arm. "Why not? In a way you are."

Rebecka shook her head. "Let me get used to this, okay?"

Steopa kissed Rebecka's hand. "Until morning."

"See you soon."

Rebecka walked down the street until she came to an alley. Then she jumped up onto the roof of a store. She leaped over the street and disappeared over the roofs.

Jimmy chuckled. “Can I do that?”

“Yes,” Steopa turned. “You can do more. Follow me.”

Steopa led Jimmy to the alley. He could smell the urine and feces a couple of buildings away. As they got closer, Jimmy covered his nose and turned pale.

“Oh God,” he said. He doubled over and dry heaved.

“Sorry,” Steopa said. “Your sense of smell is stronger now. Can you smell something else?”

Jimmy leaned against the wall. “Other than the piss and shit?”

“If it helps, you can separate the smells.”

“How?”

“It is like when you are in a noisy room and you have to listen to a friend.”

“I think I understand.” Jimmy closed his eyes. He sniffed. “Acid? No. It's a chemical.”

“Yes. Paint thinner.”

“In an alley?” Jimmy asked. “Here?”

Steopa pointed to the sign on one of the store fronts.

Jimmy chuckled. “A hobby store, I see.”

A couple of girls walked past them. One of them turned their head and smiled at Jimmy. He smirked. The girls giggled and continued down the street. Jimmy's fangs grew and he grinned. “I have to feed, too?”

Steopa glanced at the girls. They were surrounded by a bright blue shroud. He shook his head. “Not them. Some people are easier to hunt than others.”

“How will I know?”

“Did you see that cloud that surrounded them?”

Jimmy nodded.

Steopa saw a man walking toward them. This man had a dark shroud covering his body. “Look at him.”

Jimmy looked and his eyes went wide. “Whoa, that cloud, that's black.”

“That is a shroud,” Steopa said. “Anyone who is inviting death wears a dark one.”

“Cool.” Jimmy started to moved toward the young man.

“Wait.” Steopa placed his hand on Jimmy's shoulder and stopped him. “Follow me.”

Steopa led Jimmy past the young man. Then he turned onto an

empty side street. Steopa jumped onto the nearest building roof.

Jimmy laughed and jumped. He landed next to Steopa. "That's awesome."

"Want to try a longer jump?" Steopa pointed to the other side of the building.

Steopa ran. He jumped and landed on the building across the street. Steopa turned around to watch for Jimmy. Jimmy backed up to the other side of the roof and ran. He landed a few feet away from Steopa. He raised his arms up and shouted.

"I have not met a lot of young vampires like you," Steopa said, chuckling. "Most of them do not look forward to the hunt."

"Why the hell not?" Jimmy asked. "You have to eat."

Steopa smiled. "You have saved me a lot of trouble. But you have to understand, you have to drink human blood."

Jimmy paused, then shrugged. "The thought of drinking animal blood makes me sick."

Steopa slapped him on the back. "Good. We should find your prey."

He walked over to a darker part of the roof. Jimmy followed. Steopa allowed the shadows to flow over him. Jimmy watched Steopa for a moment, then stood still.

He slipped into the shadows. He whispered. "I didn't have to think about it."

Steopa nodded. "Vampires use surprise and stealth to find our meals. We use shadows and the environment to hide ourselves. We should not appear until we are ready to attack."

"Then we kill," Jimmy said.

"If we need to," Steopa said with a shrug. "The more blood you drink at once, the less you have to hunt. But the more you kill, the more chance you have of attracting attention to yourself. It is a fine line."

"So killing is optional. What happens if you don't kill? Don't they become like us? Do they remember?"

"If you are not interrupted while you feed, they will not become a vampire."

"Interrupted?"

Steopa rubbed his chin. "Rebecka became a vampire that way."

"How?"

"Another vampire stopped me."

"Really? How?"

"I had made a mistake. I hunted on another vampire's territory. He had every right to stop me. And they are friends, as well. She spoke of him earlier. Vincent."

Jimmy nodded. "Okay. What if I don't kill them, then what?"

"Humans have the ability to convince themselves that some things have never happened. If you attack them correctly, they will not remember you. But you might have abilities that can help."

"Like what?"

"Some vampires can influence how people think. Others can command them to forget."

"What can you do?"

"I knock them out."

Jimmy laughed.

"Then I take their money."

"Why?"

"Because when they wake up and find their money missing-"

"They are going to think they were mugged. Brilliant." Jimmy nudged Steopa. "Over there."

Steopa looked. A woman walked down the street, the shroud hung around her like a black blanket.

"Good choice," Steopa said. "A person with that dark of a shroud will be easy to hunt."

She limped below them on the sidewalk. She would step, then lean on one side, then take another step. The woman paused at a garbage bin and dug out a couple of soda cans. After putting them in a large grocery bag, she continued down the street.

Steopa left the roof. Jimmy followed. The woman walked into an empty lot. She pulled her handbag over her shoulder, then went into a walkway between two of the buildings. This led to a dead end. Steopa and Jimmy landed in the mouth of the walkway and blocked the entrance. The woman walked down to the wall at the end and put her bag down on the blacktop. Jimmy glanced at Steopa. Steopa nodded.

Jimmy blurred. He had the woman by the neck before she had a chance to react. With one hand clamped over her mouth, he drank. Steopa grinned. He learned as fast as I had, he thought.

Jimmy pulled away from the woman. He didn't let the body drop. Instead, he assisted her tumble to the ground. Her heart had raced, but as Jimmy rested her head on a bag of bottles, her heart returned to a steady beat.

"I didn't think I should drink all of her," Jimmy said, after he joined Steopa.

"That was good," Steopa said.

Jimmy smiled.

"Today, you will stay with Rebecka and I. We will find you your own place soon."

Jimmy looked surprised. "When's the sun up?"

"In a few hours, but we should return."

"Will it really burn me?"

"If you are injured, yes."

Steopa turned to walk back to Konakove. Jimmy caught up with him.

"Where you taught like this?" Jimmy asked.

Steopa shook his head. "No. I had killed the one that made me. I had to learn everything on my own."

"That must have sucked."

Steopa nodded. "But when I changed, people still believed in vampires. The first night I woke up in a coffin, a rosary on my head and garlic in my mouth. The village were coming out to stake me."

"Wow."

Steopa raised his eyebrow. "Now it is easier. No one believes we are real. That makes hunting simpler."

Steopa hurried across the large parkland that held the old poorhouses. Steopa's stride was double the length of Jimmy's, but he stayed next to Steopa. As they came to the first large building, Steopa felt the presence of another vampire. He stopped Jimmy.

"There is another vampire here I am not familiar with. We should be careful," he said.

"Why?"

"Etiquette," Steopa said. "You do not approach an unknown vampire mindlessly. You must make your presence known. But first, you must make sure that you want to. But this part of the city is not hunted by any vampires I know; he or she could have just claimed it."

"A territory?"

"Hunting areas, yes. Too many vampires in one area draw the

wrong sort of attention." Steopa turned to Jimmy. "Stay behind me. Stay quiet."

Jimmy stepped behind him. Steopa faded into the shadows, then he walked to the poorhouse. The windows on the lower level had been covered with large pieces of plywood. Steopa jumped to the second floor. He found an open window and went inside the building.

As he stood up, he heard voices. The voices drifted in from the other side of an open doorway. Steopa approached it. He stopped at the door and listened. The voices halted.

Jimmy opened his mouth. Steopa raised his hand to silence him. He checked the corridor and did not see anyone. Steopa made sure not to make any noise as he walked into the hall.

"Hold him." A female voice echoed.

Steopa followed the voice. He came to another open door. Inside was a large room with two levels covered in dust and broken glass. An upper level formed a semi-circle around the lower level. It reminded Steopa of an operating theater, but there were no places to sit on the upper level.

On the lower level, a man had been tied to a table. The table had been tilted on one side so his head laid higher than his feet. He pulled at the ropes on his arms, making his muscles bulge. He strained and groaned, but the ties did not stretch.

A red-headed female vampire stood next to the bound man. She grabbed the bound man's face and turned it from side to side, studying his features. A smaller vampire, with a scarred head and face, hurried behind them. He sat a large cup on a table. Alongside it a piece of cloth had been unrolled. Inside it were small bottles, tucked into pockets.

The smaller vampire looked over his shoulder. The scar that ran down the side of his face had been accented by the shadows in the room. "Take off his gag," he said.

The female vampire did.

"What the fuck!" The man strained against the ropes. "Let me go, you sick motherfuckers!"

She slapped the man. The man's head bounced against the table. Blood trickled over his lips from his nose.

"I don't know if he is worth it," she said.

"Hmm?" the scarred vampire rubbed his chin. "Yes, he is

perfect. Since his sister did not last."

The bound man swore again. The female vampire raised her hand. He laid his head back on the table. "Your sister wasn't strong enough. You should be," she said.

The scarred one mixed the contents from the small bottles into the large cup. He brought them over to the female. She opened a vein on her wrist and let the blood flow into the cup.

"What are you doing?" the man shouted.

"You wouldn't understand. But in a short time, your life will change."

Her blood dripped, then stopped as her wound healed. She pulled her arm away and smiled at the man.

"It's almost ready." The scarred vampire turned around, swirling the cup in his hand. He walked around the table and stood in front of the man. "Open his mouth."

The female clamped her fingers around the man's chin. She dug her fingernails into his skin and forced his mouth open. Jimmy tapped Steopa on his shoulder.

"What are they doing?" he whispered.

"I am not sure," Steopa lied. They would not, he thought.

The scarred vampire tipped the cup, pouring the blood mixture into the man's mouth. The man coughed and gagged. Most of the blood flowed down his face and down his clothing. The scarred vampire pulled the cup away. The female clamped the man's mouth shut.

The man struggled. He coughed. Blood sprayed out between his lips, but she held onto his jaw. The man swallowed. Steopa felt a growl form in his throat. He stopped it before it became audible.

Steopa pulled Jimmy away from the edge. The female vampire stepped back. The man's body shook. He screamed. His veins bulged out of his arms and neck. Steopa heard the man's heart beat faster. It became a solid sound, then stopped. His head lolled to one side as his last breath rattled out of his mouth.

The scarred vampire checked his watch. "Sixty seconds."

The female sniffed the bound man. She stood back. "He seems stronger," she said.

The man opened his eyes and his mouth. His fangs pushed the other teeth aside and took their place in the front of his mouth. The female undid the ropes. The scarred vampire motioned to the man.

"You come with me."

The new vampire stumbled away from the table, following the scarred vampire. The female vampire picked up the ropes, then walked to the table and rolled up the fabric with the bottles in the pockets.

The scarred vampire lit a rolled up piece of paper and threw it on the floor. A fire burned, spreading into a circle in front of them. Steopa could make out letters and symbols along the edge. The scarred vampire led the man through the flames.

The flames rose up, obscuring the two inside the circle. Smoke swirled around as if it had been caught in a whirlwind. When the flames died, the two vampires were gone.

Steopa leaned forward. The female laid the ropes down on another disused table. Jimmy watched her with his mouth open and his eyes wide. He glanced at Steopa. His face fell.

"That's not normal, is it?" he asked.

"No."

"I heard you before," the female vampire said. She had not turned her head. "Why don't you come down here?"

Steopa motioned to Jimmy to stay. He vaulted over the rails, landing in front of the other vampire. The female stood back to crane her neck. Then she held out one hand, while flipping a strand of her red hair back with the other.

"I'm Adelind."

"Steopa."

"Why doesn't your friend join us?"

"I told him to stay."

"Ah." She smiled at Jimmy. "Is this your place?"

"It has not been claimed by anyone."

"Then why?"

"Why are you making a drudge?"

Adelind laughed. Her laugh was as warm as winter on the Baltic Sea. "If this is not your place, then it is none of your business, Mr. Rodovitch."

"I did not tell you-"

"You didn't need to. You are famous in Europe, you know. The one who killed the vampire that attacked him, while still human. The giant that slaughtered the frozen troops. Now that I see you, I can see they are not stories."

“I have not heard of you.”

“Your loss.” Adelind walked up to Steopa. She ran her fingers down his lapel. “I have heard so much about you that I should offer you an arrangement.”

Steopa shoved her hand away. “I am linked.”

“Oh, that is simple to fix. Kill her.”

“Insolent slut!” Steopa slapped her. Adelind's face snapped back. The red hair she had piled on the top of her head tumbled to her shoulders and in front of her face. She turned, flinging her hair back. Her eyes flickered yellow.

“That is how you feel?” she scoffed, rubbing her cheek. “That is your last mistake.”

Steopa growled. She snapped her fingers. Fire rose up in the burned area of the floor.

“We are alike in more ways that you will never know.” Adelind stepped into the flames and disappeared.

Jimmy jumped to join Steopa. “You bitch-slapped her,” he said.

Steopa stared at the fire as it died out. I have seen those before, he thought. But how do they know how to use them?

“I know who that guy was. He's a fullback for the university's football team.” Jimmy shook his head. “What did they do to him?”

“They made him drink vampire blood.”

“They turned him into a vampire.”

“A drudge.”

“What is that?”

“A slave.” Steopa walked to the burned area. The circle had faded. He ran the tip of his boot over the floor. The letters and the symbols were etched into the tile.

“The sun is coming.” Steopa turned to Jimmy. “We will worry about this later.”

“Should we worry?”

Steopa turned. “We will see.” He motioned to the doorway. Jimmy glanced at the table, then left the room. Steopa followed him.

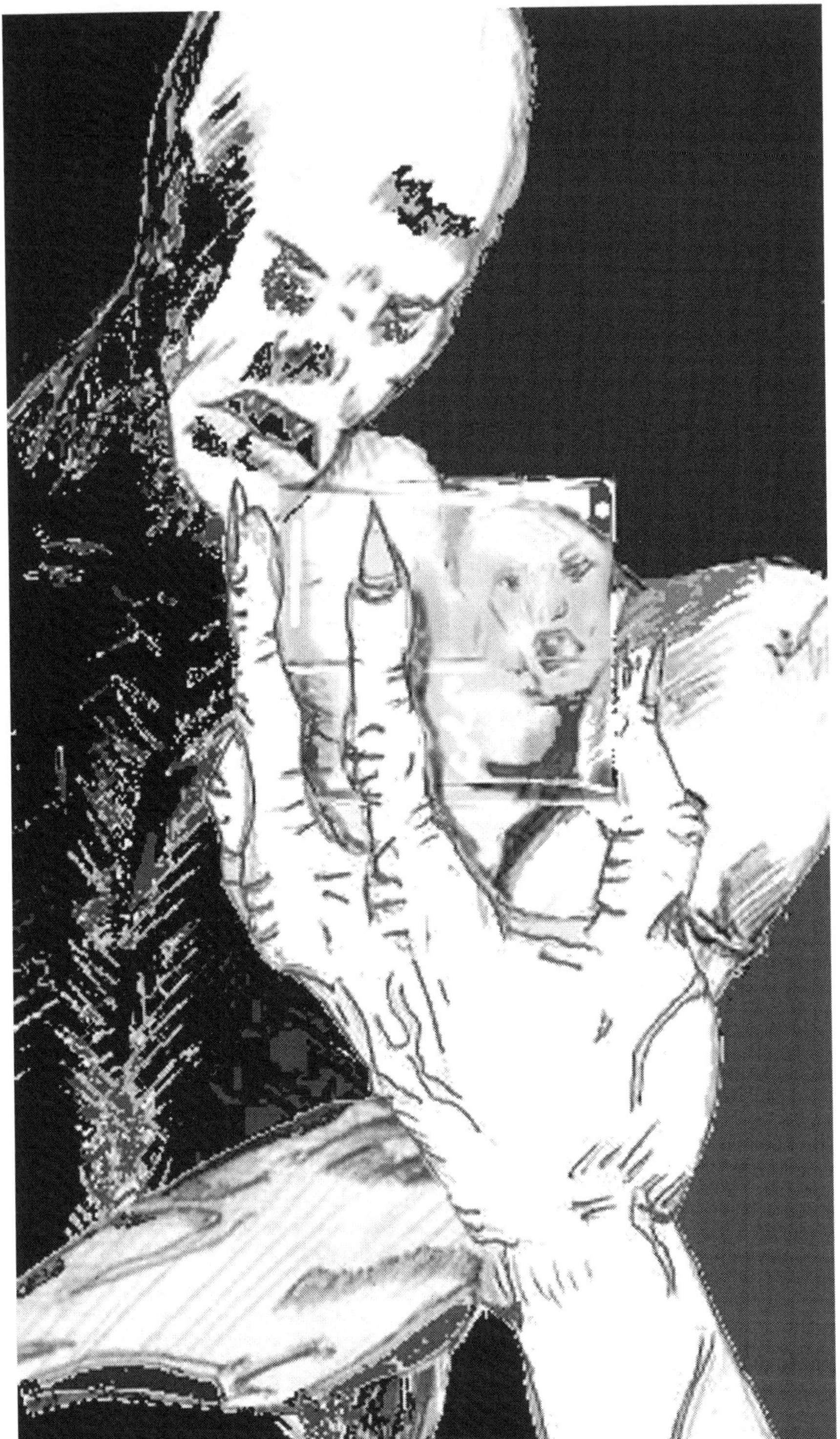

CHAPTER 4

Steopa laid looking at the ceiling in the lair. The image of the young man becoming a drudge replayed through his head until he could no longer stay in the stupor. He felt the bed move.

Rebecka rolled on her side. Her breasts slid and rested against each other on the bed. She reached over with her hand and brushed his long hair out of his face. Steopa pulled her close. He kissed her cheek then her lips. Rebecka ran her hands down his back, fingering the old scars that had never healed.

He pulled away and stroked her curls. "Do you ever...?"

"Ever what?" Rebecka laid her head on his chest.

"If we could do more?"

"More?"

Steopa nodded. Rebecka lifted her head. Her brown curls fell around her face. "You mean in bed?"

Steopa nodded.

"No."

"No?"

"I'm fine with this, Steopa." She kissed his cheek and wiggled out of his arms. "I have a feeling we should check on the coiree."

That cup, he thought. Steopa swung his legs over the bed and stood. "That would be a good idea." He walked over to their large vault-like door.

Rebecka giggled.

Steopa turned. "What is it?"

"Jimmy's out there."

Steopa looked down at his naked body. "Ah, yes."

Rebecka shook her head, and reached into his wardrobe. She moved the hangers around for a moment, then handed Steopa a blue shirt. He smoothed out the sleeves.

"Is this one your favorite?" he asked.

"No, that's the green one, but you haven't worn that in a while."

"I suppose they will be looking for Jimmy?" Rebecka said as she started to dress.

"The swamp is deep," Steopa said. "They will think he is missing in the mud. Besides, I can ask Perun to make their search difficult."

Rebecka buttoned up her blouse. "Where did you meet him?"

"Perun?"

She nodded.

He glanced around the room. "It is a long story."

"We have time."

"I thought you wanted to check on the coiree?"

Rebecka stood in front of Steopa. "You are avoiding the question."

"I am not."

She nodded. "Yes, you are."

"I met him here."

"In Deerbow?"

Steopa shook his head. "In this building."

"I always thought this was a bank vault."

"It is a vault, but it was used to store valuables for the people who worked here."

Rebecka stepped back. "What?"

"You told me about the stories of the base. This is part of it."

Her mouth fell open. "This is part of the secret military base. The one that everyone talks about like it's Area Fifty-one?"

Steopa nodded.

"It's for real?"

"Yes. Perun, Teodor, Jeremiah, and I were... specimens."

Rebecka sat back down on the bed. "What sort of place was this?"

"What do the stories say?"

"Many things, it was an underground weapons lab. It was used for hiding the former Nazi scientists who were not working on the atom bombs." She shrugged, then giggled. "That is, unless the one about the Illuminati using the base to take over the world is the truth."

"The truth is stranger. We had been captured and studied. And other beings like us," Steopa said.

"What sort of creatures?"

Steopa pointed to the door. "We have a guest, we have to talk about this later."

Rebecka stared at him for a moment, then shrugged. Steopa opened the door.

Jimmy put the bullet-ridden Nazi helmet on his head, then reached for the broadsword on the wall. Steopa placed his hand on the top of Jimmy's head and took off the helmet. Jimmy looked up and grinned.

"Sorry," he said.

"You need different clothes," Steopa said. "Then we are going somewhere special."

"Is that real?" he asked, pointing to the helmet.

"Yes."

"Where did you get it?"

Steopa placed the helmet on the bureau. "Off a dead Nazi, after I had convinced him to kill himself."

"How did you do that?"

"I told him to shoot himself."

"That's all?"

Steopa nodded.

Jimmy motioned around the room. "This is a cool place. What is it?"

"It's weird," Rebecka said.

"It was a vault," Steopa said.

"Do you have a coffin?" Jimmy asked.

"I never had one."

Rebecka patted Steopa's arm. "Me, neither."

"I think I'm gonna get one," Jimmy said.

Rebecka laughed as she sat down at the desk. "For real?"

"Why not?"

Steopa shook his head and pulled his green overcoat off the hook. He laid it across his arm. "Coffins are convenient. But if I did not have this vault, I would have found something else to keep the sunlight out."

"I still think it's a cool idea," Jimmy said.

"Whoa," Rebecka said, looking at her computer screen. "Baldman has been trying to get a hold of me."

"Who?" Jimmy asked.

"A hacker I know." She closed the lid. "I'll call him later."

They left and walked to the consignment store that Steopa used for his clothing. He rang the bell. The owner's daughter leaned over the balcony.

"She's ill," she said.

"I am sorry to hear that," Steopa said. "This young man needs clothes."

The daughter turned her head. She had a quick conversation with someone, then she went inside the apartment. A few moments later she opened the door to the shop.

"Mom said I better let you."

Jimmy walked over to the men's section. Rebecka stayed by the door, punching buttons on her phone. Steopa leaned on the counter. "How ill is she?"

"The flu, but it could get worse."

Steopa's shoulders sagged. "She has gotten old."

"She has made me promise to keep this store open and to let you take whatever you want."

"I never take the clothes. You will be compensated."

"I know."

Jimmy came back to the counter with his arms full of clothing. "Hi," he said.

The daughter rang up the clothes. Steopa paid her. Jimmy picked out a pair of black jeans, a black t-shirt, and a denim jacket. He smiled at the woman, then went to the dressing room. She lowered her head and wiped a tear from her cheek.

"What is it?" Steopa asked.

"Mom isn't doing to well. She wants to see you, but I don't think that would be a good idea."

"I understand."

"Baldman, slow down," Rebecka said from the doorway.

Steopa looked over his shoulder. Rebecka rolled her eyes. "That was months ago. I don't know what happened to the children."

Jimmy came out of the dressing room with his old clothes in his hands. He stopped at the counter and pulled off a patch that had been on his old pants. He put it in his pants pocket, then he tossed his hair with his hands. "Too emo?"

Steopa cocked his head. "What?"

Rebecka shook hers and covered the receiver with her hand. "I think you need some eyeliner."

Jimmy smiled. "I need to get a coat like yours," he said, pointing to Steopa's overcoat.

Steopa glanced down at the sleeve. "You would have to talk to a Communist officer."

Rebecka came over to the counter. "I am not near my computer now. I will take a look when I can." She closed her phone.

"Tell your mother hello for me," Steopa said to the woman.

"Thanks," Jimmy said.

They left and crossed the city to the cemetery of Forest Grove. As they came up to the gates, Jimmy sighed.

"I've been here before. A class trip, boring."

"It's not that bad," Rebecka said.

They crested the hill to the large monuments section. Rebecka pointed to the miniature copy of the Notre Dame cathedral. "That's where we are going. The Dysart Memorial."

"I've seen it," Jimmy said.

"Have you been inside?"

"Inside?"

Steopa chuckled. "There are many secrets in this place."

Jimmy ran past them and scaled the pyramid and stood at the point. He walked around the point, giggling. Steopa and Rebecka stood alongside the angel statue and watched Jimmy. He leaned forward, glanced at Steopa, then stood back up.

He joined them. "There are a few people coming this way."

Rebecka jumped to the top of the Memorial. She scanned the cemetery, then jumped down. "They're not kids."

Jimmy grinned. "We could take them."

Steopa rested his hand on Jimmy's shoulder. "Wait, we have to see if they are a threat."

Rebecka reached for the angel statue. Steopa shook his head. He pointed to another memorial. This one had been designed to look like a Roman temple. Empty alcoves sat behind the columns where statues had been.

"We could hide underneath," she said.

"Or we might find a meal," he said.

She smiled. Steopa motioned Jimmy and Rebecka to follow him. He slid behind one of the columns and squeezed into the larger alcove. Rebecka and Jimmy did the same. The two people came closer. Steopa felt another vampire approaching, but this one felt further away.

The two people came around the pyramid. The older man with a gray beard wore a tattered trench coat and a backpack. The younger man carried a suitcase. He sat the suitcase down on a bench and opened it. He moved something around in the case for a few moments. A high-pitched whirring noise, like a set a gears running, raised in pitch. He lifted out a crossbow with a small motor on it. The older one took it after dropping his backpack to the ground.

Steopa tensed. The bolts glinted silver in the moonlight. Hunters, he thought. I have not seen vampire hunters since the Red Revolution.

"Randy," the older one said. "Start scanning."

Randy ran his hand over his prematurely balding head. He reached back into the suitcase and pulled out parts of a strange looking object. As he assembled the item, it looked like a coin detector, or a bomb sniffer. He turned on a small screen on the handle of the detector. He swung it over the ground in a systematic walk around the monuments.

The older one propped the crossbow up, and opened his backpack. Inside were silver-tipped stakes, small vials of water, and an ax. Steopa held back his growl. Are they real hunters? he thought. There have been too many pretenders in the last few years to be sure.

Jimmy moved in the next alcove. Steopa almost warned him to stop, but Jimmy became still again. Steopa felt Rebecka's excitement rise. He could take them. Rebecka had learned a lot -- she would be formidable -- but Jimmy was new.

"Gene," Randy said. "There is a large opening below the Dysart Memorial."

"The smuggler's tunnel?" Gene asked.

"Possibly. Can I have the wand?"

Steopa raised his eyebrow. Gene threw Randy a piece of brass tubing. On one end of it, two l-shaped metal rods were attached. Randy put down the detector and walked over to the Dysart Memorial. He held up the wand and walked over to the wall with the rose window. The bent pieces of metal swung together and pointed to the location of the altar on the other side of the wall.

Steopa saw Rebecka start.

Gene's head snapped up and scanned the alcoves with his eyes. Steopa faded deeper into the shadows. Gene picked up a flashlight.

It had two lights on it. A normal white light and on top of it, a blue one. Gene turned it on and shined it over the alcoves. It passed over Rebecka, then Steopa. The blue light blinded and burned him. Steopa bit his lip and stood still.

As the light moved off him, the burning sensation ended. Gene moved the light over to the next alcove. The light stayed on the alcove for a few moments. Jimmy yelled in pain.

Gene kept the light on Jimmy. Jimmy screamed. Randy grabbed an ax. He ran to the alcove while lifting the ax. Steopa stepped out and grabbed the ax out of Randy's hand. He swung it around and brought it back into Randy's chest. Randy's body lifted up and slid down on the ax head.

Gene dropped the light and grabbed the crossbow. Steopa pulled the ax out of Randy's body. He tossed it into his other hand and advanced on Gene. Behind him, he heard Rebecka run out of the alcove and over to Jimmy. Steopa felt the other vampire coming closer. He paused.

Gene shot the bolt. It hit Steopa in the shoulder. The silver tip burned. The pain started cold then heated until it felt like a branding. Lowering the ax, Steopa reached for the bolt, as his fingers curled around it, it exploded.

He dropped to his knees and felt his shoulder. His hand, now missing a few fingers, covered the gaping hole where his flesh had been. He heard Rebecka scream. It could have shattered glass. Gene turned his head away, wincing from the sound. He grabbed another bolt and fumbled with it as he tried to load it. Rebecka grabbed her shoulder, as if she had been hit.

Gene spoke into a small mouthpiece that hung off his ear. "Tell her we found the giant."

Steopa slammed the ax into the ground, using the handle to push himself off the ground. Exploding stakes, that is new, he thought. Jimmy jumped over him. He raised his claws. Gene pressed the crossbow against Jimmy's chest. Jimmy looked down, surprised.

Rebecka came to Steopa's side. Her face had lost any color it had. She favored the same shoulder that had been injured on Steopa. She tore off her jacket and tied it around Steopa's wound. The other vampire felt closer. Steopa could almost name who it was. "Help Jimmy," he whispered to Rebecka.

Jimmy did not move. Gene pulled back the trigger. Behind him the shadows dissipated. A shotgun barrel came out of the fading shadows and rested against Gene's head. The chubby vampire holding the gun shoved the end into Gene's cheek.

"Okay motherfucker, are you faster than my shotgun?" the vampire asked.

Gene's finger twitched. Both barrels exploded. Gene's body, now headless, fell with a thud on the ground. The chubby vampire wiped the blood and brains out of this cropped hair. His eyes rested on Steopa.

"Steopa," he said. "Oh shit."

He ran over to Steopa.

Jimmy stared at the headless body. The bolt in the crossbow exploded, destroying most the crossbow. He dropped the crossbow, staring at the body.

Steopa reached out with his good arm. "Jeremiah?"

"Shit, you're gonna need a lot of blood to heal that," Jeremiah said, laying the gun on the ground.

Rebecka lifted her head, her face streaked with bloody tears. "Blood?"

Jeremiah knelt down to help pick Steopa up, "Yeah, damn, I don't know if we could get enough." Jeremiah pulled Steopa to a standing position. "I don't know any blood banks."

Rebecka looked back at the memorial. "I have a better idea."

Jimmy snapped out of his daze. "That head just evaporated," he said. "Fucking awesome."

Jeremiah looked over his shoulder. "Hey kid, come here. Get under his other side."

Jimmy slipped his arm under what was left of his shoulder. Steopa fought back the pain. Rebecka picked up Steopa's dropped coat. Then she ran to the angel statue and shoved it. Steopa grunted then bellowed.

CHAPTER 5

The secret entrance of the smugglers tunnel had opened part way when Rebecka ran inside. Jeremiah and Jimmy glanced at each other, then at Steopa.

"You need a blood bank," Jeremiah said.

"BRING HIM DOWN HERE." Rebecka's voice echoed through the tunnel and out into the cemetery. Steopa smiled. Her command voice sounded stronger. He winced. The pain from the wound spread down his arm.

Jimmy lifted Steopa and attempted to move into the opening, but Jeremiah wouldn't move. Steopa fought the pain, and his body shutting down. "Listen to her," he said, forcing the words out.

"What's down there?" Jeremiah asked.

Steopa growled. Jeremiah lifted Steopa's side. They helped Steopa down the tunnel. Rebecka left the door open. She pointed to the couch.

"Lay him there." She jumped through the hole in the ceiling.

Jeremiah guided Steopa to the couch. Steopa looked at the wounds. The flesh had seared and blackened from the stake. His blood would fill the wound, then drip down his chest. The bones on his fingers had regrown, but muscles and sinews had not.

"You need blood," Jeremiah said. "What the hell are we doing here?"

"Trust Rebecka," Steopa said.

"We are in a pit and-"

Rebecka returned with the coiree. She hurried over to Steopa. "It filled, just like it did with Vincent."

Steopa looked into the gold-rimmed cup. The blood filled the shallow bowl. The large mouth of the cup would have been hard to drink from, even if he had not been injured. Steopa closed his eyes as he drank the warm, sweet blood. The more he drank, the more his body filled with warmth. He drained all the blood from the coiree. Rebecka took the cup out of his hands and placed it on the floor.

"Steopa," she whispered, resting her head against his.

Steopa pulled her closer with his good arm. She ran her fingers through his hair. Then she kissed his forehead. "Are you all right?"

Steopa nodded. "Yes."

He looked at his shoulder. The blood had stopped flowing. The wound healed, but not as fast his other wounds. The fingers on his other hand had also healed. He kissed Rebecka's lips.

She stood back, then picked up the coiree.

"I'll be right back," she said.

"Jeremiah, thank you," Steopa said.

Jeremiah sat down on the chair next to the couch. "She's nice."

Steopa sat back as the flesh knitted together. "We are linked."

"Linked? I thought that was a myth."

Steopa rubbed his hand over the wound. The muscles had returned to normal. "No, it is not."

Jeremiah reached into his coat and pulled out a handgun. He checked the chamber. Jimmy watched every move that Jeremiah made. Jeremiah lowered the gun.

"How many guns do you have?" Jimmy asked.

Jeremiah shrugged. "Two. That shotgun, and my old service piece." He held up the handgun. "I know, stupid, right? Vampires shouldn't use guns."

Steopa waved his hand, motioning to Jimmy. "Jeremiah, this is Jimmy," Steopa said. "He turned last night."

Jeremiah reached over Steopa to shake Jimmy's hand. "Nice to meet you. Steopa, you have been busy."

"Jimmy is..." Steopa glanced at Jimmy. "I did not make him."

"But you are teaching him?" Jeremiah nodded. "Good. If it hadn't been for you, my first few days would have been nuts."

Rebecka returned. She wiped her hands on her pants and smiled at Steopa. He held out his hand. She sat down next to him, then checked the wound.

Steopa moved his injured arm. The wound had closed. It felt stiff, but no pain.

"You were already on your way here?" he asked Jeremiah.

Jeremiah nodded. "I knew you would have some hunters after you. They stopped at the truck stop, that one I hunt at most of the time. They were asking a lot of strange questions. That one waitress that's sweet on me. She saw the crossbows, and thought they were after me. I got into their truck." Jeremiah reached into his coat. He pulled out a small pile of papers. "They were looking for you."

Steopa took the papers. He read the first page, his birth date, the location of the village where he had grown up, when and where he had attended university, and the date he died. His whole life, condensed onto one page.

He flipped to the next page. His family tree had been plotted. Beside the name of his descendants were notes. Some had addresses and locations. Not all of the names had information. Steopa quickly looked over the names.

Next to his daughter, Nastenka, was an address with the notation, "Needed." His grandsons, Misha and Sasha, had no information, except for a question mark notation by Sasha's name. Steopa forced a sigh of relief. Whoever had compiled the list may have found some of their names, but not much information, he thought. Next to his name were the words Konakove and Burgundy Rathskeller.

Steopa put the pages down on his lap. Rebecka must have sensed something from him. She pulled her cell phone out of her pocket.

"Rebecka, check on your brother," he said.

Rebecka nodded, dialing the phone as she ran up the smuggler's tunnel.

Her name is not on the list, but they have enough information to find her, Steopa thought.

"You said she has a brother. Is he a vampire too?" Jimmy asked.

"No." Steopa gave the papers back to Jeremiah. "Do you understand what this is?"

Jeremiah nodded. "Yeah, you told Perun and me once, remember?"

Steopa felt his shoulder. "Sasha is impossible to get a hold of, but after my injury, he will show up."

"Why?" Jeremiah asked.

"He would have felt it."

"I got a sharp pain in my shoulder, too," Jimmy said.

A polite cough came from the doorway. Steopa turned to look. Ogden leaned on his cane. His blue eyes swept over the room, then he motioned to the tunnel.

"I saw two dead bodies and Rebecka running outside," he said. "What did I miss?"

His eyes scanned Jimmy and Jeremiah again. They rested on Jeremiah's handgun. Steopa reached over and pushed the barrel of the gun down.

"Vampire hunters, Ogden," Steopa said. He pointed to Jeremiah. "You met Jeremiah when Vincent had his trouble. And Jimmy is new. This is Ogden."

"Vampire hunters? In America? That's odd." Ogden walked inside. He pointed to the wound on Steopa's shoulder. "Looks like you were struck."

"Thank you, Captain Obvious," Jeremiah said.

Ogden ignored him. "That is too large of a wound for a simple stake."

"It exploded."

"Messy and unnecessary. Are you sure they were professionals?"

Steopa glanced at Jeremiah and Jimmy. "They were interested in this building."

The small smirk that had been on Ogden's face faded. His eyes flickered to the upper levels. Steopa nodded once. Ogden held up his hand and turned around slowly in the room as if he was searching for something. "You used the cup?"

"You pick that up or something?" Jimmy asked.

Ogden shook his head. "No, Steopa was injured. Our little prize fills with blood."

"That's a handy cup," Jeremiah said.

"I think it only works for a few of us." Ogden lowered his hand. "Could you excuse Steopa and me?"

Jeremiah glanced at Steopa. Steopa nodded. Jeremiah put his handgun away and stood up.

"Did you find out who employed the hunters?" Steopa asked.

Jeremiah shook his head. "But then I haven't rifled through the bodies upstairs." He pointed at Jimmy. "Why don't you come with me."

After they left, Ogden came over to Steopa and checked his wound. "That would have killed you, if it had been dawn."

"I know," Steopa said.

"So, is Jimmy your grandson?"

Steopa stared at Ogden.

Ogden waved his hand in front of his face as if he was trying to disperse Steopa's glare. “The family resemblance is uncanny. He is a relative?”

“I would rather not talk about it.”

“I have a family, too,” Ogden said. “Manas, my driver, is a direct descendant of mine.”

“Is he?”

“Yes.” Ogden sat down. He removed a handkerchief from his pocket and cleaned the top of his cane. “Were they looking for the coiree?”

“They were looking for something in the cemetery. They used some sort of instrument to find the chamber down here.”

“Vampire hunters looking here? Have you checked on the coiree?”

Steopa pointed to his shoulder.

Ogden nodded. “Yes. Are you healed enough?”

“Yes.”

“I will make sure that our protections are in place, then I will join you outside.”

Steopa waved Ogden away. “I have to rest for a moment.”

Ogden stood up and headed upstairs. Steopa closed his eyes. Someone had hired vampire hunters to come after him and his family. Who? He thought. Steopa went through a list of names of possible enemies. Most were dead or would not dare to show their faces around Steopa again. Jalmari had been the last one, and Rebecka had helped kill him.

Someone had found out about his descendants. Who could be after me now? Steopa wondered. What if they were not after me? Steopa opened his eyes. Rebecka stood in front of him.

“John's okay,” she said. “We have been invited over. Vincent insisted.”

Steopa folded his hands on his lap. “Someone knows about my family.”

Rebecka shook her head. “I didn't even know about most of them, until last night.”

“Someone that does not have your name, but has the Rathskeller listed as a possible place of rest,” Steopa said.

“That's why you wanted me to call my brother?”

Steopa nodded. "They do not know about Jimmy, of course, and a few others, that I know of, but I cannot protect them all."

Rebecka sat down and placed her hand on his arm. "Who would have found this out?"

"I do not know."

Rebecka took his hand. Her fingers disappeared into his hand as he closed his around hers. "We should warn them at least."

"I can try," he said. "But many would have felt my injury."

"We have friends that would help, you know that."

"No."

"You don't think Vincent and Ogden will help us?" she asked.

"They do not need to," Steopa said. "It is my family. I have to protect them."

"If they know about the Rathskeller, that means my family is on the list too, or will be. I have to involve Vincent."

"No," Steopa said.

"You know how protective he is of that club," Rebecka said. "If we don't tell him, and something happens, he will be very upset."

"All right, we will talk to him. But please do not mention my family."

Rebecka nodded. "All right."

The wind blew harder than earlier. Steopa tried to put on his overcoat. His shoulder gave him a sharp pain. Rebecka helped him with the heavy coat. Ogden came out of the smugglers tunnel. He moved the angel statue back to its place on the dais.

"Is everything all right?" Steopa asked Ogden, putting his good arm around Rebecka.

Ogden nodded. He pointed with the tip of his cane. "Jimmy?"

Jimmy looked up from the collection of weapons around him. He held up one of the silver-tipped crossbow bolts in his hand that he had wrapped with a piece of cloth. "Yeah."

"You should put those down," Ogden said.

"Jeremiah said that they're safe. The explosive is stable until they are put into the crossbow."

"Jimmy," Steopa said. He surprised himself with how sharp his voice sounded.

Jimmy looked up. He put the stake down, then he motioned to the rest of the weapons. "What are all these?"

"They are used to kill vampires."

Jimmy picked up a small cloth bag. He opened it and held it up. "Mustard seeds?"

Ogden chuckled. "Some people think that if you throw those on the ground a vampire will have to count them."

Jimmy closed the bag and dropped it on the ground. "They must have had some serious funding. The silver alone is a few thousand."

"How can you be so sure?" Rebecka asked.

"Mommy by adoption was a jeweler." Jimmy reached into the duffel bag. He pulled out a vial of water. "I don't think this is holy water. I never saw any that looked like this."

Steopa took the vial. He held it up so the moonlight shown through the glass. "None of the holy water in my church looked like this."

The water glimmered. Particles of something metallic floated in it. Steopa shook the vial. The light off the particles intensified, then faded. He lowered it out of the moonlight and shook the vial again. The particles did not glow.

"May I see that?" Ogden asked, lowering his hand from his chin.

Steopa handed him the vial. Ogden laid it in his left palm. With his right hand, he made strange motions over it. After a moment he closed the vial in his left hand.

"Datura wrightii. The Sacred Datura," Ogden said. "This little flower is lovely in the moonlight. And has the unlikely effect of causing us to fall into a stupor, even at night. The seeds of it anyway, and that is what is in here."

"Seeds?" Rebecka asked.

"Properly prepared. This is strong magic."

Steopa scoffed. "I have never heard of a plant that can do that."

"That is the odd part. Not only is it strong magic, but rare magic as well."

Jeremiah walked over the hill, cradling the shotgun in his arm. He waved to the south of the cemetery. "Their truck is a few blocks down the road." He smiled. "Jackpot."

He came closer and held up a cell phone. "Satellite phone."

"Can I see that?" Rebecka asked.

Jeremiah tossed it to her.

She flipped through the menu. "I'll have to look at this later," she said, sliding it into her pocket.

"Why do you want that?" Steopa asked.

"Baldman. He will have a ball messing with it. We could find out a lot."

Jimmy flipped over the suitcase. The bottom popped open. Jimmy whistled in surprise. "Serious coinage," he said. He pulled out a handful of diamonds.

"Whoa." Rebecka covered her mouth with her hand.

"I never heard of diamonds hurting vampires," Jimmy said.

"They don't," Jeremiah said. He squatted down next to Jimmy and took a couple of diamonds in his hand. "I think this is their hard currency. Whoever hired them wanted to make sure their money was good no matter where they went."

"Without an electronic trail," Rebecka said.

"Yeah," Jeremiah said. "All they would have to do is take one of these to a shady jeweler and get cash."

Rebecka leaned closer to Steopa. "With no electronic trail, no one will be able to trace them." She paused. "Unless they got traffic tickets or something like that. I could get the VIN number and the license plate-"

Jeremiah stood up. "Already checked. VIN number has been scratched out and the license plate is gone."

"When we get to the Rathskeller," Rebecka said, "I will contact Baldman."

"Who?" Jeremiah asked

"A friend with better computer skills than me."

Jeremiah scratched his nose, then he turned to Jimmy. "Help me pick this stuff up. I don't want the police getting their hands on this stuff."

Ogden squatted down and ran his hand over the diamonds. He cupped his hand and scooped up a pile. "Their employer is very well-funded. No reason to let this money go to waste."

He handed the diamonds to Steopa. Rebecka shook her head. "That is a lot of money. Who would have that much?"

"Corporations, churches, smaller countries, some military, and a few people would," Ogden said. "I could, for example."

"Whoa, really?" Jimmy asked.

"You have heard of Phelps Medical, haven't you?"

"Yeah, my adopted dad had done some advertising for them."

Ogden smiled. "My name is Ogden Phelps. I am a silent owner."

Jimmy nodded then chuckled. “I see.”

“Any military would have sent their soldiers,” Steopa said.

“Are you sure?” Jimmy asked.

Both Jeremiah and Steopa nodded.

“Can we talk about this later? Vincent wants us to come over, and the Rathskeller was on that list,” Rebecka said.

Ogden held up the vial of water. “I would like to take this home. A little study?”

“I sure as hell don't want that,” Jeremiah said. He slung the hunter's duffel bag over his shoulder.

“Thank you,” Ogden said. He turned to Steopa. “Remember the door to my house is always open to you and yours.”

Shadows swirled around Ogden and he disappeared. Jeremiah shook his head. “Is he always that high and mighty?”

Steopa raised his eyebrow. “Be mindful of him, Jeremiah.”

Jeremiah shrugged. “I'll show you the truck.”

He led the way out of the cemetery. They walked through the section of the cemetery where the stones dotted the landscape in an eye-watering grid of plots. Every stone had the same shape. The beauty of the cemetery had been turned in to a mass-produced storage area of death. A tall black metal fence separated the plots from the road. On the other side of the fence sat a black truck.

“What the hell was in that oversize trophy cup?” Jeremiah asked.

“Blood,” Rebecka said.

“Whose?”

“It does not matter,” Steopa said.

“It was a little weird.”

Jimmy laughed. “Weird?” He shook his head. “I've been a vampire for a day now. We had vampire hunters in a cemetery. I have seen three vampires disappear in front of me. The linebacker from the college turned into a dirge, and you are complaining about a cup that fills with blood.”

“Dirge?” Jeremiah asked.

“A drudge,” Steopa said.

“Wait, when was this?” Rebecka asked.

“His first night.”

Jimmy nodded. “Yeah, we cut through the poorhouses and ran into these other vampires. He bitch-slapped the woman.”

Rebecka's mouth fell open. "Why?"

"She suggested I kill you," Steopa said.

Rebecka scoffed. "Oh, all right."

"That cup is a handy thing. Where did you find it?" Jeremiah asked.

"Sorry, we cannot tell you," Steopa said.

"Steopa, really? After-"

"Jeremiah, please." Steopa held up his hand. "I made a promise. I keep my promises."

"I understand," Jeremiah said.

A truck flashing red and yellow lights pulled up to the black truck. Steopa pulled Rebecka into the shadows of the hedges. Jeremiah did the same with Jimmy. The truck backed up to the hunter's truck, making a loud beeping noise. When it stopped, the driver got out and lowered the bed of the truck.

Rebecka sighed. "Somebody must have called in the truck."

Steopa glanced at Jeremiah. Jeremiah shook his head. "Nothing much to see in it anyway."

"Rathskeller?" Rebecka asked.

Steopa nodded. He watched the tow truck driver attach chains to the van. Rebecka tugged on his arm. That is odd, he thought. I have seen cars sit for months before they are towed. He tried to read what tow company the truck belong too. There were no signs on the truck as to who owned it.

SABER INK ®
inc.

CHAPTER 6

The sign for the Burgundy Rathskeller hung over the ramp to the basement entrance. Above the sign on the side of the building the faded words "Meat Processing" could be read. As they walked down the sidewalk toward the ramp, Steopa could smell blood coming from Saber Ink, the tattoo parlor. Next to it, the store Third Eye Curios had its doors open. The smell of charcoal and mint mixed with the blood.

At the bottom of the ramp, Swen stood up behind the counter in the bouncer cage. He crossed his arms and stared at Jimmy and Jeremiah. The short-sleeved shirt showed off his muscles and tattooed arms. Because of his nature of being a berserk, when Steopa saw him, Swen looked as if he could not keep his shape. He would see Swen the man morph into the bear form and back again. Tonight, Swen looked more like a bear.

He sucked in air through his teeth and made a noise. "Vincent said you were coming, might be better if you go through the back," he said. His eyes fixed on Jeremiah. "No guns." He pointed to a large wall safe in the back of the cage. "Check them in, and I'll let you in."

Jeremiah shrugged and handed over his shotgun and handgun. Swen picked up the handgun. He spun it, flicked out the clip, checked the clip, slid it back in, flipped the gun again, pulled back on the barrel, and put on the safety. He opened the chamber on the shotgun, then put it against his leg and checked the magazine. He nodded. He locked both guns inside the safe. When he returned, he eyed Jimmy. "And what is this kid's story?"

"They are with me," Rebecka said, giving Swen a strange look. "I just want to talk to John."

"Ah," Swen said. He looked over the monitors. "Yeah, he is still at the DJ booth." Swen sighed. "I'll radio him and tell you to meet him here."

"Swen," Vincent appeared in the back of the cage. "I'll take them to my room."

Swen never took his eyes off Steopa's group, but he nodded. “All right. I just don't want trouble.”
Vincent laughed as he walked to the front of the cage. He pulled off his top hat and held it in front of him. “Trouble? Here?”
He smiled. His long brown hair came to his shoulders. With his goatee and mustache, the top hat made him look like the ring master of a strange circus. He held his arm out and opened the door to the club.
Rebecka turned to Jeremiah and Jimmy. “Swen is a good bouncer. He is only looking out for the club.”
Jeremiah nodded. “But-”
Jimmy rubbed his eyes. “I feel sick,” he said.
“Yeah, that bouncer?” Jeremiah asked.
Vincent chuckled. “You could have warned them,” he said to Rebecka.
She shrugged. “That's Swen.” She tapped Vincent on his shoulder. “When did you redo the club?”
“A few months ago. Lorelei got sick of looking at the same four walls.”
Steopa glanced around the club. Along the balcony, the mannequins wore rubber outfits. Neon had been added to the walls and the ceiling. Around the empty stage, video screens had been added; they were not turned on this night. Lined up in front of the entrance, a cannon pointed to the door.
At the bar, Lorelei hurried back and forth to fill drinks. She flung her green hair back. For a moment, Steopa's and her eyes locked. The color drained from her face. She turned, throwing the bar rag down, and hurried into the back room of the bar.
Rebecka waved to John at the DJ booth. He nodded, then banged his head back and forth to the music. His dredlocks bounced around his head. He turned and picked up a record.
“I thought he would be at the tattoo parlor tonight,” Rebecka said.
“What?” Vincent asked, yelling over the music.
“Johnny's not upstairs.”
“Our regular DJ's wife had a baby this morning, so John came down.”
Jeremiah tapped Steopa's arm. “I'm surprised you come here.”
Vincent laughed and motioned to the door marked private. “Are

you kidding? Most of our patrons want to look like him." He held open the door. "Go in."

Vincent's private room in the Rathskeller had been decorated and designed to look like a private drawing room at a gentleman's club. The deep dark wood paneling lined the walls, covering the sound proofing. A fainting red velvet couch sat against the far wall. A semi-circle of chairs faced the couch. The smell of stale blood filled the air. Jeremiah and Jimmy sniffed.

Steopa sat down on the fainting couch, smoothing out his coat as he did. Rebecka joined him. Jimmy sat down on the chair with the carved lion's feet. Jeremiah did not sit down. He stood by the door, watching Vincent.

Vincent sat down and flashed Jimmy a smile. "My name is Vincent and I'm a vampire. It's been thirty minutes since my last feeding."

Jimmy leaned forward, his body shaking with laughter.

Vincent grinned. He straightened out his velvet overcoat. "So, social call, or is the world coming to an end?"

"You asked us to come," Steopa said. He made the introductions.

"True. We had two freaks show up here at the opening of the club tonight," Vincent said.

Steopa stared at Vincent. Vincent shrugged. "Don't worry. Swen kicked them to the curb. That's why he's so jumpy."

"What were they doing here?"

"Asking questions about you, actually. You've got to give Swen credit. He has the greatest poker face. They had a drawing of you. Swen took a look and asked them if they were joking."

"A drawing, not a photograph?" Steopa asked.

"Yeah, looked like a police sketch. I have no idea who they were."

"Hunters," Jeremiah said, before Steopa could stop him.

Vincent looked surprised. "Really? I've never had the pleasure before."

"It is not a pleasure," Steopa said, harder than he meant. Rebecka jumped. Steopa waved his hand. "I realize that now, vampire hunters are rare. I have had my share of fights with them."

"You are also talking about America," Vincent said. "The last vampire dug up and staked was in Rhode Island, of all places."

"The ones we ran across tonight were well trained, but nothing like the ones in the old country. They were foolish. They came at night to look for us."

Rebecka shook her head. "No, they were looking for an open chamber. We just happened to be there."

She had a look on her face, the look that she got when she had been thinking about something for a long time. She continued, "I mean, they could not just come to Forest Grove in the daylight with a coin sweeper. And they were not really that well-armed, either. What about the ghouls? Fire works best on them. There was nothing in their bags that would burn."

"So they knew about vampires, but not ghouls." Vincent said, he rubbed his goatee. "Sloppy."

Jeremiah nodded. "Yeah, you're right. If I was sending someone out to hunt vampires, I would have them pack for ghouls, too."

"What the hell are ghouls?" Jimmy asked.

"Nasty things," Jeremiah said. "They end up in cemeteries."

"Vampires that don't drink human blood," Rebecka said.

"What?" Jimmy asked.

"Think of zombies," Vincent said. "Only they don't stop at the brains. We have hunters. Nice." He rolled his eyes.

Rebecka turned to Vincent. "I don't think you are in danger," she said. "They only had information on Steopa."

"But they had the address of this club," Steopa said.

"I see," said Vincent. "Some trouble from Russia? Or just some random idiot?"

"Not an idiot," Jeremiah said. "Too much information."

"Well, if things get too weird out there, you can hide here. And don't worry, Rebecka. I'll make sure your brother is okay. He's my main food source, I have to protect him."

Rebecka smiled. "I shouldn't worry."

Steopa stood. "Thank you, Vincent. And I am sorry if we imposed." He motioned to Jeremiah and Jimmy.

"More the merrier," Vincent grinned. "Stay a while."

"Cool, I've never been in a night club before," Jimmy said.

"You be careful," Steopa said. "You may still have people looking for you."

Vincent chuckled. "I thought you looked familiar. I saw the report on the car wreck. They wanted to dredge the swamp, but they lost the machine. It sank into the swamp and they can't find it."

Jeremiah laughed. "That would have been Perun."

"Who?"

"A friend," Steopa said.

"So I can't go out there?" Jimmy asked.

"I don't see why not. You're supposed to be dead." Vincent chuckled. "There's a nice table to the back. I'll join you."

Rebecka shook her head. "I have to make a stop upstairs to use John's computer." She pulled out the satellite phone.

"Why don't you use the one in the office?" Vincent said.

Rebecka got up and gave Vincent a quick hug. She left the room. Vincent held the door open for the rest of them. He pointed to the back of the club. Steopa led the way to the table. When they had sat down, Andi came over to the table. She smiled at Steopa.

"Chuck and his dad say hi," she said. She put down her serving tray. "Friends?"

Steopa introduced her to the other vampires.

Andi flung her braided ponytails back and smiled. "I'll bring you some water, so you get no stares."

Steopa nodded.

After she had left, Jeremiah leaned closer to Steopa. "She knows?"

"You could not smell it?" Steopa asked.

"She smelled like a dog," Jimmy said.

"She's not? Is she?" Jeremiah asked.

"A werewolf?" Steopa nodded. "I was invited to her changing ceremony."

Jeremiah shook his head. "But she is too small to be a werewolf."

Steopa chuckled. "Do not say that to her."

Andi came back. She set the glasses on the table and turned to serve another patron, pulling down her latex mini skirt as she did. Jimmy stared.

"She is marrying a werewolf, Jimmy," Steopa said.

"And she's too old for you," Jeremiah said. "That's the last time someone will say that to you."

Steopa slid the glass of water away from him. Then he felt a strange sensation. As if in the back of his mind, he felt frightened.

He concentrated. The fear wasn't from him, it was from Rebecka.

"Wait here," he said.

He hurried across the dance floor. The dancing couples moved out of his way as he passed. Andi hurried behind the bar as he flung open the door to the back room. She put down her drinks and followed him.

"Lorelei, speak to me," he heard Rebecka say.

Steopa stopped at the office door. Rebecka sat on the floor next to Lorelei. Lorelei's hands clenched over her chest. Her eyes had turned solid white. Andi pushed passed Steopa.

"What happened?" Andi asked as she crouched down beside Lorelei.

"I had just turned on the computer. Lorelei was sitting at the desk rubbing her head. I connected with Baldman and she fell over"

"I see them," Lorelei said. "The children are killed and changed."

Vincent appeared next to Steopa. "Whoa."

"Saber? Are you there?" A man's voice came from the computer.

Rebecka jumped. She picked up the microphone at the computer. "Sorry, Baldman, I have an emergency."

"They are coming for all of us, they won't stop," Lorelei said. Her eyes returned to their normal state. She looked around the office. "Not again."

Andi sighed. "Are you all right?"

Lorelei sat up. She waved Andi away. "Fine, fine, just give me some air."

"Are you sure?" Vincent asked.

"I need to be alone, okay?" Lorelei glanced at Steopa. She turned her head away.

Rebecka picked up the microphone. "Sorry, Baldman, I have to go. Send me the info."

"Yes, well, I will," Baldman said over the speakers.

Lorelei nodded. "I hate it when this happens."

Andi helped Lorelei stand. Lorelei leaned on Andi while her legs shook. Then she ran up to Steopa and hit him in the chest.

"What the hell are you playing at? You are putting all of us in danger!" she yelled.

Steopa stepped back. Vincent put his arm around Lorelei. "Hey, settle down."

"I do not know what you are talking about," Steopa said.

Lorelei scanned his face. "No, you don't. I'm sorry. But it all made sense a few seconds ago."

"What did?"

Lorelei shook her head. "I've forgotten. I hate these visions. Now I am getting a migraine. Get out!" She pointed to the hallway.

Steopa pulled Rebecka into the hall. Vincent shut the door. He shrugged. "Sorry."

"What happened?" Steopa asked.

"She can see things, sometimes," Vincent said. "But she hasn't had one of those fits in years."

"Psychic?"

Vincent nodded.

"I never saw her do that," Rebecka said.

"It can be worse," Vincent said. "But she is always right. If you can figure out what she is talking about."

He met Steopa's gaze, then shrugged. "But what are you going to do? Hide from the future?"

Steopa scoffed.

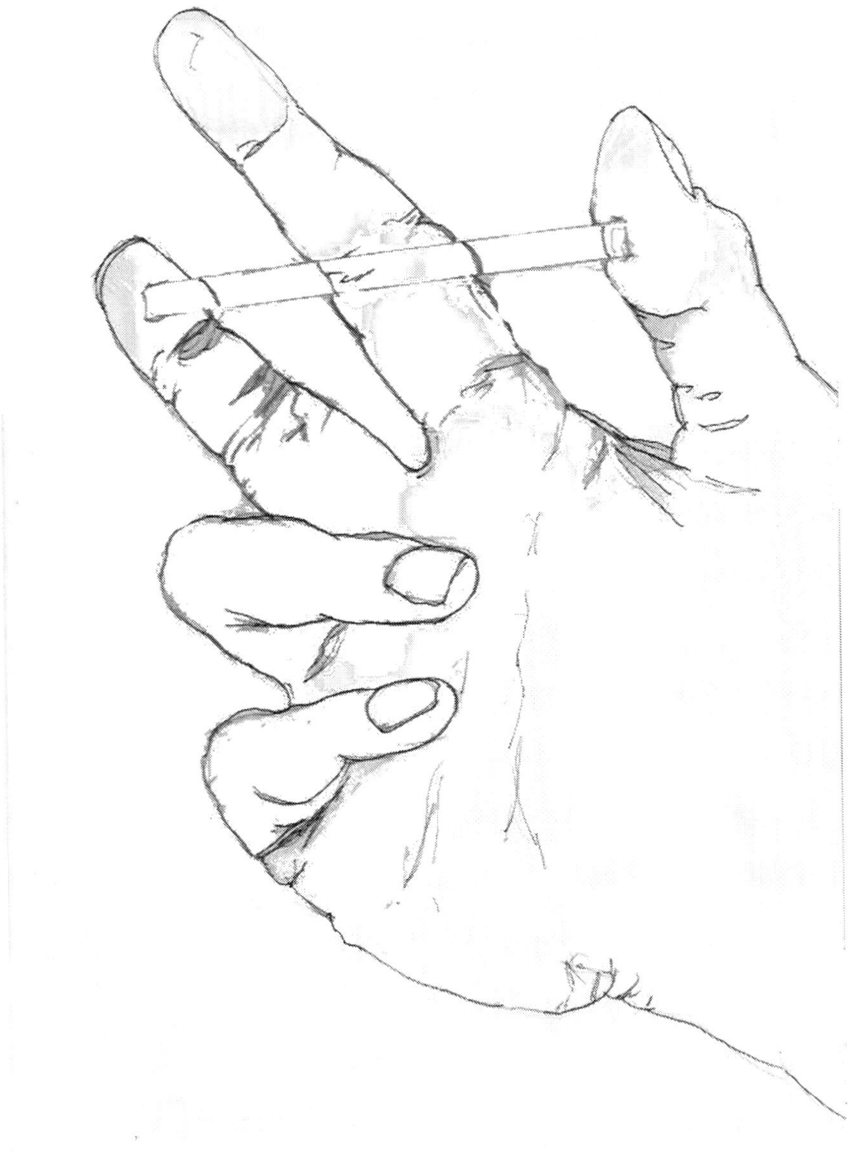

CHAPTER 7

The next night, Steopa woke up to see Rebecka sitting on the edge of the bed. She flipped her hair back and looked over her shoulder. He sat up. She leaned back and kissed his cheek. Steopa heard muffled singing on the other side of the door.

"Jimmy's got a good voice. He woke me up," she said.

"Did you sleep well otherwise?" he asked, kissing her forehead.

Rebecka nodded. Steopa stood up and went to his wardrobe. As he pulled out his clothes for the night, he could feel one more of his descendants coming. Sasha? How could he have gotten here so fast? he thought. He hung his head for a moment. Rebecka noticed, and curled her arms around his waist.

"What is it?"

"More family is coming. We will be running out of room. I should speak to Teodor."

"He already has a full house. What about here? You said it was a base."

"Most of it has been destroyed."

"Any other ideas?"

Steopa turned. "I might talk to Perun."

"Again, you should ask Vincent."

"Where would they stay? In the basement?"

She winced. "I see your point. I don't think the rest of the apartments have been worked on, and that basement would not be comfortable. We'll figure it out. It will be okay." She opened the door and left Steopa.

Steopa sat on the bed, holding his clothes. The hunters had come at night, without all the protection they needed, and they had been asking questions. Scouts? Not real hunters? Steopa wondered.

Who hired them? In the past, it would have been a town or the church. Today? No one believed in vampires. Steopa rubbed his back, feeling his scars. He remembered the hunters he had run into at Saint Petersburg. They had been hired by an older vampire to run the younger ones out of town. Steopa smiled. He had found that older vampire and watched him burn in the sun the next morning. That vampire had screamed that they had won the war.

The rumors that he had heard at that time, most of them had turned out to be false. He went to Greece, because there were supposed to be five ancient vampires sealed in a crypt on the island. He had seen interesting monuments, nothing more. Another rumor said that somewhere the oldest vampire walked among humans, and controlled entire governments. Steopa shook his head. Yet the one that said there had been a civil war among the vampires seemed realistic, he thought. After I killed that vampire, I became the oldest in Saint Petersburg; there were not many older vampires left.

He dressed, then opened the door to the main room of the lair. Rebecka had her laptop open on the desk. He could see the silhouette of Baldman. Her friend never showed his face.

Steopa walked passed Jimmy. "More of our family are coming."

"Oh, that's what I have been feeling," Jimmy said. "Like I know someone is coming for a visit. But I can feel them getting closer."

"Yes."

"So what did you find out?" Rebecka asked.

Steopa turned. She moved her microphone closer to her mouth. He walked over to her. She had a map on the screen. In another program, numbers ran on the small black terminal. The last program had the image of Baldman. He sat in the shadows, his dark round glasses obscuring his eyes. Baldman leaned back. For a moment, his face became illuminated by the glow of his screen.

Steopa leaned over to get a better look. Baldman looked familiar. Steopa stared for a moment. It cannot be, Steopa thought. He would be ancient by now. Baldman moved his head back into the shadows.

"Are we going to hunt tonight?" Jimmy asked.

Steopa did not take his eyes of the laptop's screen. "No, Rebecka and I have a few errands to run."

"Why would they use such a fancy phone just to call local?" Rebecka asked.

The man on the screen pointed. Rebecka turned her head. "Sorry, he gets nervous."

Steopa walked to the other side of the room. I have seen that man before, he thought. Steopa tapped his fingers against the metal wall. But he has not aged. It can't be him.

"Okay thanks. Baldman... What? I told you about him...All right. Talk to you later." Rebecka took off her headphones and shut her laptop down.

"That was odd," she said.

"What?"

"Baldman asked about you."

"He did?"

"He said he has seen you before."

Steopa took his coat off the hook. "He might have seen me when you were talking to him."

"Maybe, but it sounded like he knew you."

Steopa did not say anything. She walked over to the door and put her arm around Steopa. "This is kinda nice."

"What do you mean?"

"Having Jimmy here." She smiled at Jimmy. "It's like I have a little brother now. John and I did not have the best family. This feels nice."

"You did have a good father," Steopa said.

Rebecka nodded. "Yeah, but after he died. Except for John, the family wasn't much of a family."

"That had to suck," Jimmy said.

"You have no idea."

Steopa lifted her head with his finger. He kissed her. When he ended the kiss, Steopa bit her lip playfully. "I think Jimmy should meet Teodor."

"Who's that?" Jimmy asked.

"An old friend. Andi is marrying his son."

"Oh! He's a werewolf too?"

Steopa nodded.

"I thought vampires and werewolves were not supposed to get along?"

"Some do not. Teodor and I have never had any issues."

Steopa took a longer route to Teodor's so he could stop at his favorite deli that served pirogies. Steopa stopped and bought two servings. He ate one as they walked. Jimmy wrinkled his nose when Steopa opened the bag.

"I swear they are your drugs," Rebecka said.

Steopa swallowed. "I like them."

"You don't need them."

Steopa grinned. "No, but they are worth it." He held one out for Rebecka. "Cabbage stuffed."

She sniffed at the pirogi. "They used milk, not cream."

"You can eat food?" Jimmy asked.

"It's like junk food, fills you up, but not needed," Rebecka said.

Steopa held the pirogi out for Jimmy. "A taste?"

He sniffed it and grimaced. "No, thank you."

Steopa popped the pirogi in his mouth. "You should enjoy the things you used to love."

Rebecka shook her head. "Unfortunately, there isn't much."

"What about now?"

Rebecka stopped. She took one of the pirogies. "I am enjoying what I love."

"What is that?"

She stuffed the pirogi in his mouth. "Guess."

Steopa kissed her forehead. Jimmy giggled.

Teodor lived on a large empty block. Between his home and the empty factory, brushes and grass had come back. The large Victorian sat on a maintained lawn, surrounded by bikes and cars. Every window shone, lighting up the otherwise darkened area. On the porch sat Andi and Silvia. Silvia, Teodor's only daughter, picked up a magazine. Andi waved to Steopa as they approached.

Silvia looked like her mother. She had pulled her blond hair back into a pony tail. She glanced up from the pages of the magazine and smiled. Her dark eyes looked black in the dim light of the street. She stood up and waved.

Andi wore a tank top and jeans. The top showed off her muscles. With her hair down, she looked older. "Hey guys! Rebecka, you have to see these wedding dresses."

She held up a picture of a model sitting on a rock wearing a wedding gown. Steopa thought the gown made the model look like she sat in the middle of a pile of white frosting.

Andi made a face. "This one is gross."

Rebecka sat down on a porch step and picked up a magazine. Steopa held the door for Jimmy. Bill, one of Teodor's sons, stretched out on the couch holding a game controller in his hands. Bill had dark hair and a narrow, pointed face. His blond twin, Nick, sat at a desk reading a college textbook.

Nick waved at Steopa, but did not look up from his book. "Dad's in the back."

"What game is that?" Jimmy asked.

"Shock Team," Bill said, yawning.

"Need a second player?"

Bill paused the game and threw Jimmy a controller. Jimmy sat on the floor. The game started again.

Steopa walked into the next room. Chuck and Trucker were in the room. A computer with the case off and parts laying all over the table sat in front of Trucker. Chuck, another blond son of Teodor's, held out his hand as Steopa passed. Steopa tried to shake it, but Chuck slapped his hand against Steopa's. Steopa raised his eyebrow and continued on.

In the back room, Steopa found Teodor. Teodor looked the same age as his children. He wore his dark hair short but spiked in a style that Steopa had seen on some of the young men in the town.

He looked up from his project. A half-finished coat hung off a dressing dummy. "Hey, Steopa, welcome to the mad house."

He spit the pins from his mouth into a free hand.

"Everyone is here?" Steopa asked.

Teodor sat back on a chair behind him and thought for a moment. "No, Jamie had to work tonight."

"My family has started to arrive," Steopa said.

Teodor stuck the pins into a pin cushion. "All of them?"

"I do not know. I can only feel one coming."

"Whoa, why?"

Steopa told him about the hunters and the list. Teodor stood up. He looked out to the dining room, then came back. "Downstairs."

He led Steopa down the wooden steps to his basement. Teodor walked to what had been the coal storage room for the house. Now he had converted it to dry document storage. Teodor found a book. The Cyrillic letters were faded on the cover.

"So we have hunters," he said. "Damn, now it's gonna be silver bullets and wolfsbane. Like wolfsbane ever worked... You know, I was hoping my kids would not have to deal with that stuff."

"I am sure they are after my family, not yours," Steopa said.

"They had information on you. We were in the siege together. We were caught by both governments. It won't take long for them to make that connection."

He flipped through the book. "Any idea who it could be?"

Steopa shook his head. "But they were well paid." He handed a few diamonds to Teodor.

Teodor looked at the gems in his hand. "Wow."

"I need some places to hide my family for the day. Rebecka suggested our home, but I told her the rest of the base had been destroyed."

"I don't blame you for not using the base." Teodor pointed to another room that had been made in the basement. "I have some room here. Or the old factory, when the rest of them show up."

Steopa looked around. "This will be appropriate."

"Are you sure it's a good idea to have your family reunion now?" Teodor asked. "You've got hunters."

"I can not stop them," Steopa said. "When I was injured, all of them were called."

Teodor nodded. "I remember. How is Jeremiah?"

"The same. I saw Perun a few days ago."

"I see him a lot. The kids and I go running in Greenwoods every so often. He'll join us sometimes."

Steopa and Teodor talked some more, then they went upstairs. Steopa paused at the doorway on the porch. He watched Rebecka looking over the wedding dresses with the other two women. Silvia pointed to a dress that was styled after the fashions from the latter half of the nineteenth century.

"You would look so beautiful in this," Silvia said.

The bodice would have looked wonderful on you, Steopa thought.

Rebecka waved her hand, as if to make the image go away. "A wedding is not in my future."

Silvia giggled. "I don't know, Steopa is very sweet on you."

Rebecka reached behind her. Steopa placed his hand in hers. "I know."

"You are coming to Chuck's and my wedding, right?" Andi asked. "We're having it at the Rathskeller, so that should not be a problem."

"Rebecka," Steopa said. "We have to go."

Rebecka stood up. "It's been fun. Don't worry Andi, we will be there."

"Good, 'cause my folks are flipping out that I am having it at a bar."

Rebecka said her goodbyes. Jimmy joined them. Steopa began to walk toward the river. He wrapped his arm around Rebecka's waist.

"Why are we heading to the river?" Jimmy asked.

"Because that is where my descendant will be."

"Why?"

"I have to warn you about Sasha."

"Who's she?" Rebecka asked

Steopa chuckled. "He. Sasha is a man's name."

"What about him?"

"He is my grandson. He was not much older than you when he died." He nodded to Jimmy. "He died at sea."

"So?"

"He was buried at sea. Do you understand?"

Rebecka shook her head. "No."

"He changed in the water. He is not like any other vampire you have met."

"I haven't met that many."

"He is different. I wanted to prepare you." Steopa paused at the corner. "But I do not know how to explain him."

The street lights changed color. They crossed the road.

"Andi told me something interesting tonight," Rebecka said. "Basically, Chuck and her are already married, according to the pack. She is just having the official wedding to shut up her family."

"Yes," Steopa said. "They could have chosen another way, but it could have been dangerous."

"She drank poison. How much more dangerous can you get?"

Steopa paused. "Teodor met his wife Amanda when we were brought to the United States. They fell in love. She became severely injured. He found her; I could smell death on her. He sliced off a small part of his forearm and made her eat it."

"What?"

"If a human ingests werewolf flesh, they become a werewolf."

Jimmy groaned. "That's sick."

"Andi said something about sex."

"Werewolves have brutal sex."

Rebecka giggled. "Sorry," she said, covering her mouth while she snickered. "But have you ever seen *The Howling*? That one scene just played in my head."

"I have seen that movie. The reality is much worse."

"Ouch."

"How much worse?" Jimmy asked.

"Brutal."

Jimmy laughed. He jumped up on the guardrail and walked ahead of them. He placed his feet toe to toe like a trapeze artist. Steopa waited until he had walked a block ahead of them. Rebecka laid her head against Steopa's chest.

He turned to her. "Do you wish that we could-?"

"No, never thought about it."

"There are times, I wish..."

"Why?" Rebecka asked. "According to Vincent, we aren't even supposed to hold hands. I'm happy. You don't have to worry about that."

Steopa stopped. He picked her up and gave her a long kiss. When he put Rebecka back down, he caught the stares of some of the people on the street. One woman had covered her mouth and giggled. Rebecka gave him a hug.

They caught up with Jimmy, then walked into the park that followed the river along most of its course in the city. Rebecka stopped.

"Ah, Steopa. This is Ogden's territory. I don't think he will like the fact that there are so many of us here."

"It will be for a short while," Steopa said.

Rebecka pointed to the other side of the parking lot. Ogden's car sat on the other side.

"I did not feel him," Steopa said.

"You were worried about your family," she said, shrugging.

"Meet me at the look out," Steopa said. He walked over to the car. Ogden rolled down his window.

"Do you have an explanation for your sudden interest in my section of town?" he asked, with his crisp British accent.

"It is a private matter," Steopa said. "We will be here a short time."

"A private matter on my territory." Ogden leaned closer to the window. His eyes glowed blue from the lights in the parking lot. "I could chase all of you out this instant."

Steopa leaned on the car and lowered his head down to speak to

Ogden. "There are hunters in town, remember."

"Ah." Ogden sat back. "But you are still having your little meeting on my territory. Why?"

"We are waiting for another member of my family. Then we will leave."

Ogden opened the door. Steopa slid into the car. The door closed behind him with a quiet click. Ogden folded his hands over his knees. He looked up at Steopa with a pensive look. "There have been rumors. I have correspondence in England and India that tell me that trouble is starting. Your name has come up."

"Do you know why?" Steopa asked.

"All I know is that there has been a vampire asking about you, and asking about the elders," Ogden said. "A bothersome type. Most other vampires would not speak to her. But if she is behind the hunters, then she deserves to be destroyed."

"She? I recently met another vampire. A female. Could it be the same one?"

"I don't have any information that could help you identify her. But using hunters is a poor tactic."

"I agree. Why could she not face me alone?"

"And asking about the elders? I would say she is a fool as well. Who has seen an elder? I personally think they do not exist, at least in the way that most vampires talk about them."

Steopa nodded. "Did you find out any more about the holy water?"

"Interesting thing. No matter who was hit with it, there would have been a reaction."

"Like?"

"We would have been forced into a stupor. A werewolf would have lost control over their shape. A human," Ogden smiled. "would have lost control of their bodily functions."

"Odd weapon to have."

Ogden tapped the top of his cane to his chin. "I will find out more. For now, I suggest you talk to Verina."

"Verina?" Steopa asked. "Why?"

"She is one of the oldest vampires I know. But she will kill you if you call her an elder."

Steopa pictured Verina in his mind. She wore short skirts, high heels and smoked cigarettes. "How can she be?" he asked.

Ogden gave Steopa a small smile. “She is. Over a thousand years old, I have been told. She has always been a bit of a black sheep. I think she is very smart. No one with ideas of finding an elder would think of looking for her.”

Ogden pressed a button. Steopa's door opened. “Remember to talk to Verina.” He said to Steopa as Steopa climbed out of the car. “I will stay here a few moments.”

Steopa nodded. He closed the door behind him. Rebecka took his hand. “What was that about?” she asked.

“Ogden had to discuss a few things.”

Rebecka gave Steopa a questioning look.

“Do you know if Verina is in town?” Steopa asked.

“I could find out.”

“Please.”

Steopa felt Sasha. “Come, Sasha will be here soon.”

“Where?” Rebecka asked.

He pointed to the river.

CHAPTER 8

A set of stairs traveled from the lookout to the bank of the river. The recent rain storms fed the river, swelling it close to flooding. The water flowed by the boardwalk, sloshing up on the wooden planks.

Jimmy stopped on the stairs. "It's running water."

"Scared?" Steopa asked.

"Isn't running water suppose to harm us?" Jimmy asked.

"No."

Jimmy looked relieved. He took one step forward. The water churned along the boardwalk. He jumped back up the set of stairs. Under the water a humanoid shape could be seen, multiple colors flowed across its skin. A pale green hand rose out of the water.

Steopa stifled a laugh. Rebecka gripped his arm.

Her eyes went wide. "Is that Sasha?"

Water sprayed from the river. The cascade of water stopped like a sudden rain shower. Sasha stood on the boardwalk. His long black hair flowed over his thin body in wet strands. His solid green eyes looked like fish eyes. He blinked. His eyes looked human. He flung his hair off his face with a webbed hand. He smiled. Instead of the small set of fangs, he had an entire row.

Rebecka slipped behind Steopa; Jimmy stared.

"Hello," Sasha said. He spoke with a thicker accent than Steopa.

"Welcome," Steopa said. He introduced Jimmy and Rebecka.

Sasha wrung his hair, spraying droplets of water over the wooden walkway. "By the looks on your faces, Grandfather did not explain about me."

He wiped the water off his body. As he did, the green glow disappeared. The more water that dripped off him, the more he looked like the young man he had been when he died. The scar on his chest, from the harpoon, stood out against his pale skin. He smiled again. Two fangs glistened in the darkness.

Steopa hugged Sasha.

Jimmy found his voice. “Water? You flew out of the water.”

Sasha laughed. “Long story short, I was killed on a whaling vessel and buried at sea.”

Rebecka bit her lip. Steopa put his arm around her.

“An underwater vampire. That is...” Rebecka stared at Sasha.

“That is awesome,” Jimmy said.

“I think Sasha is the only vampire that can survive underwater,” Steopa said as he started up the stairs.

Ogden's car drove up to the group. He rolled down his window. “I hope you are not having any more come. I don't think this town has enough blood,” Ogden said out the window, with a slight smile on his face. He studied Sasha, then rolled up his window.

“Grandfather, why did you call me out of the water?” Sasha asked.

“I will explain on the way,” Steopa said.

Sasha ran his hand down the thigh of his tattered leather pants. “I need to look human again.”

Steopa took off his coat and handed it to Sasha. “Come,” he said. “We have a lot to discuss.”

As they walked along the streets, any women they passed would stare at Sasha; some men as well. Sasha tossed his black hair back as a woman approached. He gave her a sad look. She stumbled on her heel, then hurried past them.

Rebecka caught Steopa's gaze. “He's never met Vincent, has he?”

Steopa shook his head.

They passed a clothing store. Sasha stopped and went back to the window. “Can we go?”

“I use a different shop for my clothes,” Steopa said.

“It's not the clothes. I'm hungry.”

“How can you tell out here?” Jimmy asked.

Sasha tapped the side of his nose. “I have to move faster than the sharks.”

They went inside. Black covered every surface. Shades of black clothing hung on the racks. Grinning skulls, silver jewelry, and red velvet did add some brightness to the darkness of the shop. The merchandise had been packed in every space. Sasha walked up to the only person in the store. She stood at the counter.

The young woman with black and red hair leaned forward. The

corset pushed her breasts up and nearly out of the satin. She did not take her eyes off Sasha.

Sasha tilted his head.

Her eyes clouded. "Can I help you?"

"Da," Sasha said. "I have some clothing waiting for me."

"Right," she said.

The woman left the counter, she walked over to a rack of clothes and picked out an outfit. She held it up. Sasha shook his head. She put the clothes back and found another one.

Steopa and Rebecka wandered to the other side of the store. Steopa grabbed Jimmy's arm and brought him along with them. Jimmy watched Sasha with his mouth open.

"Are you trying to catch flies?" Rebecka asked.

Jimmy shut his mouth. He leaned closer. "How did he do that?"

"I told you," Steopa said. "Some of us have other powers."

Sasha moved closer to the clerk. She turned her body so she could show him her cleavage. She picked out an entire outfit for him to wear. Sasha winked at Steopa and Rebecka.

"Why don't you help me try these on?" he asked.

The clerk followed Sasha into the dressing room. The door swung shut.

Rebecka held a blouse up to her chest. "What do you think?"

"I think Sasha could teach Vincent a few things," Steopa said.

Rebecka giggled.

Steopa heard a soft gasp from the dressing room, then silence. Moments later, Sasha came out, fully dressed. The clerk laid crumpled on the floor. She moved her hand and moaned.

"Nice girl," Sasha said, as he bent over to buckle his boots. "I might have to come back here."

He stood up with a wide grin. "Much nicer than the normal dock worker or fisherman."

As they were about to leave the shop, Sasha turned around and snapped his fingers. The clerk opened her eyes and looked around confused for a moment. Sasha blew her a kiss and the door swung shut.

"Hunters," Sasha said after they left. "I still have aches from the last one I dealt with."

"Where was that?" Steopa asked.

"Belize City." Sasha pulled his hair through a tie. "Remember the ones in the old country? The ones in Belize could have put them to shame. And you are right, I think you had scouts. They send the scouts out to do research. If they come back, they are trained to do the actual killing."

"So more will be coming?" Rebecka asked.

"Sooner than later, I would think," Sasha said. "If they are being paid that well, then you have some very determined hunters." He stopped. "What was written about me?"

"A question mark," Steopa said.

Sasha smiled and nodded. "Good. Then we can surprise them. But I wonder if they knew that injuring you would call all of us here."

"Get their eggs in one basket, so to speak," Rebecka said.

Sasha nodded. "Da, that is it."

Steopa spun away from them, swearing under his breath. He punched the air and swore louder. He growled and hit the brick wall. The bricks turned to powder. He pulled back his fist. "Whoever is funding this vendetta wants all of us out of the way. Only I cannot think of who it could be."

Sasha nodded. "Grandfather, I have heard many things. Misha found me a few weeks ago. There are rumors that some elders are awake now. A younger vampire took it upon herself to awaken them. A family like ours would be considered... abnormal."

"I find that hard to believe. There are no elders." Steopa growled.

Rebecka's face turned paler. "You mean all of us would be killed, because we aren't considered normal vampires?"

Sasha nodded. "I still hunt in Europe. It is much different here than it is there. Many vampires still follow the old rules, like avoiding people that wear the crucifix."

"Crucifix?" Jimmy asked.

"Stories say that at one time," Steopa said, "that the Catholic church had made a deal with some vampires to only attack the Protestants."

"You're kidding," Rebecka said.

"They are only stories," Sasha said. "Like the ones about the elders. I don't believe any of them."

Rebecka scoffed.

"What?" Steopa asked.

"Do all vampires gossip like old women?"
Sasha laughed. "She is right."
"We could ignore most of the stories," Steopa said. "We are still in danger."
"That is true," Sasha said.
Steopa took Rebecka in his arms. "I will protect you." He kissed her.
"And that is another thing," Sasha said. "I have met a few linked vampires. None of them act like you two do. I wonder if that was another reason for us to be targeted."
Rebecka's ring glowed red. She pulled away from Steopa. "No!" She lowered her voice from the shout. "I am not having some euro trash tell me I am unworthy! Steopa and I are close, so what? They have no right to come here and force their rules on us!"
"Hell, yeah! This is the United States," Jimmy said. "They have to follow our rules."
"Precisely," Sasha said.
"Tomorrow, we should find out if any other hunters have been here," Steopa said. "And speak to Verina. Ogden said it would be a good idea to speak to her."
Sasha turned to continue the walk. "Whatever you need me to do, I'll do. It would be nice to have some fun out of the water."
They went back to the lair. Steopa led the way down the stairs to the maintenance tunnel. He smelled her before he heard her. Ahead in the black tunnel, she moaned.
"Who was that?" Rebecka asked.
Steopa could make out the shape of Dorn laying on the floor of the tunnel. Her blood had been smeared on the walls. Her bloodied hand prints glowed red against the darkness. Steopa crouched down and picked up Dorn's head. Blood had soaked through her mass of gray hair.
"Dorn?" Steopa asked.
Her breath rattled. "Radovitch?"
Steopa rolled his eyes. "Dorn? What happened?"
She shook her head. "What am I doing here?"
"Who is this?" Sasha asked Rebecka in a low voice.
"A crazy homeless woman," Rebecka said.
Blood covered Dorn's body. Her midsection and her head had received most of the wounds. He could not see any deep gashes.

Someone had beaten her. Steopa could see the drops of her blood forming a trail out of the tunnel.

"Why did you come here?" Steopa asked.

"The specimens," Dorn said. "I needed to check on the specimens."

"There are no specimens."

Dorn's eyes focused on Sasha. She smiled. "Another Radovitch?" She looked at Rebecka. "A big brother for the new one?"

Steopa sighed. "Rebecka, take them inside. I will take her to the hospital."

"Are you sure?" Rebecka asked.

Steopa stood, then picked up Dorn. She weighed less than he expected. "Yes, I will be home before dawn."

Rebecka touched Steopa's shoulder as she passed. Sasha stared at Dorn for a moment, then followed Rebecka down the tunnel.

Steopa adjusted Dorn in his arms. He followed the drops of the blood out of the tunnel and down the street. Dorn had not come far. She had been at the nearest park. Steopa laid her down on the park bench, then he looked for where she had been attacked.

He found it.

The blood was splattered across the trees and the bushes. Steopa could see the tracks of two other people. They had beaten her between two trees. Steopa could see the little area where Dorn kept her meager personal items. None of it had been touched.

He went back to Dorn. She sat up and rocked herself back and forth.

"Dorn, look at me," Steopa said.

Dorn shook her head.

"LOOK AT ME."

She stopped rocking.

"Was this attack like before?"

Dorn shook her head. "No, no, no punks. Men, trained men."

"How do you know?"

"Taught like I was taught. I forgot how."

They could have killed you, Steopa thought. "I will take you to the hospital."

Dorn shoved Steopa away. "No, no papers, no doctors, no!"

Steopa growled. He flung his hand in the air and swore. "*Mne po khuy*!"

He stormed out of the park, he stopped at the street. "There are times I wish I had killed you!"

Why do I bother with her? Steopa thought. She should have died. Why did she wander into the tunnel? He kicked a trash can across the street. It crashed through a shop window, setting off an alarm.

The lightening of the sky reflected in the window that it had not broken. Steopa swore. He ran back to the parking garage and down the steps to the maintenance tunnel. The door opened as he reached it. Rebecka smiled at him.

"Is she all right?"

"Yes."

Steopa hung up his coat. Jimmy had lain down on the couch. He had already slipped into the stupor. Sasha sat down on the cushioned chair. He had a thick novel open on his lap.

"Have you heard from mother?" Sasha asked.

Steopa shook his head.

"I need to contact Misha. He might have some idea where she is."

"You have not seen her?"

Sasha shook his head. "But a few days ago, I thought I felt her. Then she shoved me away."

"We will discuss this tomorrow, the sun is coming up," Steopa said.

"I know." Rebecka took Steopa's hand and led him into the other chamber.

"Who beat her up?"

Steopa undressed.

"Steopa?"

"It does not matter." He sat down on the bed.

Rebecka sat down next to him. "Are you all right?"

"Not with my family in danger."

"We are safe here."

Steopa nodded. "No one has found this place. Even the explorers that do come down the tunnel. They never make it to my vault."

She kissed his cheek. He turned his head and kissed her mouth. She laid down on the the bed and pulled him closer. Steopa laid next to her. He could feel the sun rising. He wrapped his arms around Rebecka and let the stupor take him.

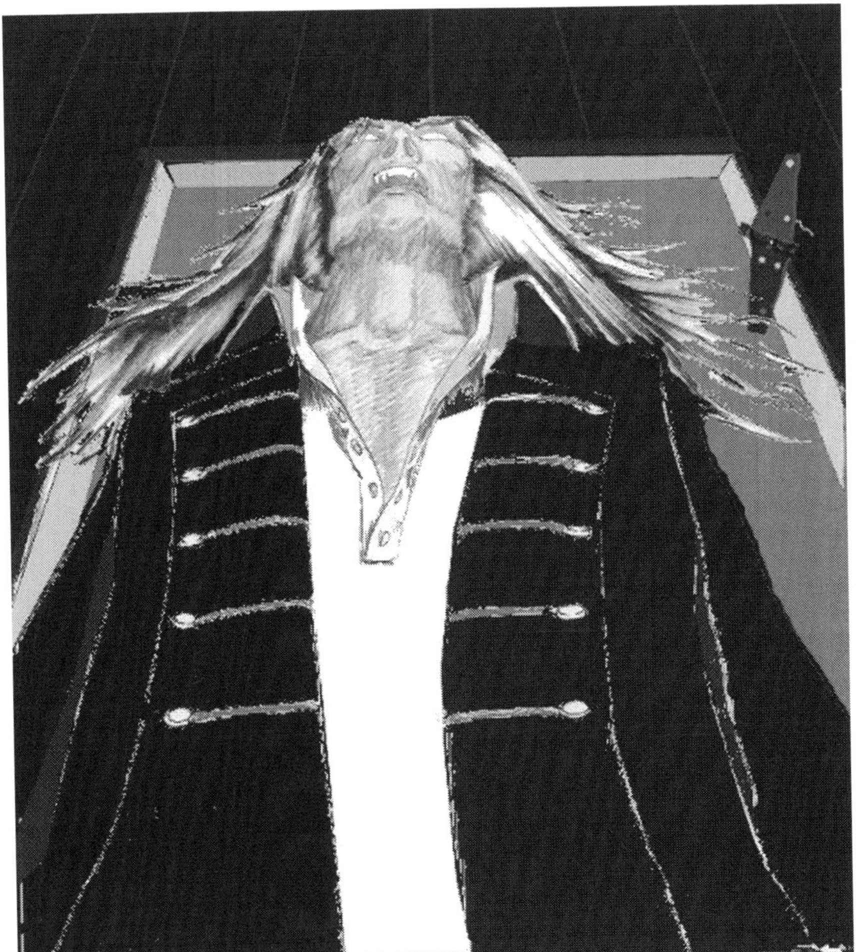

CHAPTER 9

Memories could be more vivid than reality. The wind whipped around Steopa. He looked over the familiar view of his farm. At least the farm as it had been when he had come back for the last time. Across the sky dark clouds rolled. In the distance, the clouds flashed on and off with lightning. A light mist hung in the air, but Steopa did not feel wet.

Rebecka took his hand. “Where are we?”

Steopa pointed down the hill. “This was my farm. I owned most of the land that you can see here. My father gave me half of my inheritance when I married.”

“This is Lithuania?” Rebecka asked.

Steopa nodded. “Officially, Lithuania did not exist at this time.

“When?”

Steopa looked over the familiar landscape. He had been thinking of this night. He gripped Rebecka's hand harder. “The night I had to rescue my daughter.”

He pointed to the farm. Two horses, tied to a post, stood in front of the house. Even with the wind whipping around them, he could hear raised voices. “Ana, my wife, had not recovered from my death. Then she had Nastenka,” he said. “The village accused her of sleeping with the devil. I had heard rumors where I hunted. But I do not know why I came back this night, but there I am.”

His self from the memory walked across the garden. He paused outside the house.

Steopa turned to Rebecka. “If I had known, I would have came back sooner.”

“You said you had to rescue her?” she asked.

Steopa nodded. “We will move closer.”

He took Rebecka's hand and climbed down the hill. They walked up to the house. Arguing voices became louder as they came closer to his home.

“Ana, that is not your daughter. Give her to me.” It was a deep male voice.

"He will kill her, Ana. Do not listen to him," the other male said.

"That is my father," Steopa said. He stepped through the wall so he stood in the middle of the house. Rebecka joined him.

Ana rocked next to the fireplace, holding his daughter to her chest. Nastenka fussed as Ana shook her head. Steopa's father's boots dripped with water. He had not removed his riding cloak. The rainwater pooled around his feet. He stood between Ana and a priest. The priest took a step toward Ana.

She screamed, waking up Nastenka. Steopa's father pushed the priest back.

"I know what you plan to do!" his father shouted. "Murderer!"

"That is not a human child. We all saw Steopa dig himself out of the grave."

"The grave you did not consecrate."

Nastenka cried. Ana lowered her. She looked up at the priest. "But she is all I have of him."

"That was not Steopa!" the priest shouted.

"You said it was!" Steopa's father shoved the priest back. Steopa had inherited his large build from his father. His father's shove had forced the priest into the kitchen. The priest stumbled and hit the table. Framed in the window of the kitchen was Steopa from the memory. He turned his head. Steopa remembered hearing more horses approaching. He knew then that the priest had called hunters.

Nastenka cried. Ana stared at the infant. His father came over to Ana, he placed his hand on her shoulder. "Ana, regardless of what you think happened with Steopa, whether he is dead or not, Nastenka is your daughter, your child." He pointed to the priest. "He wants to kill an innocent."

He knelt near her. "I know what the villagers say. I have arranged for a safe place for both of you. Come with me."

"Ana, he let Steopa go. He let the demon leave!" the priest shouted and pointed to Steopa's father.

Steopa's father turned. "What did you do? Ana ran to the church when Steopa died. And you filled her head with nonsense."

"We saw him leave the cemetery. You stopped us from doing our duty."

"I stopped you from being a fool!"

The priest's face turned red. "This village has been plagued with deaths. Your son is responsible!"

Steopa's father stood up and rushed over to the priest. He stood a few inches away. "Idiot! My son was killed like the rest!"

"You are the fool!"

"Careful, Father, remember it was my grandfather that built the church. My family is the reason you are here. Speak carefully."

"Rodovitch, you would not dare..."

Steopa's father grabbed the priest's shoulders and spun him around. "Leave!"

Nastenka cried, turning red in the face. Ana lowered the baby. "But Steopa..."

"That was not Steopa!" The priest threw Steopa's father off him. "Steopa died at the battlefront. It was a demon that slept with you. That is a demon child."

"You are a fool!" Steopa's father tried to pull the priest back.

The priest spun around and stabbed Steopa's father in the shoulder. Rebecka moved. Steopa stopped her. He nodded toward the door.

Steopa from the memory slammed the front door. His eyes glowed green as he glared at the priest. The clouds behind him exploded with lightning. The wind blew his hair around his head. He growled. He looked liked the demon he had been accused of being. He crossed the floor and yanked the knife out of the priest's hand. The priest raised his crucifix, Steopa slapped it away. The cross flew across the room and hit the fireplace.

"That did not protect me. Do you think it would protect you!" He picked up the priest by his neck. "You attacked my family!"

Nastenka bawled.

"Not my baby! Not my baby!" Ana screamed.

Steopa from the memory tossed the priest. He rolled out the open doorway. Steopa's father winced and checked his wound. Steopa ran to the door and kicked the priest. He turned. Ana backed up to the wall and held Nastenka with white fingers.

Steopa's father stopped Steopa from the memory from approaching Ana. "Do not. Her mind is confused. Let me talk to her."

"My child?"

Steopa's father nodded. "Nastenka."

"After my mother?"

"Yes."

Ana wailed. She slid down the wall, clutching Nastenka. When she hit the floor, she glanced down at Nastenka with a horrified look on her face. She opened her arms, dropping the baby as if she had been burned. Nastenka tumbled to the floor. Steopa from the memory moved fast. He looked as if he had blinked from one place to another. He caught Nastenka with one hand before she hit the floor.

He held the infant up to Ana. "Our child. Ana, look at me."

Ana looked. Her eyes traveled from Nastenka to Steopa's face. She screamed. She clawed at Steopa. "GO! AWAY! DEMON!"

He pulled Nastenka closer and slid away from Ana. She clawed at the air where he had been. She cried out like a wild animal, then she rocked on her knees and prayed. Her body shook as she recited the Lord's Prayer. Steopa stood up holding Nastenka. She cried, but with the shuddering sobs of a child trying to stop.

"There is a place waiting for both of them. Can you take Nastenka there?" Steopa's father asked.

"Where?"

"The nunnery. They have a foundling hospital."

"Do they think this child is a demon?"

"They do not agree with this priest. Everything is set."

Steopa from the memory nodded. He wrapped Nastenka in his coat. It wasn't the long coat he wore now, but the tattered outer coat of his military uniform. He turned.

Ana stopped praying. She opened her eyes and looked around. She patted and felt the floor as if she lost something. "My baby? Where is my baby?"

She looked up and locked her gaze with Steopa. He remembered, for that moment, he saw the eyes of the woman he had married. For a second, she looked as if she understood. She nodded once, then the madness took her. She scratched her face and screamed.

Steopa's father went over to her and pulled her hands away from her face. "Careful, Steopa, there was talk in the village of hunters coming."

"For me?"

Steopa's father shook his head. "For Nastenka."

Steopa from the memory growled. He pulled a strand of his hair out of Nastenka's hand. “An infant? They would kill an infant?”

“Yes. Go! Please!”

Steopa from the memory ran out the door with Nastenka.

The memory faded. Rebecka turned to Steopa. “Did they really send hunters?”

Steopa nodded. “They did.”

The landscaped changed around them. They stood on a road lined with ruts from carts. The rain turned the hard dirt road into a muddy mire. Four horsemen rode toward them, staying on the sides of the road. Each of them was armed with a crossbow and a sword. One of the horses carried three large stakes and three smaller ones tied to its saddle.

Rebecka gripped Steopa's hand tighter. “Those are the hunters, right?”

Steopa nodded.

Out of the woods, Steopa from the memory ran. He jumped across the road in front of the hunters. The horses reared. The first hunter, armed with a pole arm, pulled on his reins. The horse shook its head. He turned the horse onto the small path into the woods.

Rebecka dropped Steopa's hand. She ran down the path. He ran after her as the other hunters turned their horses to follow the path.

“Rebecka,” Steopa called.

She stopped.

Steopa from the memory turned around and lunged forward, grabbing the horse's reigns as he did. The horse slipped and fell on its side. It rolled, crushing the hunter underneath. He pulled out the pole arm with one hand and cradled Nastenka with the other arm.

Nastenka did not cry. She chewed on a strand of his hair. Steopa from the memory changed his handhold on the pole arm. Nastenka giggled.

The second horseman barreled down the path. Steopa from the memory threw the pole arm like a javelin. It hit the horseman in the middle of the chest, knocking him off the horse. The pole arm pinned him to the ground. Steopa pulled the pole arm out of the man's chest and stepped on his throat. The neck collapsed. Nastenka gurgled. He looked down; she looked up at him.

The other two horsemen galloped down the path. He held the pole arm out and knocked the first off his horse. The other shot a crossbow bolt. He twisted his body to protect Nastenka. The bolt hit him in the upper back.

That hunter jumped off his horse and hit Steopa with a packet. The small seeds flew out across Steopa's face. He growled.

“Get the spawn!” the hunter shouted.

One other horseman still lived. He pulled himself up using a tree for support. He chanted a prayer as he threw himself forward, reaching for Nastenka. Steopa grabbed him with his free hand and snapped his neck.

The last horseman pulled out a large silver crucifix. He held it in front of Steopa's face. Steopa snatched it from the hunter.

He shoved it in the hunter's face. “What does this do to you?”

The hunter made the sign of the cross and prayed.

Steopa felt a button on the back of the crucifix. He pressed it. An ash stake poked out of the foot of the cross. Steopa slammed the stake through the hunter's neck. The stake punctured his throat.

Nastenka gurgled as the last hunter fell to the ground. Steopa kicked the body away.

“Let me take you to the nunnery, little one,” he said.

Nastenka reached up and patted Steopa on his cheek. Steopa placed his hand next to hers. She wrapped her fingers around his one.

“I cannot take you. I could not take care of you.”

She did not let go of his finger. Steopa wrapped his coat around her and continued down the path. The memory faded along with the bodies, leaving the woods empty. Steopa from the memory disappeared.

Rebecka shook her head. “They were going to kill her? She was a baby!”

“I know.”

“That's horrible.”

“Yes.” Steopa lifted Rebecka's face. “The nunnery protected Nastenka. She heard the same rumors, but the nuns never let anyone accuse her of being a demon.”

Steopa smiled. “They baptized her as soon as I brought her in. I held her in my arms as they preformed the rite. Neither of us burned.”

Rebecka looked up at him. “I assume they used holy water.”

“Yes.”

“Did any get on you?”

"Yes."

"And you didn't burn?"

Steopa shook his head. "The idea that religious artifacts can hurt vampires is not true. There are some vampires that will behave as if they are burned or that the cross repels them. But it is an act."

"Those hunters we met had holy water."

"Ogden told me, it was not the water that was the dangerous part. The holy water is for the humans, not for us."

Rebecka thought. Her brow creased. "So what you are saying is that the holy water, crosses, prayers... all of that is to make the humans feel more powerful. To make it seem like they could kill one of us."

Steopa nodded. "Yes, yes, that is it."

The memory faded.

CHAPTER 10

A smell made Steopa force himself out of the stupor. He sniffed. A strange chemical odor filled the room. He sat up, careful that he did not wake Rebecka. She rolled over and wrinkled her nose. He sniffed again. His eyes watered. He shut his sense of smell down. Steopa pulled on his pants, then opened the door to the other vault room.

Sasha sprang from the couch and stared at the entrance door. Steopa's eyes watered. Even though he could no longer smell it, the fumes affected him. Jimmy coughed. He sat up and covered his mouth. Sasha pulled his shirt above his nose. Along the bottom of the outer vault door a small puff of smoke rose, followed by a longer tendril.

Steopa grabbed one of his swords off the wall. He reached out and touched the vault door. He pulled his hand back. The tips of his fingers blistered from the heat, but healed.

Sasha lowered his shirt. His nose flattened against his face, leaving two slits instead of nostrils. He opened his eyes. Another set of eyelids blinked over his solid white eyes. Sasha smiled, showing his rows of fangs. He pulled another sword off the wall. He nodded to Steopa.

Jimmy reached for another weapon. Steopa swatted his hand away. He pointed to the other room. Jimmy's shoulders sagged. He didn't move. Steopa motioned with his head and grunted. Jimmy shook his head and went into the room. Rebecka patted him on the shoulder as he slouched by her.

Steopa grasped the round handle and turned it. He paused. On the other side of the door, he heard a voice. He did not recognized the words, but he recognized it as a European dialect. The talking stopped. Steopa turned the wheel a few inches, then he heard the sound of metal scraping, like something being etched. He glanced at Sasha.

Sasha took off his overcoat and glowed. Multiple colors rippled over his skin. The hues changed from blues and greens to whites and reds. Steopa turned his head away. The colors hurt his eyes. He touched the door. The edges had become hot. He smelt his flesh burning before he felt the pain.

Steopa spun the wheel and pulled the door open. On the other side, three men wearing night vision goggles stared back at him. They had paused in mid-movement. One reached for his sidearm. A high pitched noise made Steopa wince. He realize it came from Sasha. The noise made the men cover their ears. Then a bright blue glow filled the hallway. The glow came from Sasha as well. Steopa had to turn his head away. The three men tried to cover their goggles from the light.

The light faded. The men were dressed in public utility employee uniforms, but their equipment gave away their profession. No employees of any utility would have six-foot stakes or silver rope. Steopa lifted his sword up and cursed in Lithuanian.

Sasha laughed and rushed forward as Steopa did. The nearest man lost his head to Steopa's sword, the next to Sasha's blade. The third man started to run down the access tunnel. Steopa grabbed him and pulled him back into the vault. Sasha slammed the door behind them.

The man struggled in Steopa's hold. He reached in his pocket and pulled out a handful of dust. He blew it Steopa's face. The pain was intense. Steopa let go of the man to try to wipe the dust off his face. Sasha ran his sword through the man's upper arm, pinning him to a bookcase.

Steopa dropped his sword. The dust burned his eyes and mouth. Sasha twisted the sword in the man's arm. The man reached in his pocket again. Sasha was too quick for him. Sasha grabbed his hand and pounded it against the vault's wall. Then Sasha opened his mouth and screamed.

No sound seemed to come out, but the hunter cried out in pain. Blood dripped from his ears. Sasha closed his mouth. The color had drained from the hunter's face.

"What the hell?" Rebecka lowered her hands from her ears.

"A hunter," Steopa said, blinking.

The human shouted at them in the language Steopa did not understand. Then the shouting turned into a chant in Latin. Steopa picked up his sword and ran it through the other arm.

Sasha smiled, showing all of his teeth.

The hunter froze. “What the fuck are you?” he asked in a thick-accented voice.

Sasha growled and dislocated his jaw. He moved in to tear out the man's throat. Steopa stopped him. “Nyet.”

Sasha stopped as if he had been struck by a whip. Steopa patted him on the shoulder. “We should ask him some questions, no?”

Steopa stepped between the man and Sasha. “You are a hunter?”

The man prayed again. Steopa struck him across the face. “You are a hunter?”

The man nodded, but did not stop praying.

Steopa heard Rebecka walk past him, and the vault door opened. Sasha leaned up against the wall next to the man. He looked like a normal human again. The man glanced at Sasha. Sasha grinned, showing his rows of fangs.

Steopa hissed. “Who is paying you?”

The praying continued. Sasha shook his head. Then put his finger to the hunter's lips. The man stopped praying.

“Good,” Sasha said.

“Who is paying you?” Steopa asked.

Rebecka's voice came from the access tunnel. “Someone named Simon Cooper.”

“It can't be the same one,” Jimmy said. “Simon Cooper is the linebacker.”

“It could be the same,” Rebecka said.

“But why?” Jimmy asked.

The man closed his eyes. His shoulders shook and tears ran down his face. “I can't tell you more, they will kill me.”

“Fair enough.” Steopa motioned to Sasha with his head. Sasha opened his mouth like a snake and tore into the man's neck.

Rebecka held a cell phone in her hand. This one was not like any that Steopa had seen before. She held the screen up to show him. The name Simon Cooper highlighted. Rebecka flipped the phone over. “The last text message was; We have found the giant's lair. Attempting now.”

Sasha wiped his face with one hand. With the other, he tossed the man to one side. “Who is Simon?”

“It could be an alias,” Rebecka said.

“I know,” Jimmy said, raising his hand. “I told you, that one we saw made into a drudge, that was Simon Cooper. But he's a football player, I don't know what he would be doing with this."

"Wait, Cooper," Rebecka tapped the phone against her teeth. "He's not related to the Coopers that own Cooper Computers?"

Jimmy nodded. "Yeah."

"He would have the money."

"Not that much."

Rebecka thought. "That's true. His father still runs it. But wasn't there something that happened lately to them?"

"Yeah, it did-"

"Did you find anything else?" Steopa asked.

Rebecka nodded. "They got some serious hardware out there. Give me a few minutes."

Sasha pulled one of the swords out of the man's arm. "I hate the daylight," he said.

Rebecka came back into the room with the hunter's laptop. She opened it and turned it on. Her shoulders sagged. "Um, I can't read this."

Steopa walked over to her. He looked at the screen. "It's Russian."

"I should have paid attention to your lessons."

Steopa patted her shoulder. "You are learning."

Sasha sat down next to her on the couch. "Can I help?"

She nodded. Steopa picked up the dead body and put it outside with the other two. He noticed a backpack. He grabbed it and went back into the lair.

He watched Rebecka and Sasha for a time. His head felt light. His arms felt heavy. He shook his body, trying to dislodge the stupor.

Jimmy sat down next to him. "Why do I feel drunk?"

"You know what that feels like?" Steopa asked.

"I drank a fifth of rum and ended up in the hospital."

Steopa shook his head. "What you are feeling is the stupor. You can fight it off in the day."

"It's daytime?"

"Yes."

The hunters' phone beeped. Rebecka picked it up. "A message from Simon," she said, then she read it out loud. "Report on the lair."

She looked at Steopa and Sasha, then spoke as she typed.

"Mistake made, will search tomorrow."

The phone beeped again. "Meet me at airport tomorrow," she read. She hit a few more buttons on the phone. "Whoa! This is interesting."

She held up the phone. A grainy video played on the small screen. Two men sat at a table in a room that looked like it was in a basement. The two men, Steopa recognized, were now dead, laying outside the vault door. A third man entered. Steopa recognized him as the drudge. In the low-quality video, you could see his fangs glint in the low light.

They began to speak. Sasha translated for Rebecka.

"We don't understand why you are hiring us."

"I need a rival taken care of," Simon said.

"How can you be sure we will not hunt you down afterwards?"

"You will not. I have friends that will see to that."

"What did he do to you, anyway?"

"He killed my sister."

One of the hunters sat back. "We only work for one."

"I will pay you more."

The video stopped.

"Did you kill his sister?" Jimmy asked.

"No."

"Then why did he-"

"Because he is a drudge. The vampire that made him, she told him to say those things. What was her name?"

"Adelind."

"Was she the one that told you to kill me?" Rebecka asked.

Steopa nodded.

"I hate her already."

The phone beeped again. Rebecka flipped it over. "From someone called Pawid. Werewolves are in this town as well."

Steopa stood. He slammed his fist against one of the walls. "If they hurt any of Teodor's family."

Rebecka pulled out her cell phone. "I'll call him." She left the vault room.

Sasha shook his head and rubbed his face. Steopa paced the room a few times, then the room spun around him. He sat down in the easy chair. He leaned forward and put his head in his hands.

"Why would he care if you killed his sister?" Sasha asked. "No, that's not what I meant to say. Why would he say that? It would be easy for the hunters to verify."

"He did have a sister," Jimmy said. "She disappeared last year, when she was on a trip in Europe."

"That is why you asked."

"Well, yeah."

"Adelind could have found that out and told him that I killed his sister." Steopa rubbed his chin. "A drudge would not think for himself, so he would not have questioned it. When Rebecka became one of us, there was a runt of a vampire named Jalmari. He used drudges to fight his battles."

"What happened?"

"I cut his head off."

Sasha grinned. "Sometimes I miss being on the land."

Rebecka came back to the room. "Okay, Teodor has been warned."

She lost her footing. Steopa reached out to steady her. "I suddenly feel very drunk," she said.

"It's the stupor," Sasha said.

Steopa pulled Rebecka on to his lap. "That is why they came now." he said. His voice slurred. "They knew it would be hard for us to react."

Rebecka put her head on Steopa's shoulder. "If they come back?" she asked, her eyes closing.

"I just fed," Sasha said. "I can fight it a little longer."

Steopa nodded to Sasha. When the night comes, he thought, I am going to drink more than my fill, and I will find those hunters and kill them.

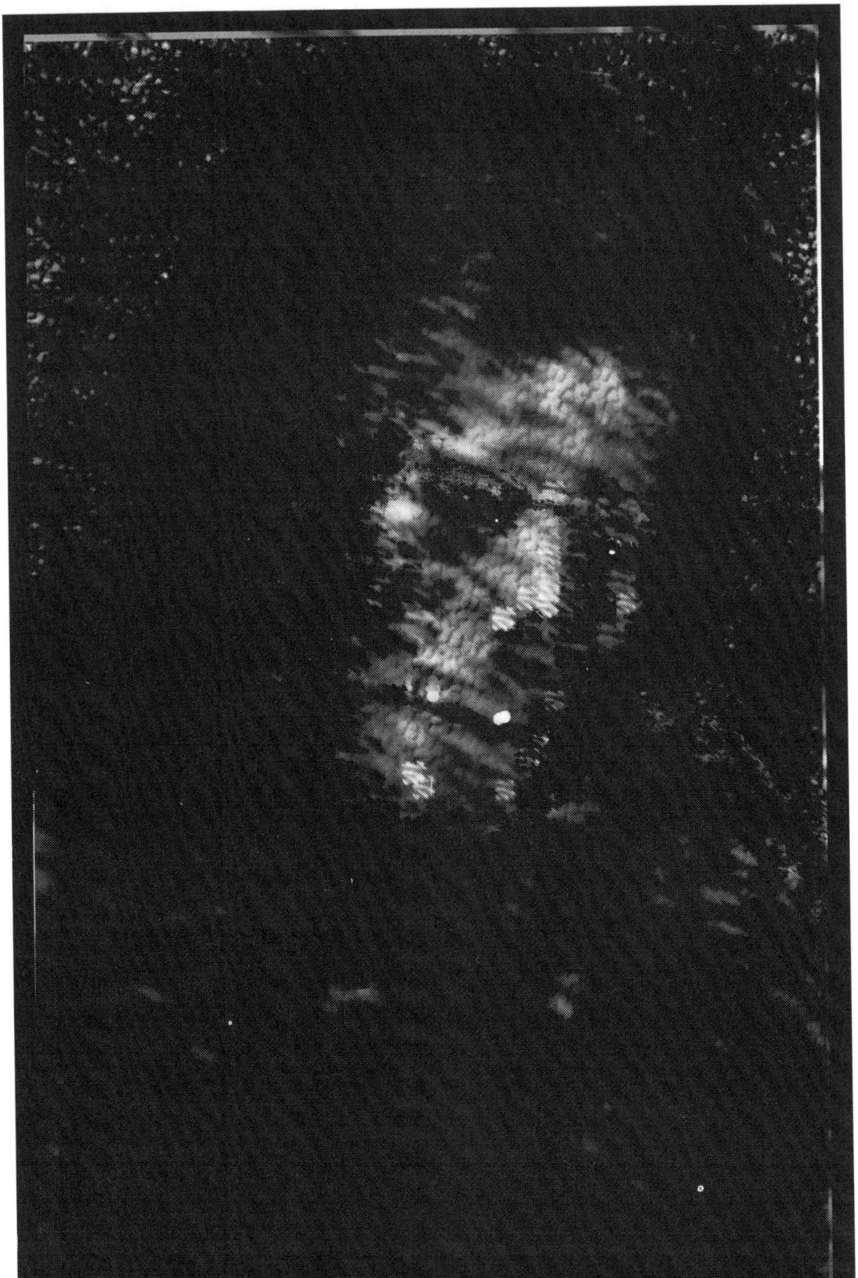

CHAPTER 11

Rebecka got off his lap. Steopa opened his eyes and listened to the tunnel outside the vault. He heard the street above them, and the sounds of the cars leaving the parking garage. Nothing sounded unusual.

"Rebecka," he said, "I need you to find Verina."

Rebecka nodded. She walked into the bedroom and shut the door.

Sasha blinked his eyes. His inner eyelids disappeared. "What now?"

"We need to get rid of the bodies," Steopa said.

Sasha rubbed his chin. "I wonder if they have someone watching this place. Where could we go?"

"There is an alcove that leads to the city's sewers, down the tunnel. We will take them there."

"Much easier in the water," Sasha motioned with his hands. "I just let them float away."

"I was wondering," Jimmy said. "How did you get here?"

"I swam."

"All the way? Where did you come from?"

"I was hunting along Cape Cod this year. Tourist season is always good for a quick meal."

Jimmy looked confused. "But we are so far inland, how did you get here?"

"There are ships that travel from your Eastern seaboard into the Great Lakes. I hitched a ride on one of those, and swam the rest."

"All the way?"

Sasha chuckled. "Except for the part where I hitchhiked. She was nice too, tasted like apples."

Rebecka came out, dressed. She stopped at her desk to pack up her laptop. "Baldman wants me to get in touch with him, too. I would like him to do his magic on the hunter's laptop. If he can break into the CIA's mainframe, he can help us with this."

"He did?" Steopa asked.

Rebecka nodded. "I'll get the hardware ready, then go to Cassie's shop. It might take all night. And don't worry, I contacted Vincent. We are in luck, Verina is in town."

Steopa went into their room and changed. He came back out and picked the saber off the wall. He placed it under his long coat so it could not be seen.

Rebecka slid her backpack over one shoulder. She went over to the door and opened it. The smell of stale blood filled the room.

Sasha picked up one of the bodies. "Where is the access tunnel?" he asked.

Steopa pointed down the tunnel. "It is blocked by concrete."

He went to the large block that fit almost flush to the wall. He hooked his claws on the edges and pulled. Behind it, another tunnel opened. This one had been made with bricks. Piles of bricks were on the floor where the ceiling had started to collapse. He smelled the sewers as soon as he moved the block.

Jimmy picked up one body. Steopa picked up the last and threw him over his shoulder. He walked the short distance to the sewers and threw the body into the water. The swarm of rats on the other side scattered. Jimmy dropped his burden.

Another splash as Sasha threw the other body into the sewer. He sniffed the air. "We aren't the only ones using this for bodies."

Steopa nodded. "I know." He pointed down one way of the tunnel. "Down there, the homeless will gather for winter. A few of their bodies have ended in this water."

They went back to the main tunnel. Steopa replaced the large concrete block. Rebecka had cleaned up the hallway except for the blood stains. She held a device in her hands. It had a long handle and a readout on the top.

"I know how they found us," she said. She held up the tool. "See, it reads any active currents, like the ones I use to power my stuff."

"The power lines you laid down?" Steopa asked.

Rebecka nodded. "I thought I had hidden the splice well enough."

"Or they could have followed that woman down here," Sasha said.

Steopa flung his hair back. "Dorn? Yes, that is possible."

"Is there another way in?" Sasha asked.

Steopa did not answer. I do not want to open that door, he thought.

"Is there?" Rebecka asked.

"What do you think Baldman can find out for you?" Steopa asked, turning to leave their lair.

"I asked him to trace the satellite phone." Rebecka hurried to catch up with Steopa. "He traced it to this city, but he thought that they used a relay."

Steopa pushed the door open to the electrical room below the parking garage. "Anything else?"

"Diamonds have been appearing in a lot of cities lately."

"What is strange about that?" Sasha asked.

"Baldman read it off one of his conspiracy newspapers. They think it has to do with redistributing wealth before another economic collapse." Rebecka shrugged. "He found it odd because of the cities mentioned."

"What cities?" Steopa asked.

"Here, Saint Petersburg, Bucharest, Helsinki, some others."

"I do not see the connection."

"Neither do I, and Baldman won't tell me."

They walked out of the parking garage. Rebecka paused. She tilted her head for a moment. "That was Vincent," she said, pulling her cell phone out of her pocket. "He told me where Verina was. I'll give her a call."

"Good," Steopa said.

Sasha paused.

"What is it?" Steopa asked.

"I thought, no," Sasha said.

Steopa turned to face Sasha, while Rebecka talked to Verina. "What?"

"There was a vehicle parked down the road. It is gone now. But I thought I saw it last night." Sasha shook his head. "I could be wrong. I can't tell the difference between them. Now, if it was a boat..."

"So are you going to be there later?" Rebecka asked.

Steopa could hear Verina's voice from the cell phone. "Yeah, I will."

"Thanks, Verina." Rebecka said.

"Where is she?"

"She is going to meet us at the Rathskeller later." Rebecka said. "Why do you need to talk to her?"

"Because she is as close as we will ever get to an elder."

"Why is that important?" Rebecka asked. "We have hunters on our backs."

"Because a vampire has been asking about me," Steopa said. "Verina knows more than we do."

"Elders?" Sasha scoffed. "Nothing but fairy tales."

"I have it on good authority-"

"She might be old, but you know the tales, Grandfather. The secret meetings, how they want to control all of us. Have you ever met one? Or seen one? Other than the one we are meeting?"

Steopa continued down the street and nodded. "One time, in Saint Petersburg."

"One, possibly two." Sasha caught up with Steopa. "Haven't you wondered why there are not many vampires older than us?"

"I have, but it is no matter."

"It might be," Rebecka said. "If, like you said, this other vampire has found the elders and is asking for help."

"What can they do?" Sasha asked. "The only difference between us and them is that they are older. They have survived. We all have."

"We should not speak to her?" Steopa asked.

"I think it is a waste of time."

Rebecka shook her head. "No."

"Give me one good reason to go."

"My brother is there." The ring on Rebecka's finger glowed. "Don't you think that if they find out about me, he will be a target, too? They had the Rathskeller on that paper."

Sasha didn't respond for a moment, then he nodded. "Yes, he would."

"We have to go," Steopa said.

"Why aren't there any elders?" Jimmy asked.

No one answered, then Sasha sighed. "Old stories. Some say they are gone, killed themselves. One story says there was a civil war and most of the elders were killed off. But I think, after a while, it gets too much, and they lay in the ground, letting the stupor take them forever."

"So is this Verina really old?"

"I don't think so," Rebecka said. "She doesn't act like it."

"I have been almost everywhere," Sasha said. "I have never met a vampire much older than... you, Grandfather."

"That has been my experience as well," Steopa said.

As they came closer to the Rathskeller, Steopa could see the line forming around the building. Rebecka shook her head.

"We should have known, there's a band playing. No wonder Verina wanted to be here," she said. "I'm going to Cassie's shop after checking in with John." She tilted her head. "Vincent will meet you in the back. By the bus."

Steopa motioned to Jimmy and Sasha. "Follow me."

After Rebecka left, Jimmy looked confused. "How does she know what Vincent is doing?"

"They can talk with their minds," Steopa said.

"Can we all do that?"

Steopa shook his head. "And Rebecka can only communicate with Vincent."

He led them around the back of the club. The tour bus blocked the entrance to the alley. Small crowds of people filled the space between the bus and the back of the club. The women turned their heads as they passed.

Steopa paused by the ramp to the club. He smirked.

"What is it?" Sasha asked.

Steopa pointed to the wall. A large section of the bricks and been broken and fallen away. "They still have not repaired that."

Sasha raised his eyebrow.

"This is where I... 'met' Rebecka," Steopa said.

Sasha chuckled. "Why did you stop feeding?"

"Another vampire stopped me."

"Who?"

"The one that is meeting us here." Steopa walked up the ramp. A member of the band's security stopped him. Steopa straighted up and towered over the man. The man looked up, but did not move.

Behind the man, Vincent appeared out of the shadows. "He's cool," Vincent said. "He works for me."

"These two are with me," Steopa said.

"Hey, Vincent," Jimmy said.

The security man stood aside. Steopa nodded to him as he passed. Vincent hurried down the hall. He spoke over his shoulder as they walked. "Verina is waiting for you in my room."

They weaved past the type of people that seemed to fill up the backstage at any concert. Vincent smiled at two groupies that blocked the door to his room. They smiled back and moved out of the way. Vincent opened the door. The smell of cigarette smoke wavered out of the room.

Verina sat cross-legged on one of the velvet covered chairs. "So, Steopa, Rebecka tells me we have hunters."

Steopa nodded. "And I was told you are an elder."

Verina gave him a small smile. "A lady never reveals her age." She pointed to the fainting couch with her long fingers. "But it is true."

Steopa took off his coat and sat down, folding his coat over his knees.

Verina smiled at Sasha. He sat down on the chair next to her. Jimmy stared. He missed the chair he tried to sit on. He jumped up and sat down again. "Sorry," he said, grinning.

She pulled down her skirt, then pointed to Steopa. "I also know that some vampires have been made aware of you."

"How do you know?" Steopa asked.

"I have friends in Europe. Most are just curious if you are real. A human that killed the vampire that was feeding off him. That is unheard of."

"It did not stop me from becoming a vampire."

"And that is why some of the vampires are nervous. If you could take out a vampire with your bare hands as a human, they have no idea what you could do now."

"What does this have to do with Simon Cooper?" Steopa asked.

"Simon?" Verina asked, thinking over the name. "I have never heard of him."

"He is the drudge that hired the hunters," Sasha said.

"What did you do to him?"

"Nothing," Steopa said. "He claims I killed his sister."

"But she disappeared in Europe," Jimmy said. "Germany, if I remember right."

"So he sends hunters?" Verina asked. Steopa almost answered, but then he realized it was an open question. She folded her long fingers on her lap.

"There is another vampire. Adelind." Steopa watched Verina.

"We saw her make Simon into a drudge."

The corner of Verina's mouth twitched. "Red hair?"

"Yes."

"I know her." Verina took a drag of her cigarette. "She keeps to herself most of the time, but then there are times she crosses the line."

"No one has taken her out?"

"They have tried. She is stronger than she looks. We fought once." Verina chuckled. "Stupid reason. But I did take a chunk of her hair."

"Simon is her dirge," Jimmy said. "Wait, I mean drudge."

Verina grinned. "What a moron. She makes a drudge to hire hunters. They won't stop with you, unless there is another reason."

Steopa pointed to Sasha and Jimmy. "I have family. Some have become vampires."

Verina arched an eyebrow. "Interesting, that is even more rare. Now-a-days, anyway." She paused. "Okay, this is what I think is going on. That Simon is weak. Adelind is using him to take you out of the picture, for whatever reason. But she talked to some other vampires. They are aware of you, and possibly your family. So they are letting her do this, to test you."

"And if I dispose of Simon?" Steopa asked.

"You get rid of a drudge," Verina said. "But you still have to deal with Adelind and try not to expose your family."

"What about the rumors of the elders?" Vincent asked.

"Most of them are nothing to worry about. They want to survive, like the rest of us."

Sasha grinned. "I thought so."

"But there are few that think that their age means that they can control the rest," Verina chuckled. "The last time they tried to govern all of us, most ended up dead."

"You did not?" Sasha asked.

Verina stretched out her fingers. Her long fingernails had been painted green. She waved them in front of her face. "The elders that ended up dead deserved it. Although the slaughter did not stop there. I was smart and I was quick."

"Why haven't we heard about this?" Vincent asked.

"There were entire bloodlines that were wiped out, including other vampires families. The winning side does not talk about it.

They do not want the younger vampires to know. In case one of them gets ideas."

Steopa hung his head. "What about my family? This will expose them. All of them felt the call to come here when I was injured."

Verina's eyes went wide, then she shrugged. "I don't know. I don't think the elders are your problem. The hunters, Simon, and Adelind, those are your problems."

Steopa chuckled. "The hunters that he has sent all are dead." He lifted his head. "Thank you."

Verina stood. She picked up her pack of cigarettes and placed them in her handbag. She patted Steopa on his shoulder. "I wouldn't worry too much. When Simon rears his head, I know you will rip it off."

Vincent giggled. "Who said he would stop at the head?"

Verina laid her hand on the doorknob. "I'm sure he won't." She smiled. "Is the band on yet?"

Vincent checked his watch. "They better be."

"Can we stay for the show?" Jimmy asked.

"You can. I will go see Rebecka. If we do not come down before dawn, wait for us outside the door," Steopa said.

"Why don't you come with me," Verina said, motioning to Jimmy. "I always get the best seats."

Jimmy and Sasha left the room with Verina. Vincent waited until the door closed.

"Sasha looks a lot like you. Son?"

Steopa shook his head. "Grandson."

"Do you have a lot?"

"What?"

"A lot of family?"

Steopa nodded.

Vincent rubbed his beard. "I think Verina is wrong. I think it's jealousy."

"Your meaning?"

"You have a family, you have a woman you are linked to. Damn, I'm jealous."

"So this Simon is being used to destroy my family because Adelind does not have one?" Steopa asked. "She is an idiot."

"Do they know about Rebecka?"

"I am not sure."

“This sucks.”
Steopa nodded.

Third Eye
Curios®
inc.

CHAPTER 12

Steopa left the club through the back door. He weaved around the small groups of people outside of the club. The line in front of the club had thinned. Some people milled around the doors of the two businesses that were open. A crowd stood outside Third Eye Curio's door, blocking anyone from entering. Steopa walked up to them. They moved aside as he walked past them.

Cassie looked up from the counter. She motioned with her head to the back room. The customer at the counter glanced at Steopa, then returned to looking at the crystal necklaces in the glass case. Cassie held up her hand.

"I want to talk to you," Cassie said.

"About what?" Steopa asked.

"Later, when we aren't so busy."

Steopa glanced around the shop. There were no empty stools at the coffee counter. A group of loud teenagers sat around the table in the back of the store. He walked around two people talking near the tarot cards. One woman looked in his direction. She stepped back and made the sign of the cross.

He stopped. She tugged on the other woman's sleeve. Her face turned white. She said a little prayer in Ukrainian. Steopa bowed his head and continued to the back room. He smiled. That has not happened for a long time; she knew what I am, he thought.

He opened the door. Rebecka looked up from her laptop. The hunter's laptop sat on the desk, its lid open and the screen saver running. A cord ran from her laptop to the satellite phone.

"Why are you smiling?" she asked.

"A woman recognized that I was a vampire."

"And that made you smile?"

"It has not happened since Russia." Steopa sat down next to Rebecka. "What have you found out?

"We are dealing with a well-funded vampire, or whoever is paying them." Rebecka clicked on a window. "Baldman had to call help in, that is how hidden the financing was, but one place keeps showing up. Kiel."

"Kiel, Germany?"

Rebecka nodded.

"That is on the Baltic Sea."

"Is it?"

"Yes."

"Anyway. I am waiting for Baldman to come back with some info. He thought he stumbled onto something nasty,"

"What?"

"He didn't say. Except that he was concerned that he would have to call in the authorities." She turned back to the laptop.

Steopa watched Rebecka for a short while. How much did she know about her friend? He thought. Baldman did look familiar...

"Does he know you are a vampire?" Steopa asked.

"Who?"

"Baldman?"

"Do you think I would tell him that?" Rebecka scoffed. "That man believes that aliens are trying to take over the world. If I give him proof that there are vampires, he'll have a heart attack."

Steopa chuckled. "That would be unfortunate."

A window blinked on Rebecka's laptop. She clicked on it. The bald-headed man in the video window smiled, then sat back so his face was in shadow.

"It's all right Baldman," Rebecka said.

"Ah, yes," Baldman rubbed his hand over his head. "I have found some disturbing things. Are you sure you want to, um, know?"

"Baldman, you know it's important."

Baldman sighed. "Interpol is following a ring of child traffickers. Kiel is one of the cities on the list. Simon's name is listed as a possible suspect."

Rebecka closed her eyes, the ring glowed on her finger.

Steopa leaned forward. "Remember the children we found."

Rebecka nodded. "Baldman, is that why you asked about them a few days ago?"

"Yes."

"But Simon-" Steopa stopped. "How did they find out?"

Baldman's mouth fell open. "Well, um, I think, yes, I think they had been watching an exchange. He was named by a woman they captured. Odd, odd thing is, the authorities don't think Simon is involved. They want to bring him in for questioning, if they can find him."

Rebecka glanced at Steopa. "We are pretty sure the Simon we are following and the one that Interpol is following might not be the same person."

"Why is that?" Baldman asked.

"Because he-" Rebecka bit her lip. "How recent was that intelligence?"

"Last night."

"He disappeared a few nights ago from here. This doesn't make sense."

Baldman adjusted his glasses. "His name came up before. When his sister disappeared. She had been seen with a woman. Ah, yes. Here."

A photo popped up on the screen. Two women stood in a stairwell facing each other. Steopa growled. He recognized one of them.

"Adelind," he said. "Can I speak to Baldman?"

"Baldman?" Rebecka asked.

He rubbed his head. "Yes."

"Steopa wants to talk to you."

Baldman made a strange face, then nodded.

Rebecka walked over to the other side of the room. Baldman rubbed his face. He grimaced, then tapped his fingers on his desk. Steopa sat down in front of her computer.

"What do you think?" Steopa asked.

"I have worked with Rebecka enough to know that there are people that want to keep secrets. I like finding their secrets. And these are nasty. What? What do you plan to do with him?"

"I didn't tell him anything," Rebecka said.

Steopa sat back. "He has tried to kill me."

"I don't want to know now," Baldman said.

"Can you tell if he is working with others?"

Baldman nodded. "That is a certain, I just cannot find proof on who they are."

"That woman and a bald, scarred man."

"How do you know?"

Steopa sat back. "I thought you did not want to know."

Rebecka reached over Steopa, she put her finger on the mouse. "Baldman, if you could look at the files I downloaded from the phone, please."

"Of course, Saberdragon. Of course."

She clicked off the screen. "Motherfucker!"

Steopa put his arm around Rebecka. "Baldman?"

"No! Do you think they are messing with that trafficking?"

"The children?" Steopa pulled her closer.

"Why does she or he want them?"

"Does it matter?"

Steopa felt the heat coming off her ring. "If he is feeding off them, he will have more than me to worry about. Children as a rule do not have shrouds."

"What if it's something else?" Rebecka pushed Steopa's arm away. "We have met sicko vampires before."

"Then we have more reasons to kill him."

"Thats all we have! We are not sure where he is! Why he is using human hunters?"

Steopa stood up. "What do you want me to do?"

"You? Us!"

Steopa stood back. "What?"

"This isn't just about you, this is about me too. This is about Sasha, and Jimmy. This is all of us."

"Rebecka, he attacked me!"

"He attacked all of us. I felt that explosion. I felt your pain. Your descendants did too. He or she knew it would happen!"

The door to the room opened. "Um guys, you okay?" Cassie asked.

"Yes," Steopa said.

Rebecka turned around and closed the laptops. "Sorry, Cassie."

"Are you sure?" Cassie asked curling her brown hair around her finger.

"Yes." Steopa left the room.

Cassie followed him. She tapped him on the back. "Wait."

Steopa spun around to face her. "What!"

The customers in the store turned to stare. Cassie stepped back. "I need to speak to you."

Steopa's shoulders sagged. "I am sorry. What is it?"

Cassie curled her finger. "I saw this, I couldn't believe it."

Steopa followed her back to the counter. Cassie pulled an old book from behind the cash register. She opened the book to a marked page. She turned the book around and pointed to a photograph.

He recognized the scene. A bombed street in Saint Petersburg. The photo had been taken at night, a group of people were gathered around a fire. Behind the group, Steopa saw two familiar faces. Steopa pulled the book closer.

"That's you?" Cassie asked, lowering her voice.

Steopa nodded.

In the photo, he stood next to Teodor in a doorway. Steopa's face had been obscured by his hair, but Teodor's face could be seen clearly. The wall next to the door had been blown apart by a bomb. He picked up the book. The caption of the picture did not tell him anything except the year.

"What is this about?" Steopa asked.

"It's a collection of accounts of World War Two. I got it in a shipment by accident," Cassie said.

"Can I have it?" Steopa reached for his wallet.

Cassie nodded, but she waved her hand when he pulled his wallet out of his pocket. "No, it's yours."

"Thank you."

Rebecka joined him at the counter and did not look at him. Steopa slid the book into his coat. "Do you want to go to the club?"

Rebecka shook her head.

They left Cassie's store. Steopa walked behind Rebecka. The ring on her hand glowed, but not as bright as in the store. When she gets angry that rings glows, he thought. I wish we knew more about it.

A cat jumped between him and Rebecka. It meowed. Steopa glanced at it. It sat down and cleaned itself. The tips of its ears were green. Steopa stopped.

"Perun?"

The cat looked up and meowed. Rebecka stopped. She turned around and came back. "How do you know that's Perun?"

"The green ears."

The cat meowed and hurried into another alley. Steopa followed. He heard Rebecka scoff, but she walked into the alley. The cat sat down, then changed into Perun. A scowl crossed his normally smiling face.

"Why are you here?" Steopa asked.

"I have a problem. I'm glad I found you," Perun said. He looked around. "I hate the city. Come with me."

"What is it?" Rebecka asked.

Perun opened his shirt, three long scratches went from his neck to his groin. "It's a vampire, but I have never seen one like him."

"You are not healing," Steopa said.

Perun nodded. "Hurry. Jeremiah and Mak are trying their best."

CHAPTER 13

"Who is Mak?" Steopa asked as they ran over the bridge to Greenwoods.

"Makkapitew," Perun said. "He lets Jeremiah and I live in Greenwoods. You saw him."

"The Native American?"

Perun nodded. He jumped off the bridge and down to the bank of the river. Steopa took Rebecka's hand and they jumped. Perun bounded up the bank and into the woods.

Steopa caught up with Perun. "Who attacked you? Was it a light-haired vampire?"

Perun shook his head. "No, bald and as big as you. I doubt you ran into this one before."

He ran up a wooded hill, jumping over the Native American vampire as he rolled down. Perun twisted in midair and landed next to the vampire.

"Mak." Perun rolled Mak over to his back.

Mak shook his head. His brown eyes glowed red. "It is a monster."

Steopa ran up the hill. Rebecka gasped when she got to the top. "He's right."

"Da."

The vampire in the hollow below them stood as tall as Steopa. His head and face had no hair, including no eyebrows. His muscles were unnaturally large, like they had been inflated. The beast roared.

"What type of vampire is that?" Rebecka asked.

Steopa shook his head. "I have never seen one-"

Jeremiah dodged the fist of the monster vampire. For being a heavy-set vampire, Jeremiah moved fast. He rolled and jumped to the side. The beast turned. It looked like a mountain of flesh rotating. It roared again. The noise made Steopa's fangs grow. Rebecka dropped her backpack. She growled.

Perun helped Mak up the hill. Mak fingered the open wound on his chest. “He sounds like a bear.”

Perun nodded. He turned to Steopa. “He found the village. Don't ask me how.”

Steopa took off his jacket and pulled his sword out of the scabbard. “I will ask him.”

The monster spun to face Steopa. Jeremiah plowed into the giant's back. The large beast swung his arms, trying to knock Jeremiah away. Steopa swung the sword. The monster grabbed the blade. He smiled.

Six sets of fangs glistened from the inside of his mouth. He laughed; a low, rumbling noise like rocks being churned in a bucket. The blade cut into his hand, but he did not release it. He sniffed.

“Rodovitch!” he bellowed, yanking the blade toward his chest.

Steopa stumbled forward. He let go of the sword just before the monster could grab him. The monster threw the sword into the woods.

Jeremiah dug his claws into the monster's head. He reached behind his head, grabbed Jeremiah with one hand and flipped him over the top of his body. Jeremiah hit an oak tree and slid down to the ground, landing on his shoulders. He rolled onto his back and coughed.

The monster swung his fist. Steopa ducked. The fist connected with Rebecka, sending her back after Steopa heard bones snap. She hit the ground and did not move. Steopa roared. The monster did the same. They rushed toward each other and hit so hard Steopa felt the ground shake. Steopa changed his handhold to try to fling the monster into the trees. The large vampire matched his holds.

They were at a standstill. No matter what move Steopa tried, the monster could match him. He saw a movement out of the corner of his eye. Rebecka stood. She hissed. The monster's eyes focused on Rebecka. He grinned.

“She will be easy to rip apart,” the beast said.

“No!” Steopa yelled.

He head-butted the monster vampire. The beast stepped back. Steopa slipped his foot around the large vampire's lower leg and tripped him. The monster flipped his body upright.

He heard a wet sound, like a knife drawn out of a swamp. Then Jeremiah appeared behind the monster. He slammed his forearm against the back of the beast. The monster's head twisted at an odd angle, then tumbled down his chest. The body fell to the ground. The blood turned from red to black as it flowed over the ground. Jeremiah held his arm up for a moment. A white bone slipped back into his skin.

"They still sting," Jeremiah said.

Rebecka stared at Jeremiah's arm. "What the hell?"

He looked at his forearm. "That? An extra-large claw, that's all"

"But-?" Rebecka's mouth fell open.

Steopa picked up the monster's head and showed it to her. "I have never seen a vampire like this."

Mak limped up to Steopa. He squatted down and picked up the large vampire's hand. "I have not either. He was not a normal vampire."

"No shit," Jeremiah said.

"Can you not feel it?" Mak asked. "There is magic here."

Perun walked around them, humming to himself. He waved his hand over the body. "Mak is right. There is magic. A type I don't recognize."

Steopa studied the head in his hand. The skin had stretch marks along the cheeks and neck. The heavy brow and the wide cheek bones reminded him of a Neanderthal's skull. He pulled up the top lip. There were six sets of fangs and no other teeth. Odd, Steopa thought, even we keep our other teeth.

"Where did it come from?" Rebecka asked.

"I don't know," Perun said.

Mak dropped the hand. "I saw it come from the old poorhouse."

Steopa growled.

"Thats where Jimmy and you saw Adelind?" Rebecka asked.

Steopa nodded.

Jeremiah kicked the large vampire's headless body. "No way this is a drudge."

The arm on the body jerked. Jeremiah jumped back. Mak chuckled.

"It said your name," Rebecka said to Steopa.

Steopa nodded. "Perhaps we need to worry about more than hunters now."

"We need to take the body back to the village," Mak said.

"Why?" Jeremiah asked.

"The vampire's spirit is still there. I could try to speak to it."

Steopa turned to look at Mak. "What do you mean?"

"When Mak was alive he was a shaman." Perun smiled, then winched. "That is why he knew what I am."

"You can speak to the dead?" Steopa asked.

"Yes, but it is odd that this one has his spirit still. When a vampire is destroyed, their spirit is as well."

"How much could he tell us?"

"I don't know."

Jeremiah picked up the headless body. "Fine, I'll carry this."

Perun led the way through the woods, limping.

"What is wrong?" Steopa asked.

"That damned vampire," Perun said. "I can feel the poison."

"Poison?" Rebecka asked.

"When it swiped me. Must have been under its nails." Perun touched the wound and sucked in his breath. "I got some herbs at that church that will help."

The path to the village had been cleared. Mak pointed to the ivy-covered fountain. "Put the body there. I will be back shortly."

Jeremiah dumped the body on the ground. He rubbed his wrist. Steopa threw the head. It rolled and hit the wall of one of the homes. He looked up to see Perun grab the door frame of the church. Perun rested his head against his arm, his shoulders sagging. He lifted his head, shook it, then went inside the building.

"Wait for me," Steopa said to Rebecka.

"Where-?" she reached for his hand.

Steopa shook his head. "Something is wrong with Perun."

He hurried to the church. At the entrance he stopped. The inside of the church had been transformed. The pews had been removed and logs laid down in their place. The crucifix laid on its side along one of the walls. Instead of an altar, large pots had been arranged. A different plant grew out of each one.

Perun looked over his shoulder. "It's not consecrated."

"Even if it was..." Steopa walked up the aisle. "Are you sure it's poison?"

Perun nodded. "I never felt this kind before."

"It is affecting you, that should not happen."

Perun shrugged. "Things affect me, I usually shake them off."

He limped to the plants. Humming, he held his hand over a

planter. The plants bloomed. Along the back of the church, primroses opened. The air filled with their sweet smell.

"You and her," Perun said. His eyes twinkled. "I never thought you would take a mate."

"Do not call Rebecka a mate."

Perun chuckled as he picked some leaves and flowers off different plants. "Mate. Wife. Whatever. The thing is she is yours. And you are hers."

"We are linked."

"Linked? That's what vampires call it? No wonder you don't have sex."

Steopa growled.

Perun sat down on the steps to the altar. He picked up a copper bowl and tossed the pieces of the plants inside it.

"We cannot have sex," Steopa said. "Because we do not reproduce that way."

"No, you reproduce by biting." Perun shook his head. "That's rabies, not reproduction."

"I saw Dorn. She came down the tunnel to 'check on the specimens' after someone had beaten her," Steopa said. He hoped Perun would take the hint and change the subject.

"I thought she would have died already," Perun said. "Has she ever done that before?"

Steopa shook his head.

"You could send her my way," Perun chuckled.

"She is an old woman."

Perun crushed the plants in the copper bowl. "She is still a woman."

"Disgusting."

Perun laughed. "You were alive once." He pulled back his shirt. The wounds had bruised and turned black on the edges. "Shit."

Steopa could smell the decay on Perun. He usually smelled like fresh cut grass and musk. The black edges of the wounds spread across his chest in spider web-like patterns. Perun grimaced.

"This poison isn't natural. I know that." He rubbed the crushed plants on his chest and sighed. "That feels better."

Rebecka walked into the church. She pointed to the fountain. "Mak's ready."

Perun smiled. "You have to see this."

Steopa walked over to Rebecka. He slid his arm around her waist. Perun wrapped his arms around both of them.

"You two do make a good couple," Perun grinned.

Steopa thought Perun's eyes glowed green for a moment. The scent of the primroses became stronger. He pushed Perun's hand off his waist.

"This is not the time," Steopa said.

Perun laughed. He grabbed Steopa and hugged both him and Rebecka. "Why not?"

It felt as if a current flowed through Steopa's waist. He started. Perun chuckled. Rebecka shook her head, as Perun left the church.

"Is he always like that?" she asked.

"Most of the time."

He walked with Rebecka outside to the fountain. His lower abdomen felt as if he had eaten something that not agreed with him. He paused. Rebecka rubbed her stomach. She looked at Steopa and shrugged.

The head had been propped up on the rim of the fountain. Mak sat by the headless body. Between the body and the fountain, a small fire burned. Mak threw a handful of dried herbs on the flames.

A sweet-smelling smoke rose up and billowed over the decapitated body. Mak spoke in his native language. He chanted and sang while holding his arms above his head. The smoke gathered over the body, forming a humanoid shape, a smaller shape than the beast that had attacked them.

Perun leaned against one of the buildings. "Ask Mak anything you want to ask the vampire."

Steopa walked closer to Mak. "Where is he from?"

Mak repeated the question.

The smoked swirled and solidified. The words sounded as if they came from the air around Steopa. "I don't know." It was a child's voice.

Steopa raised his eyebrow. "How did you get here?"

"I was sent."

"Who sent you?'

"My mather."

"Mather?"

"Adelind."

Rebecka swore.
"Why don't you ask him, what the hell is he?" Jeremiah asked.
"I am legion."
"What?" Jeremiah stood. "That's sounds like the old testament."
"Legion is what I am called. We are all called legion."
"How many more of you are there?" Steopa asked.
"Many."
Perun nodded. "There is magic here. Someone is making them."
"How?" Steopa asked. He turned to Perun. But the the smoky form answered.
"I earned my place, and then they picked me for the change."
Rebecka walked up to Steopa. She scoffed. "This is no good. I bet it can't remember anything."
"I remember... I remember my home."
"Where was that?" Jeremiah asked.
"Chicago. I was taken when I was eight."
"How old are you now?"
"Twelve."
"Oh, God." Rebecka turned to Steopa. "Remember Lorelei's little fit?"
"She said something about a birthday present," Steopa said.
Mak shook his head. "The spirit is leaving."
"Did you get anything you could use?" Jeremiah asked.
"Maybe." Steopa rubbed his chin. So the missing children and Adelind are related, he thought.
Rebecka tapped Jeremiah on his shoulder. "I have to ask you a question. What the hell is up with your arm?"
Perun and Jeremiah both looked at Steopa. He nodded. "She knows about the base."
Jeremiah held up his arm. The white-silver bone slid out of his forearm. "A little present from the base."
"How did they do that?" Rebecka asked.
"How much does she know, Steopa?"
Steopa turned Rebecka toward him. "Trust us when we tell you what happened to us down there, will not be repeated."
"They experimented on you, that's obvious."
"And worse."
"What could be worse?"
Perun walked over to them. "We buried that place for a reason.

Leave it buried."

"I sleep there," she said. "How buried?"

"Rebecka, where we rest is safe. We need to worry about the hunters and whatever that vampire was," Steopa said. "And how we are going to fight them."

"You're right." Her words came out harsh.

Steopa raised his hand, then dropped it. I made a promise, he thought. I will tell her when the time is right.

Her cell phone rang. "Sorry," she said, still with a bit of bile in her voice. She walked to the other side of the village, holding the phone to her ear.

Perun smirked. "You didn't tell her everything?"

"Yeah, you didn't, did you?" Jeremiah asked.

"I could not." Steopa watched Rebecka talking on her phone. "She would not believe me."

"I thought you said you were linked," Perun said. "Can't she tell if you are lying or not?"

"I have never lied to her."

"Not telling her is lying to her," Jeremiah said.

"No, it is not."

"You haven't been around women a lot have you?" Perun chuckled.

"But she is staying with you? There?" Jeremiah rubbed his forearm. "She will figure it out. She doesn't look stupid."

Rebecka came back. "That was John. Vincent is putting Sasha and Jimmy up for the day."

"We should go," Steopa said.

Perun pointed to the horizon and shook his head. "Sunrise is coming."

"We won't make it back in time," Rebecka said.

Perun held out his arms. "Which basement do you want?"

The buildings in the old village had held up even with the neglect. Only a couple did not look safe.

Jeremiah pointed to a small home. "I suggest that one. There is a separate wood room. No sun at all."

Steopa wrapped his arm around Rebecka's waist. "We will retire."

"Don't do what I wouldn't," Perun said.

"No! Do it!" Jeremiah laughed. "We need some entertainment."

Rebecka covered her mouth and giggled. Steopa took her other hand. "Jeremiah..."

"Come on, have a little fun."

Mak kicked dirt over the remains of the fire. "I will go to the poorhouse tomorrow and look around."

"I'll go today, you rest." Perun pulled back his shirt. The wounds were pink. "See. All better."

Steopa led Rebecka into the small house. The trap door entrance into the basement had been left open. Steopa went down first. The wood room had a dirt floor. A few shelves of home canned items lined one wall. The contents of the jars had congealed into masses of strange shapes.

Rebecka came down the steep stairs. "I already miss our bed."

"I never showed you how to hide in the dirt," Steopa said.

"No. You haven't."

Steopa stood behind her. He took her hands. "Can you feel the earth?"

"What do you mean?"

Steopa opened her arms. "Look at the ground, see the dirt. Can you feel it? The moisture?"

She nodded.

"Think about making a place to lay down. A hole large enough for you. A dry place."

The ground moved in front of Rebecka. The dirt piled itself along a hole that formed. When it was large enough, Steopa lowered her arms.

"There."

"How did you figure that out?" Rebecka asked.

"I remembered the old stories and tried it one morning."

"That hole is only big enough for me."

Steopa waved his hand. One side of it expanded. "Better?"

Rebecka nodded. "I still miss our bed."

He laid down in the hole and held out his hand. "It will be dry."

"But dirty." Rebecka laid down next to him. She laid her head on his chest. "Did you feel something earlier?"

"When?"

"When Perun hugged both of us."

"I felt something."

"It felt like I got a shock."

He nodded. “I did too.”

“Is that normal?”

“I think he tried something.” Steopa stroked her hair. “I will ask him tomorrow.”

She laid her hand against his thigh. He motioned his hand and the dirt covered them like a blanket. The scent of primroses filled his nostrils as the stupor came.

CHAPTER 14

Something made him edgy; his fangs grew. The hair on the back of his neck rose. The sun had not set, yet Steopa shook the stupor off him. He moved his hand. The dirt rolled off him and Rebecka. In the back of his mind he could feel another of his descendants coming closer to the city, but that would not set off his fangs.

Rebecka jerked awake. “The coiree!”

An image of the coiree forced itself into Steopa's mind. He could smell burning stone. He heard a high-pitched drilling noise. Rebecka grabbed his hand. Her eyes tinged red. He felt a pain, as if a drill bored into his head.

“Someone is trying to get to the coiree,” he said.

He jumped up, pulling Rebecka as he did. The red and orange sunlight drifted down the stairs. He shielded his eyes as he ran up to the ground floor. Through the large broken window, he could see the clouds had turned red due to the sunset.

Steopa shook the dirt off his coat. “The sun is setting. We should be safe.”

Rebecka made a strange noise behind him. He turned. She held her hand up, shielding her eyes from the sun. The top of her hand looked as if it had a bruise. Steopa moved to block the sun. She lowered her hand. The bruising disappeared.

“Does that happen to you?” she asked.

“No. Are you-”

“I'm fine. It felt strange.”

She moved. A small beam of sunlight hit her face. It seemed to bruise where it shone on her cheek. He reached over and touched the area.

“It doesn't hurt,” she said.

Steopa studied the mark. It was not a bruise. She had tanned, but only where the sun had touched her. “You still surprise me,” he said.

The smell of a hot stone blocked all other smells, then the sound of the drill filled Steopa's ears. He opened the door. The trees and brushes blocked most of the sunlight. Small patches of it dotted the ground.

Perun stood up on the porch of the house across the abandoned street. "What are you doing? The sun is up."

"We have to leave," Steopa said.

"I found something at the poorhouse."

Steopa paused. The sound of the drill hurt his head. Rebecka took his hand and pulled at his arm.

"I am sorry, Perun. I will be back as soon as I can."

"All right." Perun pointed to a small path. "Follow that one out. Don't leave the path."

Steopa nodded. When they got to the clearing, the trees behind them rustled as if a strong wind had come through forest. Steopa glanced behind him. He could no longer see the village through the trees.

When they got to the main road that went past Forest Grove cemetery, Steopa felt his descendant again. He could tell it was Misha; Steopa paused.

"What is it?" Rebecka asked.

"Misha, my other grandson. I can feel that he is close. He has never left his home before."

"Maybe because you were injured."

"No. Misha never leaves."

Rebecka glanced down the street toward Forest Grove. "Why don't I go ahead, you find Misha."

Steopa turned to the direction where he felt Misha. A sharp pain struck him across the forehead. He rubbed his temple. "I do not think the coiree will let me."

"Run?"

Steopa grabbed Rebecka's hand. The ground blurred underneath them as they ran. He slowed before the fence that surrounded Forest Grove. Ogden stood below one of the winged gargoyles.

"You felt it too?" Ogden asked.

Steopa nodded.

"Me too," Vincent said. He stood on top of the fence. He shook his head and dropped down next to Steopa. "Someone is digging next to the memorial."

"Workmen?" Ogden asked.

"I doubt it."

Ogden motioned to Manas sitting in the driver's seat of the Bentley. The car drove away. Ogden adjusted the grip on his cane. “Let us introduce ourselves.”

At the memorial, three men dressed in denim overalls used a large concrete drill against the bricked up rose window. Two more men walked around in the valley. They stopped at a statue. One of them shoved it. Steopa growled.

Ogden pulled out a pair of opera glasses, he lifted them to his eyes. “Definitely not workmen. Crossbows, crosses, and what looks like an elephant gun.”

The high-pitched whine of the drill hurt Steopa's head. He hissed. “We have to stop them.”

“I'm with Steopa,” Vincent said. His necklace glowed. Flames ignited around his hands. “Lets kick some butt.”

Steopa jumped. He landed next to the drill. He swiped his hand across one workman, taking the man's head off with the blow. One of the men shouted in Latin. Rebecka grabbed his head and twisted it. The bones snapped and she let his body drop. His body shook after it hit the ground, then he was still.

Steopa heard Vincent laugh and smelled burning flesh. The third man pulled a stake out of a holder on his belt. Steopa grabbed the man's hand and plunged the stake into the man's heart. Steopa pulled the stake out and looked for Ogden.

Ogden stood over the body of the fifth man. The man looked as if he had been mummified.

Vincent chuckled. “What did you-”

Something screamed. Another monster vampire jumped down from the top of the memorial. It knocked Rebecka to the ground, then spun around to face Steopa.

“You legion?” it asked. The tone of its voice made it sound female.

Steopa growled. “No.”

She picked Rebecka up by the head. “Then I kill you.”

Vincent jumped on her back and hugged her with his burning hands. “Try it, bitch.”

She shrugged him of as if he were a bug. Vincent did not hit the ground. Instead he bounced and twisted his body. He landed on the slope of the pyramid.

Steopa rushed the legion. She swung Rebecka, using her as a

shield. The ring on Rebecka's finger burned bright red. Rebecka reached up and dragged her claws through the legion's lower arm. Ribbons of blood remained attached to Rebecka's claws. She pulled her arm back to attack.

The legion let her go. She dropped and rolled. Steopa swiped at the legion. The legion blocked his blow and struck him. Steopa hit the memorial.

"Excuse me," Ogden said.

The legion turned. Ogden hit the legion with the point of his cane. The beast raised her hand and swatted the cane away from her body. Ogden jabbed it back against her chest. He shoved it deeper into her flesh. The veins under her skin turned black. Her flesh turned papery and tightened around her. She fell to her knees.

Ogden pulled his cane away. Rebecka swiped her claws at the legion's neck. The legion looked surprised as her head rolled to one side. Her body collapsed.

"What the hell was that?" Vincent asked.

"They call themselves legions," Steopa said.

Ogden rubbed his hand along his cane. "Strong magic."

"That's what we were told," Rebecka said.

"What sort?" Ogden asked.

"I know."

Steopa knew the voice, but he had not seen the speaker for decades. Misha came out of the shadows. He looked like his brother Sasha. The same dark hair, but Misha had kept his short. He had passed when he was older, older than Steopa. Misha would always be on the edge of middle age.

"Misha?" Steopa stepped forward.

"Who is this?" Ogden asked.

"My grandson."

"How many do you have?" Vincent asked.

Steopa did not answer.

Ogden motioned to the legion. "What magic?"

Misha lowered his head. "Some of this is my fault. I am afraid I allowed some of my personal books to be stolen. I could not stop them from entering. No one has ever done that before."

Steopa crossed his arms. "What happened?"

"I will speak privately."

Steopa glanced around him. "You can speak plainly here."

Misha glanced at everyone around the memorial. “A few years ago a vampire came to my house. She wanted to see my collection. I refused. While I was in the stupor, she sent someone to my home and they stole part of my collection.”

“I thought no one could get in your house?”

“I did too.”

“What did they take?” Steopa asked.

“A few books.”

“That's all?” Vincent asked, scoffing.

Ogden shook his head. “Some books are dangerous.”

Misha nodded. “She did not steal the whole set. I think she misinterpreted a passage in one. And that is why our family is being hunted.”

“What book, or books?” Ogden asked.

“Chronicles of the Lamiae Noblis.”

Ogden's mouth dropped open. Then he covered his mouth and coughed. “Can we continue this conversation inside?”

Rebecka squeezed Steopa's hand. “I'm going to look around.”

Steopa shook his head.

She motioned to Vincent. “Vincent will stay with me.”

“Yeah, sure,” Vincent nodded.

“Besides, this sounds like family business,” Rebecka said.

“But Rebecka-” Steopa pulled her hand up to his chest.

She pulled her hand away. “Come on, Vince. Let's see what I can hack into.” Rebecka walked over to the drill with Vincent.

Steopa motioned to Misha to follow him. Ogden had already slid the angel statue to the side. Steopa led Misha down into the basement of the memorial.

“What is this place?” Misha asked.

“The upper floors were a chapel and burial chambers. This floor was used to smuggle whiskey, I believe,” Ogden said. He sat down on the chair next to the bookcase. “How did you get a hold of those books?”

“I have my ways,” Misha said, sitting on the couch.

“What prophecy?” Steopa asked.

“In one of the earlier volumes a prophecy is recorded, warning the Vulgaris that the Altus will return to power. When a family of vampires comes into being.”

Ogden nodded. “I do remember reading that. But in a later

volume that prophecy was stated to be an old tale."

Misha nodded. "She did not steal that volume."

Steopa stared at Misha for a moment. "So you think that this Adelind is attacking us because of a lie!"

"Adelind?" Misha asked. "Yes, that was her."

"From Germany?" Ogden asked.

"Yes," Misha said.

"She tried to get into my library as well."

"When?" Steopa asked.

"Ages ago." Ogden tapped the top of his cane. "She is interested in magic, but has no skill."

"I sensed that as well," Misha said.

"When I saw her, she had another with her," Steopa said. "He was the one that mixed the blood for the drudge. And he did something to the floor. He disappeared through a ring of fire."

"A target seal," Ogden and Misha said together.

"A what?"

"It's a way to travel a long distance," Misha said. "It's how I got here tonight."

"I am not familiar with the legions," Ogden said. "What are they?"

"Specialized drudges." Misha rubbed his knee. "They are loyal to their maker, but unlike regular drudges, they can think for themselves to a point. And their bodies have been altered."

"I was wondering about that."

"From what I have read, the human has to be young. Their bodies should still be growing."

Steopa growled. "It is starting to look like Rebecka's friend did make the correct connection. The child trafficking."

"Child trafficking." Ogden looked up. "Would a child be usable?"

"They would be perfect. As long as they were changed before puberty."

"But there is no proof. The creature that we just killed is larger than Steopa," Ogden said. "I am having a hard time accepting that she had been a child."

Rebecka came into the room with Vincent behind her. She had another laptop in her hands. "I think they want me to find this stuff. It wasn't even password protected." She sat down next to

Steopa. "Don't worry. I disconnected the wireless. And scanned for any hardware that could give away our location."

"You can do that?" Misha asked.

"She could tear it apart and put it back together, blindfolded," Vincent said.

"Anyway." Rebecka turned it back on. "More messages from Kiel. But I don't speak or read German either."

"Mine is very rusty," Vincent said.

"I can help with that," Ogden said. "Could I see it?"

"Good. Misha, come with us." Steopa stood up. "We will talk some more."

Rebecka handed the laptop to Ogden. Steopa waited for her and Misha at the top of the tunnel. He kicked aside one of the hunter's bodies.

"You still left your house," Steopa said to Misha. "Why?"

"I cannot find mother."

"Nastenka?"

Misha nodded. "I lost track of her just before the theft."

"And you did not tell anyone?"

"She has blocked me before. But I am concerned because of recent events." Misha nodded toward Rebecka. "I am sorry, but you are..."

"This is Rebecka." Steopa lifted Rebecka's hand to his lips and kissed it.

Rebecka smiled.

Misha looked away and smoothed out his shirt. He cleared his throat. "The others are here?"

"Two." Steopa pulled Rebecka close to him. "Sasha, and a new one named Jimmy."

"Where are they?"

"Vincent said they are still at the Rathskeller," Rebecka said.

"We should meet them."

Steopa nodded.

"But what about the hunters? They were coming after the coiree," Rebecka said, pointing to the bodies.

"I know."

"That damned cup."

"It saved me."

"I know."

Steopa touched the side of her face. “That cup is the least of our concerns.”

“Until it feels threatened.”

He lifted her chin. “Do not worry.”

“I do.”

“But-”

Steopa kissed her.

“Coiree?” Misha asked. “You found the coiree?”

“You know of it?” Steopa asked.

“I thought it was a myth.” Misha removed his cap.

“I never heard of it until we found it,” Steopa said.

“Grandfather, if this is the same object that I am thinking of, then she will be after you. The prophecy makes it clear that the new bloodline will arise out of the one vampire with access to the coiree.”

Rebecka scoffed.

“I do not believe in prophecies,” Steopa said.

“Besides, he is not the only one with access to it,” Rebecka said.

Misha smiled. “But it would be hard for the prophecy to come true. Physically impossible for our kind.”

“That is true.”

“But you two are linked? That is the closest any of us will be.”

“It's not too bad.” Rebecka threw her arms around Steopa. He picked her up. She kissed his cheek. Rebecka brushed his hair off his face. “I should go home, talk to Baldman. See if he found out anything else.”

“What if we went to Teodor's? Could you talk to him there?”

Rebecka nodded.

Steopa lowered her down. “Call your brother, tell him to tell Jimmy and Sasha to meet us at Teodor's. Andi or Chuck can take them there.”

“Wait, let me get the laptop,” Rebecka said. She ran back to the memorial.

“Teodor? Your werewolf friend?” Misha asked. “What are you planning?”

“Nothing,” Steopa lied.

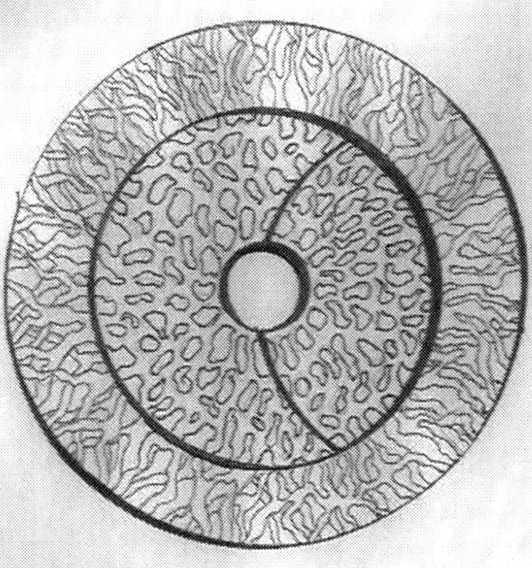

CHAPTER 15

Sasha greeted his brother with a long embrace on the steps of Teodor's house. They went inside with Jimmy and a couple of Teodor's sons.

"Misha?" Teodor asked as he sat down on the steps of his porch. "He never leaves his home."

"That is why I am concerned," Steopa said. He reached over and took the bottle of vodka out of Teodor's hand.

"Yeah." Teodor leaned back on his elbows. "I can tell. What is going on?"

"I cannot put my finger on it. We have a vampire, Adelind, that uses magic. She made a drudge out of a local football player, and he is the one sending the hunters after me. And now the coiree..."

"What's that?"

"I never told you about it."

The screen door opened behind him. The twins, Jamie and Chuck, walked out, followed by Jimmy. Jamie pointed to the old factory.

"We're going across the street," he said.

"Why?" Teodor asked.

"We want to show Jimmy around."

"Yeah, they are going to show me some werewolf things," Jimmy said.

"Really?" Teodor shook his head. "I don't know, are you sure this is a good idea?"

Chuck shrugged. "Nothing is going on in there, except Rebecka and Trucker being computer geeks. And the other two vampires are talking in Russian, ignoring us."

"Still, be careful."

They left. Steopa opened the vodka. "Thank you for letting us come here tonight."

"No problem. It's crowded, but then it's always crowded here."

A small car pulled into the driveway and its motor shut off. Andi got out of the passenger seat, while Silvia got out of the driver's side. Andi ran over to Chuck and gave him a kiss on his cheek. Then she pulled her handbag's strap over her shoulder and walked up to the porch.

"Is Rebecka here?" she asked.

Steopa nodded. "She is with Trucker."

"Damn, I was going to show her my bridesmaids gowns."

"They make everyone look like lemon meringue pie," Silvia said as she walked by.

"No, they don't."

"Dad, the dresses are lemon yellow with white ruffles on the top. What do you think?"

"I thought all bridesmaids were supposed to look stupid," Teodor said. "To make the bride look more radiant."

Andi smacked him with a bridal magazine.

"Hey!" Teodor raised his arm. "I'm not a dog."

Andi growled at him then stuck out her tongue. Silvia and her went inside with a slam of the screen door.

Steopa chuckled and shook his head.

Teodor sighed. "I wish Amanda could have seen this."

"She would have liked Andi," Steopa said.

Teodor scratched his head. "You were going to tell me about something called the coiree?"

"When Rebecka had just become a vampire, Vincent showed us what is underneath that nightclub. It is not a normal basement. In one of the rooms, we found a large gold cup. Like a communion cup." Steopa drank. He put the bottle down. "I was injured a few days ago. My shoulder blown apart by an explosive stake. The coiree filled with enough blood to heal me, before the sunrise, you understand?"

"So it's some sort of vampire thing?"

"Yes, Jalmari wanted it. Adelind has been sending her hunters through Simon to find me and that cup."

Two loud shouts, then laughter echoed from the empty building across the street. The vodka bottle slipped out of Steopa's grasp. He caught it before it left his hand. He drank more. He held the bottle up, turning it so the clear liquid caught the light. "I do not know why I still drink this."

"I've wondered. Although it was fun when you would have those drinking bets."

Steopa chuckled. "Of course, I would offer to walk them home when they lost."

"But they never made it."

Steopa shook his head. "No."

Teodor laughed.

Trucker came to the screen door. "Rebecka wants you," he said.

Steopa stood up, he placed the empty bottle of vodka on the window sill and opened the door. Trucker led Steopa to a side room. Three desks had running computers on them. Rebecka sat to the side, with her laptop open on a file cabinet.

"Trucker found some scans of old books on the hunter's laptop. I sent them to Baldman," Rebecka said. "And emailed Ogden, but I don't know if he uses his computer."

Steopa stood behind her, placing his hands on her shoulders.

On her computer screen Baldman rubbed his face. He nodded. "Yes, Saber sent me the books. I am going to send something to you. For you, Steopa."

Steopa placed his finger against his lips. She pulled out the plug to her microphone.

"What have you told him?"

"Nothing," Rebecka glanced back at the screen. "I have only told him your first name. Nothing else."

"Nothing?" He raised his eyebrow.

Rebecka looked hurt. "I told you before, he thinks aliens are trying to take over the world. I would not tell him the truth about us."

Trucker sat down at one of the desks. The screen in front of him had lines of code running. He pushed his glasses up. "Believe me, when he asked to see you, she didn't want him to talk to you."

"I did not tell you," Steopa said. "But Baldman looks familiar to me."

The file opened. Steopa leaned forward. He read the top line. "The Orphans of Vril and the Black Sun."

"Orphans of Vril." Rebecka sat up and snapped her fingers. "Remember Jalmari?"

"I do."

"Who?" Trucker asked.

"That short vampire that cut my head off," she said. "The Orphans of Vril were a secret society or club thing that he had found out about."

She plugged in the microphone. "I still have the photo, hold on."

Steopa leaned over and adjusted the microphone. "Baldman."

"You don't have to speak so loud," Rebecka said. She opened her backpack.

"Yes," Baldman said.

"I am familiar with both," Steopa said.

"I thought so."

Rebecka brought over a manila folder she had pulled out of her bag. She handed a photograph to Steopa.

"Remember, this was the guy that owned the slaughterhouse that the Rathskeller is in now." She pointed to a large man with a thick mustache wearing dark-colored robes. "But we never found out who the others were."

"Can you send me a copy?" Baldman asked.

"Maybe. Trucker do you have a scanner?"

"Yeah, give me a minute. It's buried." Trucker scooted his chair over to the bookcase.

"We have run into the Orphans' handiwork before," Steopa said.

Baldman nodded. "I have discovered that they were active in many cities. Mainly in Europe."

"In Germany?"

"They were the most public there, yes, but other cities and towns as well." Baldman rubbed his chin. "What about the Black Sun?"

"I cannot talk about it," Steopa said.

Baldman smiled. A feeling of deja-vu hit Steopa. Baldman exaggerated a wink. "I understand."

"Trucker, can you excuse us?" Steopa asked.

"Sure, let me hook up the USB. There." He left the room.

Rebecka came back to the laptop. After a few moments, she opened and closed programs, cussed a few times, and sent Baldman a copy of the photo. "Under the Rathskeller is an altar room. According to a friend of ours. Those men performed human sacrifices."

Baldman grimaced. "If that is the case, they were the only group that did. At least you are not dealing with the Illuminati."

Steopa glanced at Rebecka. She rolled her eyes. "I am sure it is not the Illuminati."

"They control everything, you know," Baldman said. "Ah ha! I

recognize one of these men."
"Are you sure?" Rebecka asked.
"Andrew Cooper," Baldman said. "What would he have been doing in your city?"
"That is the same last name as Simon," Steopa said.
"Which one?" Rebecka asked. "In the picture, who is Andrew Cooper?"
"The young looking one, with the light hair," Baldman said.
"Simon Cooper was the heir to Cooper Computing, as well as being a linebacker."
Baldman's face broke into a smile. "Of course. They make two of the servers I use. His daughter disappeared, and now the son is messed up with some rather illegal things. Andrew Cooper founded Cooper Locomotion. I am sure that the company changed its name a few times through the years."
Teodor walked into the room. He dropped his bottle of vodka. He stared at the screen, then bent over to pick up the bottle.
"Excuse me, who's that?" Baldman asked.
Rebecka glanced at Steopa. "Teodor-"
"Navarro?" Baldman asked.
Steopa pointed at the screen. "It is you! But you should be an old man!"
Baldman grimaced. "I am an old man. But you know where I worked. There were... side effects."
Rebecka glanced between Steopa and Baldman. "What the hell is going on?"
"Your friend was the only human to escape with us."
"We had Dorn, too," Teodor said.
Steopa shook his head. "She was our prisoner."
"This is about the base?" Rebecka asked.
Baldman nodded. "You see, Saber, I am not as crazy as I make myself sound."
She covered her face with her hands and shook her head.
"It's nice to see you are alive," Teodor said.
Baldman shrugged.
"All right," Rebecka said, her hands still covering her face. "You three were in a secret base. Andrew Cooper was an Orphan of Vril. One of his descendants goes missing, the other is forced to become a drudge by a vampire out to kill Steopa." Rebecka slid her hands

down her face. “I'm in the freaking twilight zone.”

“Are you all right?” Steopa asked Rebecka.

“I am going to get some air.” Rebecka walked out of the room.

Teodor took her seat. “Baldman? That's a weird handle, are you still using your real name, S-”

Baldman waved his hands in front of his face. “No! Don't say it. I cannot take the chance of being traced.”

Teodor glanced at Steopa. Steopa pulled the microphone closer. “When did you know that it was me?”

“The first time I saw you in the background. Steopa, you are unique looking.”

“Why haven't you tried to contact any of us?” Teodor asked.

“I can't take that risk.” Baldman coughed. “I am sure there are still some people that, um, want to know why my place of employment exploded.” He glanced down. “Oh dear, Sorry, I have to, um, yes.”

The screen turned black. Teodor sat back and chuckled. “That is one face I thought I would never see again.”

Steopa shook his head. “He has known about me since Rebecka turned, and has not said one thing. That man has a very devious mind.”

“Thank the stars he was on our side.”

“I should see to Rebecka.” Steopa stood up.

“Weird night.” Teodor joined Steopa at the door.

They went into the living room. Sasha and Misha were arguing in Russian. Sasha flung his hands in the air. His skin turned bright green, then red. Misha shook his head.

Steopa went outside. Rebecka sat on the porch swing. She hugged her knees to her chest. He sat down next to her. She leaned over and laid her head on his shoulder.

“He knew. This whole time, he knew about you,” Rebecka said.

“Yes.”

“Who was he?”

“An engineer. One of the few humans that did not look upon us as 'specimens.' He was as trapped as we were down there.”

“He never told me about the base.” She shook her head. “I doubt I would have believed him. He talks about aliens, corporations running the world, and gamma rays all the time. He never said anything about vampires, werewolves, and whatever Perun is.”

Steopa chuckled.

"He could have said-"

Four gunshots echoed from the factory. Someone screamed. Teodor jumped through the door and bolted across the lawn, changing into his half human, half wolf as he did. Steopa stood, then blurred down the street. He slammed his body into the warped plywood covering one of the factory entrances.

The plywood hit the ground. A man ran into Steopa. He fell back as if he had hit a wall. Jamie ran up to the man and pressed a handgun against the man's forehead.

"Bastard tried staking Jimmy," Jamie said.

Steopa slapped the gun away from the man's head before Jamie pulled the trigger. The bullet ricocheted off the concrete floor.

"What the hell did you do that for?" Jamie asked as he brought the gun back to the man's head.

"We should ask him questions."

Jamie slid the gun into the waistband of his pants. "All right, but I rather blow his brains out."

Steopa picked up the man. "What is your name?"

The man answered in Spanish. Steopa looked around. Teodor ran up to Steopa. The man spoke again. Steopa recognized a couple of words.

"I think you can talk to him," Steopa said.

Teodor shook his body and returned to his human form. The man closed his eyes.

"Sorry, I don't answer prayers," Teodor said. He asked the man a question.

The man answered.

"He doesn't want to talk to me," Teodor said

"What did he say?" Steopa asked.

"He's praying to Saint Eustace."

"Who?" Jamie asked.

"Patron Saint of Madrid and of hunters," Teodor said.

"He was cooked to death," Steopa said, "if I remember correctly."

The man spoke. Teodor shook his head and answered. The color drained from the hunter's face.

"What did you say?" Jamie asked.

"I told him I wasn't hungry." Teodor chuckled. He waved Chuck and Jimmy over. "He's lucky our pack doesn't eat living human flesh. Take him to our house. Basement would be the best, I think."

Steopa handed the man to Chuck.

"He almost got me," Jimmy said, fingering a hole in his shirt.

Chuck turned the man around and shoved him. "Let's go."

Jimmy pointed to Teodor. "Aren't you cold?"

"No, I like hanging out." Teodor said.

Jimmy snickered.

Jamie took off his vest and handed it to Teodor.

"Cover up. You are gonna give some of us a complex," Jamie said as him and Jimmy walked away.

Teodor started back. Steopa stayed. Teodor turned around. "What is it?"

"This is the other entrance to my home, the base."

"Right."

"They have tried the front and now the back. And they attacked the memorial tonight." Steopa kicked a large piece of debris. "This is not good."

"I'm starting to think they are after more than you," Teodor said.

Steopa nodded. "Can you talk to the hunter?"

"Sure." Teodor turned around, holding the vest to his groin.

Sasha and Misha ran up to the door.

"Who was that?" Misha asked.

"Another hunter," Steopa said.

"Spanish," Teodor said. "By his accent, close to Basque. Which is not good."

Sasha growled "Not good? They can be the most fanatical"

"I know, I grew up there." Teodor shrugged. "I better check on my kids. I don't want them getting ideas."

Steopa followed Teodor out of the factory. Rebecka and Jimmy met them at the street.

"I'll see you tomorrow?" Teodor asked Steopa.

"Yes."

Teodor bounded across the street.

"Are you heading back to your lair?" Sasha asked.

"Yes."

"We have been trying to contact mother, there is too much noise here," Misha said.

Steopa glanced back at the factory. We could go that way, he thought. But that would mean showing them the rest. He turned and walked away from the factory. Rebecka grabbed his hand. He led them back to the lair, taking the long way home. What are they really after? Steopa thought. Teodor was right. If it was only to attack his family, there would be no reason to try to steal the coiree or try to enter the base.

When they returned to the lair, Sasha sat down on the couch, crossing his legs. He placed his hands on his temples. "Much better," he said. "I will start to look for her in Vladivostok."

"She will push you away," Misha said. "I kept trying and she pushes me away."

Sasha did not answer. He closed his eyes. Misha sat down on the easy chair.

"Grandfather," Misha said. "I feel responsible."

Steopa hung up his coat. "Why?"

"My books."

Steopa shook his head. "You worry too much."

"Those were my books."

"Misha, when your mother died and turned, you hid all the garlic in the house."

"I did not want her to get hurt."

Rebecka smirked. She caught Steopa's eye and covered her mouth. Jimmy sat on the floor with an atlas open on his lap. "Sorry," Jimmy said, looking up at Steopa. "You said you were from Lithuania."

"Yes." Steopa rubbed the back of Rebecka's neck.

"Rodovitch is not a Lithuanian name."

"How do you know that?" Misha asked.

"I had a school teacher from Lithuania. We talked about surnames in class once."

"True. My family had moved there, two generations before."

"Ah." Jimmy turned a page in the atlas.

Sasha made a strange shrill noise. He lowered his hands. "Mother does not want to be found. I had her in my mind for a moment. She shoved me away. I could smell blood around her."

"I told you," Misha said.

"Do you think she is in danger?" Steopa asked.

Sasha shrugged. "She's done it before. Mainly when she doesn't want to be bothered."

“I will try,” Misha said.

He closed his eyes.

Rebecka patted Steopa's arm. “I am glad we are back here. I don't know if I like sleeping in the dirt.”

Steopa's stomach sank. “Perun. I forgot about Perun.”

“What?”

“He said he found something at the poorhouse.”

“We'll see him tomorrow.”

“Yes.” He put his arms around Rebecka. “I know dawn is not for a few hours-”

“I could retire now,” Rebecka said.

“Why don't you?” Sasha said. “If we find mother again, we will tell you.”

“I am sure if she was in danger, she would let you find her,” Steopa said. Unless she was afraid we would be in danger too, he thought.

CHAPTER 16

Another memory. Steopa rolled over on the bed as it formed in his mind. He never dreamed. Only memories would fill the daytime.

"What should I do with you?" Pavel, Steopa's father said. He sat down at the table opposite of Steopa. He poured two glasses of vodka. "I should take you outside and beat your butt."

"Sorry, Father," Steopa said.

"Sorry. You are lucky Jurgis did not castrate you."

Steopa slumped down in the chair. This memory, he thought. Why this one?

"Father, we had too much to drink at the dance and we-"

"Jurgis and I have been hoping that you and Anna would like each other, but we did not expect to find both of you at the hunting cabin this morning. And not what you were doing, either."

"Father, I-"

Pavel pushed the glass over to him. "Drink."

Steopa curled his fingers around the glass. Pavel downed his shot.

"We have plans for you. You have to go to university. You have to come back here and take over for me. Do you want to ruin it by getting Anna pregnant?" Pavel pointed to the glass. "Drink."

Steopa sipped the vodka. He coughed. Pavel chuckled. "We are in a precarious position here. My father came here to help build the church and stayed. To the villagers, we have always been the outsiders. And now that Lithuania is no longer and we are Russians, there are people here who view us with distrust. If the others find out what you and Anna were doing in the cabin, the rumors will be devastating."

"That was not my intention."

"It does not matter what your intention was, that is not what the villagers are going to think. Especially if that new priest hears about this. I forbid you to tell him about you and Anna in confession."

"You cannot tell me to do that."

Pavel slammed the bottle down. "Confess to God directly. That priest is serving his own needs, not God's."

Steopa looked at the half empty glass in his hands. "I would like to marry Anna."

"Is this because of last night?"

Steopa shook his head. "No. I have wanted to ask Jurgis for permission since the spring."

Pavel tapped his fingers on the table. "I will talk to him. I am sure we can arrange a ceremony before you leave for Vilnius. It would be easier of course, if your great-uncle were still alive. He could have performed the marriage."

"Is that why you do not like our new priest?" Steopa asked.

"No. My uncle was very old and had served God well. But he took most of our family secrets with him." Pavel drank another shot. "We own most of the land here, we built the church, and we are still strangers. Do you want to know the real reason why I sent you away for all of your education?"

"Because you did not want me to be illiterate?"

Pavel chuckled. "No, because I did not want you to hear the rumors about us, not until you were old enough to ignore them. Whatever you hear, they are nothing more than superstition and folktales."

"I have heard a few." Steopa finished his drink. He winced and put the glass down. Pavel filled it.

"One of the old women," Steopa said. "Said the devil caused me to grow so fast."

Pavel laughed. He stood up. "Jurgis will be glad to hear that you will marry Anna before you go to Vilnius. When you return, you will set up your land. Anna will stay with me until your home is ready."

The memory faded as the stupor left Steopa. He put his arm around Rebecka and pulled her closer. She rolled over and kissed him. He brushed her hair back from her face. She kissed the palm of his hand.

"Much better than dirt," she said as ran her fingers down the scars on his back. "What were you thinking about? I could almost see the memory."

He rolled on his back. "The morning after my father found Anna and I in the cabin."

"What were you doing in the cabin?" Rebecka asked. She rolled on her side, she gave him a wicked smile. "Having tea?"

Steopa smirked. "No. He and her father caught us in bed."

"Not sleeping?"

"Not sleeping."

"Married?"

"No."

"Oh dear," Rebecka giggled.

"Do you want to come and talk to Perun with me?" Steopa asked.

"I don't know. When he touched me last time I got a shock."

"I did too."

"Did you see his eyes glow green?"

Steopa nodded. She slid her hand over his chest. Steopa grinned. "What are you doing?" He asked.

"What?"

"That?"

"Nothing."

Steopa pulled Rebecka on top of him. "Nothing?"

She leaned forward. Steopa smiled at the view. For a brief moment he smelled primroses.

"Right now, I wish we could..." Rebecka turned her face away.

"So do I." Steopa placed his hand against her cheek.

Rebecka kissed his thumb, then got off him. She went over to her wardrobe. Steopa rolled on his side and watched her dress. He could tell she used some glamor. But she had never made herself look skinnier than she had been when she was alive. He did like how she smoothed out her hips.

"I wonder if Sasha found your daughter," she said.

"Why?"

"Because I would like to meet her."

"You will."

Steopa got out of the bed and dressed. Rebecka waited by the vault door. When he was done, she opened it.

Sasha sat on the couch with the atlas on his lap. He looked up. "We think we know where mother is."

"Where?"

"She did not push me away as hard as before. I saw what she

could see. She looked outside. There was a harbor." Sasha put the book aside. "It was on the Baltic. Close to the Gulf of Finland."

"How do you know?" Rebecka asked.

"The smell."

Jimmy raised his head off the floor. "Can we go to that club tonight?"

"Depends," Rebecka said.

Misha stretched in the easy chair. "The smell? You can tell which harbor it is by the smell?"

"Some of them," Sasha said.

Rebecka went over to her computer and packed it into her backpack. Steopa opened the outer vault door. He paused. He could smell that someone had been outside their door. The scent of a cigarette hung in the air. But it had not been from someone smoking. The scent was faint, as if it had been on clothing.

Sasha walked up behind Steopa. "What is it?"

"Someone was down here," Steopa said.

A cell phone beeped behind them. It beeped again. Steopa looked over his shoulder.

Rebecka picked up the hunter's cell phone. She looked up and read the message with a dry voice. "Bloodsuckers. You are trapped. Enjoy hell."

"What?" Steopa asked.

Further down the hallway, the sharp sound of a small click echoed. Steopa saw a small flame sprout up. Then it blossomed into a large ball of orange and yellow. Sasha pulled Steopa back.

The explosion sent a fire ball down the hall toward the vault door. Sasha slammed it shut, as the fire reached the entrance. Another explosion rocked the door. On the other side the sound of debris falling and piling outside. Steopa could feel the weight above him shift. Another explosion, but this one muted.

Jimmy covered his head, then lowered his arms. "What the hell?"

Misha stood up, keeping his eyes on the ceiling as he did. "I can feel more weight."

Rebecka raised her hand as if she was going to throw the phone. Steopa stopped her.

"You need that, yes?"

She lowered her hand. The room shifted. She looked up. "Are

we safe?"

"We should be."

Sasha turned to Steopa. "Is there another way out of here? It will take us weeks to dig out."

Steopa glanced over to the large oak bookcase. "There is."

"There's this room and our bedroom," Rebecka said.

Steopa pointed to the bookcase. "You did not wonder why it sat away from the wall?"

Rebecka shook her head. "I never thought..."

"I told you what this place was. I never wanted to show you the rest."

"What is it?" Misha asked.

Steopa went to the bookcase and shoved it aside. Behind it was another vault-like door, but this one looked like a normal door with heavy seals around it. "There is a lot more to this place. I doubt the hunters even found that out." He turned back. "I did not want to show anyone this. You understand."

"How much of the base remains?" Rebecka asked.

"Base?" Jimmy asked.

"A military base." Steopa went over to the wall that held his swords. He pulled his two favorites off.

"Not the underground base?" Jimmy asked. "The one everyone looks for?"

"The same," Rebecka said.

Another long rumble outside the vault door. Sasha's skin glowed red and blue. His features changed. When he glanced at Steopa, his second eyelids lowered. In the dark room, looking at Sasha hurt Steopa's eyes.

Rebecka double-checked her backpack. "I suppose we have to go through."

Steopa nodded. He turned the handle. The sound of air rushed in like the sound of a tomb being opened. Beyond the door was a simple cinder block room, with two other doors.

Three skeletons laid tumbled around the floor. The military uniforms had decayed off of the bones. The guns laid on the floor, rusted. One of the skeletons held a long stake.

"What happened here?" Rebecka asked.

"We escaped."

Sasha picked up one of the skulls. "It looks like this one had been bludgeoned."

The lair shook. The sound of rubble setting and falling outside the vault door continued for a long time. The room with the skeletons did not seemed to be affected.

Steopa took out his sword. "Follow me, closely."

He waited until everyone filled the small room, then he shut the door to his lair. He turned the handle and the door sealed. He crossed the room and opened one of the other doors.

This opened into a hallway. The smells of mildew and rotting wood overpowered the smell of dust. The old light fixtures had been torn or had fallen down due to decay. On one side of the hallway were many doors that had been locked with a single chain that ran from one end to the other. Steopa paused to listen. He heard the sound of debris settling on his lair and nothing else.

Rebecka moved ahead. She stopped at one of the doors and looked inside the little window. "More skeletons. The room looks burnt."

"The fire killed most of them," Steopa said.

"Your handiwork?" Sasha asked.

"I cannot take credit for all of it."

"Who locked them in?" Misha asked.

"I do not remember, perhaps Jeremiah."

Rebecka turned around. "You said you, Teodor, Perun, and Jeremiah? Just you four?"

"There were a few others."

"Like Baldman?"

Steopa nodded.

"Dorn asked about the specimens."

Steopa continued down the hallway.

"She was part of this?" Rebecka asked.

Steopa stopped at the door at the other end of the hallway. "She was."

"That deranged woman?" Sasha asked.

Rebecka nodded.

"What did she do?"

"She was the commander of this base," Steopa said. He opened the door.

"Cool," Jimmy said as he looked around Steopa.

This had been one of the gun turret rooms. Two turrets were in the center of the room, positioned so they could swing and cover either door. Across the small room, hung on a bulletin board next to the other door, were old postings and papers. Rebecka stopped in front of the board. She studied a few of the papers.

"These notices are dated in the late sixties," she said. "I thought the rumors were older than that."

"I had been in this place for a couple of years," Steopa said.

"How large is this place?" Misha asked.

"This is the top floor. Offices and security." Steopa looked down. "It went far deeper."

Sasha flipped his hair over his shoulder. "So this is the place you did not want us to find out about the last time I got the call that you had been injured."

"It was not your concern," Steopa said.

Sasha glanced at Rebecka. She shook her head. "Whatever, just get us out of here."

Steopa nodded and opened the other door. Three large columns of rock jutted out of the floor. Rebecka touched one. "How did this happen?" she asked.

"I told you there were others here." Steopa squeezed between two of the rocks.

"There is only one thing that can move rocks like this," Misha said. "But I thought they did not exist."

"Some people think the same of us," Steopa said.

"Trolls?"

"A troll."

"A real troll?"

"Yes."

Rebecka handed Steopa her backpack and squeezed between the rocks. "You don't think the hunters knew about this place? Do you?" Rebecka asked.

"How would he have found out?" Sasha asked.

"I grew up hearing stories about this place." Rebecka put her backpack on. "The bigger question is, why would they be interested?"

"There are places like this all over Russia," Misha said.

Steopa nodded. "First the coiree, and now here. I do not think it is a mistake anymore."

"How can they be related?"

"I do not know." Steopa pointed to the door down the hall. "We have a long walk."

Are they connected? Steopa thought. Could Adelind know something about the coiree and this place? Is she using Simon because of his family connection? We had found the coiree under the Rathskeller. While I was here, there was no mention of that cup. But then they did not tell us everything.

The door to the next section had been taken off its hinges. Steopa motioned to them to stay behind him. He looked inside the room. Nothing had changed from the last time he had been here. The tables and chairs were piled along one wall, rusted together.

"The cafeteria?" Jimmy asked. "I wish I had my camera."

Steopa nodded. He glanced at the wall that had been painted with a mural. Most of the paint had faded and peeled. He could not make out the insignia that had been there. Only the outer ring could be seen. Rebecka started to walk toward it. He stopped her.

"What is that?" Rebecka asked.

"A painting."

Sasha opened the door to the kitchens. He leaned inside and then turned around. "Two skeletons staked to the wall."

A small smile formed on Steopa's lips. "Yes, I did that. There had been some survivors after the explosion. I had to make sure they were taken care of."

"What? You came back here?" Rebecka asked. "Explosion?"

"This floor is the least damaged. You go further below and there are floors that are inaccessible."

"But why come back?"

"I had to make sure no one ever found it again. Why do you think Teodor lives where he does?"

"He watches this place too?"

"Yes."

As they continued. Rebecka fell back. Steopa recognized the look on her face. She always furrowed her brow when she was in deep thought.

Sasha helped Steopa move some debris from the front of a door. Misha walked over to the wall. He ran his fingers along the remains of the mural. He glanced at Rebecka. She took her phone out and clicked a photo of the insignia.

"What are you doing?" Steopa asked.

"This looks familiar," Rebecka said. "I want to compare it."

"Familiar to me too." Sasha nodded. "This figure in the middle. I cannot make out what it is, but these letters are angelic script. What sort of base was this?"

Steopa opened the door. On the other side of the corridor sat the last door they had to cross. "That is not important now."

Sasha walked into the next corridor. Steopa stopped him. He pointed to the top of the door.

"I have trapped it."

A large concrete pillar sat balanced on top of the door. If someone opened the door from the other side, the pillar would come crashing down on them. Steopa jumped to the top of the door frame, using the exposed steel posts as footholds. A rusty chain hung from the ceiling. Steopa grabbed it and fitted it into the iron hooks that were at the top of the pillar. Then he jumped down.

Steopa found a piece of rebar and opened the door from a distance. The pillar slid down, but jerked when the chain caught its fall. The chain strained. Flakes of rust fell off it and dust rained down from the ceiling. Sasha jumped back.

"Why would you put that there?" Sasha asked.

Steopa watched the pillar swing slowly back and forth. "Because no one should be down here."

He went through the door. The fresh air felt like a welcomed friend. After everyone joined him in the old loading dock, Steopa shut the door behind them, then laid another concrete pillar across its front.

This open room at one time had been full of vehicles, now it laid empty, except when the transients slept here. The partially open walls offered some privacy and plenty of places to enter. The sleepers had left trash strewn all over the floor. Along with the fresh air smell was the smell that all abandoned buildings get in the city: drugs, urine, and decay. A large, dark, wolf ran up to Steopa. As it got closer it changed into Teodor.

"Christ, Steopa I hoped you were here," Teodor said, not even stopping to cover up his nakedness. "When we saw the news reports of the parking garage blowing up..."

Another wolf appeared. This one bounded over the trash and jumped around Rebecka, barking happily and wagging it's tail.

Teodor laughed. "Andi is happy to see you too."

"Andi?" Rebecka asked.

Andi yipped. Rebecka reached out her hand. Andi bowed her head and let Rebecka give her a few pats between the ears.

"This is weird."

Andi barked.

"How is the hunter?" Steopa asked.

"Still alive. At least until you see him, right?" Teodor winked.

CHAPTER 17

Teodor unlocked the bike lock they had used to secure the basement door. The hunter had been tied to the wall in the darkest part of the basement. Steopa ducked as he went down the stairs. The hunter looked up, his mouth covered with duct tape. He opened his eyes wide, then lowered his head.

Silva sat on a table, studying the hunter. On the table next to her were bungee cords and duct tape. She looked over her shoulder as Steopa approached.

"He's talkative tonight," she said. "And speaking English too."

He walked up to the hunter and ripped the duct tape off the man's face. "Who told you about me?"

The hunter lowered his eyes. "If I tell you, I'm dead."

"You are dead already. Who is Simon?" Steopa asked.

The old hunter chuckled, but shook his head. "Trouble. That's what he is. We should have staked him, not worked for him. Half my crew has died."

"He is another vampire," Steopa said.

Silva cleaned her fingernails. "He was cursing that name earlier."

"Simon claims you killed his sister," the hunter said. "I think he is lying. He has another reason."

"I know." Steopa thought for a moment. "Did he say when or how I killed his sister?"

The hunter nodded. "You found her in Berlin."

Steopa growled. He motioned to Silva to leave the basement. She ran up the stairs. Steopa walked over to the hunter. He placed each of his hands on a side of the old man's head. His hands were large enough to cover the old man's face. Steopa leaned close.

"He is a liar. His sister disappeared last year. He has only been a vampire for a few weeks. Do you want to know the truth about me? I was attacked on my way home to see my wife. I had been fighting Napoleon's troops. I killed that blond *blydischa* after she tried to feed off me. Because of her I am a vampire."

The hunter looked up at Steopa with compassion in his eyes. Steopa hit the wall with his hand.

"This *skuwysyn* wants to kill me because he was told I killed his sister. I have never been to Germany!"

The old man looked away. Steopa forced the hunter's face to the front. "Where is this Simon?"

The old man swallowed. "We have him safely in a storage building. It's on the corner of Sixth and Washington."

"He would not be there now," Steopa growled.

The hunter nodded. "He's going to go to the club that we scouted."

Steopa smiled. The hunter's eyes went wide.

"He will have a surprise if he goes there." Steopa turned to leave.

"Mr. Rodovitch," the hunter said.

Steopa stopped.

"He's not acting alone. When we were hired I saw two others with him. A man and a woman."

"They will meet the same end as him," Steopa said.

"They're looking for something. That's why they sent my cousins to the cemetery."

"Do you know what?"

The hunter shook his head.

"Where were you hired?"

"Barcelona."

Steopa called up the stairs for Silva. She hurried down the stairs. He pointed to the hunter. "Keep him alive, for now."

Silva nodded. Steopa ducked and ran up the stairs and into the dining room. Rebecka had the laptop in front of her with Sasha and Trucker sitting alongside her.

"I know where he is," Steopa said. "He will be hungry. He will feed first. He will be going to the Rathskeller tonight."

"Crap!" Rebecka dialed her cell phone as she ran out the house.

Steopa watched her leave, then flipped up the collar on his jacket. "There are more hunters. Find them," he said to Sasha.

Steopa started to walk out of the house. Jimmy ran up to him. "What about me?" he asked.

"Help Sasha," Steopa said. "He can show you a few tricks."

Jimmy smiled. Steopa walked past him and onto the street.

Misha caught up with him.

"The hunter told me he worked with two other vampires. One has to be Adelind," Steopa said. "They are looking for something. Can you talk to Ogden?" Steopa asked. "Both of you like old books."

"Will he let me come to him?" Misha asked.

"Tell him I think they want the coiree."

"I will."

Steopa pointed in the direction of the university. "He lives that way."

Misha left. Steopa strode down the street. How dare that vampire! he thought. How dare he. Steopa could remember that blond vampire that changed him. The image of her had been burned in his mind. She seemed so small, but she pinned him against a tree with no effort.

As he stormed down the street, a group of young men wearing red headbands and red basketball jerseys walked toward him. The same colors the men wore when Steopa and Rebecka had found the children. Steopa sneered. He plowed through them. The cursing started behind his back.

Steopa spun around and grabbed one by his neck. "Do not start something you can not finish."

Another man tried to jump Steopa. Steopa reached back and grabbed him. He lifted the man over his shoulder and slammed him against the light post. The post shook. Still holding the one by the neck, Steopa looked over his shoulder to the third one. The third one backed away. Steopa growled at him.

The first choked. Steopa did not loosen his grip. He turned around and advanced on the third. The third backed away and tripped over a bench. Steopa pulled the first closer and drank out of his neck. The third one opened his mouth in a silent scream. Steopa dropped the body.

The third turned around and ran down the street. Steopa wiped his face and caught up with him in a few seconds. He snapped the third man's neck, then drank him empty.

Steopa turned around and went back to the second man. He laid on the ground gasping for air. Steopa picked him up by the shirt and dragged him into the alleyway. The man screamed. The concrete walls echoed the man's screams, but no one looked into the opening.

He dropped the man's drained body. As he walked out of the alley, he straightened his overcoat. An older woman looked out of her curtains onto the street. She saw Steopa and shut them quickly.

Steopa pulled his hair back. What had happened to Nastenka? he thought. When I was in the base, I pushed my family away too. It would have been dangerous for them to come to my rescue. Is that what she thinks? If we come to help her, we will be in danger?

Everything leads back to Germany. Sasha said the water smelled like the Bay of Finland. I know Kiel is a port there.

Steopa paused near a strip club. One of the dancers gave him a smile. He snarled. She opened the back door to the club and slammed the door behind her.

Why did they want that cup? Jalmari had told him it would give any vampire power. Yet, us four are not any more powerful than we had been before. Except Vincent can burn, but that is because of his necklace. The necklace that matches Rebecka's ring.

When we had first brought the cup to the memorial, Rebecka had seen something smile at her. Steopa remembered her fear. Vincent mentioned a creature that he saw in a dream who told him about the Altus and Vulgaris. The same words Misha had used.

I know what Vulgaris might mean, Steopa thought. Altus, perhaps. But why would those words be used to describe vampires?

As he passed a restaurant, Steopa remembered the old, insane vampire from Saint Petersburg. He was not a threat, so the vampires around Steopa's age would visit him. Steopa remembered it had been fun to get the old vampire talking. He would tell stories. One came to Steopa now.

"There are basically two types of vampires, did you know that?" the old one had said. "Only one now. They were killed off. We had a war among ourselves. And the side that lost, gone."

"Why did we fight?" Steopa had asked.

"Why do we ever? You should have see the ones that lost. They were the ones the humans feared. Those stories of vampires controlling the weather and destroying entire towns. That's who they were. Powerful. And the others were not. They were jealous.

"Then they won and now we have drudges and vassals and loyalty oaths, and all other types of shit. At least the others didn't ask you to worship them. They let you be. These new ones, bah, they make up things to make themselves powerful."

I thought it was a story. But why are there hardly any vampires older then me? Steopa thought. The old one had been right about the highly structured vampire societies at the time. When the Communist Revolution happened, it had sparked some of the vampires in Saint Petersburg to rise up as well.

But the loyalty and the oaths and the tests to become a vampire had never happened in North America. At least I have never found proof it did. Had the old vampire been right? Had something happened around the time America was being colonized? None of the old world vampires made the voyage over here?

Steopa looked up. He had almost walked past the Rathskeller. He stopped outside Saber Ink. Through the large window he saw Rebecka's brother John look up from a client. John waved. Steopa nodded then went down the ramp to the club.

As Steopa walked down the ramp, Swen finished patting down a person. He nodded. Chuck buzzed the person in. Steopa stopped at the cage.

"This is one crazy night," Swen said. "I caught two guys trying to break in the back when I pulled up. Now Rebecka tells me some bloodsucker is showing up."

Steopa ignored the word bloodsucker. "Where is Rebecka?"

"She went inside with Vincent," Chuck said.

Swen motioned him back up the ramp. When they were at the entrance, Swen nodded with his head toward the street. "You see that black van?"

"Yes."

"It's been here all night. I sent the plate numbers to Grady. He's sending a car over."

"Grady?"

"My friend, the cop." Swen rubbed his arms. "It has to be a packed place tonight too. So this other vampire, I take it, is not a friend."

"When he comes here, I will make him go away," Steopa said.

"As long as you keep him off the main floor."

They walked back down to the club. Steopa waited for Chuck to buzz him in, then he went to the back of the club to Vincent's private room. Rebecka hugged Steopa when he entered. He kissed

her forehead.
Vincent smirked. “When's the honeymoon over?”
“Shut up,” Rebecka said.
Steopa pointed to the open laptop. “What are you doing?”
“Showing Vincent that picture.”
“I recognized Joshua,” Vincent said.
“So you did not know the rest?” Steopa asked.
Vincent shook his head. “I didn't ask their names when they cut my throat.”
Rebecka's phone beeped. She glanced at the screen. “John wants me to come up.”
“He must be done with that special client,” Vincent said.
Rebecka patted Steopa's shoulder as she passed by. Steopa sat down next to Vincent. After Rebecka shut the door, he said, “They are after the coiree and my lair as well.”
“Rebecka told me. That's why they have been sneaking around here. They might still think it is here.”
“But they were drilling into the memorial.”
Vincent pointed to the image on the computer screen. “Actually, I do recognize a couple of them. That one, that was Richard Dysart. He's the one that had the memorial built. I don't think they know where the coiree is.”
“Why do you think that?”
“Because they keep coming back here. This is the fourth time Swen has chased them off. Chuck caught them once, during the day. They have been trying to get into the lower levels. But I would like to know, why you?”
“I have heard only rumors. Simon is claiming I killed his sister. But she disappeared last year in Europe. But then I saw him made into a drudge, maybe he was told to say that.”
“He's not going to show up here? Do you think they are going for the coiree again? We would feel that.”
“Perhaps.” Steopa rubbed his chin. “How does Verina travel? Between here and Europe?”
“Airplanes.”
“Really?”
“Yeah, she over-feeds before she leaves and takes a night flight. Why?”
“Kiel, Germany.”

"What's there?"
"My daughter, and possibly the vampire pulling Simon's strings."
"Verina's here, lets see if she's heard anything."
Vincent led Steopa out to the dance floor. At the bar, Lorelei poured drinks. Verina sat at one of the stools. She turned around as Vincent approached.
"Are the hunters bothering you?" she asked.
"What do you know of Kiel, Germany?" Steopa asked.
Verina's face fell. "I know that a dear friend of mine ended up dismembered and left for the sun."
"That is where the vampire controlling Simon might be operating from," Vincent said.
"Then watch out for those drudges that come from there. They call themselves legion. They are monsters. Those are the ones that killed my friend."
"I have already met them." Steopa sat down on the next stool.
"Yeah, me too." Vincent rubbed his head. "It still hurts."
"They are drudges?" Steopa asked
"Sort of." Verina bit her nail, then looked at her fingernail and sighed. "What I have seen, they use some spell or some such thing to make them. They aren't as mindless as a drudge. When they are changed, they are made larger, too."
"Were they children?"
Verina looked away, then nodded.
"And you did nothing to stop them?" Steopa hissed.
Verina spun on her bar stool to face him. "I do not mess with any vampires that don't mess with me first, you understand. I know they use children. If it makes you feel any better, those things are no longer children when they become legions. The child dies on the table. They only use the body."
"You are wrong."
"How do you know?"
"I heard one of them speak."
"What? Two words?"
Steopa shook his head. "No."
"Then how?"
"You would not understand."
Verina studied Steopa for a long time. "I can't stop what she is

doing. I don't understand what is going on myself. For some reason, she has it out for you. I want to stay out of it."

Lorelei came over to them and tugged on Vincent's goatee. "The band is going to start soon."

"Ah yeah, I'll be back. I have to do the introduction," Vincent said.

"Can I have a shot of vodka?" Steopa asked Lorelei.

She looked at him surprised. "Are you sure?"

"Yes."

Lorelei turned around to make his drink. Verina stirred hers. She had not drunk any of it.

"Last year," she said, "there was a lot of talk about you. Someone in Europe had been asking questions. You became the height of gossip. Most did not believe that you could have killed the vampire that attacked you. But once I told them about you-"

"What?"

Lorelei came back with his drink.

Verina ran her fingers through her dark, wavy hair. "Most were impressed."

Steopa felt a shiver down his spine. Then he felt as if he had been hit on the back of the head. He picked up the drink. Another sensation, his wrist burned. He put down the drink and rubbed his wrists.

Vincent got on the stage. He grabbed the microphone. Then stood still for a moment. He coughed and introduced the band so fast that his words rambled together.

He jumped off the stage as the band began to play and ran up to the bar. "Come on!"

An image appeared in Steopa's head. "Rebecka!" Steopa shoved his drink away.

Verina pushed her purse toward Lorelei. Steopa got to the door before they did. He slammed the door open, scaring a couple on the other side. He ran to the street.

The door to the tattoo parlor hung open. Steopa stopped. He could feel that Rebecka was no longer there. Vincent ran inside as a blur, he came back a second later.

"No John. His inks are all over."

Swen joined them. "What the fuck! I was only in Cassie's shop getting coffee. Where's that van?"

Steopa turned. Where the black van had been, a sports car sat. He closed his eyes. He could feel Rebecka's neck and wrist burn. It felt as if she was moving away from him fast.

"They went that way," Chuck pointed.

Vincent started to run with Steopa. Steopa stopped him. "No, make sure they do not come back here."

"Good point."

Steopa ran down the road, jumping over a truck as it barreled down the street. He could feel Rebecka. She wasn't scared, she was angry. Steopa growled and picked up speed. Her anger only fed his.

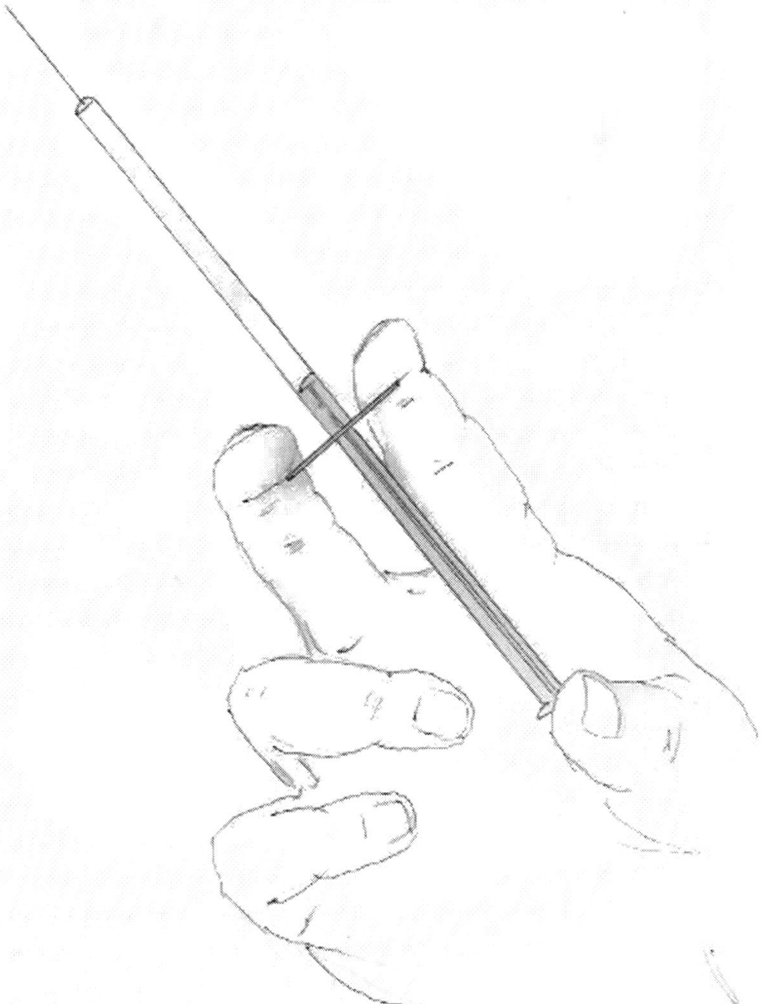

CHAPTER 18

He found the van in a small park near the neighborhood of Jacob's Landing. The windows were dark, but Steopa didn't need to see inside. He could tell Rebecka was not in the van. He faded into the shadows. He used the shadows cast by the trees from the streetlights to hide his approach. He heard two heartbeats.

Someone moved in the van. Blue lights turned on and filled the surrounding area of the van with a harsh glow. A blue beamed hit him, blinding Steopa. He raised his hand to block the light and his hand burned. He raised his long coat to shield his eyes.

Steopa jumped on the roof of the van. He tore the light off and smashed it onto the street. The engine started. The wheels spun and it took off backwards. Steopa slammed his fist through the roof of the van. The van spun and made a three point turn to turn around. Bullets flew from inside the van. They ripped and burned through his flesh. Steopa pulled back his arm, then thrust it through the roof again.

He grabbed the sides of the hole and pulled, peeling the roof of the van back like a sardine can. One of the hunters inside opened fire. The bullets cut across Steopa's chest. Two loud retorts. The van swerved back and forth. Steopa reached inside and pulled the gun out of the hunter's hands. He broke it, throwing the pieces behind him.

The van skidded and stopped. Steopa reached inside again and ripped the gunman out of the van. He threw him across the street. He dropped into the van. The driver reached for the door handle. Steopa slammed his head into the steering wheel.

"STOP!" Steopa commanded. He stood up, feeling the bullet holes heal as he did.

The driver put the van back into gear. Steopa reached around the man and wrenched the steering column up. The van shuttered to a stop. He felt his neck burn. Rebecka screamed in his head. She cursed and hissed. Her anger made his skin hot. Steopa fell to his knees.

"Rebecka!"

Steopa shook his head. For a moment he saw through Rebecka's eyes. Simon had her. He smiled and lifted a syringe in his hand.

"Simon?" Steopa asked.

The driver laughed, blood flowed down his face from his squashed nose. "Yeah, he's got her."

"Where did he take her?"

"Down there," the driver pointed back toward the Rathskeller.

"You lie." Steopa slid out his sword.

"Do you think I will-"

Steopa cut the man's head off.

He kicked the back door of the van open. Rebecka felt as if she had been thrown to the floor. He turned around feeling for Rebecka. When the feeling felt the strongest he opened his eyes. He faced the direction of the poorhouses.

A perfect place for a vampire to hide, he thought. The entire time I have been in Deerbow, no vampire had taken that part of the city as their own. There are no opportunities for hunting in the old buildings. Steopa growled.

He jumped a new chain fence, landing in a small grove of trees. He came to the remains of the old stone fence that had surrounded the buildings. He stopped to feel for Rebecka. She felt closer.

The campus spread out in front of him. Four buildings sat clustered around a central circular driveway. A large stone building that looked as if it could be a fortress sat in the middle of the other buildings.

As Steopa studied each one, he felt Rebecka in the direction of the large mansion. Of all the buildings, this one had the least damage. A faded sign in front of it announced a development that never happened.

He ran. As he came closer to the building, a legion came out of the mansion. The legion howled and ran toward Steopa. The legion swung as he ran. Steopa ducked. The legion lost his balance. Steopa tackled him and slammed the legion's head against the ground. The legion struck Steopa on the side of his face with his fist.

Steopa rolled off the legion. He sprang to his feet and raised his sword. He drove the tip of the sword through the legion's chest.

The legion laughed. "It will take more than that."

Steopa pulled it out. He swung it to take off the legion's head and stopped. Through the beast's chest a tree sprouted up. It grew and in a few moments it had expanded and destroyed the legion's chest.

Steopa looked around. A bear sat at the tree line. It raised its paw as if it waved. The bear's eyes glowed green. It ambled over to Steopa, then changed into Perun.

"Ash, right?" Perun asked, pointing to the tree. "Ash is what really hurts vampires."

Steopa nodded. "What are you doing here?"

"It's my woods. They have a lot of gull coming here. I don't think he will be getting up." Perun chuckled. "Why are you here?"

"Rebecka and her brother were taken," Steopa said.

"Your woman is there?" Perun asked pointing to the building. "The bastards."

Perun paused. He stopped Steopa. "But this has to be a trap."

"Yes it is." Steopa's neck burned. "We have to hurry."

Perun changed back into the bear. He rushed up to the building and through the open door. Steopa rubbed his neck. The burning cut through his neck. She must be in pain, he thought. He could feel that she was fighting. It was as if Simon wanted her alive, but in no shape to fight him back.

Steopa scaled the side of the building. Most of the roof had fallen onto the floor below. Steopa picked his way across the remaining floor between the holes in the roof. He could feel Rebecka below him. He stood still and listened. He heard Perun's claws clicking on the floor. Then he heard Rebecka swear. He dropped down through a hole in the roof.

The room smelled of decay and mold. He felt for other vampires with his mind. Steopa could feel that Simon was close, possibly in the hallway outside the door. He heard two sets of heartbeats. One should be John, but the other might belong to a vassal of Simon's or another hunter.

Rebecka's pain hit Steopa again. He steadied himself on a desk. Then he walked toward the door, making sure that he did not make a sound. He heard one set of heartbeats pass by. The other set echoed from the other side of the building.

A snort echoed from below. One set of heartbeats sounded as if the person had paused outside the door. Steopa pressed his hands against the door. He waited until the heartbeats had faded to the other side of the building. He opened the door. A man stood at the end of the hallway.

If it wasn't for the sound of the man's heart, I would have thought he was a legion, Steopa thought.

The man turned. He had a cell phone up to his ear. Steopa faded into the shadows. As he got closer to the man, he heard the conversation. The man spoke in German.

Steopa jumped and grabbed the man's head. He snapped his neck and let the body fall. Steopa stomped on the cell phone, breaking it into small pieces under his boot.

Steopa heard another snort come up the stairs. Perun had not changed from his bear form. His wrists felt as if they were on fire. They had turned red as if they were rubbed raw. He walked up to the door and placed his hand against the wood. He could feel Rebecka.

He stepped back to rush through the door. The door opened.

Rebecka laid on the floor. Where the ash had been wrapped around her neck, it had swollen and turned black. Down her arm along her veins, her skin had also turned black. Her brother John had been tied to a post in the room. Behind them sat Simon.

Simon smiled as if Steopa was a friend. His blond hair, cut short to his head, looked almost white. His brown eyes twinkled. Drops of blood had sprayed across the front of his ill-fitting business suit. He motioned Steopa to come inside.

Rebecka tried to roll to her side. Simon kicked Rebecka on her back.

John lifted his head. “Do that one more time, asshole.”

John's head snapped back against the wall. Steopa moved, but John shook his head. Steopa stopped.

“So you are the one,” Simon said. He raised his hand.

Steopa flew backwards and against the wall. Simon straightened out his jacket. Steopa tried to move. He felt a large weight on his chest, holding him to the wall.

Simon shook his head. “I would have thought you would have done better.”

John spit a tooth on the floor. “Watch out for him, Steopa. That's not his only trick.”

Simon nodded. “The food is right.”

Rebecka moved her unaffected arm. Simon pointed to her. Rebecka screamed. Steopa strained to look down. A large silver syringe stuck out of her neck. The same cloudy liquid that they had found in the hunter's pack glimmered inside the syringe.

"You like?" Simon said, gesturing to the syringe.

He stood up and walked over to Steopa. "I think the holy water is a bit much, but then those hunters always go back to tradition."

Simon stood alongside Steopa. "Now I see most of the rumors were not exaggerations. I never could figure out how you killed my sister, but now I see you."

"I did not kill her." Steopa said, straining to get the words out.

"That is not what I was told," Simon said. "My sister was very special to me. Very special."

Steopa strained against the unseen force that Simon had him held with. "Your issue is with me."

"No, it is not," Simon said. He shook his finger in Steopa's face. "How dare you expand your family! My mistress wants to make sure that you are gone, that all of them are gone!"

Steopa glanced down at Rebecka, she had rolled onto her stomach. She tried to reach the syringe with her good hand.

"What are you talking about?" he hissed.

"You never heard the old stories? About the family of vampires that would mark the new order?" Simon asked. "I was chosen by my elder to wipe you out. To take revenge on behalf of my sister."

"How are you supposed to do that?" Steopa asked.

Steopa's head snapped back. Simon approached him like a cat about to pounce. "I-!" He shook his head. "My mistress has given me power. I will kill you and your family."

In the hallway, the clicking of nails against the old tiles stopped. For a moment Steopa smelled bear fur, then nothing. He glanced down. Rebecka's fingertip had touched the syringe. She strained to remove it.

Simon waved his hand. The plunger pushed more of the liquid into her neck. Rebecka screamed. Steopa strained against the force.

"You must be strong," Steopa said. "You can control all of us, impressive."

"Someone has to stand up to you."

"Why you? Why did Adelind ask you? Is she too weak to face me?"

"Because I had seen the cup. I read my great-grandfather's diary." He said in a rush. Then he looked around. "The cup..."

"The coiree," Steopa said.

Simon grabbed Steopa around his neck. "How do you know?"

"That is why you have been looking everywhere in this city," Steopa smiled. "I know where it is."

"You can't."

"Kill any of us, and you will never know."

"You can't! Only I am supposed to know! My great-grandfather swore an oath to it."

"He was a human. Like you were only a short time ago." Steopa grinned. "You are a puppet."

Steopa saw John move. He had stretched out his leg. He hooked the tip of his foot under the syringe. He flicked his foot and the syringe fell out of Rebecka's neck. She raised her hand, her muscles straining under whatever force Simon used against them.

"How did you find out about it?" Simon asked.

"Another vampire like you. He bragged about it, but could not find it. Strange, I had never heard of it before, and now every upstart and pissant is trying to get it."

"Only the chosen can use it."

"Bullshit," Rebecka said.

"My mistress said you have no respect for our traditions."

"What do you know of our traditions?" Steopa hissed.

He felt some of the pressure release off his arms. He strained and lifted his right arm. Simon came closer, smirking. Steopa wrapped his hand around Simon's neck.

"I can snap your neck," Steopa said.

Simon fought against Steopa's grip. Rebecka picked up the syringe. She rolled over and stabbed Simon in the foot. Simon eyes turned white. The force around Steopa exploded. He lost his grip on Simon's neck, his arms flung down alongside his body. Rebecka rolled on the floor and was flung against another wall. The syringe shot straight up and buried itself in the ceiling. Simon steadied himself.

"I take it you've never fought a vampire that could use his mind." Simon's eyes had returned to their normal brown. "I thought you were supposed to be some sort of super-strong freak."

Steopa tried to speak, but couldn't. Simon turned his attention on

Rebecka.

"She's a mystery," Simon said. "We can't figure out where she fits into your family tree. Yet, there is her brother. Why didn't you turn him too?"

"No reason," Steopa said, forcing each word.

Simon flicked his hand again. Steopa's sword tore out of his scabbard and flew across the room. It struck Rebecka's chest. Rebecka looked surprised, but didn't cry out. She winked at Steopa and hung her head. Blood dripped from her wound to the ground.

Simon smiled. He flicked his hand, and stabbed her again. Steopa forced his head off the wall. "Did you not study your enemy?"

The blood dripping from Rebecka pooled on the ground below her. It moved across the floor like oil. Steopa tried to turn his head. He thought he saw movement across the floor. Then he saw a squirrel scurry across the floor and behind John.

Simon returned to his chair. Rebecka's blood flowed under Simon's seat. Simon smiled. "If I knew it would be this easy, I... she would have never hired the hunters."

"Your hunters were weak."

Another movement caught Steopa's eye. Behind John, Perun grinned. In his one hand he held a knife with an antler handle. In the other, John's bounds. John slid down the post and onto the floor.

Simon flicked his hand. The syringe dropped from the ceiling and hit Perun in the chest. Perun dropped John's ropes and pulled the syringe out of his chest. "You think that will work on me? Ass."

"What are you?" Simon asked.

"Where are you from, boy?"

Simon's jaw clenched. "That doesn't matter."

"Yes it does. I wanted to give you fair warning." Perun threw the knife.

Simon raised his hand. The knife turn around in mid-air. Perun ducked and the blade buried itself in the wall behind him.

"Fun times," Perun said, laughing like a madman.

Perun's loud laugh made Simon's eye twitch. Steopa felt the force lessen on his body. Steopa grinned. As long as Perun keeps Simon busy, his hold weakens on us, he thought.

John reached over and took Rebecka's hand. She did not move. But the blood under Simon's chair climbed up the legs.

"What is wrong with your mind, boy?" Perun asked. He grinned, his green eyes flashed. "There are three minds there. You are all messed up."

Simon grunted. He raised both of his hands. Something clattered to the floor. A stake rose in the air. Steopa had seen one like that before, the night he woke up in his coffin. The long stake looked like a javelin, but thicker.

Simon swung it around in the air. "Let's see," he said. "One of you has to go." He lowered it for a moment. When he raised it, his hands shook.

Perun giggled. "Wood doesn't harm me."

"No one survives getting their head chopped off!" Simon hissed.

"Are you sure about that?" Perun's mad laugh echoed through the room.

The stake spun around and buried itself into Rebecka's chest. Steopa felt the pain. He bellowed. The smug look on Simon's face faded.

Perun helped John up. John grabbed the knife out of the wall and rushed Simon. Simon turned, almost too late. John buried the blade into Simon's chest. Simon shoved John off him and into Perun. Perun steadied John and grinned. Perun's smile chilled Steopa.

Rebecka's blood gushed out. It joined the rest in the pool. Steopa swore a string of Russian, Lithuanian, and Polish swear words. Simon laughed as he removed the blade.

Perun sang.

Simon stopped laughing. "What are you doing?"

Perun sang in a low voice that sounded like a growl. The language was unfamiliar to Steopa. Perun raised his hands as if he held a drum in one, and with the other tapped out the beat. Steopa could hear the drum. The sound seemed to come from deep inside his body.

"Stop it," Simon said.

Perun raised his voice. The drumming became louder.

"Stop it!"

Blood dripped from Simon's nose. The pressure on Steopa lessened to the point he could move away from the wall. Simon grabbed the sides of his head. For a moment, Steopa felt another vampire mind. That mind tried to push back into Simon's head.

The blood from the floor flowed over Simon's lap. He looked down and tried to push the blood away. It covered his hands.

"War is the province of danger and the unknown," Steopa said.

Simon looked at Steopa like he was crazy. Perun walked closer to Simon, still drumming the unseen drum. The blood climbed up his chest and to Simon's neck.

Steopa crouched down beside him. "You should have known more about me."

"What is he?" Simon asked looking at Perun.

"A friend." Steopa placed his hand on Simon's head and made him look at Perun. "I think you are a liar. But you do not know you lie. You are a drudge, you have been told what to say. But you know the truth, deep down."

The sound of a large piece of wood hitting the floor made Steopa glance over to Rebecka. The stake had been pushed out of her chest. John slid over to Rebecka and tried to stop the flow of blood from her chest.

"Let my friend help you," Steopa said.

"I, I, I, can't. She... she wants to find you and that... thing...," Simon said.

The blood from Rebecka had almost enveloped Simon. Steopa picked up the stake.

"Rebecka can control blood. If you make her bleed, she can still fight you. So cutting her head off makes no difference," Steopa said, weighing the stake in his hands. He nodded toward Perun. "And my friend. He can disrupt anything your mind throws out."

Perun laughed. His eyes glowed silver, along with strands of his wild hair. "He thinks he knows the mind?"

"You said he had three minds. I felt one," Steopa said to Perun.

"Yeah, one is powerful. And female." Perun placed his hand on Simon's head. "But the others are his."

"What do you mean?"

"He's fighting himself." Perun slid his hand down and touched the side of Simon's face. "But you know Steopa is right."

Simon cried out. He grabbed Perun's hand. Rebecka's blood pulled away from Perun. "It was her. All her. She killed my sister. Used her blood to look for the coiree."

Steopa leaned closer. “Why?”

“I'm not sure,” Simon grimaced. Tears rolled down his cheeks. “She told me it was because my great-grandfather drank from the cup. Our blood was linked to it.”

“Why you?” Perun asked.

“Adelind found me online. Told me she knew what happened to my sister. She made me drink that blood.”

“Then she told you I killed your sister?” Steopa asked.

Simon nodded. “She used my blood, too. She's never out of my head.”

“I felt that,” Perun said.

“Please,” Simon said. He pleaded with Steopa with his eyes. “Please.”

Steopa stood up and adjusted his grip on the stake. He forced the stake through Simon. The floorboards underneath cracked. Simon struggled for a moment then laid still. The blood broke away from him in a wave. It rolled back to Rebecka. John moved out of the way, but his leg caught some of the blood.

Steopa picked up his sword and took Simon's head off with one swipe.

Steopa went to Rebecka. She had not opened her eyes. None of the blood had reabsorbed into her body. Steopa laid his head down next to hers. He could barely feel her.

“I can't heal vampires,” Perun said.

“I know,” Steopa said.

“I am sorry, Steopa.”

“She is not lost yet.”

John wiped his face. “She had her head taken off and survived.”

Steopa nodded. He lifted Rebecka's face. Her eyelids fluttered. Steopa picked her up. “Take her brother home.”

“In the city?” Perun asked.

“He lives above a bar.”

“Now you are talking.” Perun pulled John up. “Show me the way.”

Steopa cradled Rebecka in his arms. He kicked Simon's head out the window. He could see the glow from the lights of Deerbow. He ran to Forest Grove cemetery, to take her to the coiree.

CHAPTER 19

The angel statue rocked back and forth after Steopa kicked it aside to open the tunnel. He jumped down and shouldered open the door. At the upper level, Steopa laid Rebecka on the dais behind the altar. He grabbed the coiree and brought it to her. Ogden stepped back, surprised. Supporting her with one arm, he helped her drink from the coiree. Most of the blood splashed down her chest. But it filled the gaping hole from the stake.

He dropped the cup and pulled Rebecka closer. Ogden spoke. Steopa looked up.

"I asked," Ogden said, "what happened?"

"That bothersome drudge staked Rebecka."

"He did that?"

"He has been dealt with."

Rebecka moved her head. She opened her eyes, smiled, then her head rolled back. Ogden came over to the dais. He held his hand out and raised his eyebrow.

"May I?" he asked.

Steopa did not stop him. Ogden lifted one of Rebecka's eyelids. "Let her rest. She has to heal."

Steopa laid her down.

"Why are you here?" He stroked Rebecka's large curls.

Ogden picked up the empty coiree and replaced it on the altar.

"A little research," Ogden said. "I was next to the coiree when it filled with blood. You came up the stairs moments later."

Steopa nodded. "The same thing happened when Vincent was injured. And myself."

"I have been wondering if the coiree and the jewelry that Rebecka and Vincent have are related."

Steopa growled. "This is not the time to talk about this."

Ogden tilted his head. "Yes it is. She will heal tonight because of those items. Whatever is behind this artifact wants us to protect it.

But what is the cost?"

Steopa waved his hand. "I said this is not the time to talk about it."

He stood up, towering over Ogden. Ogden looked at Steopa without a flutter of an eye.

"Rebecka was almost killed," Steopa growled.

"I understand," Ogden said in a calm, even voice. "She should be ashes by now. I would not be able to survive that sort of attack."

"Rebecka is strong."

"Look at her ring."

Steopa turned. The ring glowed yellow. Steopa had seen it glow red before, never yellow. The light pulsed like a heartbeat.

The click of Ogden's cane on the marble made Steopa turn. Ogden stopped at the entrance to the stairwell. "I want to make sure we can pay the price. There are other forces at work here. Your grandson Misha agrees."

"Perhaps you should share your fears with him."

Ogden held up his hand. "I have. The legions appear out of nowhere. How? The seals."

"Seals? Like the one I saw used in the poorhouse."

"Are you familiar with any of the magical texts, like the Seventh Book of Moses?"

"No."

"They are markings that can assist in magic. The human magicians used them to bind demons and angels. Some of us have learned to use them for movement."

"So?"

"Let us put it this way, Steopa. If I had to travel to England. I would not need a jet."

"I see."

"Yes, I will leave you." Ogden looked around the chapel as if he was looking for something, then he walked down the stairs.

Steopa snorted. He shook his head and returned to Rebecka. Why would Ogden act as if they had sold their souls to the devil? Payment? Rebecka lost all her blood. How much more of a payment did she have to make? The coiree had saved his life as well. Every time they came here they left a little blood in the cup. They had already paid.

Rebecka moaned. Steopa stroked her face and laid down beside her. Dawn was hours away. He didn't care. Steopa pulled Rebecka closer to him.

He looked at the roof of the chapel. The builders had not spared the details even on the ceiling. Steopa had never noticed the mural above him. A blue sky with clouds, the shading made it look like the sun had risen in the East.

He heard a rustle, like a large bird moving its wings. Steopa glanced around the chapel. He did not see anyone, but he felt as if someone had entered the chapel. Steopa remained still. It did not feel like a human or a vampire.

Behind the coiree, the air seemed to shimmer, then wave like the air on a hot day. Through it, a white figure appeared. His black wings were folded along his back. His head had a halo of black shaggy hair. It could have been an angel, but Steopa had never been taught that angels had three fingers on their hands.

The white being turned his head and studied one of the boarded-up stained glass windows. The window showed the angel casting Adam and Eve out of the Garden of Eden. The serpent coiled along the bottom of the window.

"Why do humans believe such things?" the creature asked with a deep, rich voice.

"What are you?" Steopa asked.

The creature did not turn around, but his shoulders shook as if he laughed. "Not who? You are astute."

"I do not know many vampires with wings," Steopa said. He started to stand.

"No, stay there," the creature said. "Do not disturb her."

"How did you get in here?" Steopa asked.

"I am not here, Steopa Rodovitch. That is why it will not matter if you get up."

He turned around, but shadows covered his features. He walked over to the coiree and touched the cup. Steopa could see the creature's hand; the three fingers looked like talons.

"How do you like my gift?" the creature asked.

"Yours? Are you the one that fills it with blood, too?"

"It is a sign of my gratitude. Now, Steopa. Simon will meet the sun. Your family is safe, for now. But I want to speak to you about your other family."

Steopa sat up, resting on his elbows. "My other family?"

He smiled. Rows of sharp fangs, much like Sasha's, grinned back at Steopa. “Rebecka Saberhagen, the most unlikely vampire. She will be a fine mother.”

“What do you mean” Steopa asked.

“You had a farm, correct? So you know that breeding is essential for a good herd. Or even something as simple as a good dog. The time will come where only the ones with my blood will survive.” The creature ran his talon along the top of the coiree. “My blood is in a few humans. Stronger in some than others. Rebecka and you are from such lines. It was a chance that you two became linked. But a chance I needed to happen.”

“Are you are a god?” Steopa raised his eyebrow.

“I thought you did not believe in such things.”

“I do not. The crucifix did not stop that vampire from attacking me. There is no higher power.”

“No, I am not a god. But you should not discount such things.” The creature leaned against the altar. “But as I said, my blood flows through some of the humans and vampires on this planet. I have been waiting for this to happen. It almost happened too late.”

“Speak plainly, or do not speak at all,” Steopa said.

The creature walked around the altar to the other side. “Then I will be blunt. Most vampires that run around on this pitiful planet will never reach their full potential. They are like the runts you would get in large litters. Their powers muted, or never realized. But then there are the ones like yourself and Rebecka. Even before you were changed, my blood flowed the strongest through your veins.”

He tilted his head. “The family you have now, that was luck. And they are strong. They will survive. But the family that you two will create. That one will be the most important of all.”

Steopa scoffed. “How are we supposed to do that?”

“You were a father, I assumed you know how.”

Steopa shook his head. “We are not capable.”

“You have both drank my blood. It would have happened, slowly. But your friend sped things up. You should thank Perun.”

“You speak as if that prophecy is real.”

“It is, but it is no prophecy. It is fact. A fact that has been changed and rearranged to fit the ones in power. Or should I say the ones that want to be in power.”

"You mean the vampires like Adelind?"

"She is a puppet, all of them are. Some people that crave power will take whatever they can get, without seeing the strings attached. Those types of vampires are taking over entire cities, all of them pawns."

"Who is controlling them?"

"An outside power. One that has no reason to be on this planet."

"Forgive me, but what you are saying sounds like fantasy," Steopa said.

The creature nodded. "I suppose it does." He crossed his arms. "Let me give you some insight into your near future. As you know, Simon did not act alone. Adelind used him to smoke you out, to search for the coiree, and set him up to take the fall, when the human authorities got too close."

He fluttered his wings. "She betrayed me, and the rest that have my blood. Watch out for the one that is really pulling the strings. She has talked to a..." He paused searching for the word. "A rival of mine. He told her that it was important to find the vampire with the blood line that still flowed, to kill them."

He shook his head. "I am sure that is not what my rival said, but that is what the puppet believes."

Steopa raised his eyebrow, but did not say anything.

"To put it plainly," the creature said. "Your family was marked for extinction because of a misguided prophecy. And there are others that will step in to finish the job."

"So what now, more hunters?" Steopa asked "Do I have to watch out for dhamphirs as well?"

"As for dhamphirs, most have drank the blood. There are not many left. The ones that are, do not want to relive the old war."

"War?"

"Before your time. But it nearly wiped out the ones with my blood."

"Does this matter?"

"Not right now."

"Do you know about Adelind?" Steopa asked.

"A very traditional vampire. Of her own making, with human help."

Human help? Steopa thought. He gently moved Rebecka's head and stood. He tried to stand taller than the creature, but the creature grew. He expanded his wings.

"I know the type," Steopa said. "They are the ones that avoid the crucifix and travel with the dirt from their homeland."

"Yes, the ones that believe in the old folktales that most humans no longer do. She will be coming soon."

The creature smiled. "I know you do not believe me. I do not ask you to believe me either. Unlike my rival, I do not want supplicants."

"You are correct, you could be a dream," Steopa said. "Is she the one behind the legions?"

The creature shook his head. "No, she does not have the skill for that. The one that made those is the direct line to my rival. He was shown how. My rival likes to show a little of his power. To make the humans and the vampires think they have the same power. But it's a tease."

"What else do we have to watch out for? Mad Dutch physicians?"

"Not watch out for, but use. Talk to your friend Ogden. He knows about the seals. The ones that your friend, the wild man, found in the poorhouses." He fluttered his wings again. "I will leave you. Protect your families."

He faded away.

Steopa stood for a moment. He looked down at the coiree. It had a small amount of blood in it. Steam rose from the bowl of the cup. Steopa chuckled.

He heard the click of Ogden's cane on the floor below.

CHAPTER 20

Steopa felt Rebecka move away from him on the dais. He reached his hand out to her. When she did not take his, he opened his eyes. She smiled. Except for her bloody and torn clothes, she looked well.

"You were almost killed again," he said.

"I know. But I'm tough."

Steopa sat up and stroked her hair. A breeze blew up the stairs. The scent of primroses came with the wind. Rebecka curled his hair in her fingers.

"It's over," she said.

"For now. Vampires never go for long without fighting each other." Steopa kissed her forehead. He slid his hand down her shirt and opened it up. Her chest had healed. He ran his fingers along the insides of her breasts. Her skin felt soft. He cupped her breasts and kissed her cleavage.

Rebecka chuckled and she grasped his hands. "I had the strangest dream last night. A black-haired angel told me that I am going to be a mother." She laughed. "At least he didn't say it was a virgin birth."

Steopa looked up.

"What?" Rebecka asked.

"Describe him."

"I don't remember, because he looked like he was just shadows. White shadows. I remember his fangs and eyes. Why?"

"I saw him. I was not dreaming."

The smile drained from Rebecka's face. "I hope it's because we share each other's thoughts."

"I do not think so. Did he talk to you about Simon?"

Rebecka shook her head. "No, he said I should ask Perun why he wanted to help us."

"That 'angel' claimed the coiree was his." Steopa stood and

pointed to the cup. “Why does every vampire we meet want that damned thing?”

“I don't know.” Rebecka smoothed her blood-stained shirt and sighed. “Do you believe that winged thing?”

“I will talk to Perun first.”

“So we are supposed to have kids. How could Perun have done anything?”

“Anything to do with life, Perun can affect and change.”

“That really doesn't answer my question.”

“We will have to ask him.” Steopa heard the door to the tunnel open. “I think we have visitors.”

Steopa took off his overcoat and handed it to Rebecka. She put it on. With her frame, its hem dragged on the ground. Steopa flicked his hair back. Rebecka stared at him for a moment.

“I just realized something,” she said.

“What?”

“That you are good looking... I mean...,” she waved her hand in front of her face. “Never mind.”

“I fed very well last night.”

She shook her head. “No, that's not it. It's like I am really seeing you.”

Steopa put his arm around her. “It might be the blood from the coiree.”

Rebecka shrugged. “Or whatever Perun did. I hope John is okay.”

“He should be. Perun would have healed him.”

Someone ran up the stairs, but then fell. Rebecka adjusted her shirt. She made a face.

“Hey, you guys coming down?” Jimmy yelled. “We can't go up there. Sasha tried.”

Steopa took Rebecka's hand. “We should not tell them about the visitor.”

Rebecka glanced at the coiree, then her ring. “Strange things,” she whispered.

They walked down the stairs. Jimmy sat on one of the crypts. Sasha sat on the floor, holding his head. Misha nodded to Steopa.

“I guess the university is going to have to find another linebacker,” Jimmy said.

“Then we should think about leaving,” Sasha said. “Hurricane season will be strong soon. Good time to hunt without being noticed."

"I will stay a little bit," Misha said. "I have to take care of things."

"You don't have to leave tonight," Rebecka said. "I was just getting to know all of you."

"Grandfather," Sasha said. "What is up there? I ran up there to tell you we were here, and I hit something."

Steopa glanced up the stairs. "Only four of us can go into that room."

"Why?"

"A cup."

"That one that filled with blood, when the hunters attacked you?" Jimmy asked.

"The same."

"Is that the coiree?" Misha asked.

"Yes."

"At least we know no other vampire can take it."

Rebecka squeezed Steopa's hand. "Since Sasha wants to leave, maybe we should spend one more night together."

"The club?" Steopa asked.

"We could."

"But first, we have to speak to Perun. I have put him off for too long."

"Perun?" Jimmy asked. "That weird looking guy? That would be cool."

"You should find him interesting, Misha," Steopa said.

They left the memorial. Misha ran his fingers through his short black hair. "Your friend Ogden..."

"What about him?" Rebecka asked.

"He would be a formidable enemy."

Steopa chuckled. "What gave you that idea?"

"He could match me in a fight."

Steopa glanced at Misha. Misha had taken after his father. He did not inherit the Rodovitch build. He looked plain and with his nervous hand twitch, he gave the impression of a weak person. Yet Steopa knew that was not the case. You did not have to be physically intimidating to be strong.

"Simon could use telekinesis," Steopa said.

"What?"

"He had me pinned to the wall using his mind."

"That is unusual."

Rebecka held up her ring. "I have not figured out what this can do, but Vincent has the necklace. He can burn you by touching you. Maybe Simon had something like this."

"We could check his ashes," Misha said.

Steopa stopped. "Yes, Perun wants to see us. We will go there first."

"Back to the poorhouse?" Rebecka asked.

"Yes."

"Can I get a new shirt first?"

Steopa nodded. "The store is not far."

As Steopa approached the clothing store, he could tell something had changed. His finger hovered over the bell. The daughter looked down from the balcony.

"She passed," she said.

"I am sorry," Steopa said.

The daughter glanced at the rest of them. "I will be down."

Sasha, Misha, and Jimmy stayed outside. Rebecka walked through the racks looking at the shirts. The daughter blew her nose.

"She left me a letter. You knew her in Saint Petersburg?" the daughter asked.

"Yes."

"I didn't know she had been a photographer."

"I am sure she kept many secrets. That is why she was my friend."

Rebecka came over to the counter wearing her new shirt. Steopa pulled off a large bill. The daughter stopped him.

"I read the letter, you don't have to anymore."

Steopa laid the bill on the counter. "It is a gift. The arrangement I had with your mother does not extend to you. Unless you want it to."

"I'll think about it."

They went into the courtyard. Steopa looked back to the store. "We will have to find another place."

"That shouldn't be an issue," Rebecka said.

He hugged Rebecka. She kissed his lips. Misha cleared his throat.

"What?" Rebecka asked.

"It's strange, seeing a linked couple like you," Misha said.

Sasha shrugged. "It happens."

"Come on," Steopa said. "We need to find Perun."

The southern entrance to Greenwoods was not far away from the poorhouses. Steopa started to look for Perun there. He did not have to look long.

Perun sat next to a fire in the middle of the shell of a fountain in front of the poorhouses. He raised his hand in greeting. "I knew you would come back tonight. Rebecka, you look radiant."

"Perun these are my grandsons, and you have met Jimmy. We need to talk," Steopa said.

Perun nodded. He gathered up a few wooden discs he had scattered in front of him. "Did you bring anything to drink?"

"Not tonight."

"Come now, Steopa, you know that I do not talk for just anyone."

"Perun," Steopa growled.

"But you are an exception." Perun stood as he wrapped a deer hide around his shoulders. "Follow me. I made sure Simon burned. You can see his remains if you like."

"We would."

Perun nodded. "There is magic in here I have never felt before."

"You are a leshy," Misha said. "I met one of your kind before."

"Where?" Perun asked.

"In Russia."

Perun nodded. "There used to be more of us."

"Grandfather, you never told me you knew a leshy."

"I did not know that was important," Steopa said.

"I would love to ask you so many questions," Misha said to Perun.

"You will have to do it properly, not like-" Perun pointed to Steopa with his thumb and made a face. "You have to bring me the right tribute."

"What is that?"

"Vodka, beef, or lamb. Not the cheap vodka either."

Misha nodded. "Of course not."

Perun opened the door to the poorhouse. "I found it in the basement. I know some types of writing. Runes and the like, but nothing like this."

"Where are Simon's remains?" Steopa asked.

Perun pointed to the top of the next building.

"Sasha and Jimmy, go through his ashes, make sure that there is nothing unusual," Steopa said.

Perun led them down a set of stairs to the dank basement. Mold and mushrooms grew along the walls. The floor had been flooded with a few inches of water. Perun's eyes glowed silver as the corridor became darker. He pointed to a large room to the side.

"In there."

This room had not been flooded. The floor had been cleaned. In the middle of the room, on the floor, a strange design had been carved into the concrete. Misha held out his arm and stopped Steopa from approaching.

"It's a seal," he said.

A triangle formed the outer edge of the seal. Strange symbols had been written around the perimeter. In the center of the seal, three ovals had been drawn, overlapping each other and pointing to the corners. In the center, where they overlapped, a clay bowl had been left. The stale smell of blood and the rusty stain inside the bowl were signs that someone had bled here.

"Are you familiar?" Perun asked Misha.

"Yes." Misha took a few steps forward. "Sometimes they are trapped."

"What is it?" Rebecka asked.

"They can be used for many things. Humans try to use them to conjure demons and angels. I use them to travel."

"Huh?"

"I draw the right seal, and I can step into it and end up somewhere else. But I have never used blood."

"Is that important?" Steopa asked.

"No. I don't know why they would."

Perun picked up the cup, he smelled it. "Deer blood."

Misha took the cup away from Perun. "Not even human or vampire blood." He ran his finger along the inside of the cup. "Wait." He sniffed his finger. "Aconite. Do not have Teodor or any of his children touch this."

"Why not?" Rebecka asked.

"It's poisonous to humans. If a werewolf touches this, they could loose their pelt."

"It skins them?" Rebecka grimaced.

"Peels the fur right off." Perun mimed pulling his skin off his body.

"It makes no sense." Misha put the cup back down on the floor, and walked over to the seal. He patted his jacket and pulled out a pad of paper with a pencil.

"This is not like the one I saw Adelind use," Steopa said.

"This is a permanent one." Misha laid the paper down and rubbed his pencil along the floor. "These are harder to maintain. Which could explain the blood."

Steopa walked around the room. Along one of the walls the mold and mushrooms were gone. He reached out and touched the wall. Ash flaked off and coated his fingertips. Rebecka came over to him.

"Something burned," he said.

"I don't smell anything."

"Sometimes the humans come here and wreck things," Perun said as he came closer. "Mak and Jeremiah love it when that happens."

"But it is only on the wall," Steopa said. "The concrete has not been damaged. The floor is untouched."

"Have you mated yet?" Perun asked.

Rebecka giggled. Steopa turned around and grabbed Perun's arm. He dragged him out of the room and into the wet hallway.

"Why is it your concern?" Steopa asked.

Perun chuckled. "You're my friend, as strange as that seems."

"And my intimacy with Rebecka is your concern?"

"Why not?" Perun patted Steopa on his shoulder. "I can see that you are coupled. Linked, you call it. Mated is what I would call it. And if you are... you should enjoy each other's company."

"We do."

"You should be fucking." Perun's grin split his face in two.

"We cannot."

"Has it fallen off?"

Steopa stared at Perun.

"Has it?"

"No."

"So what's stopping you?"

"We are physically incapable, ever since the change."
"Not anymore. Not for you two, at any rate."
"I was told you did something."
Perun's smile faded. "Who told you?"
Steopa growled. "I met a creature. He told me."
"Steopa..." Perun's voice lowered. "What sort of creature?"
"It looked like an angel, but with rows of vampire teeth."
Perun stamped his foot, water splashed covering Steopa's pants. "Black hair?"
"You know him?"
"If it is who I think it is..." Perun shook his head. "What else did he say?"
"Rebecka and I were to start a new family."
"Nothing wrong with that."
"And he told me his rival is behind-"
"Fuck-me-running." Perun hit the wall. More mushrooms sprouted on the wall where his fist had slammed into the concrete. "They're here? About time they straightened out their mess."
"Excuse me?"
Perun shook his head. "Sorry, Steopa, it's hard to explain. Even to you."
"If you know anything-" Steopa shook his finger at Perun.
"I know a lot of things. And I am glad that it's you that he has contacted. I know how you feel about certain things, and you will be the one to stand up to him, if needed."
"Be plain with me."
"I can't." Perun shrugged. "It is not because I do not think you deserve to be told. It is because you have to concentrate on other things now. Whatever is brewing with that creature could take centuries to come to completion. Why become obsessed with it?"
"That is true. Would Rebecka be in any danger?"
"Not if he wants both of you to become proud parents." Perun shook his head. "I thought I was giving you two a gift and he twists it."
"A gift? We were happy-"
Perun shook his head. "The way vampires reproduce is disgusting. You two should not have to stalk the streets and infect someone if you want to have a family. That's not natural."
"We are not natural."

Perun's eyes flashed silver. “Yes, yes you are. You might not have enough life in you so I can heal you, but you are from this world. You are a part of it, just like the rocks, the animals, and the humans. You are the ultimate predator. Death avoids your kind. If you weren't natural, I could not wake things up. You would still be as flaccid as a dead fish.”

Steopa turned and went back in the room. “Rebecka, Misha, we are leaving.”

“You mean it still is?” Perun asked.

Steopa growled. Rebecka came out of the room. She took Steopa's hand.

Perun flashed her a smile. “You two are going to have fun.”

Rebecka smirked. She glanced over her shoulder and bit her lips. Her body was shaking. A giggle escaped her lips. Misha joined them.

“We will talk later,” Steopa said to Perun.

“Of course,” Perun said. “We are watching this place. I don't like those things running through my woods. You want unnatural, Steopa. those legions are. They might have been human or vampire, but they are not now.”

“I have seen enough,” Misha said. “We should join the rest.”

“Agreed.” Steopa pulled Rebecka closer to him.

When they had left the poorhouse, Perun disappeared into the woods. Rebecka doubled over in laughter. Then she stood up and hugged Steopa.

“Sorry,” she said giggling. “I don't think you could be a dead fish.”

“What are you talking about?” Misha asked.

“Never mind.” Steopa growled.

CHAPTER 21

Jimmy and Sasha found nothing in Simon's ashes. Steopa suggested the Rathskeller. Rebecka raised her eyebrow, but did not question him. I should speak to Vincent, Steopa thought. Ogden keeps too many secrets. Like I do.

Vincent met them at the entrance. Misha and Sasha went to the bar. Jimmy started to join them, but Andi pulled him to a table across the room. Rebecka excused herself and hurried to the bar. She talked to Lorelei, then both of them went to the back. Vincent chuckled.

"She's looking good for being a pin cushion yesterday."

"You heard?" Steopa asked.

"Johnny told me." Vincent walked Steopa over to one of the larger booths. He sat down opposite Steopa.

"How much longer is your brood gonna stay in town?"

"They are leaving soon," Steopa said.

"Everything will go back to normal. That's a scary thought."

"I do not think it is over."

Vincent winked at a woman as she passed the booth. "What do you mean?"

"Simon was only the puppet."

"So more problems?"

Steopa shrugged. "I hope not right away. My daughter is missing. It will be easier to search for her with them back at their homes."

"How do you know she is missing?" Vincent leaned closer.

"Her sons cannot find her."

Vincent motioned with his thumb to the bar where Misha and Sasha stood. Steopa nodded.

"Not to be personal, but how many do you have?"

"I do not know."

"Have you ever accidentally attacked one?"

Steopa shook his head. "No, one time I came upon one while I was hunting. I could tell that she was descended from me, but she was still alive."

Vincent waved. Steopa turned his head. Verina walked in with a long-haired lanky young man. She waved. The young man took off his jacket, revealing both arms covered in tattoos.

Steopa tapped his fingers against the table. "I saw that creature."

The smile on Vincent's face faded. "The one that appears with the coiree?"

"Yes."

"When you were injured?"

"No. Last night when I took Rebecka there." Steopa told Vincent about the strange conversation.

"Bullshit," Vincent said.

"I beg your pardon."

"Not you. That thing. He tells me to take this-" Vincent held up the necklace. "From Rebecka. I did. Now I can burn. But he tells you to have another family. Doesn't he know that there's nothing below the waist? There are women I have taken to my room I would have bedded in a second. But nothing now."

Steopa looked away, he shifted in his seat, then leaned forward. "Did you meet Perun when he brought John back here?"

Vincent shook his head.

"He is a leshy."

"What's that?"

Steopa thought. "A wildman? Greenman?"

"I have heard of the greenman."

"Leshies watch the woods they live in. Perun has power. He gave Rebecka and I a gift, he says."

"What sort of gift?" Vincent asked.

"He thinks we will be able to have this new family, the normal way."

Vincent's mouth dropped open. "Serious?"

"That is what he says. I do not feel any different."

"Maybe he messed up."

Steopa shook his head. "He may act like a fool, but he has a sharp mind and I have seen him do things that I have only heard about in stories."

Vincent sat back. "And if it happens? Are you going hire a nanny?"

Steopa scoffed. "I will not worry about that."

Vincent tapped his fingernail against his fang. "I hate to see what is going to happen when this gets out.

"Your meaning?"

"I mean, there are vampires in this town that are disgusted with you and Rebecka acting like lovesick teenagers."

Steopa growled.

Vincent grinned. "I like it. She's happy. But can you imagine what would happen if you two have children? The rumor would be bad enough."

"Rumor. Prophecy. It is all the same thing. Why do you think Adelind sent Simon after me to begin with? That and she was looking for the coiree."

"Why did we dig that thing up?" Vincent rubbed his face. "That's right; we wanted to put it in a safer place."

Sasha sat down next to Steopa. "Misha wants to stay. I will have to leave soon. What should we do about Jimmy?"

"If he wants to stay in town, he has to find a place."

"Here?" Vincent asked. "There's not much left."

"Who is that?" Sasha asked, motioning with his chin to Verina.

"Verina," Vincent said. "She's a friend."

"This place would be shut down if it was in Europe."

Vincent scoffed "Why?"

"Because the only places vampires are allowed to socialize have to approved."

"Still?" Steopa asked. "I thought that was done away with."

"In a few places," Sasha said. "But others have been bringing back the old ways."

"The old ways are foolish." Steopa shook his head. "If I had stuck to the old ways, I would still be in a cemetery in Saint Petersburg. It is times like this that I am glad I live in the United States. I do not have to deal with all the politics."

Sasha nodded. "Although I love hunting along the Rhine."

"What about Venice?" Vincent asked.

"I have only gone there once. Too much competition."

Rebecka came out of the back of the club with her brother. The right side of John's face had a large bruise covering his cheek and eye. There were no other physical signs that he had been tortured.

Sasha stretched out his arms. "Have you ever been to the south?"

Steopa shook his head.

"I went to Missouri once," Vincent said.

"Some of the vampires down there are insane," Sasha said. "I think it was all the revolutions."

"What revolutions?" Vincent asked.

"South America," Steopa said.

"Oh."

Sasha flung his hair back with one hand. "And the hunters are like the ones we just dealt with. Fanatics. At least in the countries where the Church is strong."

Rebecka leaned over and kissed Steopa on the cheek.

"John looks well," Steopa said.

"He feels good. I'm going to hang out with him in the booth for a while."

Steopa motioned her closer and kissed her again. She smiled, then headed off to the DJ booth. Vincent moved over. Steopa looked up. Verina stood by their table.

"May I?" she asked.

Steopa nodded. Verina sat down next to Vincent. She smiled, showing her fangs. "So he's gone. Good."

She held her hand out to Sasha. "Verina."

"Sasha," Sasha said taking her hand.

Verina leaned forward. "I got an interesting phone call tonight from my friend Sonja. Her club was shut down."

Steopa shared a glance with Sasha. "A vampire club?" Steopa asked.

Verina nodded. "Like this place, but all the vampires meet downstairs. Sonja didn't even realize there were new vampires in town."

"Where was this?" Vincent asked.

"Kiel, Germany. Sonja got away, but some of the younger ones did not."

"Are you expecting trouble?" Sasha asked.

Verina gave him a strange look. "News travels very fast. Especially now-a-days. You killed Simon and suddenly Adelind becomes nervous. When Adelind gets nervous, she lashes out."

"Christ! Steopa, who else did you piss off in the past?" Vincent asked, then laughed.

"It's not a laughing matter, Vincent." Verina gave Vincent a stare. "Adelind is stubborn, pig-headed, and violent."

"That sounds like someone we know."

Rebecka came back to the table. She took Steopa's hand. "Come on. John is about to play a song we can dance too."

"Dance?" Steopa asked. He motioned to the crowd in the club. "They do not look like the type to enjoy a waltz."

The music started. The drum hammered out a polka beat. No brass instruments; electric guitars had taken their place. The droning sound of an accordion and fiddle cut over the modern instruments.

Steopa smiled. "Polka?"

Rebecka nodded.

He slid out of the booth and took Rebecka's hand. They walked to the middle of the dance floor. She placed one of her hands on his hip. With the other she took his hand. Steopa nodded to Rebecka. He led her across the dance floor. The other dancers, if they tried to polka, attempted the simplest step they could do. Steopa and Rebecka kept up with the beats, with a different step.

It had been the one that Steopa had learned when he had gone to University. Perfect for the fast beats that echoed out of the speakers around the club. They danced close to the slam dancers; some moved out of their way. The song changed. It still had the same beat, but sounded closer to the music that they played in the club most of the time. The traditional instruments had been replaced by synthesizers.

He changed direction. Rebecka kept up with him. He picked her up and spun around with her. The other dancers on the floor moved further away. They were alone on the dance floor. The music ended with a flourish of drums and fiddle. A few people applauded. Rebecka patted Steopa's chest. He took her hand, and bowed.

"You could have killed someone," Verina said, then she laughed.

Steopa let Rebecka slide into the booth first.

"You are lucky that you don't have to breathe," Vincent said.

Rebecka nodded. "Or sweat."

Misha came over to the table. "I think I will leave, too. I have left my home for too long."

"What about your mother?" Steopa asked.

"I might be able to find her from Moscow."

"Could you get me closer to the Gulf of Finland?" Sasha asked.

"I could, but why?"

"I know that was the place I saw. I could help you look."

Steopa put his arm around Rebecka. "We should leave soon. There is a lot to do at home."

"Steopa," Verina said. "Did Adelind say anything to you when you saw her?"

"She told me to kill Rebecka."

"Doesn't surprise me. She killed the one she was linked with."

"How the hell could she do that?" Vincent asked.

"I do not know; that is what she says."

Steopa slammed his fist on the table. Glassware shook, drinks spilled. "I am sick of rumors and stories."

Rebecka nodded. "Like I said, vampires gossip worse than old women."

Verina smiled, then giggled. "Rebecka, you're right. We are horrible."

"One of these days I will end these rumors about me," Steopa said. "I am thinking that the vampires from Europe talk big, but do not want to face any of us."

Verina shook her head. "Careful-"

"Why? Why should I be the one that is careful? They come here and roust me. Next time I will not be so forgiving." Steopa sat back.

Misha and Sasha exchanged looks. Rebecka squeezed his hand. "Neither of us will be."

Steopa nodded. "Good."

Jimmy came back to the table. He glanced over his shoulder and waved to someone. "Vince, can I have that apartment tonight?"

"Why?"

Jimmy motioned with his thumb. A young woman sipped her drink at his table. Vincent grinned.

"Sure. Don't make it a habit," he said.

Sasha slapped Jimmy on his back. "Don't drain her."

Steopa stood. "Jimmy, we will have to find you your own hunting area soon."

"He can use the 'keller." Vincent said.

"Are you sure?"

"At least for a while."

Jimmy grinned. Vincent pulled a key off a large ring and threw it at Jimmy. Jimmy caught it and hurried back to the table.

Sasha gave Steopa a one-armed hug. "As soon as I find out more about mother I will contact you."

"Can you get a hold of a cell phone?" Rebecka asked.

"There are other ways."

"Grandfather," Misha said, holding out his hand.

"Another time," Steopa said, shaking Misha's hand.

Misha turned to Rebecka. "I cannot wait for mother to meet you."

He hugged Rebecka. Rebecka gave Steopa a strange look as Misha embraced her.

"You are always welcome at my house," Misha said. He put on his hat and walked out with Sasha.

"Wow," Rebecka said.

Vincent chuckled. "Simon was an idiot. You have a frickin' army with all those descendants."

"And that is probably why they were after you," Verina said. "Take out the competition."

Steopa pulled Rebecka closer. He kissed the side of her neck. "They may have more to worry about." he whispered.

Rebecka giggled.

"You two want some privacy?" Vincent asked. He snickered.

"I think we will retire," Steopa said.

Rebecka stood up and pulled Steopa's hand to her chest. "Can you say bye to John and Lorelei for me?" she asked Vincent.

"Yeah, you kids have fun." He waved them away.

Verina shook her head, but giggled.

Steopa wrapped his arm around Rebecka's waist. They left the club. When they had made it up to the street, Rebecka sighed.

"What is it?"

"Our lair, it's under tons of rubble."

"There are other ways to get inside."

"I know, but all that concrete..."

Steopa pulled her closer. "It will be very private."

Rebecka smiled. "And quiet now."

Steopa chuckled. "Very quiet."

An hour later, after stopping so Rebecka could feed, she and Steopa stood across the street from the destroyed parking garage. Steopa shook his head. The building had fallen down like pancakes thrown on a plate. The smell of explosives hung in the air. Yellow caution tape surrounded the debris. A backhoe and a grater had been brought in, but it looked as if nothing had been done.

Rebecka wiped the blood from her chin. “It's completely buried. How many people were killed?”

“I do not know.”

Rebecka pulled out her cell phone. She tapped the screen, then shook her head. “Three. Those hunters deserved what they got, killing innocent people.”

Steopa started to walk toward the factory. “They would say the same about us.”

“We don't kill just anyone. At least most of us don't...”

“We should not. But when food is hard to find...”

Rebecka smiled and took Steopa's hand. “Sometimes it's a good thing.”

“Some people would be angry.”

Rebecka shook her head. “I was, remember? If I hadn't had such a bad night, you would have ignored me.”

“It was a dark shroud around you.”

Rebecka bit her lower lip. “I was messed up. But not as messed up as Simon.”

“It was not Simon's fault,” he said. “When you are a drudge you can lose who you really are. He fought her. Couldn't you tell?”

“I was too busy losing blood.” Her phone beeped. Rebecka looked at the screen. “Baldman?”

She held the screen up and read the text as it scrolled passed. “Baldman has a photo. Simon with two other people. A woman and a man with glasses. Here.” She handed the phone to Steopa.

The black and white grainy photo showed Simon in mid-step on a brick-lined street. On one side of him stood Adelind, her hands on his shoulders. Behind them was the smaller vampire.

“Where did he find this?” Steopa asked.

“Its from a surveillance camera. Kiel, Germany. I don't want to ask how he got it.” Rebecka touched the screen and put the phone back in her pocket.

“Again, Kiel, Germany.”

“That has to be where Adelind is working from,” she squeezed his side. “That's where the child trafficking was being investigated.”

"She is killing those children."
"I know, and just for that I would like to rip her head off."
"I think she has my daughter."
Rebecka stopped. "Are you sure?"
"No, it is only a feeling."
"Well, I trust your feelings more than I trust some people's facts."
Steopa kissed her forehead. "How long have you known Baldman?"
"About ten years. He was one of the first hackers I ever met. Why?"
"He never told you about me?"
"No, he never said anything."
"What about his past?
Rebecka shook her head. "First rule when you get a hacker like him on your side, don't ask about their past."
"Did he find out about you?"
"I am pretty sure he did. He alerted me about my mother looking for me, about a year before you... we..."
"Before I kissed you."
She smiled. "I like that, 'kissed.' A painful kiss."
Steopa kissed her neck, where he had bitten her. Rebecka pulled his head closer. He ran the tip of his fang along her neck. Then he pulled away and smiled.
"Are you wearing perfume?"
"No."
"I thought I smelled... never mind."
Their walk through the factory did not seem to take as long as when they had left. Steopa snapped his fingers as he entered their vault. The candles flamed.
Rebecka laid her backpack on the couch. "It doesn't look like we got any damage."
Steopa hung up his coat and his sword. "These rooms survived the first explosion."
Rebecka slid her arms around his waist. "I heard you and Perun talking. Was he joking?"
"He jokes about many things."
"But what he did to us?"
"I do not think so."

“I was wondering, because I do not feel any different.”

“Me neither.” Steopa turned and lifted her chin. He kissed her.

She pulled away. “It's still early.”

“I know.” He pointed to her desk. “Do you want to practice some Russian tonight?”

“Can you give my tongue a rest?” Rebecka asked, then she laughed. “That sounded bad.”

“Fencing?”

Rebecka shook her head. She unbuttoned her blouse. “I better take this off, I need to hang it up.”

She took off her shirt and turned to enter their bedroom. Steopa stopped her.

“You did not get that bra at the shop.” Steopa reached over and ran his finger down the white lace.

“Andi's. Can you believe I can fit into hers?” Rebecka stuck her chest out. “Although it is a little tight. I am so glad I don't have to breathe.”

Steopa curled his finger under her strap. He pulled it off her shoulder. Rebecka reached behind her and undid the clasps. She let the bra fall to the ground. He ran his finger between her breasts.

“No scar,” he said.

Rebecka took his hand. “I'm fine.”

She moved closer to him and wrapped her arms around his waist. “I feel like laying down.”

He kissed her forehead, then her lips. “I will be in.”

Rebecka nodded. Steopa removed his shoes, made sure the old entrance had been secured, then went into the bedroom. Rebecka laid down on the cover of their bed, nude. She did not look up from her book.

Steopa leaned against the doorway. “You look beautiful.”

The candlelight flickered, casting shadows against the walls and her skin. She laid on her side, her hips curved gently into her waist. Her curls had fallen around her face and down her back. She glanced at him, then patted his pillow.

“When I was alive, a woman like you would have been highly desired. Rubens would have painted you,” Steopa said. He wrapped his long fingers around the bed post.

She looked up from her book. “What?”

“You look beautiful.”

She cast her eyes down. “I haven't done anything special.”

He sat down next to her. “There is no need.”

Rebecka smiled. She studied his face for a moment. “I like that. I like how the candles make your eyes twinkle.”

She brushed his hair away from his face. He leaned closer. He smelled primroses again. She kissed his cheek, then his lips. Steopa slipped his hand under her breasts. He felt her hands undo the buttons on his shirt. He leaned back. She put the book on the nightstand.

He turned his back to her and removed his shirt. Rebecka wrapped her arms around his neck. He felt his hair wrap around her waist. She kissed his shoulder, then she ran her fingers down the scars on his back.

“Do you ever wish these would disappear?”

Steopa shook his head. “No.”

“Why?”

“Because I got my revenge.”

She pulled his hair away from his neck and kissed it. Steopa closed his eyes. Whatever Perun thought he had done to them had not worked. Below his waist, his body had no reaction to Rebecka's kisses.

“What type of revenge?” she moved her lips down to his chest.

“Years later I ran into that commanding officer, the one that had ordered my whipping. He was a drunk, living in a cheap hotel paid for by his family. He invited me up to his room for a drink.” Steopa chuckled. “He was drunk, and he told me he wanted the young woman that worked downstairs.”

“What did you do?” Rebecka asked.

“I convinced her to come upstairs. I drank her dry, then used his knife and slit her throat. I left, calling for the police. They did not believe his story that a vampire had killed that girl.”

“Were you hungry?”

Steopa shook his head. “But he hung for her murder. And I laughed when I saw his body hanging from the gallows.”

“Cruel,” she said. She kissed the other side of his neck, sliding her fangs slid along his skin. From the back of his throat, a soft growl rose. Rebecka pulled away.

He leaned back. “What is it?”

“Why is it important for Perun and that thing that we have sex?”

“I have thought the same thing.”

“They should stay out of it. I mean, we have been very physical”

Steopa laid back, pulling her down with him. She rolled on her side so she could look down at him.

“I have enjoyed it. So why spoil it?”

“Perun thinks like that.” Steopa ran his fingers through her hair.

“It's not that I wouldn't want to have your children.” Rebecka reached down and cupped his testicles. “But until-”

Steopa shrugged. He felt a warmth along his groin matching that of her hand. “You are right.”

Rebecka curled her body along his. “Besides we have a long time to figure it out.”

Steopa nodded. The smell of primroses faded.

CHAPTER 22

Weeks passed. During the day, while in the stupor, Steopa could hear the heavy equipment moving the rubble. A few nights before, he had opened the entrance. On the other side of the vault door, dust and concrete filled the passageway.

The power line that Rebecka used had survived the explosion. She spent a few days reconnecting cables. Then she spent her time looking for any information on Simon or Adelind on the computer. Everything pointed to Kiel, Germany. She had asked Steopa if they could take a trip. He did not want to leave the lair in its current condition.

He spent most of the weeks exploring the upper parts of the base to find a closer exit. He had to re-familiarize himself with the layout of the upper floors. He refused to let Rebecka help him. The lower levels had to remain closed and he did not want her to wander into the past.

This night, he pulled a pile of debris away from a wooden door. Water had found its way down and peeled away the paneling. Steopa opened the door. The hinges broke. He let it fall to the floor.

The room on the other side of the doorway had a long table sitting in the middle. Around it, hard wooden chairs had been toppled and thrown. On top of the table laid a shoe.

The shoe, a modern high-top, looked out of place in a room that had not been open since the late 1960s. A ventilation shaft broke through the ceiling tiles and snapped in two. The shoe laid on its side, underneath the break. Someone had cut themselves on the jagged edges of the shaft. Steopa could smell the blood. It smelled old, perhaps a year or more.

Steopa pushed the table aside and peered inside the air vent. The duct opened up into a larger area. He pulled the duct away from the ceiling. The old tiles broke apart as he forced the sheet metal to the floor. The duct fell, leaving a larger area open in the ceiling.

He jumped into the exposed area. Another tunnel. He squeezed his frame through the opening. A large grate laid on the floor. A sign warned him that authorized personal were only allowed here. Steopa scoffed.

He had to lower his head. The tunnel had not been made to walk inside. Tracks ran along the floor. He came to an end. The opening led to a utility tunnel. One end of the tunnel ended in a brick wall; the other side continued away from the lair. Steopa followed it.

This tunnel avoided most of the destruction that the rest of the base had suffered. A large pipe jutted out from the floor, turned at a right angle and then went into the wall. He shook the pipe. One end of it came away from the wall. He kicked it. The pipe snapped, then tumbled to the floor.

He continued on until he came to a door. The steel door had rivets along the side. Steopa turned the handle. The rust broke off in large pieces onto the ground. He pushed the door open.

The tunnel continued. As he shut the door, he noticed someone had written in magic marker on the other side. "Floor bad, not safe."

The air smelled fresher here. He could also smell marble. He followed his nose. This plain corridor smelled damp, but not moldy. The gray concrete blocks had cracks and large chunks missing from the walls. He came to another door, but this one had been removed.

Garbage was strewn around the floor of a concrete basement, but there were no smells or other signs that this room had been used by anyone recently. A breeze hit Steopa's cheek. A ground-level window had been busted, but it was not large enough for someone to climb through the frame.

A set of metal stairs rose along one wall. He climbed the stairs. Every step caused the frame to shake. He lightened his body and continued. The door at the top had an old electric lock on it. He hooked his claws around the rusted metal and crushed the lock.

He opened the door. A large sign, hanging on its side, blocked the main entrance. The words Deerbow First National Bank had faded on the wood. The carved wood counters had been destroyed. Enough of the counters remained that Steopa could see the detail that had been worked into the wood. One of them had been set on fire in the past; half of it had fallen into ash and charcoal. The marble had survived any attempts to vandalize it. A compass inlay on the floor could be seen under a layer of dirt.

A chain wound through the front door handles; a heavy padlock was rusted to the iron. The decayed plywood peeled off the window frames. Steopa walked around the counters and into the teller area. The windows of the drive-through were boarded up, but someone had moved a section of the plywood. Steopa squatted down and looked. He smiled.

He returned to his lair.

“I found a new entrance,” he said.

“Where?” Rebecka asked.

“The Deerbow National Bank.”

“Not the original building?” She closed her laptop. “I've always wanted to see inside.”

Steopa held out his hand. “Let's find out.”

When they entered the main part of the bank. Rebecka craned her neck. “Wow. Look up there, the wood hasn't been touched.”

Carved reliefs of Greek figures looked down at him. He chuckled. “It looks like a temple.”

“It's prettier than the parking garage entrance,” Rebecka said. “But it's in Port Slue.”

“Hunting will not be good here.”

“I don't think anyone actually lives in this part of town,” She said.

“No, it is all businesses.”

“Yeah, the ones that can't afford downtown. My second to last shrink had her office down here. The one that put me on the lithium.” Rebecka giggled. “Want to stop by her office?”

Steopa shook his head. “The Scottish Fest starts tonight.”

Rebecka checked her cell phone. “Oh, by this time most of the whiskey would have been drunk.”

Steopa put his arm around Rebecka's waist. “Do you want to find food for the night?”

“You're better.”

Steopa chuckled. He pushed the boards back with his free hand. Rebecka ducked underneath. He joined Rebecka in the old parking lot. The hairs on the back of his neck stood up.

He sniffed and could not smell anything, but his fingernails grew into claws. His whole body tensed to fight. He glanced at Rebecka. She looked over her shoulder.

“What is that?” Rebecka whispered.

He turned. A light blue glow reflected off the bank's wall. The ground between the two buildings lit up like a campfire burning. A shadow obscured the glow for a moment, then a legion stood. Around his feet the blue light faded. The legion opened his red eyes. He roared.

Steopa shoved Rebecka aside and braced himself. The monster hit him like a linebacker. The legion shoved Steopa toward the drive-through window. The heels of his boots made furrows in the dirt of the parking lot. He changed his grip and got his hands around the legion's neck and head-butted him.

The legion stepped back. Steopa glanced around. He saw two more appear from between the buildings. A female legion jumped and landed close to Rebecka. She raised her hands and blocked a kick from the female legion.

The legion's fist connected with Steopa's face. Steopa rolled with the punch and brought his fist up. He slammed his fist into the legion's chin. The legion returned the blow. Steopa felt a sharp pain in his neck that traveled down his back.

He clawed at the legion's neck. He could not cut through the legion's skin. Steopa lowered one shoulder and changed his grip. He lifted the legion up and swung him over his shoulder. Steopa slammed the monster down on the ground.

A red string flew past Steopa's head. He saw Rebecka whip her hand. A strand of blood flowed from a cut in her palm. She moved her hand and the blood whipped across the female legion's face. It slashed open her cheek.

Steopa raised his foot to smash the monster's head. The legion grabbed his foot and threw Steopa. Steopa hit the pavement. Car alarms sounded down the street. The female legion's head rolled past Steopa. Rebecka screamed and jumped on Steopa's attacker before he could move. Steopa got to his feet.

Rebecka had a length of what looked like red wire in her hands. She slung it around the legion's neck and tightened it. He raised his fist to strike her. Steopa stopped the legion's fist with one hand and with the other struck the side of his head. Rebecka grunted. Her muscles had tensed as she tightened the bloody wire. The wire sliced through the legion's neck. Steopa kicked the head away.

She flicked her hand and the blood went into her body. The ring glowed green on her hand. She pointed behind Steopa.

The last legion lunged. Steopa tackled him and knocked the legion to the ground. They rolled. Steopa made the legion roll toward a pile of building debris. He reached out and grasped a wooden fence post. He rolled away, turning the post in his hands.

He planted one end of the post against his boot. The other end he held out pointed toward the legion. The legion attacked. It rushed Steopa and impaled itself on the post. Steopa lifted the legion on the post, making the body slide down the wood.

Rebecka limped over and bit her hand. Her blood dripped in a long stream. She wrapped it around the legion's neck and pulled. His head came off by falling to one side. Steopa picked it up and studied the legion's features.

"Ugly," he said.

Rebecka pulled the blood back into her body. She pointed to the space between the two buildings. "Look at the ground."

Steopa walked over to the small open space. On the ground, blue letters faded. He could not make out what type of letters they were.

"They almost look like runes," Rebecka said.

"No, they are not."

"Another seal?"

Steopa nodded. The letters faded into blackness. Steopa stood. He ran the toe of his boot over the ground, where the letters had been. "We should speak to Ogden."

Rebecka nodded. "He would know."

CHAPTER 23

Less than an hour later Ogden knelt in the parking lot. He waved his hand over the area where the writing had been. It glowed orange for a brief moment. Ogden stood up and ran the tip of his cane over the dirt. "How many legions?"

"Three," Steopa said.

"How are they amassing so many?" Ogden asked. "To control more than six drudges is nearly impossible, but to send legion after legion..."

Ogden shook his head and made a tsk noise. "They are using unstable magic; if it is the spell I think they are using. Even if you had not dispatched those legions, they would have destroyed themselves."

"What do you mean?" Steopa asked.

"I have not heard them called legions before. But they are basically cannon fodder. Sent out to clear the path before the main attack."

"How the hell do you know that?" Rebecka asked.

"I have a lot of books. The use of children is new. The spell calls for corpses."

"Wait, is this some sort of zombie?"

"If you mean the Haitian spell, no. But that is the closest explanation." Ogden squatted down and studied the ground. "There has to be more than one vampire in control. How did you dispose of the bodies?"

Steopa pointed to the top of the bank. "Their heads are there. Their bodies are a few blocks away."

"Good." Ogden nodded. He pointed to the area the seal had been. "That is not good, but there is one bright spot. The magic used here was short-lived. Those were scouts. I think it was luck that you ran into each other."

"Are you certain?" Steopa asked.

"Right now, they are looking. The placement of this target, in this secluded spot, was to hide their arrival. But if they did know where you were, they could have had this seal appear where you rest. Is this the work of Adelind?"

"We have a photo," Rebecka said, "that my friend found. Simon with Adelind and one other."

"Can I see?" Ogden asked.

"I have met Adelind and seen the other vampire," Steopa said.

Rebecka showed him the photo. Odgen nodded. "Yes, that is her. She killed the one that made her, about twenty years ago. Soon after she came to me asking me to show her magic. I refused."

"Why?" Steopa asked.

"She had killed the one she had been linked to, do you think I would take that risk? She must have found a teacher."

"Wait," Rebecka waved her hand. "She killed the one that had linked with her? How could she do that?"

"You and Steopa are different. You don't hate him."

"Because he attacked me?" Rebecka took Steopa's hand. "He was hungry. And Vincent told me I was safe."

"That is the difference. You had Vincent helping you. Imagine what it would have been like if Vincent had not pushed you in the right direction."

Rebecka turned her head away. "She must have felt as if it had been forced upon her."

Steopa wrapped his arm around Rebecka. "But why would she attack me, my family, and the coiree?"

"And-" Rebecka started, but then she bit her lip.

Ogden raised his eyebrow. "And?"

Steopa's shoulders sagged. "The base."

"Base?" Ogden asked. "You mean the stories about it are true?"

Steopa nodded. "I was a... guest."

Ogden leaned on his cane. He rubbed his chin. "What sort of experiments did they do to you?"

"Many different ones."

"Be direct with me, Steopa. If that base and the coiree are related-"

"I do not think they are."

"If you know of anything-"

"Wait!" Rebecka held up her hand. "They experimented on Steopa, do you think they would have told him why, or even the truth?"

Ogden nodded. "I see your point, but should the base and the coiree be connected?"

"I do not know." Steopa closed his eyes. "But there is someone that might know, but her mind is gone."

"Dorn?" Rebecka asked.

Steopa nodded. He opened his eyes. "This time at night she would be at Riverside Park."

"Why Dorn?"

"I told you she was the commander there."

Rebecka shook her head. "But she is senile."

"No, I did that to her."

"You did what to her?" Ogden asked.

"I told her to forget." Steopa shrugged. "I was too forceful. Maybe you can talk to her?"

Ogden gave Steopa a strange look. "Depends on what you did to her." He pointed to the street. "Manas is waiting, come."

Rebecka pulled Steopa closer as they followed Ogden to the street. Manas started the Bentley. After they got in, Ogden told Manas where to go.

"Tell me about Dorn," Ogden said.

"She was the commander," Steopa said. "When we left, we took her with us, to ensure we could leave."

"She was your hostage?"

"Yes."

"Why did you need a hostage?"

Steopa shifted in his seat. "They had been ordered to destroy the specimens. She had all the security codes. It made our escape easier."

"How did they trap you?"

"I will not discuss it."

Ogden sat back in his seat. "Fair enough."

Steopa looked out the window as they rolled through the city. Rebecka laid her head on his shoulder.

"I never heard of that cup until we dug it up," Steopa said. "And what they were studying in the base was not magic. If they are related, I cannot see the connection."

"I do know that the coiree is for our kind. I doubt humans could use its full potential. I doubt we have," Ogden said. "It has healed some of us. But what else can it do?"

Steopa shrugged. Manas turned onto the road that followed Riverside Park.

"The homeless gather at the band shell," Steopa said.

Ogden gave Steopa a stony look. "Have you hunted here before?"

"No, this is your territory."

"Then how do you know?"

Steopa pointed to a side road. "There."

Manas turned down the road.

"There are times I have to check on her," Steopa said. "Park near the picnic shelter."

Manas stopped the car. Steopa got out and held the door for Rebecka. One of the homeless men walked closer to the shelter. He paused, then turned and ran. Steopa growled. He ran after the man. A moment later he grabbed the man by his arm.

"Where is Dorn?" Steopa growled.

The man pointed.

"Why did you run?"

"I thought you were one of the monsters."

Rebecka and Ogden caught up with Steopa. The man's eyes darted between the three.

"Monsters?" Rebecka asked.

"They are as big as him." the man pointed to Steopa.

"Legions." Steopa let go of the man. "We have to find Dorn."

She wasn't far. Steopa saw her laying on the ground in front of the band shell. Her clothing had been bundled around her. Steopa walked up to Dorn. He hit her foot with his.

"Dorn."

She woke up and sat up, shaking her head. "Radovitch, what do you want?"

"Radovitch?" Ogden asked.

Steopa rolled his eyes. "Dorn, I want you to talk to this man."

She shook her mass of gray hair. "Does he have clearance?"

Ogden held out his hand. "I am Sir Ogden Phelps, Captain of Her Majesty's Army."

Dorn looked at his hand, then placed her grimy hand in his. "I am sure that will do."

"He wants to talk to you about the base," Steopa said.

"Does Britain want our assistance?" Dorn asked.

Ogden helped Dorn stand. “Yes, we are curious about an item call the coiree, have you heard of it?”

“We don't deal with the artifacts at our base, only the specimens.”

“How many vampires do you have?”

“Two. No, wait, now three.”

Ogden glanced at Steopa.

“The ghoul had been killed,” Steopa said.

Rebecka looked over her shoulder. She motioned to Steopa that she wanted to see something. He turned his attention to Ogden and Dorn.

“That's right, only two now.”

“This object is related to the vampires. Are you sure you have not heard of it?” Ogden asked.

Dorn looked at Steopa for a long time. “But I ordered your destruction. What are you doing here?”

“Answer his questions.” Steopa saw Rebecka walk behind a building.

Dorn shook her head. “The rocks fell. They grew out of the ground and blocked us! You did that! You made that troll do it.”

“I did nothing!” Steopa hissed.

Ogden stepped back.

“I did nothing but make sure that we escaped.” Steopa jabbed his finger into Dorn's face. She stepped back and into Ogden.

Ogden patted Dorn's hand. “May I?”

“What?”

Ogden placed his hand against her forehead. Her eyes fluttered. He moved his fingers. “What did you do to her?” Ogden asked Steopa.

“I told her to forget.”

“That's all?”

“Yes.”

“The damage is too great.” Ogden steadied the back of her head with his other hand. “A lot of secrets in that brain.”

Steopa could not see Rebecka.

Ogden sighed. “There is nothing. At least there is nothing about the coiree.”

“So there is no connection,” Steopa said.

“It would seemed to be.” Ogden removed his hands and pulled

out a handkerchief to clean them. Dorn stumbled back and sat down on the ground.

Rebecka came out of the brush next to the river. She ran toward Steopa.

“Legions!” she screamed.

Two barreled out of the woods. One reached out and tried to grab Rebecka. She dove. Ogden raised his cane. A blinding light streamed from the tip. The blue light struck one legion in the face. It screamed and dropped to his knees.

The other grabbed Rebecka. She punched him in his chest. Her hand went into his chest and out of his back. The legion whimpered, then cried. Rebecka rolled. She pulled out her hand. The legion stopped moving.

Ogden held the light on the one that screamed. He walked to the legion. “Steopa, could you take his head off?”

Steopa gripped both sides of the legion's head, then twisted his neck. The legion's head came off. Steopa dropped it on the ground. The light stopped shining from Ogden's cane.

Ogden took the head from Steopa. He studied it. “I think an autopsy is in order.”

Rebecka wiped the blood from her arm. “You want to cut him up?”

Ogden nodded. “Look at his teeth.”

Ogden turned the head around. He pulled back the legion's lip. At first Steopa did not see anything unusual, except for the extra fangs. Then he saw the teeth were normal, for a child.

“So she is using children,” Steopa said.

Ogden nodded. “Look at the stretch marks on the skin. This poor creature had been grown quickly.”

“That's horrible,” Rebecka said.

“Unnatural.” Ogden turned the legion's face. “If it makes you feel any better, it is possible that the children were already dead.”

“Maybe this is nothing more than petty revenge,” Steopa said. “Remember the children we rescued.”

“They were being sold to her? That is too horrible to think about,” Rebecka said.

“Children?” Ogden asked.

“Rebecka and I interrupted a man selling two children.” Steopa looked down at the legion. “If they made a legion out of a child, would they be easier to control?"

"Yes." Ogden nodded toward his car. "Rebecka, could you ask Manas for my kit, please?"

"You are going to do it here?" Rebecka asked.

"Best place. Otherwise I have to take this corpse home."

Dorn walked up to Steopa. "He is a doctor, too?"

"Yes, madam, I am." Ogden flicked his hand in her direction. Dorn crumpled to the ground and snored.

Ogden lifted the body off the ground. He went over to a picnic table and laid it on the wooden planks. He ripped open the shirt of the legion.

"Could Adelind have done this?" Steopa asked.

Ogden shook his head. "No, the skills to make legions are difficult to learn. The other one in the photograph. The one with the scar. I wonder what his role is."

"Could it be a human assisting them? They are using hunters too."

Ogden scoffed. "No. I studied magic when I was human, but I did not really know how to control it until I changed. Our minds are different. If our brains were still like a human, we would go mad."

"Some of us do."

"Yes." Ogden nodded. "Your grandson, Misha could be one of the most powerful vampires on this planet, but he chooses not to. Do you know why?"

"He is content."

"Yes, he is happy in his home. He told me he rarely leaves, even to hunt. People always have a way of showing up at his door when he needs a meal."

"That is true," Steopa said. "I have seen it."

"Can you understand what that means? It means just by thinking about it, he can influence humans around him. A rare gift. I wonder if the ones that are attacking your family know that."

Steopa placed the legion's head on a permanent charcoal grill. "They should not even know about my family."

"But they do. Which means they know about your other grandson. The one I saw jump out of the water. Aquatic vampires are a myth among our kind and there he is."

"He died at sea," Steopa said.

“And there are some vampires that are repelled by water, holy or not. Yet your grandson has made it his own hunting ground. How many strange gifts does your family have?”

“Strange? Does this matter?”

Ogden pointed at the body. “It matters to the one that is making these abjurations.”

Rebecka came back with a large black bag. Ogden took it from her and opened it. Inside were stainless steel medical tools. He pulled out a large scalpel.

“This will not take too long.”

He made a long incision in the legion's chest.

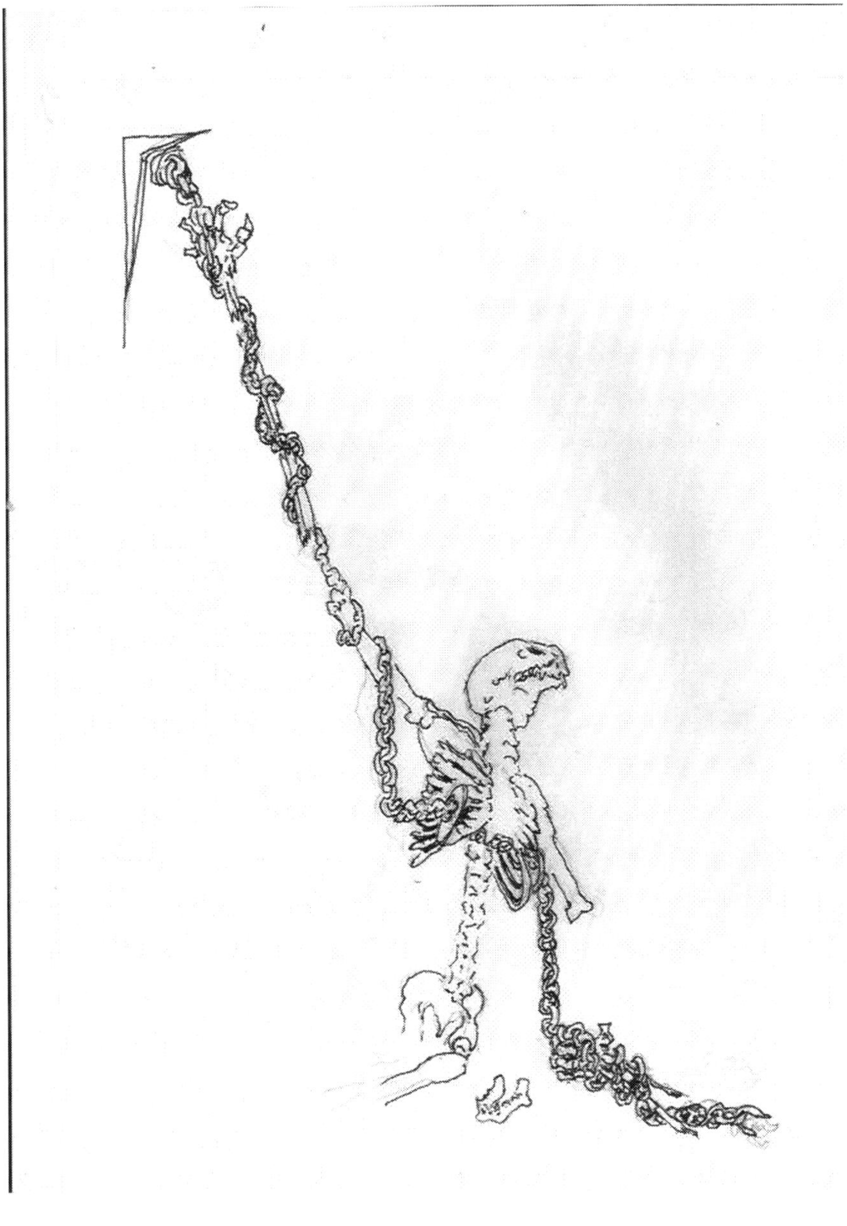

CHAPTER 24

They returned to their lair. Rebecka sat on the couch with her head in her hand, her fingers curled. She shook her head. “Horrible.”

“About the child?”

“Children.” She turned to face him. “Every legion we have destroyed has been a child. What sort of sick mind...”

Steopa sat down next to her. “At least we found out they are not looking for anything in the base.”

“Except for us.”

Her computer beeped. Rebecka sighed. “I suppose it's Baldman.”

She went over to her computer. “What's up?” she said in the microphone.

“Saber. I found something very interesting. Let me get it back up on the screen. There. I am having it translated. Ah, yes.”

“What is it?” Rebecka asked.

“A letter. Let me read it to you.” Baldman coughed. “Yes. Here we go.

"*Simon, you will do what I ask. My vision was not a mistake. We must purify the bloodline. All abnormals will be destroyed. I understand that you* -- I assume she is talking about Simon -- *I understand that you were not created the old way.* Whatever that means.”

Baldman coughed. *“You can be granted favor in the new order. If you do what I ask, I will give you Brighton, England. You must kill all of the Rodovitich spores. They are dhamphirs and must be destroyed. Dhamphirs are not to be trusted. The last time, they betrayed all of us. If we do not destroy the Rodovitches, they will rise to power and control all of us.”*

Steopa scoffed. “Is she insane?”

“Insanity is such a broad term,” Baldman said.

“What about dhamphirs?” Rebecka asked.

“The second part of her letter is full of allusions to them. And a cup."

Steopa went over to the computer and leaned over Rebecka's shoulder. "A cup?"

"Coiree. Interesting it is similar to the word coire, which means valley or hollow."

"What does it say about the coiree?" Rebecka asked.

"Whoever drinks of it will be purified and will have all the power." Baldman shrugged. "Perhaps the grail?"

"Did you find anything else?" Rebecka asked.

"Yes. Another letter. Shorter this time. Yes." He adjusted his glasses. *"Do not destroy Nastenka. We are close to discovering what is in the bloodline. And her blood feeds the legions well."*

Steopa stood up, hit the wall and swore.

"Did I say something..." Baldman grimaced.

"Thank you." Rebecka shut the chat window. "Your daughter?"

"She has my daughter!" Steopa shouted.

Rebecka winced. "Are you sure? It could be another Nastenka..."

"No." Steopa shook his head. "Somehow Adelind has my daughter. She knows about my family because of her. Nastenka has been pushing her sons away. Why? She does not want them to find her. Adelind might use her as bait."

"To finish what Simon tried to do?"

"Yes. That is why she has been sending the legions. To find us. To weaken us."

"Then why have the legions show up at Riverside Park? That's Ogden's territory. She knows we are here; she should have sent more to this spot."

"Unless there is another reason."

Rebecka stood up. "What if she is using the legions to clear the path for her? To make sure there are no vampires that can stand up to her. She is scared of you."

"And you."

Rebecka shook her head. "There is no reason to be."

"You are linked to me and you can take a legion's head off with your blood."

"We know where they are! Let's go and fight them. I don't want to sit here and keep fighting off those mutant freaks," Rebecka said.

"It matters because I have no idea how powerful Adelind is."

"I'm tired of looking over my shoulder."

"I cannot help that."

"Then there is a chance she will go after my brother too."

"Your brother?"

Rebecka growled. "Simon attacked us and took John to keep me in line. She's talking about bloodlines. Who do you think she will go after?"

Steopa put his hands on Rebecka's shoulders. "Do you think that I enjoy having my family marked for death because some fanatic thinks we should be killed?"

Rebecka slammed the lid to her laptop shut. "It's not just your family." She pointed to the door. "It's me. It's the other vampires in this town. We are all in danger."

"And it is my fault."

"No."

"How am I supposed to protect all of you?" Steopa nearly shouted.

"I don't know!" Rebecka shouted. "Why is it your responsibility? Why do you have to make it your cross to bear?"

"I did not. That *blyadischa* made it so!" Steopa yelled.

"And we have to stop her." Rebecka's eyes filled with bloody tears. "I don't want to spend the rest of my time with you watching out for crazies."

Steopa lifted her chin with his hand. "I do not want you injured."

She grabbed his hand. "I can fight."

"I will not lose you."

"I'm not weak anymore. You made me strong."

"I will not take that chance."

Rebecka turned away. "Look, I spent most of my human life begging for people to take care of me. I don't want that anymore. I can fight. I can help you take on that nut case."

"I know how strong you are now." He brushed her curls over her shoulder. "But I have seen you get your head cut off, and get staked. And each time it felt like part of me died.

Rebecka's shoulders sank. "It's a risk we have to take. But I will not stay here and just wait. I want this fight to happen on our terms."

Steopa turned her around. He moved his hands down her

shoulders and her arms. “It will never end. It is not in the vampire nature to be peaceful.”

“I don't want to lose you either.” She shook her head. “But I'm sick of hiding.”

Steopa drew Rebecka close to him. “You are right. I would have never been so cautious with a challenge before. I would have hunted Simon down myself.”

A worried look crossed Rebecka's face. “You made me strong; did I make you weak?”

Steopa shook his head. “No. What happened in this place did it.” He motioned with his hand around the lair.

“What happened?” Rebecka asked.

“Not now. When we get rid of Adelind, then I will tell you.”

“You will?”

“Yes.”

“Promise?”

“Yes.”

“Deal.” Rebecka hugged him. She pressed her cheek against his chest. “How do we end it?”

“We call her out. Make her come to us.”

“Blood duel?” Rebecka asked.

Steopa shook his head. “That worked with Vincent, but that is because his challenger liked to work alone. She does not.”

“What could we do?”

“Find her, make her come here. But we choose the place.”

“We? You and I?”

Steopa lifted her chin. “I will call my family back. But first, Nastenka.”

Rebecka nodded. “Yes, let's find her first.”

“Would you like to come to Germany with me?”

“Do I need a passport?”

Steopa chuckled. “Not the way we will go.”

“What about Jimmy? We should talk to him.”

Steopa nodded.

They left the lair and headed down the street from the old bank. The clouds to the west flashed on and off with lightning. Steopa put his arm around Rebecka as thunder rolled in the distance.

“How do you think Jimmy is doing?” Rebecka asked.

“Quite well, I am sure.” Steopa pointed to the street that headed

toward the river. “Do you want to go down there?”
“Might not be too many people out,” Rebecka said.
“We will-” Steopa heard a scream.
“What direction?”
Another scream. Steopa pointed. “That way.”
Steopa ran down the street and cut through an alleyway. Rebecka darted ahead of him. She stopped at an intersection. Steopa caught up with her. She held her arm out to stop him.
“Down there.” She motioned with her head to the bottom of the hill.
A legion raised her arms above her head. She threw a body across the street. Steopa growled. The legion's head snapped in his direction. She hissed. Steopa charged down the street. The legion ran into a dark empty lot.
Steopa followed the legion. A faint blue light glowed on the ground then disappeared. He stood in the middle of the empty lot and growled. Rebecka sat on the ground next to the item the legion had thrown. He snarled.
“What is it?” he asked.
“Another vampire,” she pointed to the headless body. “I don't think I know this one.”
“How can you tell?”
“His head is over there.” Rebecka pointed to a truck.
Steopa found the head laying next to the front wheel. He studied the face, then shook his head. “You are right, I do not know this one either.”
“The legion?”
“Disappeared.” Steopa kicked the vampire's head. It splattered on a nearby wall. He balled his fist.
Rebecka stood. She wiped her hands off on her pants. “She didn't wait long did she?”
Steopa growled. Rebecka placed her hand on his shoulder. “Why go after the others?”
“To scare us.”
“Hold on,” Rebecka closed her eyes and turned her head. “Um, Vincent wants us to come to the 'keller.”
“Why?”
“Swen just killed a legion.”
“First, we take care of this.” He pointed at the body with his

foot. “They are messy killers.”

Steopa picked up the beheaded body. As they passed a smaller tributary that fed into the Deerbow River, Steopa threw the body into the water. Rebecka wiped the back of his coat.

“Blood,” she said.

“Leave it.”

“It will stain.”

Steopa covered his face with his hand and chuckled. “Rebecka, you should be worrying about other things.”

“I am, but I don't want you walking down the street looking like you just rolled in a butcher shop.”

Steopa wrapped his arm around her. “There are sometimes I wish we would have met when I was alive.”

“You would have hated me.”

“I do not think so.”

“I hated myself. What chance did you have? Besides, you would not have noticed me.”

“You think so?” Steopa cupped her cheek in his hand.

“You turn women's heads, did you know that?” Rebecka said. “When we hunt, sometimes women see you.”

“It is the glamor.”

Rebecka shook her head. “No it isn't.”

“I would have approached you.”

“Why?”

Steopa looked down at her chest. Rebecka glanced down. “My tits?”

“Perun is correct, they are nice.”

She zippered up her jacket. “You and Perun are the only ones that ever said anything.”

“I am sure other men have have noticed.”

“Let's go to the Rathskeller, okay?” She walked ahead of Steopa.

Steopa caught up with her. “Did I offend you?”

Rebecka shook her head. “No. It's just I... I have a hard time accepting...” She looked up. “Can we go by the roofs?”

Steopa bowed and motioned to the nearest building. Rebecka climbed up the wall, he followed. She waited for him on the roof.

“What is it?”

“You didn't offend me,” she unzipped her jacket. “You know I have a hard time accepting compliments.”

"I was serious when I said Rubens would have painted you."

She smiled, then she shook her head. She raised her hand to her temple. "Sorry, Vincent is insistent. We have to go."

Halfway to the club, they landed on a roof. Steopa ran across. Something caught his eye. He stopped. He pulled Rebecka back. She gasped.

A vampire had been strapped to a ventilation shaft. His arms and legs spread out over the opening. Only the blackened skeleton remained. The skull's mouth opened with a silent scream, showing the extended fangs. Steopa reached out and touched it with his fingertip. The bones crumbled.

"He was attacked last night," Steopa said.

"The legions?"

"Who else? We have not fought amongst ourselves for as long as I have been in this town."

Rebecka picked a leather bracelet off the ground. She turned it around in her hand. "It burned off. His name was Sal."

"Come on." He took Rebecka's hand.

They made their way to the Rathskeller. Ogden's car sat across the street with a large dent in its hood. Chuck stood by the entrance to the nightclub. Behind him, yellow caution tape had been strung up between the posts.

"Missed the fun," he said. He raised his hand in greeting, then winced.

"You had a legion?" Rebecka asked.

Chuck shook his head. "No, two. Swen's in the freezer right now. I'm turning people away. Be careful when you get down there, Lorelei is beyond pissed."

"Was Jimmy here?"

"Yeah, he's below."

They walked down the ramp. The entrance to the bouncer cage had been turned to kindling. As Steopa stepped over the broken door frame, he heard Ogden speak.

"It's only a sprain. You are lucky."

"That was not a vampire!" Lorelei yelled.

"Yes it was." Ogden looked at Steopa. "Steopa has run into them before. As have I."

Lorelei sat on a bar stool while Ogden wrapped her wrist in a fabric bandage. She glared at Steopa as he walked up to the bar.

"John is by the freezer with Vince," Lorelei said to Rebecka, but she locked her eyes on Steopa. "But you stay here."

Ogden cleared his throat as Rebecka went to the back room.

"The legions attacked here too?" Steopa asked.

"No shit." Lorelei pulled her arm away from Ogden. "They messed with my bar."

"Manas hit one as we were traveling. It jumped out in front of us and tried to break into the car."

Lorelei shoved her finger into Steopa's face. "Your fault."

"What?" Steopa asked.

She blushed. "That night I had my fit, I saw your family hunted. Those things are looking for you."

"They were," Ogden said. "The one that attacked my car was very talkative. They have been told to attack any non-humans in this city."

"Not just vampires?" Steopa asked.

"Apparently, Adelind, or mother as she was called, has expanded her reach." Ogden stood.

"I wonder if she knows what she is up against."

"Vampires, werewolves, and berserks, oh my." Lorelei said. She giggled. "Sorry, I need a drink."

"I am going to check on the bouncer," Ogden said.

Jimmy limped up to Steopa. "Hey."

"They attacked you, too?" Steopa asked.

"Ha!" Lorelei said as she poured herself a double shot. "Jimmy didn't give them a chance."

Jimmy smiled and shrugged. "I jumped from there."

He pointed to the upper balcony. "I got the one that tried to attack Lorelei."

She put down her shot glass. "Then Chuck came from the side. I didn't see what happened."

Jimmy leaned closer to Steopa. "Its body is in the basement. What's left of it, anyway. Chuck threw up."

"Ah."

From the back came the sound of something large thudding against metal. Jimmy cringed.

"What is it?" Steopa asked.

"Swen."

Steopa followed Jimmy into the back room. They walked past

the office and the storeroom to the walk-in freezer and cooler that sat near the back entrance of the club. Vincent sat in a chair in front of the freezer. He leaned back on it, so the handle of the freezer could not be opened.

"I would stay back there if I were you," Vincent said. "Swen's banging on the door."

The door to the freezer bulged. The legs of Vincent's seat scraped forward. Vincent slammed his seat back.

"You okay, buddy?" he yelled.

A muffled roar came from inside the freezer. Something crashed inside. Ogden stepped back, almost stepping on Steopa's toes.

"Will that hold him?" he asked.

"It has before," Vincent said.

John chewed on a new lip ring, then shook his head. "This is the longest I have seen Swen flip out."

"Chuck was awesome." Vincent braced his feet against the floor. "I swear the legion pissed his pants."

"They're children," Rebecka said.

"What are you talking about?" Vincent asked.

"The legions were made from children." Ogden walked over to Vincent. "The one that Steopa and I dispatched earlier tonight still had a baby teeth."

"That's fucked up," John said.

"Its sick," Rebecka said.

The pounding on the door subsided. John raised his walkie. "Swen?"

"You can let me out." Swen's voice cracked from the walkie.

Vincent stood. He shoved the chair away with his foot while he opened the door. Swen walked out, without any shirt or shoes. His long red hair had fallen around his shoulders. The sweat had turned to ice, frosting his beard and hair. He rubbed his tattooed arms.

"Whoa," Swen said.

He reached for the chair, he missed and fell on the floor. John reached to help him. Swen shoved his hand away.

"Give me a minute, Johnny." Swen flung his hair back. Icy droplets of sweat flew across the back room.

"I am tired of this." Steopa turned to John. "Do you have a map of the town?"

"Yeah, in the office."

Steopa followed John to the office. He opened up a large map of the city and laid it across the desk. Steopa pointed to the large green patch on the east side of the city. "Greenwoods."

"That is a cool place to visit."

Steopa glance up from the map. "I will have a war there."

John scoffed. "What?"

"Are you serious?" Ogden asked from the doorway.

Steopa nodded. "She started it, we will finish it. I have to force her out. Or we go to her. But I do not want to leave this city."

Steopa stood and turned to Ogden. "If we can find where she is, could you send me there?"

Rebecka peeked around Ogden. "What?"

"If she wants to hunt my family, fine. If she wants to clean this city, she will have to face all of us. Lorelei is right, part of this is my responsibility. I will use myself as bait."

Rebecka opened her mouth to speak. Ogden held up his hand. She closed her mouth and shook her head.

"I might be able to get a general idea where she had that target seal cast from," Ogden said. "We know she is from Kiel, but is she still operating from there? I do not know if it would be close enough to get to her. And they only last a few moments."

"Sounds like it would be easier to hitch a ride with one of the legions," Vincent said as he slipped past Ogden and into the office.

"We are lucky that she is only using target seals right now. You can only send a few at a time. That is why the groups of legions have been small. But if she finds what she is looking for, she could send an army here in a matter of minutes."

"Are you going tonight?" Rebecka asked. Jimmy peered around her shoulder.

"No. But we will have to time it correctly. It would have to be night there as well," Steopa said.

Ogden leaned on his cane. "I think we better get a plan in order, don't you?"

"Yes."

Vincent closed his eyes and rubbed his temple. "I don't think we will have a chance."

"Why?" Rebecka asked.

"Can't you feel that? Someone has called us."

Ogden closed his eyes. "Yes, Solemn Trees."

Steopa glanced between Vincent and Ogden. “I do not feel any call.”

“Neither do I,” Rebecka said.

“I do,” Jimmy said.

Vincent raised his finger. “Wait.” He rubbed his beard, then sighed. “Because some of the other vampires want to talk about you. Verina is going to the meeting now.”

“Nothing like being the social pariah,” Rebecka said.

“Yes, well,” Ogden said. “This meeting is not proper. Therefore, I think you two should come.”

Steopa slammed his fist against the desk. The wood broke under the blow. John jumped back into the filing cabinet. Steopa growled.

“Enough!” he shouted. “Rebecka and I will go to this meeting as well. She wants us to attack each other.”

No one spoke. Steopa shoved the others away from the door and stormed out of the office.

“Hey!” Vincent yelled. “Don't you want a ride? I mean, we got a Bentley parked outside! You could show up for ass-kicking in style!”

CHAPTER 25

Manas dropped them off a few streets from the cemetery. As they approached the wrought iron gates, Verina waved to them from the graveyard. She leaned against the post smoking a cigarette.

"They are already gathered." Verina pointed her long fingernails toward Steopa. "And some of them want your head."

"If they can reach it," Vincent said.

"Who called it?" Steopa asked.

"The one with the long scar, Rolf."

Steopa shrugged. "I do not know-"

"I do," Ogden said. "Strange, he would call a meeting."

"What is he like?"

"German, aristocratic, and keeps to himself."

"Aristocratic?" Steopa growled. "It is a wonder we have not crossed paths before."

"Should we go in with you?" Rebecka asked Ogden.

Ogden nodded. "Normally, I would speak against it. But the four of us have another issue to worry about. We have to make sure nothing happens to each other."

Steopa took Rebecka's hand. "Whatever happens-"

"Don't talk that way," she said.

"The others are waiting," Verina said. She snuffed the cigarette out with the heel of her boot.

They walked across the grounds of the old cemetery. Rebecka squeezed Steopa's hand and leaned closer to him. "Have you ever done this?"

Steopa nodded.

"What happened?"

"All the vampires in Saint Petersburg gathered to decide what to do with the elder that had gone insane. She was dismembered."

Rebecka pulled herself closer to Steopa. He heard her sniff.

Vincent glanced back. "Don't worry, Rebecka, they have to get to him first."

"They didn't invite me either. We are both for the chop."

"No, the message didn't get to you because you two are linked."

Verina scoffed. "You are a horrible liar, Vincent."

Rebecka looked down, she wiped something from her face.

"I am sorry," Steopa said.

She shook her head. "Don't apologize for them. They want to get both of us, fine. They'd better do a good job."

Five vampires stood in the small valley of Solemn Trees Cemetery. On the ground between them, a large ax and two large knives were stuck into the dirt. As they approached, a few turned to look. Jeremiah hurried down from the other side of the valley.

A slender, lanky vampire pointed in their direction. "What is he doing here?" he asked, storming over to Steopa.

"You know how it is," Vincent said with a shrug. "You try to keep something a secret from someone, they find out and they insist that they have to come with you."

"He shouldn't be here." The lanky vampire unraveled a length of chain that he had wrapped around his waist. He raised it.

Jeremiah plowed into him with his shoulder. "Back off, man."

"You siding with him?"

"Dude, I don't even know why we are here," Jeremiah said. "Until I find out, you ain't touching him."

"You couldn't-"

Jeremiah raised his fist, the point of the white blade-like bone extended. "Try me. Step away!"

Ogden touched the lanky vampire's shoulder. "Excuse me, mister?"

"Jackal."

Vincent cracked up, laughing like a psychotic. "Sorry, but Jackal?"

Jackal lunged at Vincent. Vincent raised his hands, blue flames shot out of his palms. "You want to be crispy?"

"Shut up!" a voice echoed from the valley.

A dark-haired vampire had shouted. Steopa recognized him. During Vincent's duel, this had been the vampire that came with Ogden. The *schmiss* that ran from his right eye to his chin and the scar under his left eye gave him a face that was hard to forget.

"Ogden, why did you bring them?" the dark-haired vampire asked.

"Personal reasons, Rolf." Ogden walked closer. "You should have come to me about any issues you had. We could have avoided all of this."

"Then you know?" Rolf locked his eyes with Steopa's. "I want to know why we are targeted."

A thin, young-looking female vampire came closer, holding her hands to her face. "They killed Sal last night. They tried to kill me. The sun came..." She turned her head away.

Rebecka moved toward the younger vampire. Her arms outstretched like she wanted to comfort her. The tall, elegant black vampire stopped Rebecka. "And what about you?"

"What about me?" Rebecka asked.

"Are you his drudge or what?"

Rebecka balled her fist. Verina pulled her back, whispering in her ear. Rebecka lowered her fist, but did not take her eyes off the black vampire.

"Why have you put us in danger?" Rolf asked. "Since you are here, you can defend yourself if you want."

Steopa came closer to the semi-circle. He never took his eyes off Rolf. "If I want? You assume that I agree with this." He turned. "Some of you know me. My name is Steopa, for those who do not. Yes, all of you are in danger, because a vampire from the old world wants me dead."

"So why attack us?" the black vampire asked. "Two large vampires came to my territory last night. I was able to avoid them."

"Those were her legions."

The thin vampire shuddered. Jackal scoffed. "Those drudges? I vote we kill him now."

"You may try," Steopa said. "But they are not normal drudges."

"Steopa is right, the one who sent them uses magic," Ogden said. "Legions are harder to kill."

Jackal hissed. "Magic too. Now you are pulling my leg. Kill him!"

Rolf raised his hand. "Jackal, we are here to decide if that is the best course of action."

"I don't know what the problem is," Vincent said. "It's not like vampires with grudges haven't shown up, hell, I would be worried if they didn't."

“What is different is that four of us are dead now, because the vampire with the grudge is after us now.”

“Not just us,” Ogden said. “All non-humans are targeted now.”

“So?” Jackal scoffed. “Why should we care if they take out a few dogs?”

“Because there are some things in this city that would be very upset if they were attacked,” Steopa said.

“And now you are an expert on this city?” the black vampire said. “I have been here for a century.”

“Big deal,” Vincent said. “Besides, I don't see you around the city much, maybe you don't know what is here?”

“You only sulk in that nightclub.”

“No reason to leave.”

Mak appeared out of the shadows. His sudden appearance made Rolf jump. Steopa smirked. Mak walked passed Jeremiah and gave him a small nod.

“I have been here since before this was a city. And I know nothing of the vampires from the old world,” he said, walking up to Rolf. “But I have talked to her legions. She might be only after Steopa now, but she will not stop with us, or the others.”

“How do you know?” Rolf asked.

“I talked to her legions. I stay in Greenwoods with Jeremiah and another. She uses the poorhouses as a base.”

“Why didn't you stop her?” Jackal asked.

“I am not familiar with her type of magic.”

Rolf looked at Ogden.

“I told you, you should have come to me,” Ogden said. “The vampire that wants Steopa dead is named Adelind. She heard a rumor and acted on it.”

“I know the one that's hunting Steopa,” Verina said. “She will not stop with his death. She will want all of us to bend our knees to her. She's done it in Kiel.”

“Excuse me, how do you know?” the older female vampire said.

“My friend was attacked. It's like she wants to set herself up as an elder. She uses legions and other vampires to do her work for her.”

“This is not your city. Why should you care?” Rolf asked.

“I like it here.”

“And that is your only reason? You are from Europe. Maybe you are in league with her?"

"Why would I be?" Verina asked.

"Hey, she's not the one on trial here," Vincent said.

"You are right. What are these legions?" Rolf asked.

"She takes children and makes them into those monsters," Rebecka said.

"Impossible!"

The female vampire that looked like a grandmother turned around and started to walk away from the group.

"Where are you going?" Rolf shouted.

She turned. "I am not dealing with this."

"You should stay."

"No." She hurried up the hill.

"You see," Rolf said. "You brought this here."

"Why are you frightened?" Steopa asked. "You complain like a child."

"I am not." Rolf growled. "But why you? What rumor?"

"Yeah," Jackal said moving closer to Rolf.

"Because she is after my family," Steopa said. "She believes a passage in a book."

"What family?" Rolf asked. "The strange vampires that were here in the city earlier?"

"Most of them, yes." Steopa glanced at Jimmy.

Jimmy lowered his hat and looked away.

"What do you do? Hunt them down and bite them?" Jackal asked.

"It is none of your business how it happens."

"Are they dhamphirs?" Rolf asked. "Because if they are, we may have to find them too and-"

Steopa struck him. Rolf stumbled back. Steopa grabbed Rolf's head and pulled him close. "How my family came to be is not your concern. I know she attacks you! I found two corpses tonight! I will call her out and take care of her on my terms. If you want to help, you are welcome to, but if not, stay out of my way!"

Rolf's eyes grew large. Steopa growled, then shoved him away.

"Perhaps you are helping her," Verina said to Rolf. "Both of you are German..."

"That is a slanderous accusation!" Rolf said.

"Now imagine me hunting you because of that." Verina smiled, her fangs glistened. “If you wants these attacks to end. I suggest you listen to Steopa.”

“No kidding. You called everyone here tonight to put Steopa on trial without him here?” Vincent shook his head. “Big mistake.”

“What was to be my punishment?” Steopa asked, pointing at the ax and the knives. “Dismemberment?”

“If you were lucky.” Rolf straightened out his coat.

“I would like a word with Rolf alone,” Ogden said.

Steopa nodded. Ogden motioned to Rolf to follow him. They walked over to a small monument. Steopa watched them. He felt Rebecka slip her hand into his. Rolf argued with Ogden, waving his hands as he talked.

The thin vampire walked up to Steopa. “Is that woman coming here?”

“She will.”

“Why bring her here?”

“What is your name?”

“Leteia.”

“I will make her come here, Leteia. Do not concern yourself.”

“Why do you want to bring her here?” Leteia put her hand over her mouth. “Those legions killed my friend, Sal. I don't know if I could face them again.”

The black vampire's eyes flickered down to Rebecka and Steopa's clasped hands. “Yes, why bring her here?”

“I would rather fight her where I know the layout. Besides,” Steopa pointed in the direction of Greenwoods. “We have the perfect field for battle.”

Rolf returned with Ogden. “Do you think your plan will work? I think it's foolish.”

“You are in no danger. I will go to her. I will force her to show herself here. Perhaps you will be lucky and she will destroy me.”

Rebecka gripped his hand tighter.

“But why Greenwoods?” Rolf asked.

Jeremiah punched the air. “Perfect place.”

Mak nodded.

“Would you rather have her run though the city?” Steopa asked. “We can contain her there.”

“How?”

“I have friends that will help.”

"Who?" Jackal asked.

"Werewolves."

"Werewolves? There are werewolves in Deerbow?"

Vincent shook his head. "Are you a complete idiot? I employ one."

"And don't forget Perun," Jeremiah said, grinning.

"What's a Perun?" Leteia asked.

Rebecka blushed. Steopa stared. He had never seen her or any vampire blush.

Rebecka giggled. "Perun is unique."

"He is a Lord of the Forest," Mak said. "I doubt she has ever met the like of him before."

Steopa smirked. "True. He will be a surprise."

"Then there is Sw-" Jimmy started to say. Vincent clamped his hand over Jimmy's mouth.

"What if you fail?" Rolf asked, turning away from Jimmy.

"Then she is yours to deal with."

"You don't have to worry about the battle," Ogden said. "I will be there. It isn't your concern, even though you have tried to make it so."

"Why is it yours?"

"I have an agreement with Steopa. That is all I will say."

"And she trashed my bar," Vincent said. "I want some payback."

The black vampire flung her scarf over her shoulder. "Then everything looks to be arranged. I hope you succeed." She walked away.

"Whatever," Jackal said. He turned to leave, but then turned back around and raised his middle finger. "Do what ever the hell you want, but stay out of my part of the city."

He jumped into a tree and disappeared into the shadows.

Rolf looked at the group that remained. "I wish you luck, but only because I do not want to clean up your mess. If you can get the other beings in this city to fight with you..."

His body shimmered, then it was gone. Leteia lowered her hand away from her face.

"Can I help?"

"I thought you said you didn't want to face them again," Rebecka said.

"I owe it to Sal."

Steopa nodded. “After I return tomorrow, we will meet and work out the battle.”

“What are you doing tomorrow?” Verina asked.

“I will go see Adelind.”

Ogden spun his cane in his hand. “You realize I can send only one. You will be going alone.”

“But I will not be when I get there,” Steopa said.

“Are you sure?” Rebecka asked.

Steopa nodded.

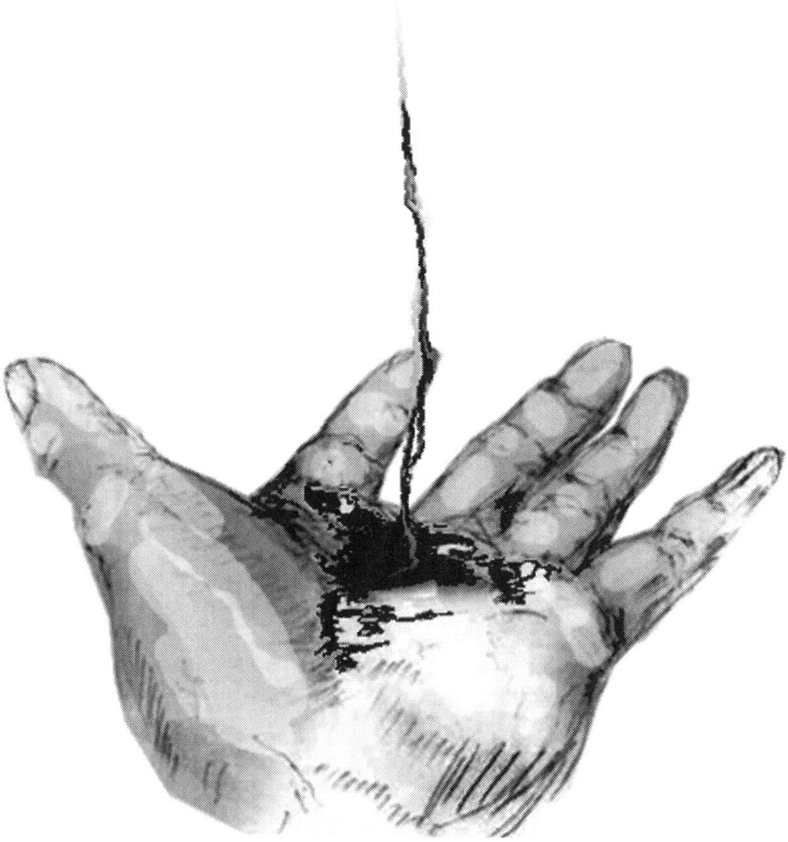

CHAPTER 26

Steopa and Rebecka returned to the deserted workers village with Jeremiah and Mak. The path opened in front of them as they walked through the trees and underbrush. Steopa held up a pine branch so Rebecka could cross underneath. As he came closer to the house that Perun lived in, he heard a sigh and a giggle. Perun sat on the porch with a young woman on his lap. She pulled down her shirt as they approached.

"You're back!" Perun waved to them. "Steopa, Rebecka! Welcome."

The young woman blushed and tried to get off Perun's lap. He held her closer, then stroked her cheek.

"Don't worry, these are my friends. Everyone, this is Linda."

"This might not be a good time," Steopa said.

"Why?"

"We have to talk."

"Sometimes you are the death of the party." Perun kissed Linda. He ran his hand over her breast. Then he pulled away. "Sorry, can you wait inside?"

Linda stood up and hurried into Perun's home. Jeremiah shook his head.

"Where did you meet her?" he asked.

"She had an argument with her boyfriend by the rock." Perun laughed. "I offered my shoulder to cry on."

"How long did it take to get in her pants?"

"Not long." Perun walked over to Steopa, adjusting his leggings as he did. "What is so important?"

"I want to use your woods for a battle."

Perun rubbed his beard. "What sort of battle?"

"The one that is using those legions. I want to fight her here."

Perun grinned. "I don't see why not, plenty of room."

"I have your approval."

"Of course. You want me to help? Or is this a vampire-only thing?"

"You assistance would be welcomed."

Perun's eyes glowed green. "There is a thicket of ash trees next to a small pond. What do you think?"

Steopa pulled out the map from his back pocket. "Show me."

Rebecka walked away from him. She headed toward the old church. Steopa laid the map down on the floor of the porch. Perun sat down by the map. He pointed to a section of Greenwoods.

"There. She will have a hard time leaving that place."

"Is this a marsh?" Steopa asked, pointing to an area south of the trees.

"Yeah, the other side of the marsh where you found that descendant of yours. Where is he, anyway?"

"He is staying with our friend Vincent." Steopa glanced over to the church. Rebecka walked around a statue in front of it. Steopa returned his attention to the map.

"She will bring her legions," Steopa said.

Perun nodded. "Mak can take care of those. You see these hills?"

Steopa nodded.

"They aren't hills."

"What are they?"

"Burial mounds."

Steopa looked over to the house where Mak stayed. Mak sat down on the steps and lit a long pipe.

"He can raise the dead?" Steopa asked.

Perun nodded. "I would like to see the legions deal with them."

Rebecka came back. Steopa pointed to the map. "What do you think?"

"I don't know." She rubbed her temple.

Perun pointed at her ring. "Where did you find that?"

"I took it from another vampire."

Perun held out his hand. Rebecka stared at him for a moment, then laid her hand in his. He ran his fingertip over the jewel. "It's not working."

"What?" Steopa asked.

"It's asleep."

"Huh?" Rebecka pulled her hand back. Perun gripped it.

"A troll would be better for this."

Steopa laid his hand on Perun's chest. "What are you doing?"

"Did you see the other pieces?"

"Our friend has the necklace. The bracelet was destroyed."

Perun ran his thumb over the stone. "You are one lucky woman. If this had been working when Simon attacked, you could have killed him immediately."

"What do you mean?" Rebecka asked.

"That blood control trick of yours." Perun lifted his thumb off the stone. It glowed red. "You could have controlled his blood."

"How?" Rebecka asked.

"Think about it. You could have pulled all of his blood out of his body."

Perun removed the knife from his belt and cut his palm. "Try it."

Rebecka stared at his hand. His blood dripped to the ground. She closed her eyes. The ring glowed brighter. The blood dripping from Perun's hand slowed, then stopped. It pooled in his palm, and a thin tendril of his blood lifted out. It rose snaking above his hand. She opened her eyes.

"Are you doing this?" Steopa asked Perun.

Perun shook his head. "She's a quick learner."

The blood dropped to the ground. Rebecka blinked her eyes. "Wow. Thank you, Perun."

"Keep this one in line, that is all I ask." Perun hit Steopa in the shoulder.

"One more thing," Steopa said. "I need to contact my grandsons."

"I should have gotten Misha's phone number," Rebecka said.

Steopa chuckled. "You can talk to Vincent using your mind, could you try to talk to Misha that way?"

"I don't think I can."

Perun patted her on the shoulder. "I'll help you. That's what you wanted, right?"

Steopa nodded.

"You realize you are keeping me away from a very sweet young lady."

"Perun, this is important."

"So is she." He laughed. "We'll make this quick. Sit by the fire."

"What fire?" Rebecka asked.

A fire rose up in the fire pit outside Perun's home.

"One moment." Perun went back to his home.

"What is he going to do?" Rebecka asked Steopa.

"Help you."
"How?"
"You remember how he blocked Simon from using his mind against us?"
Rebecka nodded.
"He is an expert when it comes to abilities of the mind."
"Like telekinesis?"
"Yes, and others."
Rebecka sat down at the fire. Steopa sat beside her. He crossed his legs with a grunt. She moved over so her back was toward him. She laid back, resting her head on his chest.
"It is a pretty night," she said.
The storm clouds broke apart, revealing the stars behind them. He could see the Milky Way band. He put his arms around Rebecka and kissed her neck. A bundle of herbs dropped into the fire. The flames turned brilliant yellow, then back to the orange-red glow. Perun sat down on the other side of the fire.
"Stay, Steopa," he said, crossing his legs. "This won't take long."
The bundle of herbs smoked. The sticky sweet smell rose from the fire and made its way around them. Perun held his hands up. One hand clasped around an invisible drum. He struck it with his other hand. Steopa could not see the drum, but he could hear it. It sounded like a slow, steady heartbeat.
"When you contact them, tell them to meet me in Kiel tomorrow evening," Steopa said.
Rebecka nodded.
He rested his chin on Rebecka's forehead. The smoke from the herbs reminded Steopa of running in a meadow when he was a child. He closed his eyes. The drumbeats filled his head. It felt like his heartbeat.
Steopa opened his eyes. Rebecka and Perun were gone. The fire had turned cold. He looked around. The village loomed around him. Steopa stood. He did not feel the air move around him. He listened. The woods were silent. He took a step. Underneath his feet, the pine needles and dry leaves should have made a noise, but they did not.
"What is this?"
A shadow moved along the ground and solidified into the

winged, fanged creature from the coiree. Steopa raised his eyebrow.

"How are you here?"

"I am not attached to that cup," he said. His wings moved, but did not make a sound. "I can come and go as I please."

"What do you want?" Steopa asked, crossing his arms.

"I want to tell you not to worry. Forcing Adelind here may not seem like the best course of action, but it has more positive outcomes than letting her continue."

"Your assurance is noted."

"You do not trust me?"

Steopa tilted his head. "Have you given me a reason?"

"I have given you that cup. Filled it with my blood-"

"I do not know your name."

The white-winged creature smiled. "That is true, but I have to keep it from you for now."

"Perun knows about you."

The smile faded. "How do you know the leshy?"

"So you are not omnipotent," Steopa said.

"He's a bit of a prick," Perun said behind Steopa.

The creature looked surprised. Steopa turned. Perun walked toward them. In this place, Perun did not look like a strange hermit. His hair had turned silver and hung in tight braids around his face. Silver antlers grew out of the sides of his head. They were translucent, as if they were made of smoke. Perun grinned. His green eyes twinkled and glowed like Christmas lights.

"You know this creature?" Steopa asked.

"We go a long way back. A very long way." Perun nodded. He pulled his belt up. An ax, club, drum, and large pouch hung from it. Across his back, Steopa could make out a quiver with a silver bow.

"How did you get here?" the creature asked Perun.

Steopa noticed no anger in the creature's voice. He sounded surprised.

Perun laughed. "I let them take me here. I felt it was the right thing to do."

"That is not what I mean."

"You mean, here, now? In my woods? You should not be so stupid." Perun pointed to Steopa. "What do you want with my friend?"

“He is now tied to the coiree,” the creature said. “Things are in motion that-”

Perun waved his hand as if taunting the creature to hurry. The creature shook his head and rubbed his chin. “We are working for the same outcome.”

“I thought you needed reminding of that,” Perun said. “It could have been any two vampires that brought back the Altus line. Why Steopa and Rebecka? Because I made it easier, right?”

“Your assistance was not needed.”

Perun nudged Steopa. “I told you he was a prick.”

“They drank my blood, it would happen.”

“Not in time. You know how important this is.”

Steopa stepped between them. “Am I a child? Talk to me. What do you mean by Altus?”

“You haven't told him about the Altus?” Perun scoffed. “Forget prick, he's an ass.”

“Perun! I warn you. By spoiling this you spoil any chance for yourself,” the creature said.

“Let me be the judge of that.”

The creature raised his wings. “Why do you insist on this?”

“It's my nature. Let me enlighten Steopa.” Perun turned to Steopa. “You see, long ago, there was only one type of vampire. But some humans became jealous of their powers and wanted the same. You know how humans are. They try to take everything. So his rivals take some of these humans and give them the same powers.

"For centuries, they never fought. The originals called themselves Altus. They became powerful, but did not interfere with humans, except for food. Most of their food came to them via retainers. They lived as families, some large enough to be called clans. And the other vampires became jealous again.

"This time it was the vast wealth the Altus had acquired. The lands they owned. They wanted everything the Altus had. So the war started. The others had convinced the dhamphirs to turn on their own families. They thought they had won.

"But some of the Altus families had hidden their children away. They lived among humans, took human spouses and raised families, hiding what they were. And once in a great while, a descendant of these would get attacked by one of the other vampires. Of course they would change, and not even know themselves that they were powerful.

"That cup, the coiree, will only fully work for an Altus. It has power, and some of the power can be leeched off it. But its full potential can only be used by an Altus."

"What are the others called?" Steopa asked.

"Vulgaris," the creature said. He shook his head. "A name they took for themselves."

"Yeah, but most of them don't even know about the war. The ones that do don't get involved," Perun said.

"True. My rival poisons the ears of younger vampires. Ones that want the power that they think they should have. Power is not given away cheaply."

Steopa nodded. "Nor should it be promised."

"Very good."

Perun patted Steopa on the shoulder. "I am glad you are involved with this. At least you will not be bowing your knee to him."

"I never ask for that," the creature said.

"Your rivals do. They want people groveling."

"Were they the ones that convinced Adelind to hunt my family?" Steopa asked.

"Yes. As you said, I am not omnipotent. Neither are my rivals. They thought the Altus line had already returned."

"Not quite," Perun said.

The creature nodded. "You have to make an example of her. Or others will try."

Steopa sighed. "I know."

"Yes," the creature rubbed his chin. "A few humans have found it and tried to get it to work for them. They failed."

"They gave it the wrong blood," Perun said. "But it remembered."

"The cup is sentient?" Steopa asked.

"No, not really." Perun sighed. "I wish our troll friend was here, he could explain that better."

"Now, Steopa," the creature said. "When the time comes-"

"I think we have had enough of this," Perun said. "I have a woman waiting, as does he."

"I only wanted to reassure Steopa. I need to keep my

involvement in this to a minimum, for now." the creature said. "You know why."

Perun waved his hand. "Don't worry." He snapped his fingers and the creature disappeared. "Enough of him."

"I trust you. What do you think of this?" Steopa asked.

"He means no harm to you. But he has to fix this..." Perun sighed. "You protect that cup and stay with Rebecka. And remember, I won't let anything happen to my friends."

"Ogden will want to know the full powers of the coiree."

Perun leaned back. "You tell him that I don't even know. It wasn't made for me. It wasn't made for humans. They will try to use it." He pointed to the house that Rebecka and Steopa had stayed in before. "Go to Rebecka. She's waiting."

Steopa turned. The world shifted around him. Sounds from the forest came back to him as if someone had turned up the volume. The dried leaves crunched under his feet. The fire had turned cold, red embers dying in the middle of the circle of stones.

He heard the sounds of love-making from Perun's home. He shook his head as he walked to the other house. He opened the door. He heard Rebecka talking. As he walked in, he saw her pacing in the abandoned kitchen. She waved to him as she talked to someone on her phone.

Steopa walked across the floor, feeling the floorboards shift underneath him. He entered the kitchen. The large cast iron stove had rusted, but still remained attached to the chimney pipe. He noticed a blackened brass plate behind the stove. He used his sleeve to wipe off some of the grime. The name Thorson and the words pauper and home could be made out.

Rebecka closed her phone. "You were sleeping."

"I was?" Steopa turned to face her.

"Yeah, I talked to Misha and Sasha. They will meet you there. When I was done, I couldn't wake you."

"I have not slept at night for centuries."

"Perun giggled about it." She glanced at her phone. "I called Ogden. He will meet us at the old bank tonight."

"Tonight?"

"It's almost dawn. Are you okay?"

"I saw that creature again."

Rebecka hugged him. "What did he say now? That we are

suppose to start a religion too?"

Steopa chuckled. "No. Perun knows him."

"Really?"

"He told me not to worry. I believe him."

The moans from Perun's house became louder. Rebecka giggled. Steopa smirked.

"I am surprised she is screwing him," Rebecka said.

"He has that effect on women. When we were in the base, they would not let female soldiers alone with him."

"You're kidding, he's so... shaggy." Rebecka snickered, then laughed.

"I do not think it is his hair that the women noticed."

Rebecka laughed. She pressed her body closer to his. Her body shook as she laughed. Steopa picked her up and kissed her. Her giggling subsided as they kissed. She wrapped her legs around his waist. She moved her lips down his neck. The smell of primroses blew into the house.

Steopa ran his fingers through her curly hair. She pressed her fangs against his throat. He growled. She pulled her head back.

"Be careful," Steopa said. "We should not share our blood."

"I know." She smiled. "But it's tempting."

Steopa kissed her neck. She made a noise in the back of her throat. She leaned back and unbuttoned her the top of her shirt. He kissed the top of her breasts.

"Do you smell that?" Rebecka asked.

"What?" He pulled down her bra cup.

"Flowers. I can smell flowers."

He lifted his head. "Morning is coming."

"It's always something," Rebecka said.

"We could fight the stupor."

"I know, but you need your rest. You have a trip to make."

"I want to take you with me."

"I know." She ran her fingers through his hair. "Next time."

"We will go to Saint Petersburg then to Lithuania. I could show you the village I grew up in."

"That would be nice."

Steopa kissed her lips. "Soon."

He carried her into the basement before the sun broke past the horizon.

CHAPTER 27

Steopa and Rebecka met Ogden at the old bank's parking lot. Ogden walked to the area where the seal had been. Ogden crouched by the spot. He waved his hand over the area. A light red glow began to rise from the ground. It glowed as much as a dying fire.

"I hope there is enough to work with," Ogden said. He moved his hands over the ground, speaking under his breath.

Steopa stepped back. Whenever he saw Ogden casting magic, Steopa's hair would start to stand on end. Ogden waved his hands outward from his body. The seal glowed bright red. The light glowed for a few moments and then burned out. Ogden used his cane to steady himself on his shaky legs. As he leaned on his cane, his knuckles turned white.

"Yes, Kiel," he said. "Near the Holstenstrasse." Ogden rubbed his forehead. "Unfortunately, I could not get the exact location."

"How long can you make the seal last?" Steopa asked.

"As long as you need it. But when you get there, you have an hour, two hours at the most, before the sun rises." Ogden sounded tired. "The ones she used were quick set-ups. They were not to last more than a few minutes."

"I got you something," Rebecka said. She placed a cell phone in his hand.

"Thank you." Steopa kissed her cheek.

Rebecka squeezed his hand. "You will be careful."

"Yes," Steopa said.

Ogden had moved around to another side and written letters around the circle as he mumbled some phrases. Steopa adjusted his scabbard. He had stopped at the lair and armed himself. He choose his old cavalry sword, and a handgun he found in World War Two. Before they left the woods, Perun gave him a hand ax.

Ogden finished drawing the seal. He stood and walked over to his leather case. He placed a small chalice on the blacktop. He measured out herbs and pieces of wood. After placing them inside the chalice, Ogden cut his hand, letting his blood drip into the cup.

"Are you ready?" he asked.

Steopa nodded. Rebecka let go of his hand, letting her fingers fall as she backed away. "Use that cell if you need to," she said, her voice barely audible.

Ogden lit a match, then set the items in the chalice on fire. He threw it on the seal. The chalk caught fire and burned blue.

"Quickly," Ogden shouted.

Steopa drew out his sword and stepped into the seal.

The ground melted away. The world spun. All the colors smeared into hues, racing by him. He felt as if he had not moved, only the world around him. Barely seconds later, the world solidified around him.

He stood at the end of a street. It looked empty, except for a street cleaner that had not seen Steopa's arrival. He stepped out of the seal. He could feel that Nastenka was close by.

He waited a moment. Misha and Sasha should be here, he thought. He watched the street cleaner. A loud, sharp whistle echoed down the street. Steopa turned around. Sasha waved to him. Misha stood up at a bench. Steopa came up to them.

"Have you been waiting?" Steopa asked.

"Not long," Misha said. "This seemed to be the best place to wait for you."

"Mother is nearby," Sasha said.

"I know, I felt her as soon as I arrived." Steopa looked around the street. The street cleaner came to an intersection and started to turn his machine around.

"We do not have much time," Steopa said.

He ducked down a side street. Misha and Sasha joined him. Steopa paused and closed his eyes. He could almost see Nastenka. He opened his eyes and looked around the street. Stores lined both sides.

"Strange place to hide," Misha said.

"Yes, very public," Steopa said. "But remember Vincent lives in a nightclub."

"True, but he is one vampire."

Sasha walked further ahead. He stood in front of a wooden door. He flung his hair back and motioned to them to come closer. The upper door mantle had been carved. Steopa gave it a quick glance, then his shoulders sagged.

Two reclining skeletons surrounded a death angel that had been carved above the door. Steopa pointed. "She does not want to be secret," he whispered. "That mark is used in some cities to show vampire-friendly places."

Misha nodded. "I have seen that before, but no vampires inside."

"It is not used much now," Steopa said.

"Let's see if we can get in," Sasha said. He knocked on the door.

Steopa stepped to the side as a panel slid open. A pair of brown eyes looked out the small opening.

"*Guten nacht,*" Sasha said, bowing his head. "I want to see Adelind."

"*Was?*" The voice on the other side of the door asked in German.

"Adelind."

"*Wer?*"

Steopa punched his fist through the door and into the speaker's chest. He wrapped his fingers around the heart. Twisting his hand to snap the arteries, he pulled it out. The body fell as Steopa removed his hand from the hole in the door. He threw it behind him. Sasha kicked open the door.

The door hit the body on the other side. It opened enough to allow them inside. Sasha went first. Steopa pulled out his sword and followed, then Misha.

They had entered a large room with chairs, couches, and a piano in the corner. The decorations would have made Lorelei envious. Paintings of torture and drinking blood lined the walls. The black smoky candles burned, even though electric lights shined from the ceiling.

The vampires in the room looked at them with bored, disinterested eyes. A gaunt male vampire stood up and sighed. He glanced at the sword, but his face remained impassive. "Why are you here?"

Steopa raised his sword. "Adelind," he growled.

No one in the room reacted. Steopa pressed the blade against the gaunt vampire's neck.

Misha whispered. "It is like we don't matter to them."

"Drudges?" Sasha whispered.

"No."

Steopa studied the gaunt vampire's eyes. Across the center of the eye a smoky film covered the iris. The vampire's pupils were dilated as well. Steopa glanced around the room. On every table a bowlful of bags of blood.

He sniffed. He could smell a scent he had not smelt in a long time. Not since his time in the base. He put his hand on the gaunt vampire's shoulder.

"We want to see Adelind. But you do not know where she is, do you?"

"She did not tell us."

"And you are to wait for her, not do anything?"

"Yes."

Steopa brought the sword around and took the gaunt vampire's head off. No one screamed. No one reacted to their companion's head and body separating. Some hadn't stopped their conversations.

Sasha placed his hand on Steopa's arm. "They don't care."

"What's wrong with them?" Misha asked.

"It does not matter." Steopa shoved the body aside with his foot. They are worse than drudges now, he thought. "We will find Nastenka first."

Misha closed his eyes, then pointed down a hallway. "Through there."

Steopa glanced down the hallway, then back at the crowd of vampires in the room. He hissed. He turned around to his grandsons. "They will not care. They are being controlled."

"How do you know?" Misha asked.

Steopa ignored him. He shouldered past them and started down the hallway. The few vampires that they passed never looked in their direction. All the doors along the hallway were locked. One opened as they passed. The vampire stopped. She stared at Sasha.

Sasha raised his hand. She tilted her head, following his hand like a snake following a snake charmer. "I am looking for someone," he said. "Can you help me?"

"Depends..."

"Adelind?"

"I don't know-"

"If you wanted to find her, what would you do?"

"I, um."

Sasha glanced over his shoulder. “Go get mother. This will take a bit.”

“She is drugged,” Steopa said.

“I can get through. Go.” Sasha's skin color rippled blue, then red, then back to his normal color.

Misha motioned with his head down the hall. Steopa handed Sasha the gun. “My friend Jeremiah made the bullets for that.”

“Then it should work.” Sasha slid the gun into the top of his pants.

Steopa followed Misha down the hallway. They came to an intersection. From another direction, a legion walked toward them. He paused, then ran. Misha waved his hand. The legion's body slammed against the wall. The legion bellowed. He rolled his shoulder off the wall. Sasha stepped back. Steopa swung his sword. He sliced through part of the legion's neck.

The legion felt the large wound. He fell forward, starting at the knees, then the hips, then the waist. He laid prone on the floor. Steopa removed the ax from his belt. He raised it and took off the legion's head. As the blade hit the floor, he thought he felt the boards shake.

The nearest door swung open. Misha glanced inside as Steopa stood up. Misha turned to Steopa. “What sort of monster-?”

Steopa looked over Misha's shoulder. Lining the walls of the room were cages. Each cage had a child inside. All the children were asleep. Plastic tubes, from IV bags that hung on the side of the cages, had been attached to each one. Steopa growled.

Misha entered the room, he opened the first cage. A young dark-haired girl laid on her side. The tube entered her upper arm. Misha touched the side of her face, and closed his eyes. She could not be older than twelve.

“There is nothing. She isn't even dreaming,” he said.

“What do you mean?” Steopa asked.

“It is like she is in a stupor.”

“And the rest?”

Misha walked down the line of cages, touching each one. He stopped after the seventh cage. “All of them.”

He pointed to a bag. “What is in this?”

“Ogden said the legions were children.”

Misha stepped back. “If we could stop this-”

"We do not have time," Steopa said. His stomach turned when he said that. "Nastenka needs us."

"Yes, Grandfather." Misha turned, he looked at the children, then Steopa. He lowered his head and left the room.

A little further down the hall, Steopa paused. It felt as if Nastenka stood next to him. He tried the nearest door. The lock broke in his grip. He opened the door. He stopped himself from running inside.

Nastenka laid in the middle of the room on a hard cot. One arm was tied down with cord, held out straight from her body. A tube ran from her vein to a large basin. Her blood dripped into the basin, splashing the ground around it. The floor underneath the basin was stained brown. Blackened skin surrounded the wound. Her black hair laid limp, dull, and brittle around her head. She did not open her eyes when they entered.

"Nastenka," Steopa whispered.

She opened her eyes. She looked around, not focusing on anything. Her former brilliant green eyes were clouded over. As she blinked, the cloudiness disappeared. Her eyes focused on Steopa. She shook her head.

"No, papa, you should not be here."

"Nastenka, hold on." Steopa stepped into the room.

"No." Nastenka raised her free hand. "She cannot find you here."

"We came to find you and take her out."

"We?"

Misha stepped into the room. He came closer. "Mother."

"My son, not you." Nastenka shook her head.

"And Sasha," Misha said.

"Leave me. Now."

Steopa used the blade of the ax to cut the cord around her arm. Then he pulled the tube out. "We will not leave you here."

She sat up, rubbing her arm. The black bruising disappeared from her arm. Steopa cradled Nastenka in his arms and picked her up. She shook her head.

"Papa, please."

"No. We can get you out." Steopa cradled her like a child.

Misha went to the door and looked out. "Here comes Sasha."

Sasha appeared in the open door with the female vampire

holding on to him. She leaned against Sasha as if she had too much to drink.

"Mama," Sasha said.

She hit Steopa on his shoulder. "Why both of my boys?"

"We were the closest," Sasha said. He nodded to the vampire on his arm. "She does know where Adelind is."

"Papa, no, do not go after her," Nastenka said.

"I have to. She has been attacking us." Steopa pulled the ax out.

"She has?"

"Yes."

"All of you?"

"She has been sending the legions," Sasha said.

Nastenka growled. "Those creatures?" She looked up at Steopa. "Kill her."

Steopa smiled. "Where is Adelind?"

The female vampire pointed down the hallway. "In her chambers."

Misha picked up the basin of blood. "Mother, what were they doing to you?"

Sasha stepped into the hallway and pulled out the gun. "Legions."

"How many?" Steopa asked.

Sasha pushed the female vampire into the room and fired the gun. A loud scream echoed from the hallway. Sasha opened his mouth and made a noise. The piercing, echoing sound made Steopa's ears ring. Sasha raised the gun and fired again.

Misha dropped the basin. He reached into his jacket and pulled out a stake. He aimed and threw the long piece of wood. No sound, then a thud.

"Come on, we go to Adelind," Sasha said.

The female vampire ran up to Sasha. She pushed him against the wall. "No, you can't."

Steopa grabbed the back of her neck and pulled her back into the room. "We will. STAY HERE."

Her head snapped back. She stumbled and tripped over the bowl of blood. Steopa slammed the door shut.

A dead legion lay against the wall, the stake protruding from his chest. A second legion had crumpled along the floor, blood flowing from his ears. Sasha kicked the body as he passed.

"Down here."

Nastenka patted Steopa's shoulder. "I think I can walk."

Steopa let her down. Nastenka leaned against Steopa, then she straightened up. "I am ready."

Sasha took the lead. He led them down the hall. He would pause and look around, then continue. Most of the vampires that passed them did not look at them. At the end of the hall, a stairwell led down.

Nastenka grabbed Steopa's hand. "Sorry, Papa," she said. "I am still dizzy."

"It is all right," Steopa said.

Sasha stopped at the bottom of the stairs. Steopa heard voices. The female voice sounded familiar. He tapped Sasha's back.

"What is down here?" he asked.

"Adelind's quarters. That's what I was told."

Steopa handed the ax to Nastenka. He moved ahead of the group. "I hear someone."

He strained to listen. He heard. "Private Reese is injured. He should have died. Steopa and Perun saved him."

"No," Steopa growled under his breath.

"Papa?" Nastenka asked.

Steopa followed the sound of the voice. "I know that voice."

He stopped outside a door. Through the wood he heard, "But it is unstable, if we send any more people through they will be killed."

Steopa opened the door. Dorn laid on a hospital bed, her arms and legs bound. She shook her head while she talked to no one. Steopa walked up to her.

"Radovitch?" she asked.

"Radovitch?" Nastenka asked.

"She could never pronounce the name correctly," Steopa said. "Dorn, what are you doing here?"

"You have to stop them, Steopa. You know what is in there. Stop them. They cannot find out about the mission."

"The mission ended decades ago," Steopa said. "And the base is destroyed."

"Good," Dorn said. She nodded. "Good. Protect us."

"Who is she?" Nastenka asked.

"Remember when I went to America, I had been captured?"

Steopa asked. Nastenka nodded. "She was the commander of the base that held me."

"What is she doing here?" Misha asked.

"Her mind is gone." Steopa patted Dorn on the side of her face. "I do not know what they think they will learn."

The door opened behind them. Three vampires stood on the other side. The short, scarred vampire looked at Steopa, then at Dorn, then back to Steopa.

Next to him was a young female vampire with a collar around her neck. A leash ran from the collar to the hand of the third vampire. Adelind. Her black eyes flickered between them.

"It's you," she said, looking at Steopa.

"Adelind," Steopa said.

The vampire on the leash growled. Her skin had stretch marks along the side of her head and down her arms, yet it was not hard to make out the resemblance to Simon. Adelind snapped the leash.

"I see you found Simon's sister," Steopa said.

"How did you get this far?" she asked.

"Your security is lacking."

"I'm sorry," the bald vampire said. His voice had a slight lisp to it. "Our residents must not have understood the danger."

Adelind held up her hand. "We will figure it out later. I want to know why you are here."

"You will stop hunting my family," Steopa said.

"I will not," she hissed. "You stand in my way."

"I do not know how."

"You cannot have the papers!" Dorn shouted. "They have been destroyed."

"Maybe we don't need them now," Adelind said. "Perhaps Steopa knows. You live in the old base, don't you?"

"It is a safe place from the sun," Steopa said.

"It's more than that," Adelind said.

"If you want to go digging around in the rubble, be my guest." Steopa stepped forward. Adelind did not move. "All you will find are remains and rocks."

"And yet you found the coiree. I doubt that was a coincidence."

"What do you know of it?" Steopa asked.

The vampire on the leash bared her teeth. Sasha moved closer. His skin turned pale. Adelind crossed her arms, resting the leash across one of her arms.

"I know it wasn't yours to have. Do you know how annoying you are? First, you have a bloodline that should not be. Then I find out that you know of and use the coiree. And last, you live in the base in which I need to find something." She sighed. "You are a pain in my side."

"I would like to know who told you about me. About us."

"It doesn't matter."

"I think it does," Misha said. "We cannot be the only family line."

"You are."

"And that scares you?" Misha shook his head. "A silly thing to be scared of."

"It took them centuries to wipe out the families!" Adelind shouted. "And then you have the audacity to bring back one. We will not bow to them again!"

Steopa glanced at Misha. Misha raised his eyebrow. "We have no idea what you are talking about," he said.

Sasha's eyes changed. He raised his hand. Between his fingers, webbing had formed. Steopa moved between him and the leashed vampire.

"That is Simon's sister," Steopa said, pointing to the leashed vampire. "You did not kill her. What is she now, a failed legion?"

Adelind spit. The bloody spittle hit Steopa's boot. "I will stop you now. Before you can become a real threat."

"With your mutant children?" Steopa asked. "That is sick, even for one of us."

"They are the new breed." She straightened up. "My creation."

"Enough!" Steopa shoved her back. "You will come to me. I refuse to play your game anymore."

Adelind unhooked the leash from the female vampire. "Really, You think you are going to leave here?"

The female vampire ran screaming toward them. Nastenka pushed Steopa aside. The female leaped on Nastenka, clawing at her chest. Nastenka snarled and flipped the vampire off her. Misha raised the handgun, pulled the trigger. The bullet took enough of the back of her skull blew out to make the beast vampire stumble back and fall.

"You were saying," Steopa said. "I am taking my daughter and I am leaving. If you want to finish this, you come see me. Tomorrow, one hour after sunset, Greenwoods."

The short vampire grabbed Adelind's arm. "I need all of her blood," he said.

Simon's sister rolled over, her brains hanging outside her head.

Adelind scratched Steopa's face. "You will not leave."

Steopa slapped her. The blow knocked her down. She stood up, rubbing the side of her face. "Wrong move," she said.

The floor shook. The sound of many feet running toward them became louder. The bald vampire pushed his glasses up and hurried out of the room. Adelind smirked. "When you become injured, your family knows. Same thing happens to me."

Legions burst through the door. Misha fired the gun. A legion grabbed his hand and threw him across the room. Sasha backed up as two ran toward him. Steopa pulled out his sword and swung. One head came off; another legion's arm hit the ground.

Adelind moved closer to the door. She smiled. Steopa ran another legion through. Two grabbed Nastenka, one with each arm. She swung her arms, knocking the legions together. Steopa sliced through another one, then he heard Dorn scream.

He glanced behind him. A legion had ripped her out of her bounds. The legion slammed Dorn against the wall. Her screaming stopped. Steopa shoved the legion off his sword and spun around. He split that legion in half.

Sasha screeched. The sound made Steopa cringe. Sasha made the noise again. Dust came down from the ceiling in thick clouds. Adelind covered her ears. The legions backed away.

Steopa grabbed Nastenka's hand. Misha ran in front, shouldering his way past the legions that held onto their ears. Steopa followed, pulling Nastenka behind him. Sasha let out one more piercing scream and followed them out the door.

"Kill them!" Adelind screamed.

They made it up the stairs before the next group of legions set upon them. Steopa let go of Nastenka's hand. He swung this blade and took one down. He heard a clink behind him, but did not take his eyes off the next legion that came toward him.

Sasha and Misha each had a legion to deal with. Steopa took another head off. Then he heard a rip. It was not the sound of cloth or paper ripping. This rip was the sound of a body being ripped. He turned, almost tripping on Perun's ax, which had fallen to the floor.

A legion had Nastenka by her neck. He had split her chest open. Nastenka's mouth was open in a scream, but no sound came. Steopa raised his sword, then lowered it. Where the legion stood, he would not get a good blow in.

Steopa bent over and picked up the ax. He threw it. It hit the legion in the lower neck. It dropped Nastenka. The ax flew back to Steopa's hand. He stared at it for a moment. Nastenka grabbed her wound, holding it shut.

Misha picked up Nastenka. “We don't have much time.”

“Back to the seal,” Steopa said. He pointed down the hall using the ax.

They entered the large room. The vampires in the room had gotten off their seats and stood between them and the exit. Steopa threw the ax. It flew in a wide arc, taking two of the vampire's heads off as it made the trip back. The vampires nearest the decapitated ones stepped back.

Misha spun around and fired into the legions behind them. Sasha screamed. The lights shattered around them. Steopa barreled through the standing vampires. He threw open the exit. He held it open until Misha and Sasha were in the street. He slammed the door shut.

They ran toward the seal. The sky around them had started to turn gray. Misha stopped at the seal. He handed Nastenka to Steopa. The sound of a door breaking open made Sasha turn around. Misha crouched by the seal.

“He made it for only one?” Misha shook his head. He patted his pockets, and pulled out a piece of chalk that had been wrapped in wire. “Give me a moment.”

“We don't have that,” Sasha said. “They're coming.”

Misha erased part of the seal, then he drew strange symbols around it. He bit his wrist and flung his blood on the new writing.

“Okay, Grandfather, you first.”

Steopa stepped into the seal, holding Nastenka. The world melted away. Nastenka moaned. Steopa stepped away from the seal when the world reappeared. He spun around.

“They were right behind us!” he shouted.

Ogden nodded. He raised his arms.

Sasha and Misha appeared in the seal. Misha pushed Sasha out of the seal as Ogden spoke in Latin. At the seal a leg started to form. Ogden lowered his arms quickly. The leg solidified, but nothing else. It fell over and hit the concrete.

Rebecka ran up to Steopa. “You found her.”

Steopa nodded.

Nastenka moaned and looked down, Steopa saw the blood. Her wound had not healed.

“Ogden, we need to get to the coiree,” Rebecka said.

He hurried over to Steopa. Ogden laid his hands on Steopa and Rebecka's arms. The world melted. When the momentum stopped. The angel statue stood in front of Steopa.

CHAPTER 28

Rebecka shoved the angel statue aside as Steopa ran into the Dysart Memorial. He jumped and landed on the floor of the burial chamber. He laid her down on the crypt with the gargoyle at its head.

"Papa," Nastenka whispered. She reached out to him.

"Wait here," Steopa said as he ran up the stairs.

The coiree sat in the middle of the altar, a small amount of blood pooled at the bottom. Steopa picked it up. No blood appeared in the cup. The blood sloshed in the cup. He slammed it down, making the cup ring as it hit the marble.

"You damned thing! You fill this with blood when Rebecka and I were injured!" He shouted.

Nothing changed inside the cup.

"Where are you?"

No sound in the crypt. The shadows stayed stationary. Steopa slammed his fist against the altar.

"Whatever you are! My daughter needs your blood!"

A shadow lengthened in front of the rose boarded-up window. "But that blood is not for her." The voice of the creature seemed to echo off the marble.

Steopa raised his fist. "You want me to father a new line of vampires. I will not abandon my current family for them. My daughter needs your blood!"

"Do you know what you ask?"

"I do."

"I cannot allow it."

"I would have her drink my own blood. She would be a drudge, but she would be alive. Is that the choice? If it is, I will no longer serve any of your needs."

"You cannot back out of this arrangement now."

Steopa lifted the ax. "You want me to spill my own blood?"

"Is that the wisest choice?" the creature asked.

Steopa held his arm out over the coiree. Then he raised the ax.

The coiree glowed red. Blood rose to the lip of the cup.

"Thank you," Steopa said.

Steopa grabbed the cup and ran down the stairs. Nastenka had rolled to her side. Rebecka stood to the side with a pensive look on her face. Steopa handed the cup to Rebecka, then helped Nastenka sit. He lifted the cup to her lips. She drank the blood. At first she sipped. Then she grabbed the cup with both of her arms and drained it.

Nastenka gave the empty cup back to Steopa. The wound on her chest healed. "Why were you yelling?"

"It does not matter," Steopa said.

Rebecka looked up, then looked away.

Nastenka's eyes had returned to their brilliant green. She tilted her head, from this angle she looked like her mother, Anna. She had her mother's lips and cheeks.

"Sounded like you were praying," she said.

Steopa shook his head. "I never pray." He turned to Rebecka. "Can you give us a few moments?"

She nodded and left the crypt.

"I am sorry," Nastenka said.

"For what?"

"For asking you to leave. Thank you for rescuing me."

"Why were you there?"

"They sent a few vassals into my home," Nastenka said. "They used ash to bind me and brought me out in daylight. It burned. But they didn't want to kill me. They wanted me to be bait for you. And that short vampire wanted to collect my blood."

"Why?" Steopa asked.

Nastenka shook her head. "I don't know. He kept me fed and bled me everyday. Adelind and him would talk about purifying the bloodlines."

Steopa sat down on one of the other crypts. "Adelind wants us dead because she considers our bloodline a threat. But she wanted the same blood for purification?"

"She's insane," Nastenka combed her hair with her fingers. "Those legions. Adelind claimed to have created them, but it was the short one."

She stood. She looked at Steopa and smiled. She had taken after him with her build, tall and slender. She sat next to him on the crypt.

"Who was that woman?" she asked. "The heavy one. The one that told you to take me here."

"Rebecka," Steopa said. "We are linked."

Nastenka's mouth dropped open. She fixed Steopa with a glare. "You told me you would never make another vampire."

"It was an accident. She was to be my meal, but then a friend of hers stopped me."

"How could he have done that?"

"He is another vampire."

"Was she his cache?"

"No, a friend."

She sat back with a surprised look on her face. "How can he have human friends?"

"He is..." Steopa chuckled. "Has a very outgoing personality."

Nastenka studied Steopa's face for a moment. "Do you two get along?"

Steopa nodded.

"Has she met the others?"

"Yes, Sasha likes her."

"Is she good to you?"

Steopa patted Nastenka's hand. "We are good to each other."

Nastenka looked around the crypt. She sighed. "I am not calling her mother."

Steopa chuckled. "I do not think Rebecka will let you."

"Are we in America?"

Steopa nodded.

"My first time."

"Your English has improved."

Nastenka shrugged. "A language school opened up near my home. I think I picked up some of it while I slept."

"Why would you not let Misha contact you?" Steopa asked.

"I couldn't take the chance that you would come and get me," Nastenka said. "I didn't want you to run into her trap. But she wasn't ready for you."

"I came to challenge her. I am tired of her sending her underlings to fight her battles. I want it to end."

"The other vampires in town are in agreement with this?" Nastenka asked.

“Some are.”

Ogden came up the ladder. “Excuse me, but it worked?” He asked.

Steopa nodded. “Ogden Phelps, this is my daughter, Nastenka.”

Ogden bowed. “Charmed.” He turned to Steopa. “Rebecka is downstairs with your grandsons.”

“Thank you,” Steopa said.

“Tomorrow is when you challenged Adelind. That does not give us much time,” Ogden said.

“Less time for her. We have most of the night here.”

“Tonight yes, but what about tomorrow?”

“Excuse me, I would like to talk to my sons,” Nastenka said. She stood up and jumped down the hole to the lowest level.

“I also have some things to arrange.” Steopa stood.

“Steopa, are we fighting Adelind or are we trying to prove something?”

“We will kill her, but there should be no doubt that we will fight for ourselves. We will protect our own.”

“We or you?”

“If you do not want to battle her-”

Ogden held up his hand. “She tried to get the coiree, that is reason enough. I want to make sure that you are doing this for the right reasons?”

“What reasons do you think I would be doing this?”

“For glory?”

Steopa scoffed. “I do not want that.” He pushed past Ogden. “My family.”

He jumped down to the lower floor. Nastenka, Misha, and Sasha had taken seats on the couch and the easy chair. Rebecka sat on another chair, away from the rest of them. Steopa came up to her and put his hand on her shoulder.

Rebecka patted his hand. Steopa leaned over. “You could join them.”

She shook her head. “It's all right.”

Ogden joined them. Nastenka glanced up and smiled. “How do you know my father?”

“We have an arrangement.” Ogden pulled up the last empty seat. “There is a fourth member, but he is detained.”

“Lorelei is probably making him clean up the club,” Rebecka

said.

"You were a prisoner of Adelind's. Is there anything you can share with us?"

"I don't know what help I can be." Nastenka shrugged. "They kept me in that room and bled me."

"Surely not to drink?"

"I don't know what they did with it."

"She has other vampires with her," Sasha said. "But they were almost like drudges."

"Why do you say they are like drudges?" Ogden said.

"They only care about themselves," Nastenka said, "as long as they are fed."

"They are drugged," Steopa said.

"How do you know?" Ogden asked.

"Because I recognized the smell of the blood. How do you think they kept me in the base as long as they did?"

"She drugs the blood?" Ogden sat back. He stared at Steopa for a moment, then he turned his head.

"I don't think she controls them," Nastenka said.

"Who does?" Ogden asked.

"That little vampire. He's the one that changed the children into legions."

Ogden picked up his cane. "I will be there tomorrow. Good evening."

Shadows swirled around Ogden, then he was gone.

Nastenka turned to Steopa. "I can't believe you got the other vampires in this city to help you. The ones in Vladivostok would not lift a finger to help me."

"Adelind forced them," Steopa said. "She sent legions and hunters to find our family. They attacked any vampires they found."

"Are you staying for the fight tomorrow?" Rebecka asked.

"Against Adelind?" Sasha said. "Of course."

Steopa pointed to Sasha. "Could you three go to Teodor's? When you get there, ask him to come to Greenwoods."

"Is that where the fight will be?" Misha asked.

Steopa nodded. "I plan to spend the day there. I will meet you there at sunrise."

"What about the rest or your family?" Rebecka asked.

“Get a hold of who you can.” Steopa said.

Misha tapped the side of his head. “No problem. I don't think any will come.”

“Try.”

Steopa held out his hand. Rebecka clasped it. Steopa waited until the rest walked into the tunnel.

“Do you want to see your brother?” Steopa asked.

“Why?”

“Because there is a chance-”

“I am already dead and I want to be with you.”

“We have one stop to make, then on to Greenwoods,” Steopa said.

Rebecka creased her eyebrows. “Something else is wrong.”

Steopa nodded. “Dorn is dead.”

“What? How?”

“They had taken her. A legion killed her.”

Her eyes flickered over his face. “But you are not sad.”

“Relieved.” Steopa kissed her hand. “She will no longer bother us.”

Rebecka shook her head. “I don't know what it is with you and some of these older women.”

“Your meaning?”

“Dorn? The lady at the shop?”

Steopa chuckled. “There are times when you come across people that it is better to have them close, so you can watch them.”

She giggled. “Scared of two old ladies?”

“Two old women with dark secrets.” Steopa motioned to the door. “We do not have much night left.”

Rebecka slipped her arm around his waist. Steopa kissed her forehead. When you are as old as me, he thought, you will have dark secrets, too.

CHAPTER 29

Perun looked up. His smile split his full face in two. "Three bottles! And not the cheap stuff either!"

He held up the vodka bottles to show Jeremiah and Mak. Steopa opened up the package wrapped in white butcher paper. Perun grinned when he saw the meat inside and danced a small jig.

"Lamb! Do you know how long it has been since I had lamb?" Perun laughed.

"You made his night," Jeremiah said. "All he needs now is to find a woman on the cross country track."

Perun laughed. He turned around and waved his hand. In the fire pit, the fire grew as he approached. "Too bad you all only drink blood. But more for me!"

Mak lowered his pipe. "What is the occasion?" he asked.

"Two reasons," Steopa said, sitting down on a set of steps. "The fight tomorrow and I have news."

Rebecka sat down next to him. Steopa pulled her closer. "Teodor is coming."

Perun looked up from pulling the meat out of the butcher paper. "Good thing you said something. I'll save a bit for him."

"What news?" Jeremiah asked.

"We will wait for Teodor," Steopa said.

Rebecka laid her head on his shoulder. Steopa patted the side of her face. She moved closer. "Are those the northern lights?" she asked.

Steopa looked up. Through the light pollution from the city, he could make out the ribbons of the northern lights. "Yes."

Perun fixed a branch he had fashioned into a spit above the fire. He looked up and smiled. "I haven't seen them in a long time. A good sign."

"The city is too bright," Jeremiah said. "The last time you had to come down to the interstate with me to see them."

"That was a few years back." Perun opened one of the bottles. "You know, some people believe the lights are the souls of the dead and if you whistle while the lights dance, you will be drawn down to the dead."

Leaves crunched in the distance. Someone or something came closer to the village. Steopa turned his head to look. A large black wolf came through the brush, holding a pair of pants in his mouth.

"Teodor," Steopa said, raising his hand in greeting.

Teodor dropped the pants on the ground then shook himself. He sat back on his heels, in his human form. He picked up his pants.

"Is that lamb?" he asked, pulling on his pants.

Perun nodded. "Steopa brought it. I saved you some."

"Thanks. It's been awhile."

"No kidding," Jeremiah said. "How's your pack?"

"Growing. Chuck is getting married."

Perun chuckled. "Watch out Steopa, soon there will be more werewolves to deal with." He opened one of the bottles of vodka and drank.

"What's so important?" Teodor asked.

"Dorn is dead."

An owl hooted somewhere in the woods. The fire crackled as the meat cooked above it, but no one around the fire made a sound. Perun put down his bottle.

"Did you finally allow her to die?" he asked.

"A legion killed her."

"I don't know how to feel about that," Jeremiah said. "She was a real bitch when she was my commanding officer, but the last few years, you kinda felt sorry for her."

"Sorry for her?" Teodor asked. "She tried to kill all of us."

"She was a good lay," Perun said shrugging.

"Ew," Rebecka said.

Perun grinned. "One time. We needed her to come with us and I overdid it with the charming, that's all."

"Yeah, but ew."

"Who was this woman?" Mak asked.

"We told you about the base," Jeremiah said. "She ran it."

"And you let her live?"

"Steopa scrambled her brains. Killing her would have been a mercy," Teodor said.

"The base is buried, she's dead, let's drink!" Perun said.

"There is another thing," Steopa said. "I ran into vampires

tonight who are drinking the same blood I had been given in the base."

Teodor growled. "So others know?"

Steopa nodded.

"That blood mixture?" Perun asked, wiping his lips. "I can fix that."

"You could not," Steopa said.

"Because they kept me away from the sun and the plants and everything. But here, I can fix it."

"Those vampires might be fighting us tomorrow."

Perun chuckled. "It won't take much. Mak can help me."

"Where is this battle?" Mak asked.

"Near the mounds." Perun pointed vaguely in a direction.

"Good place, I will ask my tribe to help."

Teodor stared at Mak. "What?"

"Many members of my tribe are buried there, they will help."

"How?"

"Mak can speak with the dead," Steopa said.

Rebecka rested her hand on Steopa's thigh. She kissed his neck. Steopa chuckled. Perun put down the first empty bottle, then belched.

"Sorry, empty stomach."

"You always have an empty stomach," Jeremiah said.

"Is that all you do with the meat and drink?" Rebecka asked. "Steopa told me that you would make the woodsman pay in drinks and meat."

Perun nodded. "If they want to use my woods, they have to pay me. Simple. And what would I do with money?" he laughed.

"Spend it on whores?" Jeremiah said.

"I never would do that. Women can't resist me." He farted near the fire. The flames billowed outward.

Teodor covered his nose. "My god, Perun, some of us have sensitive noses."

Perun laughed. Jeremiah giggled.

Steopa shook his head. He turned to Teodor. "Are you bringing your family?"

"All but Trucker and Silva. They are staying around the base."

"Why?"

"Just in case. I don't want someone sneaking in there when we are busy."

Steopa sat back. "I did not think of that."

"Toss me some of that meat," Teodor said.

Perun picked up a chunk of meat and threw it at Teodor. Teodor caught it and ripped off a piece. "There is one thing you can give Dorn credit for. She stuck most of us together on the same level."

"I don't think that was her decision," Jeremiah said.

"Whatever, I'm going to miss her."

Perun spit out his mouthful of vodka. "You're kidding."

Rebecka kissed Steopa's neck. He turned his head. "What is it?"

She shrugged.

"Hey," Jeremiah said. "How do you know that bitch vampire isn't going to cheat?"

"She will," Steopa said.

"If she tries to bring more in, through the woods, my pack will be waiting," Teodor said.

Perun nodded. "Don't worry, I'll help to keep her there."

"What are you planning?"

"There are a lot of ash trees in that area." Perun winked.

"Steopa," Rebecka whispered. "Are we staying here for the day?"

He nodded. She grasped his hand. "You stay with your friends," she said. "I have a few phone calls to make."

She stood up and pointed to the house they had stayed at before. "That one. Right, Perun?"

Perun nodded. "Any of them."

Steopa watched her walk to the empty house. She stopped on the porch and pulled out her cell phone. Her hair looked longer in the moonlight. Steopa smiled. She leaned against the wall of the house as she spoke into her phone.

Perun pulled the meat off the spit and came over to Steopa. He sat down with a grunt. "You still have my ax?"

Steopa unhooked the ax from his belt and handed it to Perun. Rebecka turned so her back was toward him. Perun nudged Steopa.

"You didn't clean the blade," he said.

"I did not have the time," Steopa said.

Perun lifted the ax. "Nice, isn't it?"

"It flew back into my hand."

"Of course, it's my ax."

“Are you going to tell me that you are the god of lighting now?” Steopa asked.

“Nah, I was named after him.” He put the ax down on the step. The blade glowed for a moment. He ate the meat off the spit. After he swallowed he pointed to Rebecka. “You should spend the rest of the night with her.”

“I will.”

“No, now.”

Steopa raised his eyebrow. Perun pointed. “Go.”

Rebecka turned around as she tapped the screen of her phone. Steopa stood. He nudged Perun with his foot. “If you spy on us-”

Perun chuckled. “No, I will be too busy with these three. We have to get the grove ready.”

Steopa smiled. He went over to Rebecka. She looked up and slid her phone back into her pocket. “That was Baldman. He saw you on the security cameras.”

“What do you mean?”

“He's hacked into the surveillance cameras around the area where he had been looking for Simon. He saw you tonight. After you disappeared, that small vampire appeared.”

Rebecka held her phone so he could see the screen: A grainy black and white photo of the small vampire. Rebecka touched the screen. The image grew. The bald vampire looked worried.

“He tried to remake the seal, and look what happened.”

She showed Steopa another photo. The small vampire had raised his arms to protect his face from the tall, human-shaped flame next to him.

“When was this taken?” Steopa asked.

“Just after daybreak. Either that legion was very injured, or they go up like tinder.”

“If it is the latter, she will want to finish the fight as soon as possible.” Steopa took Rebecka's arm. “We should go inside.”

“One more thing. Baldman got into their computers tonight. He said he found the recipe for the tainted blood.”

Steopa's jaw clenched. “Is he certain?”

“He told me to tell you, it's not the same as the one they used on you. This one has an older date on it.”

“What does he mean?”

“He thinks she uses the original recipe. The stuff they made in the base for you was an alteration. He said it proves that there were other research bases like that one."

"There were."

"Why?"

"During war, any advantage over the enemy will be considered a good thing."

"It's horrible."

"Rebecka, the humans experimented on other humans they considered lesser than themselves at the time. Do you think they cared that we were not human?"

"I don't know who are the monsters anymore."

Steopa hugged her. She laid her head on his chest. He glanced over to the rest of the group. Perun turned his head away as if he had been caught spying. Steopa chuckled.

They went into the house. Bunches of herbs hung along the ceiling. Steopa lowered his head as he walked inside. A bundle of herbs tangled in his hair. He reached up to pull it out.

Rebecka sniffed the air. "Smells like Cassie's shop." She paused. "Should I be nervous?"

"About tomorrow?"

She nodded.

"You have been in fights."

"Not like this one."

He nodded. "That is true."

Rebecka stood on her tip toes and gave him a deep kiss. Steopa pulled away, slowly.

"It is all right to be frightened," he said.

"It's not me that I am afraid for. I am scared for you."

"Why?"

Rebecka looked away. "It's stupid."

"What?"

She bit her lip. "It's just that since I found out about the base, I have had this nagging thought. And..."

Steopa lifted her chin. "You can tell me."

"How did they capture you?" She looked away. "I have seen you do amazing things. I can't see you caught like a rat in a lab."

Steopa looked down, then he glanced out the window. Teodor, Jeremiah, and Perun walked away from the village.

"Because they found Teodor and I when we were at our weakest.

We were crossing the Bering Strait. I had not eaten for a long time. Teodor tried to help, but the ice was not his normal place to hunt." Steopa's shoulders sagged. "The moment we stepped into Alaska, we were caught. I slipped into a stupor. When I awoke, I was in the base."

"You could have escaped then?"

Steopa shook his head. "That blood, the same type of blood I smelled at Adelind's, sedates you. I never wanted to raise a hand against them. And they did treat me well. I had books. I could read the newspapers. A few of the soldiers were good chess players. It was not a bad place to stay."

"And you never thought of leaving? What happened?"

"They used us, and I drank fresh blood. It felt like waking up from a dream."

Rebecka hugged him. "I understand."

"You do?"

"Remember those pills I used to take? The night I changed, it felt the same way."

Steopa wrapped his arms around her and pulled her close. She laid her head on his chest. He closed his eyes and rested his chin on her head.

"If anything happens to you, and we can't get you to the coiree," she said. "I will stay with you."

"When the sun comes I might burn."

"I don't care. I'll burn with you."

"I do not want you to do that."

"Why? I would not be able to live like this without you."

"You would survive."

She shook her head. "I choose not too."

Steopa lifted her chin. "If you burn, I will join you too."

"We'll burn together."

"Along with any prophecy."

Rebecka chuckled. "I never believed in those things anyway."

The smell of the drying herbs seemed to become stronger. The smell of primrose, mint, and sandalwood drifted around them. The light from the fire flickered across the walls. Steopa felt Rebecka's hands undo his belt.

"What are you doing?"

She grinned. "Taking that sword off."

"How well can you control your blood?"
"Which way?" she asked.
"You enveloped Simon."
Rebecka scoffed. "I had been staked first." She removed his belt. The sword dropped. Steopa caught it with one hand. He laid it on the old counter. Rebecka pressed herself closer to him as he turned back. Then she stood back.
"There is something different," she said. She laid her hand on the front of his pants.
Steopa laid his hand on top of hers. He raised his eyebrow. "Damn that Perun," he said, chuckling.
Rebecka giggled. "So you feel it too?"
Steopa undid her top button. "This might be the only time."
Rebecka moved his hands away. "I know."
She unbuttoned the rest of her shirt. Steopa took off his. He placed his hand on her shoulder, then slid her shirt off. He ran his hands down her sides, as the shirt fell. She moved closer to him. He undid the zipper to her pants.
"What are you doing?" Rebecka asked.
"Nothing."
"Nothing?"
He slid his hand between her legs. Rebecka shuddered. Steopa kissed her neck. "I had to make sure."
She wrapped her arm around his waist. "Don't stop."
He pulled her pants down with his other hand. She made a noise like a purr as he squeezed her butt. Rebecka reached for his pants. He stopped her with one hand.
Outside he heard a door slam. He glanced outside. Mak walked passed their window and disappeared into the darkness of the woods. The common area of the village laid empty. The fire had turned to red coals. When he turned his head back, Rebecka stepped out of her pants.
Rebecka looked different. Her curves had smoothed. Her breast were fuller. She laid one hand on her hip, and smiled.
"You are beautiful," he said. He finished undressing.
Rebecka looked out the window. "How long do you think we have?"
Steopa walked up behind her and kissed her neck. "Not long."
She slid one of his hands to her breast. He cupped it, then

squeezed. She made a noise like a purr in the back of her throat. Steopa turned her around. She surprised him, by pushing him down.

"Lay back," she said as she straddled him. Steopa ran his fingernail from her cheek to her cleavage. She leaned forward. "Your eyes are glowing."

Steopa laid his head back and smiled. He let her do whatever she wanted. He fought the urge to bite her and drink her blood. The urge became more intense the longer they made love. Rebecka bit his shoulder, but she pulled back her mouth before he bled. The pain made him grab her hips and thrust harder.

When they had finished, she curled up along his side. Steopa comb her hair with his fingers. She rested her hand on his hip.

"Sorry about your shoulder," she said.

"I enjoy it."

"Really?"

Steopa nodded. "Should you tell Perun or should I?"

"Tell him what?"

"That we mated."

Rebecka laughed. Steopa chuckled. She rolled on her back.

"I hope this was not the only time."

"Me too." He watched the herb bundles sway above them, then smiled. "I do not think it will be. Give me a moment."

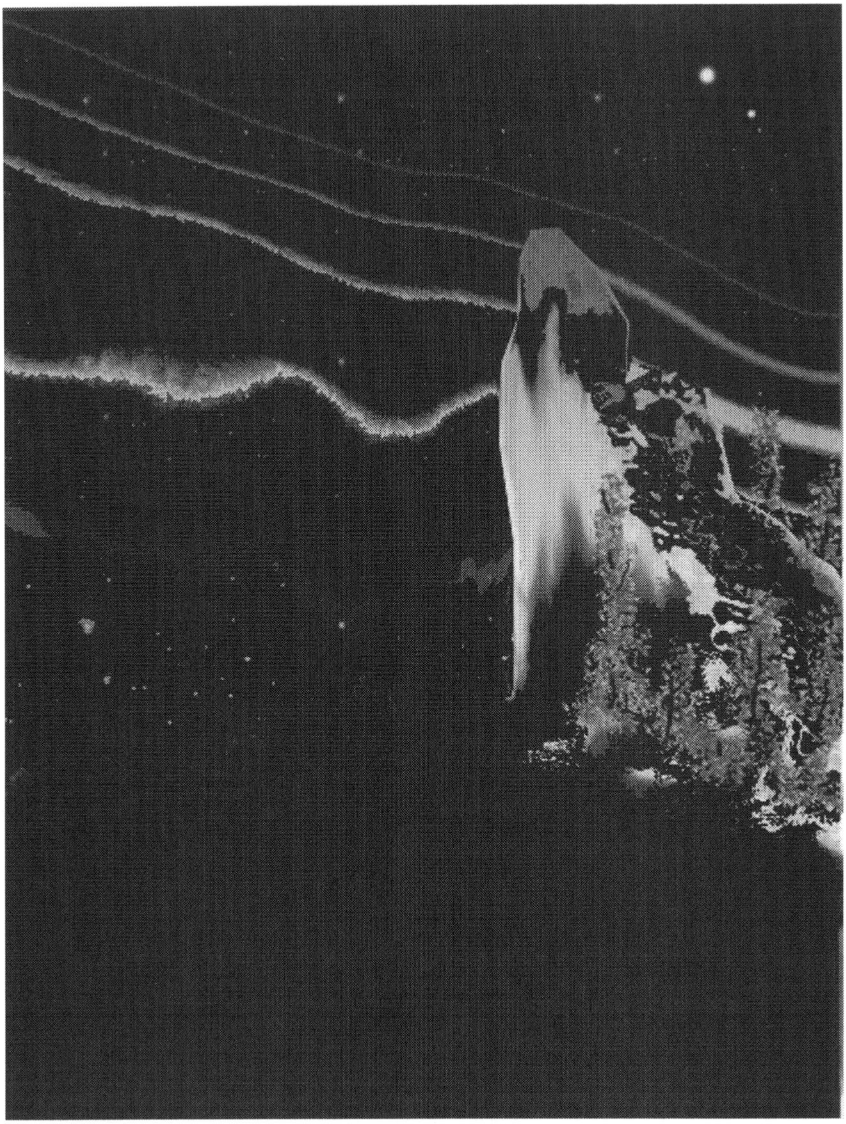

CHAPTER 30

Steopa forced the stupor off him before the sunset. He lifted Rebecka's arm off his chest, placing it on hers. The dirt slid off him, leaving Rebecka buried. He sat. He could tell that the sun had an hour left before it went below the horizon. In the basement, none of the late-day sunlight could reach him. He glanced up the steep steps. The first floor had long shadows on the wall.

He shook off his jacket, then slid on his belt and scabbard. He glanced back at the mound of dirt covering Rebecka. She had no weapons except her claws and teeth. She should not fight, he thought. But she will not let me tell her that.

He knelt down by the mound of dirt. He uncovered her face, brushing the dirt off her lips. She did not look dead or sleeping. Her complexion had taken on a waxy look and feel. He leaned over and kissed her lips.

Above him, the floorboards creaked. Then he heard Perun singing. Steopa left Rebecka's face uncovered. He stood up and smoothed out his coat. After putting his hair into a ponytail, he climbed the stairs and walked into the living room.

Perun had his arms above his head as he cut down a bunch of dried herbs. He sliced through the string.

"Finally, eh?" Perun said, winking.

"What?" Steopa asked.

"I can smell it. You two mated." He dropped the bunch of herbs. "Good for you."

"Now will you stop asking?"

Perun raised his arms again. "It's been a busy day for me. It took a lot of persuasion to get the trees to agree."

Steopa stared at him. "What?"

"To move." Perun cut the string on another bunch. "I can ask a bear to do a tap dance, no problem. But asking a tree to move? Some of them are quite arrogant."

Steopa shook his head. "You had to ask-?"

Perun nodded. "The trees around the village like to keep it

hidden. But those ashes, they had no idea what I wanted. But I finally convinced them."

"Trees?"

Perun chuckled. "That surprises you. I thought vampires could control the weather. Trees should be no problem."

"What are they going to do?"

"When the battle starts, encircle the grove, so any vampire that leaves will have to climb through the brush. All ash."

"They will burn." Steopa smiled. "I like it."

Perun threw the bundle on the floor on top of the large pile of herbs at his feet.

"What is that for?" Steopa asked.

"For the drugged ones." Perun turned a bundle in his hands. He moved to the next one. "After these start to burn, they will awaken."

"Are you sure?"

Perun nodded, then shrugged. "I hope."

"Perun?"

"Yes."

Steopa place his hand on Perun's arm so he stopped cutting the bunches. "If something happens to either Rebecka or me, can you make sure we stay together?"

"I can't heal you."

"I am not asking you to heal us."

Perun lowered his arm. "I see."

Steopa looked out the window. The sun had moved low enough that the trees blocked any rays from it. The sky turned red. "She told me last night she would rather burn than stay a vampire without me. I feel the same way."

"You could always find another," Perun said. He bent over to collect the bundles.

"No."

"I'm only saying that... I have had more wives than I can remember. Each time one passed away, I swore I would not find another."

"No."

Perun shrugged. "Maybe it is different for you." He stood up with the herbs. "I'll do it. I won't like it, but I'll do it."

"Thank you."

Perun dropped another bunch. "Mak spent the day at the mounds. I think he talked to the dead there."

"We do not have much time to gather," Steopa said.

"Then help me with this." Perun motioned to the outside. "The sun is almost down." He shoved a pile of herbs into Steopa's arms.

Steopa followed Perun. Perun threw the bunches of herbs into a large iron pot. Steopa could see dried mushrooms and berries lining the bottom of the pot. He sniffed. He recognized the smell of the mushrooms.

Perun pointed to a large tree branch. "Hand me that, will you?"

Steopa gave him the branch. "I know what type of mushrooms those are."

"Fly Amanita, the humans call them."

"What are you making, something to make everyone hallucinate?"

Perun shook his head. "That's what the humans think about. It won't affect vampires."

"What about werewolves?"

"Not them either."

"So why add the mushrooms?"

Perun smiled and started to pound the dried mixture. "You don't understand how the mind works. We need a way in. Those mushrooms will open it."

A door slammed. Steopa turned around. Rebecka stood in the doorway. She smiled. Steopa held out his hand to her. She came over and clasped his hand.

"We have to make sure everything is ready," Steopa said.

"Do you think she is here yet?" Rebecka asked.

"I haven't heard anything." Perun stopped pounding the herbs. "I will see you at the grove."

Steopa nodded. He led Rebecka through the woods. She paused when they found the cross country trail.

"I didn't realize how close we are to the university," she said.

"We will be deeper into the woods." At the end of the path, Steopa could see the lights of Deerbow shining across the river. "But do you think the humans will notice or even care?"

"It doesn't matter to them." She waved her hand. "That's how we can hide among them."

"True, if they could see-"

"They don't."
Steopa pointed to the tall rock outcropping. "There, at the base of that rock."
"The High Tower?" She stared at the white and red rock. "That's the battle ground?"
"Yes."
She smiled. "I would hate to be your enemy. That can be a nasty piece of ground, with the pond nearby."
"If Perun has had his way, it will be worse tonight."
They made it to the parking lot closest to the rock called the High Tower as the last of the sun's rays disappeared. The moon had not risen, leaving the woods covered in blackness. Steopa could feel other vampires approaching. He heard two car engines. The rest of the vehicles were far away.
Perun appeared for a moment at the edge of the woods with a large sack in his hand. He pulled out a deer skull and placed it on the ground. Then he filled the skull with some of the dried herb mixture. He stood up and disappeared into the woods.
"What is he up to?" Rebecka asked.
"He is giving us an advantage," Steopa said.
Two vans pulled into the parking lot. From one emerged most of Teodor's family. From the other, Vincent, Swen, Jimmy and Steopa's descendants. Andi ran over and hugged Rebecka.
"This is gonna be weird," she said.
"Andi? Are you sure you are okay with doing this?" Rebecka asked.
"No problem." Andi grabbed Chuck's arm as he walked up to them. "Chuck and I will be together."
"I owe some bruises back to those legions," Chuck said.
"And I should take her to court to have her pay for the repairs to the 'Keller," Vincent said.
Swen walked up to Steopa. "When's the fun?"
"If you are here," Rebecka asked. "Who's watching the Rathskeller?"
"After that damage, Lorelei closed it for a few days. Don't worry, they are with Cassie."
"Where's Cassie?"
"Up at a bike rally."
Steopa raised his eyebrow. "Is that safe?"

"Three hundred bikers." Swen shrugged. "Safer than in the middle of the city. Besides, Vince told me she was sending her goons out to attack any non-humans. I think she would include me."

"Yes."

"I think she is trying to set herself up like an elder. What a bitch," Verina said behind them.

Everyone turned. Verina walked across the parking lot, smoking a cigarette. "I mean," she blew out the smoke. "What she thinks an elder is."

Teodor shook Steopa's hand. "Where do you want us?"

"Make sure they do not leave, or bring more reinforcements," Steopa said.

Teodor stretched. His body elongated, his face changed from human to the hybrid of human and wolf. Andi did the same. Rebecka stepped back. Teodor howled. The rest of his family joined the howling.

"Whoa," Jimmy said. He looked around. "They don't mess around, do they?"

Rebecka pointed to Jimmy. "What do you got there?"

He lifted up a duffel bag. "Remember the hunter with the explosive stakes? I got his crossbow."

"Do you know how to use it?" Steopa asked.

"Point, shoot, and wind it up."

Vincent rubbed his goatee. "You've been practicing on the walls in your apartment, haven't you?"

Jimmy shrugged.

"When we get through this, you are patching them up." Vincent grinned.

"Any sign of her?" Nastenka asked.

"Nothing yet," Steopa said.

"Too bad this wasn't closer to the river," Sasha said.

"There is a large marsh there," Rebecka said.

Sasha winced. "Marsh? How much of it is open water?"

"I thought you could use any water."

"Marshes have a lot of vegetation, slows me down. I would have better luck in a bathtub."

"There is a large area of open water."

"Good, that's something."

"It is getting late. Let's move," Steopa said.
"Wait!"
The vampire from the meeting ran across the parking lot. She looked at the group and gave them a small smile. "Sorry, I almost didn't come."
"Thank you, Leteia," Steopa said.
"None of the others came?" she asked.
Rebecka shook her head.
Vincent scoffed. "Not their problem."
Theodor's pack ran into the woods. The rest followed Steopa as he made his way down to the clearing. Along the way, he saw more deer skulls full of the herb mixture. A light flared in the darkness in front of them. Perun's eyes were illuminated by the flame.
"Can you still do your fire trick?" Perun asked. "I have to light all of them."
Steopa snapped his fingers. Around the grove, small fires lit up in the deer skulls, then faded out. Sweet and pungent smoke poured out of the skulls. Perun smiled, but it had no mirth in it.
"Good, the smoke will cover what Mak has planned."
"What does he have planned?" Steopa asked.
"You will have to see." Perun disappeared into the woods.
"What was that?" Nastenka asked.
"A leshy," Misha said. "Having him on our side almost makes this battle unfair."
"So they are real?" Nastenka asked. "These woods can become dangerous, then?"
"I've seen him before," Leteia said. "When I was a student at the college."
"Then you were lucky," Steopa said. "He will not let anyone see him." He heard brush move. Ash trees had seemed to appear around them. He nodded. "Yes, the woods are about to become more dangerous for our kind. If we do not hurry, we will get caught in it."
"Did those trees move?" Jimmy asked.
Rebecka nodded.
"Crap," Jimmy said.
Steopa pushed some of the brush aside and walked into the grove. The large rock towered over the grove and marsh. Ogden stood in the middle, watching a ridge. He glanced over to Steopa.

Then he picked up his cane and motioned Steopa over to him.

"I made sure to come here at sunset," Ogden said. "I didn't want her to get the better ground."

Steopa looked over the clearing. On the west side, a small pond shimmered in the middle of the marsh. To the north, another marsh. To the east a pile of rocks, large boulders that had been left by the glaciers eons ago. The High Tower rose up out of the rocky ground. The woods that they had exited from laid to the south.

Mak and Jeremiah walked into the clearing. Mak paused by the rocks, then removed his shirt as he came closer. "This is a very good place." Mak motioned to the east side of the clearing. "I have kinsmen buried over there. I have persuaded them to help."

Ogden raised an eyebrow. "What type of help? They are long past."

"Their spirits are still dangerous."

Sasha wandered away. Steopa watched him walk around the small pond. Rebecka slipped her hand into his.

"Maybe she isn't coming," she said.

Sasha jumped into the water. The smoke from Perun's herb mixture poured over the ground. It curled around Steopa's feet. The smell reminded Steopa of church when he was a boy. The sweetness of the smoke almost blocked out the other smells in the grove.

Mak pointed to the pond. "Who is the one in the water?"

"Sasha," Steopa said.

"He can assist me," Mak said. He walked over, then sat by the lake.

Perun came back to the group. He dropped the empty bag on the ground. "I'm ready."

"I am worried that she will set up more seals. She might bring in reinforcements," Steopa said.

Ogden shook his head. "I have already thought of that. I will destroy any she has."

"I will help," Misha said.

"Good." Steopa looked over his shoulder into the woods. "It would be a good idea to hide our numbers."

"Our small number," Vincent said.

Steopa raised his eyebrow.

Vincent shrugged. "You know the rest of them in the city are watching this. They won't step in to help. So screw them if they don't want to help."

"They are opportunistic," Ogden said. "We fail. They hope Adelind will leave. And they will have the city to themselves."

"I would have done the same," Steopa said. He motioned Perun over. "How far back are the ash trees?"

"About as far as the parking lot."

Steopa took one more look around the grove. "Yes. In a few moments, I will meet Adelind for a quick parley before the battle." Steopa pointed. "Verina, Vincent, and Perun, come with me. The rest of you, hide along that tree line."

Rebecka squeezed his hand then walked away. She bit the fingertips of her left hand. Why is she doing that? He thought. The blood dripped down into long thin red ribbons.

Ogden picked up his cane. "You don't want me to come?"

"You need to stay here and watch for anything unusual."

Ogden nodded.

Vincent cleared his throat. "There she is."

Steopa turned around. Across from them in the clearing stood Adelind. Her vampires and legions appeared one at a time with a blue flash along the ground. Steopa studied the line forming behind Adelind. We are outnumbered, he thought, but would any of them move without Adelind telling them what to do, if she went down?

Adelind walked to the middle of the clearing. The bald vampire hurried to keep up with her. Verina raised her hand to her face and snickered.

Perun glanced over to Steopa. "Are you ready for this?"

Steopa stepped forward. The others fell behind him. They walked down to the middle of the clearing. Adelind stood with her chin held high. Steopa's eyes fell on the short vampire. He stood behind Adelind, rubbing his hands together. Adelind walked up to Steopa.

"You are outnumbered," Adelind said. "Do you really think you have a chance?"

"It will end here, one way or another," Steopa said. "You have made more enemies here than me."

Adelind shook her head. "I should not even speak to you. Who is the eldest?"

Verina blew the smoke in Adelind's face. "I am."

Adelind sneered. “You are the eldest?”
Verina tossed her hair back. “Yes.”
“You will allow this, in your city?” Adelind asked.
“It's not my city,” Verina said. “So I really don't care, but your mutants ruined my night and my nails.”
Vincent grinned. “I would like to talk to you about some damage your goons did to my club. Where would you like me to send the bill?”
“You have no respect,” Adelind hissed.
“Damn right.” Vincent said.
“What is that?” Adelind asked, staring at Perun.
“I can't believe it, Steopa,” Perun said. “You found a woman I wouldn't fuck.”
Adelind growled. “You are a fool.”
Perun's eyes glowed green. “You are in my woods. I would say you are the fool.”
“We will not stop until you are dead,” Steopa said.
Adelind scoffed. She motioned to the bald vampire and turned around. Steopa motioned with his head to the tree line. The rest walked back. Steopa drew out his sword.
Nothing made a noise, except for Mak singing at the edge of the lake. Steopa watched Adelind's side of the clearing. The bald vampire walked among the legions, shoving some back. The other vampires had gathered to the front. None of them looked as if they were ready to fight. They stood on the slight rise, looking disinterested. The smoke from Perun's herbs drifted into Adelind's numbers. Adelind called the short vampire over. She snapped at him. The short vampire held out his hands as if he was apologizing.
Steopa grinned and raised his sword.

CHAPTER 31

The little vampire waved his hand and the vampires that were with Adelind broke from their group and ran toward Steopa. As they ran, their legs cut through the gray smoke rising from the deer skulls. The mist rippled like water. The smoke rolled up on one. When it cleared, that vampire could not been seen.

Steopa did not yell charge. He did not give any order. Yet every vampire that was not along the tree line rushed forward with him. Vincent turned to a mist and disappeared into the smoke as a vampire from Adelind's side tried to jump him. Steopa swung his sword, but as the blade almost came into contact, the vampire in front of him flew back. Perun chuckled. He held his hands as if he was holding a bat, but Steopa could not see anything.

"They're not too bright, are they?" Perun said. He pointed.

Another vampire rushed Steopa as he held his sword out straight. The vampire impaled himself on the blade. Perun laughed. He skipped away into the smoke.

Steopa viewed the battlefield and caught sight of Adelind yelling at the short vampire. He crouched in a servile manner and slunk away from her. The legions had not moved. They would move forward as if they wanted to fight, then the bald vampire would shout at them and they would move back.

Unsteady, Steopa thought. She may not be as well-prepared as she needs to be. He glanced over his shoulder. The rest of them were still hidden. A vampire swiped at him. Steopa kicked him back and swung his sword. The blade sliced through the vampire's chest. On the back swing he sliced through the vampire's neck.

He raised the sword and yelled. From the tree line, the rest of them appeared. They appeared out of the shadows, moving in one line. When they were free of the tree line, they came running into the clearing, except for Misha, who appeared next to Steopa. Shadows swirled around Misha and he blurred up the side of the hill into the trees.

Adelind screamed at the bald vampire. He shouted. The legions ran forward. A few of the vampires to the back of their line were knocked down as the legions passed. The ones that were not knocked down, hurried into the trees.

Something brushed past Steopa's leg. As Steopa raised his sword, the smoke rose up over the vampire in front of him. The smoke settled down and the vampire disappeared. Steopa felt the body hit his leg, then a hand grabbed his calf. Steopa felt something pulling on the vampire that held on to his leg. Steopa sliced his sword down through the gray smoke. The vampire's hand remained, but the rest of him disappeared into the trees.

He kicked the hand off his leg. Another vampire raised his claws to strike. Verina appeared quickly between him and the vampire. She struck out with her hand, slicing though the vampire's neck with her fingernails. He looked surprised before his head rolled off his neck.

One of the largest legions ran toward Steopa. As he came closer, two crossbow bolts struck his chest. The legion lowered his head and picked up speed as he ran. Every time his foot hit the ground, it shook. He screamed. Steopa swung his sword, just as the behemoth hit.

The tip of the blade disappeared into the legion's chest. He pushed his body up Steopa's sword, opening his mouth. The two pairs of large fangs glistened. Steopa raised his foot and pushed against the legion's pelvis. The legion grabbed Steopa by the shoulders as Steopa tried to push back, using his leg as leverage. The legion connected his forehead with Steopa's.

Steopa felt his skull crack. He shook his head. The legion changed his grip on Steopa's shoulder. Steopa fell backward, taking the legion with him. As he landed, he kicked the legion off. Steopa rolled. The legion kicked Steopa's midsection. Steopa snapped his sword up and through the legion's groin.

The legion screamed. The smoke billowed around them. A red ribbon wrapped around the legion's throat and head. The legion tumbled to the side. Steopa jumped to his feet.

The ribbons flowed back to the cuts on Rebecka's wrists. She came rushing toward Steopa, then past him. Steopa spun around, looking for the next attacker. He saw Jimmy loading the crossbow. He grinned at Steopa, then raised the weapon.

The next legion that crossed Steopa's path had Vincent on his back. Vincent held onto his neck. The veins in the legion's neck turned red. Smoke started to roll out of his mouth, ears, and eyes. The legion burst into flames. Steopa had to jump over the body as it fell forward, still running. Vincent misted. Steopa lost track of him as Vincent disappeared into the smoke.

Steopa took down a vampire and another legion. Then he glanced over the grove to Adelind. She still had not joined the fight. Beside her was the bald vampire. He jumped when screaming started outside of the battle area. Howls from Teodor's family and the screams of the vampires surrounded them.

A legion plowed into Steopa from the side and grabbed Steopa's neck. Steopa dropped his sword. He clawed at the legion's eyes. The legion tightened his grip on Steopa. The legion's fingernails touched Steopa's spine. Steopa stuck his claws in the legion's chest, forcing his hand into the rib cage. His fingers felt something hard. Steopa pulled. The legion roared. Steopa yanked hard and pulled out a section of a spinal column.

Steopa pushed the body off him. He rolled over and picked up his sword as he stood. He sliced the head off. The head rolled into the smoke. The top of it was visible for a moment, then the smoke covered it. When the smoke moved away, it was gone.

Leteia grabbed one of the drugged vampires and whipped her into a tree. Another vampire tried to grab her. Leteia slipped out of his grasp and struck him across the face. Her claws left deep cuts over his cheeks.

Steopa raised his sword to block another attack. A large bear barreled past him. The remains of a leather vest hung off the bear's back. Swen? Steopa thought. The bear reared up and swiped the vampire with his large claws. The vampire's head hung off a strip of skin. The body fell backward. Steopa backed away, keeping an eye on Swen in his berserker rage. But Swen ran on, taking down the drugged vampires as he did. Steopa heard singing. He turned.

The smoke over the pond remained still. Mak sat on the ground, the smoke and mist covering most of his body. He chanted, his eyes closed, rocking back and forth. Nastenka appeared next to him. Three legions ran toward Nastenka, fighting on the other side of the pond. One legion disappeared with a splash. The other two stopped. The body of the first legion flew through the air, his throat opened with a large, gaping wound. A loud splash of water, another legion disappeared into the pond. This one screamed until the water covered her head.

Ogden backed into Steopa. Another legion forced him back. The legion raised her claws to swipe. Steopa brought his sword up. Blocking the hand, then swinging to take the hand off. Ogden grabbed her other arm at the wrist. The legion hissed. The area around the legion's wrist turned purple, then black. She fell to her knees, then over. Her body turned to ash as the mist covered it.

"Thank you," Ogden said.

"*Da*." Steopa nodded.

Another legion cut through the smoke. It ran toward Nastenka. She spun around and tried to block the female. The female sliced through her chest. Nastenka fell back into the smoke.

Sasha jumped out of the water. He let out a shrill scream. Nastenka's attacker covered his ears. Behind him, Misha appeared out of the smoke. He struck the legion in the back of the head. The legion looked surprised before the back of her head flew off.

Steopa felt a claw slice through his back. He spun around. A drugged vampire stepped back. She blinked her eyes, staring at her hand. She looked at her claws, then up at Steopa's face. She backed away.

Jeremiah appeared behind the vampire. She backed into him. He grabbed the female with one hand. The white, bone-like blade slid out of his arm. He held it against her neck.

"Hi there," he said, then sliced her head off.

Two more legions rushed Steopa. He took their heads. He glanced up and saw Adelind back up into the tree line. The bald vampire joined her, but she kicked him. He crouched and backed away like a beaten dog.

Steopa hurried across the grove. Adelind stood by herself. Steopa ran, shouldering legions as they tried to stop him. Adelind's eyes went wide and she ran into the woods. Steopa jumped. He reached the tree line. He swung his sword to clear a path through the wood and followed her into the brush.

Adelind disappeared into the trees. Steopa saw her for a moment, then the shadows swallowed her. Steopa stopped. He saw the shimmer of the leaves of the ash trees. He sniffed the air, but could not smell her.

One of Teodor's pack howled. Then another. Steopa turned. He saw Adelind run down a path away from the ash trees. He ran after her. One of Teodor's sons reared up in front of her. She jumped into the trees.

"Come around to the rock." Steopa pointed to the High Tower.

Teodor's son nodded then howled. He jumped over a smaller ash tree. Steopa heard him howl as he ran.

Adelind leaped from tree to tree. Steopa kept up with her on the ground. She broke a branch off and threw it at Steopa. He batted it away. She swung on a branch and hit Steopa in the chest with her feet.

The kick knocked him back, but not down. He regained his footing. Adelind ran up the hill that led to the rock. Steopa picked up speed to catch up with her.

Swen rushed past him, snorting as he barreled up the hill toward Adelind. She jumped into the trees. Swen stood up on his hind legs. He slammed his front paws against the tree. Adelind leaped on to another tree, heading toward the High Tower.

Steopa turned to follow her. Swen roared. He charged Steopa. Steopa skidded to a stop. He fell backward into the smoke. Something slid by him along the ground. It crossed over his chest as he tried to move away from the charging berserk.

Perun jumped. He landed between Steopa and Swen. He placed his fingers in this mouth and blew a loud whistle. Swen stopped. Perun pointed toward the main battle. Swen shook his massive head and barreled back to the fight.

Steopa stood. "Thank you," he said.

Perun shrugged.

Steopa ran toward the High Tower. The mist followed him into the woods. It snaked around the trees as if it was looking for something. Adelind stopped at the top of the hill, her back to the base of the rock. The mist swarmed behind her, rising up like a cobra.

Steopa caught up with her. She spun around and screamed, waving her hands. The smoke dissipated around her. Steopa roared. He raised his sword and charged up the small hill.

She swung her claws to strike Steopa. He grabbed her fist and spun her around. He slammed his sword against her neck. Blood welled along the blade. Steopa twisted her wrist.

"Adelind," he hissed. "Do you still want to kill me or my

family?"

"Please," she begged. "Please don't."

"Pathetic," Steopa growled.

"Don't kill me. We could work together."

"No."

"I didn't realize..."

Steopa pressed the sword deeper into her neck. "Why do you not fight your own battles, instead of hiding behind those monsters?"

"Do you think I need them?" Adelind asked, her voice turning cold. "Then you don't know me at all."

She tore his face with her claws, while she shoved the sword away. She slipped out of his grip. Steopa reached for her. She raked her claws across his chest. He felt intense pain as her nails dug into his flesh.

With her other hand, she sliced his neck. Steopa covered the wound with his free hand. The searing pain burned deep inside. He coughed.

Adelind sneered. "I don't need them. I use them, but why not? They think they will become like me."

"What are you?" Steopa spit blood at her. "A bitter woman? Killed the one that was linked to you?"

"I never asked for this!" Adelind kicked Steopa in the midsection. Her heel tore into his skin. The same pain as being staked struck him. Steopa grabbed her foot and shoved her away.

The wounds she had dealt him did not heal. Steopa swung with his sword while the blood dripped down his face. She dodged his attack.

"But I learned to embrace it! That's why I killed him! I didn't want to share this with him." Adelind grabbed Steopa's wrist. She pulled him closer. "And then I kept running into your name. How dare you interfere."

"What the hell are you talking about?" Steopa shouted. He forced his sword down. The point buried itself into her shoulder. How can she be so strong? he thought.

"You really don't know?" Adelind laughed. "Do you think you were the only one that had been experimented on?"

"You were not in the lab!"

Adelind shook her head. "Here? I was never here. I never left Germany."

She ran her finger over his wrist. Steopa's stomach turned. Adelind grinned. “Do you know where I was made? In the first lab.”

Steopa glared at her. “So?”

“Do you think they stopped there? I saw the fat male's trick with the blades. He was not the only one.”

She tightened her grip on his wrist. He felt a sharp pain in his arm. The pain shot through his muscles and into his bones. His nerves felt as if they were being pulled out of his arm. He forced the blade further into her shoulder.

A white flash blinded him. He stumbled back. Adelind did not let go of his wrist and arms. He blinked. He could see the world in negative for a moment. Adelind swung him around and shoved him into the rock.

“And you think I needed help?” She slammed Steopa against the rock again.

“Then why?” Steopa forced himself to say. The pain in his nerves made it hard for him to focus.

“They're an experiment. Because when everything comes together, I will need an army.” Adelind tilted her head. “You aren't healing. How does that feel? That you're about to be killed by a woman?”

Steopa growled. He head butted her. Adelind's head snapped back. She let go of him as she raised her hand to her forehead.

He thrust his sword. Adelind dodged his attack. She grabbed the hilt of the sword. Another wave of intense pain hit Steopa. He lost his grip on the sword. She lifted it above her head and smiled.

“I'm sick of running into you!” she screamed. She brought the sword back like a baseball bat. “Time to end this.”

“Don't you dare touch him!” Rebecka screamed.

Steopa looked behind Adelind. Through the drips of blood he saw Rebecka running toward Adelind. Adelind turned her head, just as Rebecka tackled. She hit Adelind in the midsection with her shoulder, knocking her to the ground.

Rebecka yanked Adelind's head up by the hair. She slammed it down on the ground, hitting a large tree root that laid exposed. Adelind clawed Rebecka across nose. Just like Steopa's wounds, Rebecka's did not heal.

Steopa wiped the blood from his forehead. The pain subsided

from his body. He took a step away from the rock. His legs shook. He forced himself to get closer to Rebecka.

The muscles in Adelind's neck tightened as Rebecka pummeled her face. Rebecka's blood streamed from her nose. It snaked down to Adelind's body. Adelind's hands glowed as if a light had been shone through them. A second later a white blinding light exploded in Rebecka's face.

Rebecka stopped. She shook her head, her eyes looked dazed. Adelind used Steopa's sword, cutting a large gash in Rebecka's chest. Steopa reached them and grabbed the blade of the sword. He yanked it out of Adelind's hand. Rebecka's blood flowed around Adelind and underneath her. Adelind tried to move, but the blood had formed a lasso around her.

"Try to move," Rebecka said. "Just try it and I will start to rip your blood out of your body."

"You can do that?" Adelind asked. Her voice a harsh whisper.

Rebecka slapped her. "Want a demonstration?"

One of the Navarros howled nearby. Steopa could see a blond werewolf coming closer.

"Get your family over here," Steopa said.

The werewolf raised his head and howled.

Adelind turned her head. "How many are out there?"

Rebecka swayed on her knees. Steopa placed his hand on her shoulder as he got down on one knee. He grabbed the top of Adelind's head.

"You do not know? I thought you knew all about me."

He nodded to Rebecka. She leaned back and pulled the blood back into her body. Steopa slipped his hand down Adelind's face and around her throat.

"We should get a better look," he said.

Rebecka used Steopa's arm to stand. Then he pulled Adelind up, never letting go of her neck. He pick her up until they were eye to eye. She raised her hand. He swatted it away. "You will not touch me."

Two more werewolves came through the woods. One shook his fur, Teodor returned to his human form. "Is she the one?"

Steopa nodded. "And we are going to see how the fight is going."

He dragged her to the steps of the rock. Rebecka stumbled over to the railing. She looked up to the top of the rock. "Can we throw her off?"

"It won't kill her," Teodor said.

"Repetitively?"

"Rebecka. Teodor," Steopa growled.

Teodor ran up the stairs. Steopa followed, dragging Adelind behind him. She clawed at his wrists and twisted her body. Steopa slammed her against the side of the rock outcropping. A portion of the limestone turned to powder as he body struck the rock. He felt her bones snap.

"Be still!" Steopa shouted.

At the top, the stairwell connected with a large lookout area. The large flat patio had a high railing surrounding its edges. In the distance, the lights of Deerbow city shimmered along the river. Cars moved up and down the riverside road, their lights making them look like fast-moving fireflies from this distance.

Steopa dragged Adelind to the edge of the overlook. He hung her over the side. Below them the mist covered the grove. The legions had been pushed back to the hill where they had appeared. The rest of the drugged vampires ran into the trees. Their screams drifted up to the top of the High Tower.

"Call your mutants off," he ordered.

Adelind shook her head. "I can't. I don't control them."

Steopa growled. "The little one? That bald vampire controls them?"

Adelind nodded.

"You are an idiot! You do not know how to control the legions."

She choked. Steopa threw her on the floor of the lookout. Adelind rolled over and laid on her elbows. "It won't matter if you kill me. What is in place will happen." She coughed; blood splattered on the floor.

"Another prophecy?" Steopa scoffed. "How can you believe in them?"

Adelind shook her head and chuckled. "How can you be so blind? That cup is not what you think it is."

"You assume much, and what did you mean, 'when the time comes'?" Steopa asked.

"You think that cup will protect you? It didn't before."

Steopa glanced at Teodor.

Teodor shook his head. “She's insane.”

Rebecka's face turned red. “You know some of us don't have the luxury of having been around for years. So old bitty, why don't you tell us straight!”

Adelind pointed to Steopa. “You should not have killed the one that bit you. She could have told you all about this.”

“I fought her and killed her.” Steopa growled. “Whatever romantic notions you have about how I became a vampire are wrong.”

“And if you knew what you were, you wouldn't be hiding in that base. Altus.”

“Altus?” Steopa said. The smug look on Adelind's face faded. He continued, “I have heard that name before. And I do not care.”

The lookout shook. Steopa looked up as a legion jumped over the top step. As he slammed his foot down on the wooden platform. Vincent jumped on the legion's back. The legion opened his mouth to bellow. Vincent misted. The mist snaked into the legion's open mouth.

The legion growled. His took a step, then his head snapped back. His arms flung around and he moved as if he had been drinking too much. The movements were stiff and sharp. He tore at his own chest, then at his own neck.

Adelind pulled herself away from the legion. Rebecka slammed her foot down on Adelind's arm to stop her from moving. Steopa raised his sword.

“Why don't you attack?” Teodor asked.

“Vincent's inside,” Steopa said.

The legion stopped shaking. He stood rigid, then the sound of bones being snapped in two was heard. His chest expanded. The skin stretched and broke. A fissure opened at the top of his chest, ripping his torso apart.

Blood sprayed the lookout. Steopa raised his hand to protect his face from the gore. Rebecka ducked behind him. The legion's body fell in two pieces on to the floor. Vincent stood in the middle of the pieces, covered head to foot with gore. He wiped the blood out of his eyes, then picked a piece of brain off his damp hair.

“Ugh,” Vincent said, stepping out of the pile of intestines, bones, flesh, and blood.

Teodor wiped the blood from his body. “They smell worse then

they look."
"The fight is over," Vincent said. "Most of them disappeared in the smoke."
Jeremiah joined them on the lookout, dragging his foot behind him. "Kill her," he said. He coughed, then spat out a fingertip.
She pointed to Jeremiah. "But we are the same. What they did to you."
He raised his arm, the long white blade came out. "This? This is just a big claw, that's all."
"But they..."
"They messed with me." Jeremiah shook his head. "But they didn't make me."
Steopa grabbed Adelind by her shirt. "We are going to do this properly. Adelind, you will die, but I think we should decide how."
"I vote for cutting her head off," Rebecka said.
Steopa smeared the blood from the back of his hand on Adelind's cheek. "We will take her below and decide there."
"Almost everyone is waiting," Jeremiah said.
"We will be done shortly," Steopa said.
Jeremiah lifted his injured foot, rotated it, then put it down. "Better. I'll go tell them."
He left, followed by Teodor. Vincent came up to Adelind and smiled. His fangs glistened while the bloody mess dripped down his face. "I think Steopa will treat you nicer than my lawyers."
Adelind stared at Vincent. He patted the other side of her face. It made a sticky, wet sound. "See you below, sweetheart."
"Rebecka, could you go with Vincent?" Steopa asked.
Rebecka hurried to catch up with Vincent. Steopa spun Adelind around and yanked her close to him, so his arm hooked both of her arms behind her. He waited until they were alone on the top of the lookout.
"I want you to know one thing: Other vampires will know of this. Not because you tried to fight me, but because you attacked my family." He shook her with each word. "No one harms my family."

CHAPTER 32

The smoke pulled away from the base of the High Tower. Steopa could not see Perun, but he could hear his rough voice chanting somewhere in the woods. Everyone had gathered around the base of the rock. There were three missing, Leteia, Mak and Swen.

Steopa shoved Adelind against the rock. "We need to decide what punishment she deserves."

"Flaying?" Vincent asked.

"I vote for leaving her there until the sun hits," Sasha said.

"Who will make sure she burns?" Ogden asked.

The sound of Perun's rough singing floated over the group. Steopa shook his head.

"Perun is burying Mak," Jeremiah said. "I think we should bury her alive."

"Where's Swen?" Vincent asked.

"In the pond," Jeremiah pointed.

"And Leteia?" Rebecka asked.

Jimmy shook his head. "A legion got her. But she ripped his arm off before he killed her. At least she took one down fighting."

Verina gasped. She twisted her arm back to its normal angle. The bruise that ran from her shoulder to her hand disappeared. "There is an old punishment."

Adelind twisted her body. Steopa struck her with the blunt side of his sword. Then he pressed the point into her neck. When she stopped moving, Steopa turned to Verina. "What is it?"

"Make her pay with her flesh," Verina said.

"Dismemberment?"

Verina nodded. "But done in a particular way."

Vincent walked closer to her. The blood and the gore still covered his body. Verina's eyes traveled up and down his body, then she moved away.

Adelind stopped struggling. Steopa removed the tip of the sword from her throat. "You will die on this rock."

She screamed. "You can't do this. I will be an elder. I command you to stop."

Verina slapped Adelind across the face. Four deep gashes ripped across Adelind's cheek. "You are not an elder. I am." Verina's voice changed. It became deeper, rougher, the type of voice that made people listen.

"You think you know what it takes to survive." Verina grabbed Adelind's chin. "Every vampire that tries to control another vampire ends up ashes. The ones that survive, the ones like me, that have seen upstarts like you rise and fall over and over again. We know that to survive, we do not bow to another. We fought you, not because Steopa asked us, but because you had crossed us as well."

Verina shoved Adelind's head back. "Creating those legions just to use them, that is poor leadership. Making them out of children makes you a monster more terrible than the humans claim we are. You are not worthy of the blood in your veins."

The woods fell quiet after Verina's outburst. She pulled her hand away from Adelind's face. She glanced at everyone, then turned to fix her hair.

"Could you clean up a little?" she asked Vincent with a sharp tone.

Vincent misted. For a moment, the blood that had been covering his clothes and hair kept the shape of a man, then splattered to the ground. Vincent solidified on the other side of Verina, without any blood on him. "Better?"

"We have a few hours before sunrise," Steopa said to Adelind. "We will take it slow."

"Can you talk some sense into them?" Adelind asked Ogden, her eyes brimming with bloody tears.

"Consider yourself lucky it wasn't up to me," Ogden said. "Steopa wants you dead tonight. I would make it last a few weeks."

"Steopa," Rebecka said. "Simon attacked my brother, under her orders. I want a piece of her too."

Steopa shook his head. "None of us will take any part of her, except for Verina, who will make sure other vampires hear of this."

"Of course," Verina said.

"But the rest of us will not take trophies. Because you are no more than garbage," Steopa said. "Sasha, Misha, come here. Each of you take an arm."

Misha slammed her arm against the rock. Sasha took her other arm, his skin rippling with phosphorescence. Steopa stepped back and adjusted his grip on the sword.

Perun appeared beside him. He came out of nothing. He laid his hand on the sword blade. "Don't ruin your weapon with her blood," he said. He pulled his ax from his belt. "Use this. It has done this sort of work before."

Steopa sheathed his sword and took the ax. This one had the handle made from a deer antler. Pictographs, runes, and other images had been burned into the handle. Steopa tested the blade. His fingertip brushed the sharpened end and split open. He rubbed the blood between his fingers, then nodded to Misha.

"Hold her arm still," Steopa said.

Misha adjusted his grip on Adelind.

"You are all aberrants. You need to be wiped out," Adelind screamed.

Steopa brought the ax down. The head cut through her arm as if it had been paper. It bounced off the rock. Her left forearm dropped to the ground. Adelind screamed. Misha kicked the arm away.

Her blood gushed out of the wound for a few moments, then the flow stopped. Her skin grew over the wound and healed. Adelind stared at the stump, her eyes wide. She turned her head and spit at Steopa.

Steopa laid his hand on Rebecka's shoulder to stop her from attacking Adelind. "No. Wait. Soon the pain will make her shut down."

He nodded to Sasha. He held down her other arm. Steopa raised the ax. Her other forearm rolled down the hill as she screamed.

"Someone hold her leg," Steopa said.

Jimmy grabbed her leg and held it out for Steopa. He aimed and cleaved her calf. Adelind opened her mouth to scream again, but no sound came out.

"The last time I witnessed something like this," Perun said with no hint of his usual merriment, "they tied off his arteries so he would not bleed to death before the punishment was done. You should be thankful you can heal."

Adelind lifted her head, her skin had turned ashen. "Why don't you stop them?"

Perun walked up to Adelind. He took her chin in his hand. “Take a good look at me, sweetheart. What do you see?”

Adelind's eyes focused on Perun's. She shuddered. Then she struggled. “No!” she screamed.

“That's right, you see. How could you betray your own? How could you betray your world?”

“Perun?” Steopa tapped the bloody ax head in his hand.

“You should be thankful, this is mercy.” Perun stood back. He glanced at Steopa. Steopa felt his skin crawl. He started at the sight of Perun's solid black eyes. Those were not Perun's normal shining green eyes. These felt as if something very old, older than even the rock, looked at Steopa.

Steopa turned his attention back to Adelind. He felt a chill, as if he had looked into an abyss. He raised the ax and chopped off her other calf.

Between each blow, Steopa waited until the wound healed. Adelind passed out when he took off her left arm at the shoulder. Misha and Sasha moved away from her now. She had only her torso left.

The sun would be rising soon. Steopa wiped the blade of the ax on the grass. He had only one more blow to make. “I could stop now,” he said. “She will not survive the sunrise. But this has to be done properly. Any other vampires with delusions of grandeur will think twice about coming here.”

He stood up and turned around so he could see the group behind him. No one had spoken since Perun. He weighed the ax in his hand.

“This is our place,” he said. “This city is open to any vampires, and that scares ones like her. All you need are your teeth and your claws. You do not need underlings. And there are things here that we have to protect.”

He glanced at Vincent, Ogden, and Rebecka. The coiree. We do not know all its power, he thought. But we protect it, from the likes of Adelind. Steopa snarled.

“And protecting our family,” Rebecka said. Nastenka hugged Rebecka's shoulders.

Steopa nodded.

He brought down the last cut. The head rolled down the hill. At the bottom it struck a stump. Perun rubbed his beard, then hurried down the hill after the bloody trophy.

Nastenka looked around. "Where's the little one?" she asked.

"Who?" Sasha asked.

"The little, bald one. The one that collected my blood."

"I thought he ran toward the pond," Rebecka said.

Sasha shook his head. "I never saw him."

"We can't look for him," Vincent said. "Daylight's coming."

The sky had started to lighten. Birds sang in the woods. Perun came back to the group. He had her head.

"I've got a good place for this," he said. "Unless you want it."

Rebecka took Steopa's hand. "I want to go home."

Steopa nodded. "You keep it, Perun. And I am sure Teodor has enough room," Steopa said to his descendants.

Teodor nodded. "All of you are more than welcome."

Nastenka shook her head. "No, we should go. This city can't feed us all."

"One more night," Ogden said. "I don't like that we cannot find the bald one."

"I will go to Germany. If that one returned, I will find out," Misha said.

"Then come to my house tomorrow," Ogden said, "if you decide to look for him."

"Now?" Nastenka asked.

"Why not?" Misha shrugged. He walked toward the tree line. Stopping part of the way.

Vincent held his arm out for Verina, "Do you want to get some coffee?"

She lit a cigarette. "I need to rest."

"Hold up. I'm going back with you," Jimmy said.

Verina bent over and picked up Adelind's hand. She pulled off a bracelet. "Her hand won't survive the day," she said holding the cigarette in the corner of her mouth. "But this might be proof enough."

Vincent motioned to the pond. "We have to get Swen out of the water."

Swen walked up to the group, his body soaked. "I'm here."

Vincent waved and walked away with his group. Misha stood up. Around him blue light flared up, and he was gone.

Perun stopped Steopa. "You should stay at the village, today."

Rebecka squeezed Steopa's hand. “Why?” She asked.

Perun tilted the head in his hand. He reached into the neck and pulled out a small object. It looked like a blue metallic pearl.

“This isn't normal for your kind.” Perun rolled the object between his finger and thumb. “I thought I would make you something with it.”

“Why do we need to go to the village?” Steopa asked.

Perun grinned. “You want me to make it right, don't you?”

Rebecka sighed. “It is closer.”

Steopa wrapped his arm around Rebecka. “All right, Perun. We will stay.”

Perun hurried ahead. Steopa glanced back at the small clearing. The smoke cleared. Bodies dotted the ground. He shook his head. A waste, he thought.

CHAPTER 33

Steopa woke up from the stupor. He reached over to curl up with Rebecka. He felt empty ground. He moved the dirt off of him. He found her sitting on the floor by the stairs.

"I couldn't sleep," she said.

"How long have you been awake?"

"Most of the day. There was a thunderstorm, so I went upstairs for a little while. Perun can be sweet."

"What did he do?" Steopa stood.

"Nothing much. He kept me company. Told me stories."

"He likes to tell stories." Steopa brushed off his coat. "We have to go to Ogden's."

Rebecka didn't move. She hugged her knees. Steopa stopped at the stairs. "Rebecka?"

"I don't want to go."

"Why?"

"Because I am tired and hungry." She leaned forward and put her chin on her knees.

"We can feed after-"

"No, I can't wait any more."

"This is important."

Rebecka shrugged. "Is it?"

"That little vampire-"

"Did nothing other than what Adelind told him to do. I know he collected Nastenka's blood. But..."

Steopa held his hand out to Rebecka. "And that reason enough."

Rebecka looked at his hand but did not take it. She shook her head. "You can go, but I'm satisfied."

Steopa studied Rebecka's face. She had dropped her glamor. In the few years that she had been a vampire, her real look had changed. Her cheeks and eyes had sunken. She moved her hair out of her face. As she did, Steopa could see that her skin had turned waxen.

"What is wrong?" Steopa asked.

Rebecka stared at the dirt floor. Her shoulders sunk. “Last night, we dismembered another vampire. We have killed... but what we did felt like murder.”

“We had to extract a punishment.”

“No trial? No judge? Do we have the right?”

“She attacked my family-”

“And mine.”

“That gives us the right.”

“She said that she did not want to have our type rule again.”

“She was mistaken.”

“But...” Rebecka looked up, but did not remove her chin from her knees. “But what if what we did last night did happen a lot in the past? That punishment is something tyrants would do.”

Steopa grunted as he sat down next to her. “I do not want to rule anyone. She was delusional. Do you think she would have been nicer if the situation was reversed?”

“I don't know,” Rebecka said. “You assume we would have wanted to attack her like she did to us. We wouldn't have.”

“Yes. I went to her. To give her one chance to leave us alone. She refused. What happened to her was her choice.”

Rebecka did not respond. Steopa laid his arm around her shoulder. She moved away.

“Rebecka-”

“We could have ended her life quickly,” Rebecka said. “We made her suffer.”

“That was the point.”

“And now you want to go to Germany and find that little one and do the same to him. Where does it stop?”

“It does not stop,” Steopa said. “It is not in our nature.”

“You think I am still thinking like a human, don't you?”

“Possibly.”

“Don't get me wrong. I know she had to die. She would not have stopped any other way. But we butchered her. If you find that little one and do the same to him, will that satisfy you?”

Steopa laid his hand next to hers. She took his.

“We are predators, do not forget that,” he said. “Predators have to fight for every meal. In this city we have it easy. Not enough vampires to make hunting a competition every night. But the amount I saw in her lair would have made hunting difficult. Instead of fighting for her own place, she controlled the rest. It was only a matter of time before a challenger rose up and tried to end her."

"If it hadn't been you, would the others have butchered her?"

"It is one way. We are hard to kill. The ways that work, seem like torture. There are far worse ways to be killed."

"Such as?"

"In Saint Petersburg we bound and froze a vampire in the river, then took the frozen body to the top of the nearest church. When the sun hit, they burned."

"That doesn't sound as bad."

"You should talk to Sasha about what happens to vampires in freezing water. It is like the stupor, but you are fully aware. It is a strange hibernation."

"So when the sunlight hit them, they could feel the burning?"

"Yes."

"But they could not get out of the hibernation?"

"Yes."

"Horrid." She lowered her head. "I don't think I could ever do what you did last night."

"I did not enjoy it."

"I know."

Steopa tried to put his arm around her again. This time Rebecka let him. "I hope you never have to, but never appear to be soft around a vampire you do not know. They might think you are weak."

"Predators go for the weak and the ill. Just like bullies," she scoffed. "I'm tired."

Steopa pulled her closer. "I need to find out for myself where the little vampire went to."

Rebecka pulled her phone out of her pocket. "Let me introduce you to a wonder of modern technology. This is a cell phone."

Steopa chuckled. "Rebecka." He hugged her shoulders.

"Look. Here is Misha's phone number. Watch, I am going to call him." She put the phone to her ear.

Steopa nuzzled her neck. "I thought it was a magic box."

She handed him the phone. "Here he is."

Steopa placed the phone to his ear. "Misha?"

"Grandfather."

"What happened?"

“He returned. Earlier this evening at the lair, there was a fire.”
“Did you see him leave?”
“I did not, but I do not feel any more vampires in that building.” Misha paused. “One of the local vampires did not like me being here until I told him that Adelind is dead. He is grateful. They could not touch her.”

Rebecka's phone beeped. Steopa looked at it, then returned it to his ear.

“Do you think he is still there?” Steopa asked.

“*Nyet*, he is either dead or hiding.”

“Thank you, Misha.”

“I will be returning home.”

“Goodbye.”

Steopa handed the phone back to Rebecka. She looked at the phone in her hand.

“Perun did tell me the blood you drank at the base made you seem like a pet.”

He nodded. “I suppose.” He rubbed his chin. “Adelind told me that she was in the first lab.”

Rebecka scrolled through her phone. “Then the text Baldman sent me makes sense now.”

She held up her phone. Steopa read, “Found her name on a manifest. 1943 First made vampire?”

Rebecka slid her phone into her pocket. “So more humans experiment on our kind. Typical.” She looked sighed “Are you still going to Germany?”

Steopa shook his head. “There is no reason now.”

“What now?”

“Tonight?”

“Yes.”

“How hungry are you?”

Rebecka shrugged.

“We will go see my descendants, say our farewells, then hunt.”

“Are you two decent?” Perun shouted. “Even if you are not, I'm coming down.”

Steopa stood. He held his hand out to Rebecka. She grasped it and stood next to him. Perun bounced down the stairs. “I didn't interrupt anything, too bad.”

“Thank you for your hospitality,” Steopa said, “but Rebecka and

I need to return to our home."

"I understand." Perun held out his hand. "Remember that rock I found in Adelind's head? Here it is."

He opened his hand. The pearl-like stone had been weaved into leather straps. "I thought you would like this. A little thing to remember her by."

Steopa took the woven band. "Thank you, Perun."

"Hey, make sure you come by more often than every ten years." Perun hugged Steopa. Steopa embraced him with one arm.

Perun backed away and held his arms out to Rebecka. "And when you get tired of that guy..."

She hugged him. "That's not going to happen."

They left. Rebecka called Teodor as they walked toward the city. She handed the phone to Steopa.

"Nastenka wants to talk to you."

Steopa held the phone to his ear.

"Father, do you need us tonight?" Nastenka asked.

"No, Misha verified that the little one is gone."

There was silence.

"Nastenka?"

"Is he sure?"

"He could not feel him."

"All right," Nastenka clicked her tongue. "Then that is it."

"Yes."

"Sasha and I will leave. I would like to see you again, but..."

"But?"

"I have been gone from my home too long. I need to see if it is still standing."

"I understand."

"Goodbye, Papa. Give Rebecka a hug from me."

Steopa said goodbye. He handed the phone back to Rebecka. Then he hugged her. "From Nastenka."

"We're not going?"

"No."

"Pity."

Rebecka took his hand. "Are you going to miss them?"

Steopa started to shake his head, then he nodded. "We cannot stay together."

"There are others?"

"Yes."
"Have you met them all?"
"No."
"Maybe we should."
Steopa slipped his arm around her shoulders. "In time."
Steopa walked with Rebecka to Ottoville. They walked through the large park, then across the strip malls' parking lots. The buildings became taller the closer they came to the downtown. They left the ground and took to the roofs. On the outskirts of the downtown, he stopped at the top of a smaller skyscraper.
"The city looks beautiful up here," Rebecka said as she walked along the edge of the roof.
Steopa held her hand. He walked alongside her. "I do like this city."
"More than Saint Petersburg?" Rebecka asked. "You spent so much time there, that-"
"It was a place, that was all."
Rebecka stopped. "Just like this city."
"No, not like this city."
"Why?"
Steopa pulled her off the edge and closer to him. "Because we met here."
His hair wrapped around her shoulders as the wind picked up. A strand curled around her back. Rebecka ran her hands along his sides and under his long coat.
"Suppose," she said. "Suppose that Adelind's little nightmare came true, and you became that ruler. What then?"
"Nothing."
"Nothing?"
"I would not want it."
Rebecka smirked. "I thought that is why all the other vampires are frightened of you... of us. We can do something they can't. Therefore they think we are going to... take over the world." She giggled.
"I do not think being capable of having sex makes you a ruler."
Rebecka laughed. She laid her head on his chest, her shoulders shaking. Steopa ran his hand down her curly hair. She looked up at him with a wide smile.
Steopa leaned over to kiss her. This is where I want to be, he

thought. And damn anyone that tries to take it from me.

About the Author

Mari Miniatt lives in Syracuse, NY with her husband, sons, and two cats. She is still a working artist, sharing the lifestyle of her vampires by working only at night.

15572259R00182

Made in the USA
Lexington, KY
08 June 2012